aiseal Mór was born into a rich tradition of Irish storytelling and music. As a child he learned to play the brass-strung harp, carrying on a long family tradition. He spent several years collecting stories, songs and music of the Celtic lands during many visits to Ireland, Scotland and Brittany. He has a degree in performing arts from the University of Western Sydney and has worked as an actor, a teacher and as a musician.

Also by Caiseal Mór

THE
WELL
OF THE
GODDESS

BOOK TWO OF THE WELLSPRING TRILOGY

CAISEAL MÓR

POCKET
BOOKS

LONDON · NEW YORK · SYDNEY · TORONTO

First published in Great Britain by Pocket Books, 2004
An imprint of Simon & Schuster UK Ltd
A Viacom Company

Copyright © Caiseal Mór, 2004

Internal design: Caiseal Mór

1 3 5 7 9 10 8 6 4 2

Simon & Schuster UK Ltd
Africa House
64–78 Kingsway
London WC2B 6AH

www.simonsays.co.uk

Simon & Schuster Australia
Sydney

A CIP catalogue record for this book is available from the British Library

ISBN 0 7434 6858 9

Typeset by SX Composing DTP, Rayleigh, Essex
Printed and bound in Great Britain by
Cox & Wyman Ltd, Reading, Berkshire

Acknowledgements

any thanks go as always to my literary agent, Selwa
Anthony. Her support and generous advocacy has
ensured I'm still able to follow my chosen vocation.

Julia Stiles has edited every one of my novels since she was
Commissioning Editor at Random House Australia in 1994. It
is rare that an author is blessed with such a strong on-going
relationship with an editor. Thanks Julia.

I'd also like to thank all the folk at Simon and Schuster UK
especially Kate Lyall Grant who takes care of my novels at
Pocket Books.

I'd also like to extend my gratitude to all the readers who
enjoy my novels and to those who e-mail me or visit my website
(www.caiseal.net). It's great to receive so much mail from so
many readers. For those who haven't seen my web-page it's a
great place to find out publication dates and availability of the
music I've composed to accompany this trilogy. I look forward
to hearing your comments on my work.

At last I'm in the midst of my favourite part of the story of
Sianan, Mawn, Isleen, Lochie, Sárán and Lom. Guy d'Alville
has been after his revenge for a long time. Ever since I wrote
'The Tilecutter's Penny' he's been waiting in the background
to deal with Robert FitzWilliam. At last he's got his chance.

Caiseal Mór
May 2004

If you wish to write to the author, Caiseal Mór may be contacted at the following e-mail address:
harp@caiseal.net

For information about other books and music by Caiseal Mór, please visit his website at:
www.caiseal.net

The Compact Disc of music composed and recorded by Caiseal Mór to accompany *The Wellspring Trilogy* may be ordered through amazon.co.uk or visit his website www.caiseal.net for details.

Pronunciation Guide: The Well of the Goddess

Aoife	eef-ah
Aenghus	ah-noos
Anamchara	ah-num-kara
An Té a bhi	
agus atá	un chay a vee agus ah-taw
Aoife	eef-ah
Aontacht	ohn-tahkt
Áilleacht	Ah-lee-akt
Banba	bahn-va
Ban Righ	bahn-ree
Becc Mac Dé	beg mac jay
Bláni	Blah-nee
Boann	boh-an
Borumh	boh-roo
Branach	bran-akt
Brehon	breh-in
Bride	bree-dah
Caer Narffon	Car-nar-von
Caitlin	kotch-lin
Caoimhin	kay-vin
Cenn Maenach	ken mee-nahk
Cruitne	krit-nee
Curragh	koo-rah
Cymru	kim-roo
Dair Eolas	jayr olas
Dearg Uila	deruk-hoola
Derbáil	der-vahl
Draoi	dree
Dulogue	doo-loge
Dun Righ	dun-ree
Dun Sidhe	dun-shee

Eagla	ah-glah
Eber Finn	ayber-finn
Eirinn	ay-rin
Eoghanacht	yo-an-akt
Eolaí	yo-lee
Éremon	ay-ra-mon
Eterscél	ay-ta-shkayl
Eriu	ay-ree-oo
Fánaí	faw-nee
Feni	fee-ni
Flidais	flee-daysh
Fodhla	foh-lah
Gaillimh	gahl-iv
Gusán Gelt	gooh-sawn-gelit
Inisfail	inish-fahl
Inis Mór	inish-mor
Isleen	ish-leen
Leabhar Fál	lebar-fawl
Leoghaire	leeh-ree
Lochlann	lok-lan
Lom Dubh	lom-doov
Mallacht	mal-ahkt
Maolán	mwee-lawn
Marcán	mahk-awn
Míl	meel
Molaise	mohl-aysh
Morcán	mork-awn
Morrigán	moh-ree-gawn
Muirdeach	mew-ah-juk
Nathair	nah-hair
Nathairaí	nah-hair-ree
Neart	nart
Oidche	eeh-ha
Ollamh	oh-lahv

Órán	ooh-rawn
Ortha	ort-ah
Rián Ronán Og	ree-awn-roh-nawn-oge
Ruathar	roo-hahr
Samhain Oidhe	sah-win-eeh-ha
Sárán	saw-rawn
Scathach	skah-hah
Sciathan Cog	skee-ah-han-koge
Scodán	skoh-dawn
Segais	sha-gaysh
Sen Erainn	shen-ay-rin
Sianan	shan-nan
Sidhe	shee
Síla	shee-lah
Slua	slah
Sotar	soh-tah
Srón	shrohn
Tairngire	tah-eerun-gee-ree
Tigern Og	tee-gern-oge
Tóla	tooh-lah
Tóraí	toh-ree
Tuatha-De-Danaan	tooh-ah-hah-jay-dah-nahn

to the killibegs

castle lanfranc

lough gur

wexford

Ireland according to Binney.

The Well of Yearning

She sits in her cold stone tower, alone. Waiting. This fair maid of noble birth has a mind to be married. She longs for a lover, a man of high renown. Her nut-brown hair is braided. Her gown is of the finest blue velvet. Her eyes are so full of hope. Surely he'll be along soon.

A fresh breeze whistles through the window. Our maid looks up from her embroidery, and on this fine morning, so full of promise, a familiar scent wafts up to her. The roses are in bloom.

In an instant she's thrown down her needlework to stand at the window. There she sees the sight she's dreamed about all her life. There she glimpses the hope of her heart. A horseman is riding across the meadows toward the castle tower.

He's dressed in mail armour with a bright helm upon his head. His lance is tipped with a red pennant, his black horse bedecked in red leather harness. A wealthy prince? A nobleman's son? A crusader hero returned from the Holy Land with riches in store and a reputation of good standing?

Her heart flutters. At last her prayers have been answered. At long last she will be free from the tedium of her shuttered existence. She'll travel the world. She'll stand by her illustrious husband at court. She'll bear his children.

She's down the winding stairs in a flash and waiting in the great hall for the man of her dreams to enter. After what seems an age the two oaken doors are flung open as the knight forces his way into the hall. The chamberlain greets him with a bow then turns to announce the visitor.

'Sir Piers de Courcy.'

The young woman bows her head to him and is just about to welcome the gentle gallant knight when he cuts her off.

'This'll do nicely. I had no idea your father had such a tidy little tower at his disposal. If I had, I would've murdered him years ago.'

The knight removes his helm and tosses it to the chamberlain. His face is disfigured with a great scar that cleaves his left cheek from ear to jowl. His eyes are leering, his expression arrogant. He's filthy from the road.

'Draw me a bath!' he commands the chamberlain. 'Then have the lady waiting for me in her bedchamber. If we're going to be married I want to find out what sort of a mare I've been landed with.'

'My lord,' she protests with more than a hint of nervousness. 'My father will return shortly. Surely you should speak with him. You are mistaken if you think I'll marry you without his consent.'

'Your father is dead. I'm the lord now. You are my wife. Now go to your room and prepare yourself.'

'You're not the knight I've been dreaming of!' she shouts. 'You're not the man of my dreams. You're not what I've been praying for!'

'Just be thankful I've decided to take a bath,' the ugly fellow shrugs. 'A lot of men wouldn't bother.'

Make no mistake about it. Chivalry is dead. And it was the bloody Normans who killed it. All their talk of high knightly ideals and devotion to the service of God. All that rubbish about courtly romantic love and unswerving dedication to heart's desire. What a barrel-load of badgers' bollocks!

Few among the Normans ever adhered to those ideals,

except when it suited them. Don't worry, I'll let you know the truth about those treacherous bough-splitting bastards soon enough. But out of respect for the thread of my story we'll talk about them later on, if you don't mind.

Now give ear to the tale of the War of the Otherworld. If you marvelled at the story of Caoimhin and the Killibegs, your jaw will drop with wonder at what I am about to tell you. Last night I spoke of the Well of Yearning from which all mortals drink.

Tonight I'll mention other wells. Come closer. Huddle in by the fire so I don't have to strain my voice. Some things are best spoken of in a whisper. And the name of Aoife, Queen of the Night, is one of them.

She it was who stirred up the Redcaps to war, she who tempted the Normans to come to Ireland. She tricked many of their finest warriors into fighting for her cause. She awoke the monstrous Nathairaí. She schemed her schemes and played out her plans. And to what end?

Aoife had a mind to become a goddess. That's it indeed. You heard me right. She had ambitions of attaining the rank of deity.

Don't look at me like that. I can tell what's in your thoughts. You're doubting the veracity of my tale before I've even begun. Well that just shows how ignorant you are and how stupid our folk have become in less than two generations.

When I was a girl everyone knew the tale of Aoife. Everyone understood what kind of creature she was. She was an immortal. Her kind weren't common by any measure, but we'd all heard the tales of the Danaans and the Fir Bolg who had shared the cup of immortality.

The Danaan Druids were cunning at their Draoi-craft. When our ancestors, the Gaels, first landed here in Ireland they brought war. The Danaans knew they could not match the Gaels at battle-craft so they convinced their people and the warriors of the Fir Bolg tribes to partake of an enchanted liquor.

The Brew restored all who drank it to perfect health and youth. Neither blade nor plague would touch those who tasted the juice of the Quicken berries. Thus was death banished and decay forestalled.

But if any who had taken the Brew were to have their head separated from their body, then, and only then, would they know the sting and slumber of sweet death. This was kept a secret known only to a few, until with the passing of the countless seasons even the immortal Danaans and the Fir Bolg forgot this was their one weakness.

But Aoife hadn't forgotten.

My dear friend Caoimhin wrote down her story in the tale of the Watchers. He took some terrible liberties with the truth and he ignored many important facts. But his rendering of the tale is close enough for me to recommend it to you.

Aoife was a spoiled child who was gifted with the Quicken Brew and became an undying eternal child. She cared for nothing and no one but herself. Those who opposed her were eliminated. Those who supported her didn't fare much better, especially if she got bored with them.

As her life dragged on she learned many skills. She could conjure dæmons, some folk said. She could shape-shift her own form and the outer appearances of others. That's a fact. But it was her ambition which eventually became the single driving focus of her life.

She had heard there was a mystical spring which had its source somewhere in the Otherworld of the Faerie folk. The waters of this place were said to confer the power and majesty of a goddess upon any woman who tasted of them.

Now it's not surprising Aoife acquired a powerful yearning to drink from that fabled Well of the Goddess. She wasn't satisfied with immortality. She wanted more. But she'd heard that no one may approach the sacred Well of the Goddess who is not already worshipped by the mortal kind as such.

But she misunderstood what drinking from the well entails. She thought a mere cup of water from a sacred spring could change her destiny. Any storyteller worth her salt will tell you that to drink from the Well of the Goddess is just a pretty turn of phrase.

Don't take it literally or you'll miss the meaning. As you'll see I drank from the Well of the Goddess. But you'll have to listen to the whole of my tale to hear how that came to pass.

So our Aoife, Queen of the Night, Sovereign Lady of the Redcaps, set about bringing all the people of Ireland to her shrine. And how did she think to do it? First of all she planned to extinguish every hearth fire in the land on the eve of All Hallows Day. In the darkness that followed, her Redcaps were to spread fear and havoc throughout the country. To help them, she had prepared a mighty snowstorm with which to harass the folk who relied on fire for their survival.

But it was the last part of her strategy that was the most devilish of all. This cold and fearful night filled with raiders and restless spirits would not end with the coming of the dawn. There would be no sunrise.

Aoife had enlisted ravens, Redcaps, the two worm Nathairaí, dæmons and mortals to her cause. This host were to harangue the countryside with war and death until the queen called them off. Then she would bring in the dawn.

Only then would the fear be lifted. Only then would she declare herself the protector of the people of Ireland. Only then she would accept their praise and thanks.

It was an audacious plan. But you have to ask yourself, why would anyone, immortal or not, aspire to becoming a deity? The answer is simple. As I said, she had already tasted of immortality. The flavour of eternal life had become bland to her by then. She had learned the craft of Draoi-enchantments and this discipline had kept her attention for a long while. But eventually she lost interest in that pursuit. Not before she became a true master of the Draoi-craft, mind you.

So in the earnest desire to be distracted by new distractions, visit new vistas, attain new attainments, Aoife discovered a burning hunger within her. It was a hunger for power.

Now the kind of power one may wield with Draoi-craft is nothing compared to the awesome capabilities of a goddess. So it was only a matter of time before her mind turned to that path.

She made one mistake. To be fair, it was an easy blunder to make. She imagined that it had been her own idea to aspire to the rank of goddess. In fact the ambition had originated with two spirits who had been with her since birth.

They were a Frightener and an Enticer.

I heard your question. You don't have to repeat it. I'm old but I have my hearing yet. I might move slower than you do but I'm not slow-witted. I'll return to the Frighteners and Enticers later if you prefer.

You asked me what the Otherworld is like. And I'm just the right woman to give you an answer. I love nothing better than to speak of my youthful past now the tally of my days has grown so great.

I have called myself an eedyit over and over ever since that Samhain Eve all those years ago. And though Aoife was the originator of all the trouble, it was my eedyit self and none other who turned things round the way they ended up.

There aren't many left such as me. I'm known as Binney the Bookbinder who consorted with King Caoimhin. I can tell you anything you wish to hear, whether or not it be true in the minds of some or false to the understanding of most.

So hear me. Pay close attention to what I have to tell you.

The Otherworld is in many ways exactly the same as this

one. It's a wide realm. There are many dangers. Some folk you meet there will be among the cruellest encountered anywhere. Others are the very breath of warming kindness.

Some of the inhabitants of that place are exceptionally greedy. Many are inexplicably compassionate. Most are alike in more ways than they are different. As I said, the Otherworld is not unlike the world of mortals.

Have you noticed that this world at times appears dreamlike? Has it ever struck you that things are not always quite what they seem?

I can see it written all over your blank face. You don't know what I mean, do you? You've never thought of your waking life as dreamlike, have you? Well consider this. How many coincidences do you brush off each day? Haven't you ever brought an old acquaintance to mind only to have them suddenly appear out of nowhere as if summoned by your thoughts? When was the last time you met a stranger and, though you were certain you'd never encountered them before, you could not shake the notion you had met them in another life? How often have you woken from a deep sleep and been so profoundly affected by your dream that you've expected to find it continuing on in the waking world?

Few of those who wear flesh understand these things of which I speak. So your ignorance is not a poor reflection on your character. For the mortal span of years is short, whilst the measure of the Kingdom of Peace is so great no embodied soul may breach it. That's why those who reign in splendour seem forever youthful to those of us who draw breath. A lifetime spent here in Ireland would be but a day to any among the Shining Company.

As I said, few mortals have any understanding of these things. Our space is too short. Our vision into future days is clouded by worries of the past and all the hurt of the here and now. That is to say, there are few of the Earthborn who ever glimpse that which is truly the Otherworld and no mere elaboration in their own wild imagination.

Those mortals who do see the truth are the chosen ones among their people. They have been gifted to find the gate through the fence separating the Land of Plenty from the Plain of Painful Lessons.

I will tell you now, if you would listen, how I came to be renowned amongst those fortunate few to walk the Forests of Feasting.

If you were listening last night you would have heard me speak of the Well of Yearning, that mystical fountain all the mortal kind partake of before their soul-journey into this world. Those waters grant us longing, ambition and homesickness, without which our voyage would be worthless.

There are other wells also. There is the Well of Forgetfulness of which every soul drinks when leaving this world at death. There is the Well of Segais, which is the source of all wisdom. There is the Well of Storytelling where all the great tales are born.

And then there is the Well of the Goddess. Aoife, immortal daughter of the ancient King of the Fir-Bolg, sought to taste of that well. She desired to be elevated to the status of deity. She yearned for the praise, adoration, affection and awe of ordinary folk.

But she made a mistake. She misunderstood. The Well of the Goddess is not what you might expect. I should know. I drank from it. Yes indeed, I did. I'll tell you all about it this night, if you would listen.

FISH OF THE FOREST

Two wary scouts edged their way along the path through Aoife's uncanny woods. They carried only bows and slim-shafted arrows for weapons. They were weighted down with twenty empty water-skins each, slung across their shoulders.

They had discarded their armour before they set out so they could travel swiftly. Believe me when I tell you nothing would have made them happier than if they'd been able to keep their war gear. But those water-skins had to be filled and once full had to be carried back to their comrades of the Sen Erainn.

In any case, what good would their armour have done them in the Otherworld? Trust me when I tell you that a closely linked mail coat is no better protection than a linen tunic when it comes to enchantments.

Drooping branches completely canopied the two warriors. Any fading daylight filtering down through the leaves was tinged with green, so the faces of these two fighters seemed sickly-looking and pale. The woman in the lead signalled with a hand gesture to her companion. He silently acknowledged her.

You heard me. A woman warrior. There had been woman warriors in Ireland ever since the ancient days. Didn't you know that? As a matter of record, it was the women who trained the men at feats of arms.

9

On the island of Scathach to the north-east by the coast of Alba which the Normans call Scotland there lived a community of women warriors. By day they schooled the men in the arts of war and by night they tutored them in the arts of love. If only more of the Normans had taken their education in that place.

But here I am only a short way into my tale and you've distracted me again. This will have to stop. You must learn to curb your curiosity or I'll never get to the end of the story. You'll just have to take my word for it that there were women who took up arms in Ireland. I'll grant you that among the Irish it was no longer a common practice. But these folk weren't Gaels. They were Sen Erainn.

If you'd seen them you would have known that immediately. Their brown hair was knotted together in fine long locks resembling the braids Norman ladies sometimes wear. But they were not braids. The hair had been locked together for practical reasons. These people were fisher folk.

Their shoulder-length hair was rubbed with beeswax and salt to keep it out of their eyes on the open ocean. And to allay the stench of dead fish. Likewise their clothes were suited to the work of hauling nets. Their tunics, britches and undershirts were of fine doeskin. This was soft, light, strong and very water-resistant. Both warriors wore a carved walrus tooth on a leather thong at their neck. All sea-peoples are fond of such charms.

Their knee-high boots were made of the skin of the king otter, a black creature twice the size of any other ocean-going otter. The fur was turned out. On their heads they wore brown caps cut to the same design as the headgear of the Redcaps but not dyed with the blood of their victims.

The Sen Erainn were cousins to the Redcaps. They'd once been the same people. But I'll tell you more of that later.

The warrior in the lead stopped to wipe the sweat from her

brow. When she'd decided to set off on this adventure she'd hardly considered the dangers. Much like the rest of her people she'd been caught up in a frenzied fever for war, stirred by their chieftains' speeches.

Now that she was squatting here deep within the borders of the land of their enemy she began to wonder whether it'd been wise to leave home at all. The trees closed in around her. She felt crowded and stifled in the thick forest. Never before in her life had she travelled through a wooded land.

Any forest would have been an unnerving place for this warrior-woman. But to give her her due, this particular wood could have reduced a seasoned veteran to quivering brine.

'One may learn a lot from fish,' she whispered to herself as she held her bow tightly against her body for reassurance. She was quoting a popular proverb of her people. 'Mark you well when they refuse to cross a stretch of water. Only a fool would set his course to traverse such perilous seas.'

Her companion crept closer.

'It's a wise saying,' he agreed. 'I haven't seen a fish for days. I swear these waters are swarming with less agreeable creatures. Where the fish don't go the wise should not venture either.'

That was another proverb of the Sen Erainn.

'Of course you haven't seen any sea folk!' the woman retorted sharply. 'There are no fish in the forest!'

'That's exactly my point!' he pressed quietly so his voice didn't carry too far. 'That's what makes my blood run cold. No fish. No salt. No sea-song. It's eerie. It's not natural.'

The woman put a hand out behind her to silence him but he didn't notice.

'I fear my boat is too tiny to weather the waters of this place. This herring is ready to swim home to the shoals he holds dear.'

'I swear if you make another sound you'll be a *pickled* herring,' the woman hissed. 'Stay your ground. Summon your courage! We've got a job to do. Our people are counting on us.'

'If I *were* a herring,' the other warrior shot back in the poetic manner of his fisher ancestors, 'I'd stay well clear of this queen's net. We've drifted too close to where her herring boats gather. So don't talk to me of pickling. If I'm going to be stacked in a pickle barrel, I'd prefer not to be pressed up against you.'

'Be quiet!' the woman insisted.

'Srón,' the other warrior pleaded, 'what hope have we if danger strikes? We can't take on all the Redcaps of the North alone. We're too far ahead of the warriors of the Slua Sen Erainn. If we encounter the enemy, we're finished. There's safety in great numbers as they say. Hear the wisdom of the ocean-dwelling shoal fish.'

'If I were a fish,' Srón replied, losing her patience, 'and I loved the seabed where my kinfolk dwelled, I wouldn't be concerned whose dinner plate I might end up on at the end of the day. While I have teeth in my head no net will hold me. While I have strength in my fins no predator will outswim me. While I have flap in my gills no fisherman will make a soup out of me.'

She turned to face her companion, a hint of a mischievous smile shaping her lips. 'Come now with me, Scodán. We'll dart among the deep-sea fishing nets and fill the ocean with our farts.'

He laughed. 'You're a poet, Srón. And no mistake.'

You'd probably have to be one of the fisher folk of the Sen Erainn to appreciate their way of looking at the world. If your ancestors had spent three thousand winters on that bleak island of theirs, you'd probably have little else on your mind other than fish.

Apart from pickled herring, there's nothing those people love more than witty spontaneous verse. It was probably inevitable their culture would find its purest expression in fish poetry.

Of course you understand their dialect is quite different

from mine. So I hope you'll excuse my renderings of their words. I'm sure the poems are much finer in their own tongue.

Srón was just about to compose another tongue-in-cheek retort intended to urge her companion on ever deeper into the forest, when a tremendous hum stole her attention. The two warriors looked into one another's widening eyes.

'Sea folk sing no such scare-songs,' Scodán hissed urgently, his eyes flashing wildly now. 'The fish of the forest are upon us and that is the battle call of their queen. She has found us! We'll be ensnared!'

'Don't swish your tail about so much!' Srón shot back. 'You're stirring up the water with all your flapping.'

'You're the one who wanted to fill the ocean with our farts!' he reminded her indignantly. 'Well this tight forest is no sea haven. The current won't bear us away to safety. Our stink will surely linger. We must flee!'

The hum grew in intensity before Srón had the chance to tell him to shut up. Instead she dragged him further into the shadows. The two scouts crouched down beside the path in the deep shade of a mighty, ancient yew. Her companion looked up at the tree in awe.

'This seaweed may not be our friend,' Scodán noted as he brushed away a low leafy branch. 'But there's no better place to shelter than among the sturdy kelp when the waves are rising.'

'Still your tongue!' his companion hissed desperately.

Sadly, it was already too late to silence him. His last fisherman's quip had been enough to seal their doom. They had been noticed.

The humming grew to a strident buzz and the buzz raised its pitch until it resembled a shriek. Just when the two poor scouts thought their ears were going to burst, a cloud of stinging insects descended on the path. A few landed on Scodán. He brushed them off as though they were flies.

But these were not flies. They were the fish of the forest.

13

One of the insects landed on the back of his hand. The warrior stared at the black and yellow bands across its belly in dismay as it lifted its sharp tail end purposefully. It stabbed down hard to sting him deep into the flesh. Scocán flinched and swore. In a second he'd flicked the insect off him.

'Bees!'

He spoke the word as if it were a curse. Then he sucked the wound where the insect had stung him.

'Bees,' Srón repeated with resignation as she made a token attempt to keep the tiny winged creatures off her. 'There's no fish with a sting in its tail like a honey-gatherer. That's why our ancestors chose to draw their living from the ocean. Bees are not friends to our folk. They do not come to Aran's isles.'

As she spoke a vast cloud of swirling, screaming insects congregated before the two warriors. Each creature was crying out with the full intensity of its tiny high-pitched voice. Scodán covered his ears, only to find there was blood flowing out of them.

He searched frantically in the cloud of insects for his companion. Srón was on her knees, her back straight. There was blood at her ears and nose as well. He thought she had the look of a land-locked salmon about her, or a fish that has not got the strength left to dart away from the trawl.

'I won't sit here waiting to be made into a side dish at some seafood feast!' Scodán shouted defiantly.

With that he moved around the tree, intending to make a dash along the path back in the direction they'd come.

'I'll see you in the soup,' Srón told him by way of farewell.

'If I end up in the queen's soup I'll make sure my bones stick in her teeth and cut her gums,' he promised.

The terrible thing is that he hadn't taken three steps before the enormous swarm engulfed him completely. In less time than it takes a bee to sting, his form was lost in the furious flight of tiny wings.

14

Srón thought she heard him scream, but she couldn't be certain above the swarming insects. She certainly wouldn't have blamed him if he had. The honey-makers' thrumming frenzy was intense, ear-splitting and vicious. When their fury had abated they swirled around again. At length they spiralled up off the stiff form of the Sen Erainn warrior.

Where Scodán had once stood there was now a carved wooden idol such as those worshipped in ancient days by the Old Ones. The transformation was incredible. Yet a hint of the warrior's character remained. A long herring tail had been added to his form, perhaps as a mocking final touch.

As Srón watched his woody remains teetering off balance, the mass of bees converged in a thick pillar of honey-wings. In a few breaths they'd coalesced into a shape vaguely resembling a tall proud woman. Suddenly the noise of their flurry ceased. Then the bees disappeared almost completely, subsumed into the form of a lady with long red hair, fine white skin and piercing green eyes. She shook out her green gown and cloak as one or two lingering insects buzzed away into the forest.

Srón knew what manner of woman this was and bowed till her forehead met the earth.

'Greetings, lady,' Srón offered before the bee-woman had a chance to speak. 'Truly you are as terrible as all the old tales tell. You are the Queen of Terrors.'

'Who are you?' the woman growled, ignoring the poorly concealed insult. 'What arrogance brings you to my forests uninvited?'

The warrior looked up just as her companion's wooden form toppled forward to land with a crunch face first beside the path.

'I am called Srón. My name means the prow of the boat. I'm a scout for the Slua Sen Erainn.'

The bee-woman squinted. 'Do you know who I am?' she asked in a menacing tone.

'You are called Aoife. Some name you Queen of the Night.

15

You consort with Ravens and Redcaps. You are the enemy of my people.'

'How many march with the hosts of the Sen Erainn?'

'More than there are sands on the beach.'

Aoife smiled, amused.

'More than there are fish in the sea?' the queen added. 'I beg you to keep your quaint island metaphors to yourself. The poetic nuances of the Sen Erainn are of no interest to me. No more fishy tales please. I want the truth.'

'Nine hundred there are,' Srón shot back, her eyes suddenly burning with defiance. 'Nine hundred fisher folk who love the sea and their island home. Our poetry may not be to your liking but your conceited haughtiness is not to ours.'

Srón stood up proudly. She wasn't going to spend her last few moments of freedom cowering to the enemy.

'Only nine hundred of us have come to give you battle for the wrongs you have done us and the evils you would do to us if we gave you the chance. But nine hundred Sen Erainn are worth nine thousand Redcaps of the North. For we are fighting for our homes. What are you fighting for?'

'My people are fighting for their loyalty to me,' Aoife explained as if talking to a child. 'I'm a goddess. Or at least I will be on the morrow. Your petty rebellion will come to nothing. You can't hope to stop me.'

'Bring on your Redcaps, my lady,' Srón declared. 'We'll face them and they'll find us as unyielding as the jagged rocky shoreline of our island. We'll tip their boats over in the gale of our battle rage. Then we'll drag them down beneath the foaming waters to be food for fishes.'

'I don't need to raise the Redcaps to my defence!' Aoife snapped. 'I'm a bloody immortal! I can look after myself. How do you think I got this far? I certainly wouldn't have achieved much if I had to rely on the Redcaps. They're a stupid race. But you'd know that. They are your cousins.'

'Very distant cousins,' Srón corrected. 'They took the Quicken Brew. Our folk did not seek immortality. We remained pure.'

The aspiring goddess smiled again, softening the expression on her face as she approached the proud scout.

'I know all about Flidais,' the queen informed her prisoner. 'I know she called in the Sen Erainn as her allies in this rebellion.'

'I am a simple warrior,' Srón replied. 'When I'm not wearing a mail coat I push an oar at my brother's leather fishing boat. The chieftains of our people do not share the details of their alliances with their lowly scouts. I know nothing of Flidais except that she is renowned as the Goddess of the Hunt.'

'She is raising all the disaffected peoples of Ireland against me!' Aoife hissed with contempt. 'She thinks she can overthrow my ambition to replace her and all the other ancient deities.'

'You wish to replace the ancient deities?'

'Every one of them.'

The queen could plainly see the horrified expression on Srón's face and it pleased her.

'Danu is an old fool,' Aoife laughed. 'She's become forgetful. She sleeps most of the time. Samhain Oidche has come and gone nine times since she last attended the festivities. Her reign is finished. All the old ones have declined. It's time for new blood.'

'Danu will stand against you and you will fail,' Srón answered grimly. 'The people of Danu will rise up. Flidais has called on all those who are loyal to Danu to gather in resistance to your plans.'

'So you do know about the treachery of Flidais?' the queen smiled as the Sen Erainn warrior realised her mistake.

'You will fail,' Srón shot back.

'I will not. The Christians have one god. They recognise no other authority. Soon Ireland will have one goddess.'

'The Christians eat their god,' Srón smiled. 'They grind his body into flour then bake him into bread. They drink his blood.'

'There'll be no more cannibalism in Ireland when I'm a goddess,' the queen promised. 'We'll drive the heathen Christians and their dæmonic rituals into the sea. I will be a just goddess. I will be worshipped for my even-handedness. I will rule this land as it should be ruled.'

'Not while there is breath in my body. Not while the host of the Sen Erainn have sickles of iron.'

'You've got a stout heart,' Aoife complimented. 'I could do with more warriors such as you. Join my hosts. Serve me. Lead a company of my Redcaps. In return you shall have whatever you wish for. It's not often I offer a reprieve. I advise you to accept.'

While Srón considered Aoife's words she glanced apprehensively over at her companion, now a statue crudely carved out of wood. He seemed lifeless but the warrior-woman could sense he was still conscious within the casing of that distorted timber. The very thought of such a fate appalled her. She didn't want to spend the rest of her days here in the midst of the forest far from sight or sound or scent of the sea.

Her people made their home on a flat rain-soaked island surrounded by the broiling briny ocean. It may have seemed only a barren stretch of damp rock to anyone else, but to those born on Inis Mór the island was a paradise. Srón stiffened her resolve. She reminded herself that if she sided with Aoife and was spared the wooden fate of Scodán, she would never be able show her face again at the hearth of her kin.

Either way she was doomed to banishment from her beloved homeland forever. So she did a very Sen Erainn thing. On the spot and as jittery as she was, she composed a poem.

'Ask a fish where he lives and he'll tell you he dwells in the sea. His scales are bright and shiny when he's at home. And with all that flashing silver about him he may seem like a pretty companion to share the long winter nights. But a fish need only be away from the sea for a short while before he begins to stink. This fish has already wandered from home more than a week. The longer you keep me, the more I'll get on the nose.'

Aoife put a hand to her forehead in frustration as she tried to work out what the warrior was on about.

'Are you going to join me or not?'

'Even if you salted my flesh or pickled my body, this is one herring who will never nourish your ambitions.'

'Very well,' the queen sighed. 'If you're going to persist with that awful poetry, you leave me no choice.'

In a flash the Queen of the Night transformed into a swarm of bees again and was gone. Behind her she left another wooden idol leaning heavily against the yew as if it had been abandoned by some long-forgotten people.

And, by the way, Srón had guessed rightly about what it might be like to be encased in wood. Though she was trapped in the form of a motionless lump of timber she was still conscious of everything about her. Indeed her awareness of the world had doubled.

What had seemed a small noise before was now a resounding rumble. What might have startled her in the past set terror in her splintery bones. Just as well Srón was not the kind to lose heart. Though her familiar outward form was utterly gone, one thing hadn't changed.

At the very centre of her being there was a dim memory of the salt breeze and the sea air. In fond recollections of the ocean's lapping embrace, Srón found comfort. And so she settled down to face the rest of eternity separated from all that was dearest to her, utterly exiled from the abode of her soul.

Of course just at that moment she didn't realise she'd already beaten Aoife's punishment. You see, so long as Srón held her home in her heart she could never be parted from it. Thus it mattered not that she seemed to be little more than an abandoned old idol.

The Jester and the Oak-Knight

uy d'Alville was once described to me as a black-hearted fiend walking about in flesh. And that was a generous appraisal in my view.

I hate talking about the blaggard. My skin crawls at the very thought of his dark wet eyes so full of smouldering confidence. But since he's important to this story I'll tell you a little more about him before I go on.

He'd once been a high-ranking Hospitaller knight, but by the time he landed in Ireland during the course of these events he'd had all honours stripped from him.

In his younger days he'd been touted as a future grand master of his order. Yes. He had all the right qualities a chivalric society sought in a commander and spiritual leader. First and foremost he was an utter bastard. He was handsome, charming, wily, sly, devious, self-serving, I'll grant you, but he was first and foremost a bastard.

Those qualities immediately marked him for the inner circle of any knightly company. But he had other notable attributes as well. He was cruel, arrogant, greedy, lascivious, ruthless and vengeful. He was a superb military tactician and an accomplished musician. He was fluent in Greek and Arabic, a competent cook and an avid reader on all matters alchemical and philosophical.

His skilled horsemanship earned him the praise of both king

21

and caliph. His eye for the cut and colour of a tunic reduced both harem- and high-born ladies to fluttering swoons. The Knights Templar feared him. The orders of Teutonic chivalry courted him. The Church tolerated him. The Order of the Knights of the Hospital praised him as an ideal warrior. For a while.

Only one cloud obscured the horizon for this rising sun. There was a rumour Guy dabbled in black magic. Unfounded it was and certainly blown out of proportion through the jealousy of his peers. But it was enough to hold back his advancement to the highest office of the Hospital.

What pope would have chanced the scandal of having a devil-dealing dark-master in charge of the Hospitallers? What if Guy turned out to have more skill at the black arts than the Holy Father? That could have been most embarrassing for the papacy.

So I'm sure you'll appreciate the irony of the situation. This one charge was probably the only accusation which couldn't be laid at d'Alville's feet. But it was enough to keep Guy languishing at the perimeter of the inner circle waiting for elevation to the highest ranks.

When Guy chanced on Robert FitzWilliam his whole life took a turn for the worse. I won't go into detail. You can read Caoimhin's account of their first meeting in the Tale of the Tilecutter's Penny. The upshot was that Guy was expelled from the Hospitallers, stripped of all titles, lands and privileges. Then he was cast out from the tight-knit circle of his knightly peers.

Now I'll say this for him, any other man might have been reduced to begging in the street. A lesser soul might have ended his days walking the cloister clothed in a penitent clerical cloak. But Guy was, as I mentioned earlier, a vengeful man. He wasn't the kind to look too closely at himself when he had someone else at hand he could conveniently blame for all his woes.

With a view to recovering his fortune for a start, Guy signed on as a mercenary in the employ of the Emperor of the East in Constantinople. In less than a year he'd earned enough gold to hire a small band of his own warriors. Driven on by the wild tradewinds of vengeance he set off to the north-west toward the land of Robert's birth.

Ireland.

Along the way Guy plundered, pillaged and generally spread havoc throughout the lands he chanced upon. So by the time he arrived in Normandy he'd saved up quite a tidy sum. He hired more foot soldiers, dressed them in his own livery and then he did a most audacious, some would have said cheeky, thing.

He offered the services of his company to the Knights Hospitaller who were under the command of an old acquaintance of his, a certain Bishop Ollo. This cleric had been planning an incursion into Ireland for some time. All he'd lacked was an experienced war-leader to drive the troops on to victory. Guy was his man.

It must be said that Ollo wasn't so much interested in imposing the rule of Rome. He may have been a bishop but he wasn't much of a Christian, if you take my meaning. He'd bought his bishopric then set about expanding the taxable lands which lay under his sway. That's why he was drawn to our country.

At that time much of Ireland was still up for grabs as far as the foreigners were concerned. Ollo had a mind to drain some tribute out of us, the poor inhabitants of this much-invaded country. Along the way the bishop set his sights on a few other treasures he'd heard could be found here. But I'll tell you more of that later. I'll concern myself with Guy for the moment if you don't mind.

Ollo's main military force was made up of Hospitallers. I told you last night those black-coated warriors landed at

Wexford in the south-east a few days after my dear departed darling Caoimhin, who is called Saint Caoimhin these days, first set foot on the sacred soil of his ancestors.

Guy assembled his force in the west near the old Norse town of Limerick. I won't go over everything I told you yestereve. I'll just remind you where we left proud Guy.

Aoife had used her skill at enchantments to change him into a tree. That's right. The ways of this immortal woman may seem incredible to those of us who are doomed to die. Her mastery of the magician's art may challenge the understanding of mortals. But by Saint Bride's bookshelf, Aoife knew how to humble a man. Her one concession to Guy's pride was that she gave him the form of a strong oak tree; a bending willow would have been the ultimate blow to his manhood.

So there, after all his other adventures, stood Guy. His journey had come to a halt at the edge of the wooded lands which Queen Aoife claimed as her own domain. His feet were planted deep down in the moist soil. His arms stretched out in frozen, impotent gestures of defiance. But, much like Srón of the Sen Erainn, his heart and mind were unchanged.

Aoife was a wily one, I'll give her that. She knew what it takes to tame an unruly subject. She understood how to break the spirit of an arrogant bastard like Guy d'Alville. There was only one thing she hadn't counted on and it would return to bite her on the backside later.

And what was that?

I'm not going to tell you yet. Be patient. It'll all come out in due course.

Nine hundred warriors on the march make a terrible din. Noise and war go together, so they say. It's also true that warrior passion poisons the hearts of those it touches. And there's a weariness which descends on any fighter when forced to march far from hearth and heart-folk. These nine hundred were already showing signs of disgruntled, impatient tiredness.

They itched for a fight but every one among them would have liked a bit of a sit-down first and a hearty meal. None of them knew it then, but it was going to be a long, long while before they tasted any food or drink. And they would have to wait a while for their fight too.

It takes a certain breed of person to decide to become a warrior. It was believed by the Romans that sword folk either hold no fear whatsoever or they thoroughly enjoy the uncomfortable quivering sensation of their bowels turning to water. That's why they seek out war, fighting, strife and the like.

There may be something in that observation as far as the Romans were concerned. It's well known they were a perverse people who regularly indulged their obsessions, often unto death, or unto dirty undergarments at least.

But I have a notion it takes more to make a warrior than a hunger for quivering fright or a thirst for bubbling blood. Anyone who's stirred up to the defence of their country, kin and cattle may just as passionately take up the blade. I've seen enough of war to know it's those with most to lose who fight the fiercest.

These nine hundred fighters who've just trudged noisily into my tale had the fires of their ferocity fuelled by a threat against their homeland. It so happened that Aoife had demanded the allegiance of these sea folk on pain of subjugation, slavery, slaughter or nasty combinations of the three. These warriors were Sen Erainn, cousins of the Redcaps who had flocked to Aoife's service, and she thought they'd be hers for the asking. But make no mistake, they had walked a different road down the countless seasons since they'd parted company with their kinfolk.

These Sen Erainn had not shared the life-giving Quicken Brew. So their seven chieftains had not been so easily led along by the wily, sly, devious taunts of the Queen of the Night.

They were an island people and there was no voice so loud in their ears as that of the ocean. When an upstart like Aoife attempted to enforce her authority over this proud folk, they rose in arms against her. They weren't going to wait for her Redcap fighters to land on their precious rain-soaked rock. These people had weathered the mightiest storms the sea could throw at them. In their time they'd seen great gales blow rolling wave-crests right across their island from one side to the other. If the full force of the angry ocean hadn't dislodged them from their home, you can excuse their pride if they doubted whether Aoife could do so.

So in the time-honoured tradition of their forefathers, the Sen Erainn had gathered their warriors. All able folk took up arms and sailed across to Ireland in a mighty fleet. Once they were all landed they set out to attack the stronghold of the Queen of the Night before she had an inkling of their arrival.

That's how they came to be making so much noise in the midst of the forest where Aoife held sway. I'll give them this much, they were a plucky people. I don't how any of them imagined nine hundred fish-stinking fighters laden down with weapons, pots, pans and dried herrings were going to sneak past our Aoife.

It so happened that as their leaders chose a resting place among the trees on a slope above a dark pool, Aoife encountered Srón and Scodán. That's how she learned of their intentions. You can take my word for it that she was incensed these upstarts had come to challenge her in her own garden.

Nevertheless she calmed herself. She waited till they'd settled down round their campfires for the night before she made her move. She's a patient one, our Aoife. She doesn't like to rush anything she finds enjoyable.

So you can imagine the chieftains' fire that night. The Sen Erainn have crossed the ocean to Ireland in their leather boats. They've marshalled their fighters to march south and east toward the heartland of the Redcaps. They've built their rage to fever pitch, a hovering storm-front swelling before the first lightning strike. There are rumbles in their ranks but their thunder hasn't sounded yet, not by half.

Then a sentry gives the shout. His cry becomes a gurgling scream of terror. The whole war band rises to their feet to face the direction of the hideous noise. A few short breaths pass in silence.

'Who goes there?' their War-Druid bellows.

But the answer he receives is not like anything he expects. It comes down upon his people as a curse.

And if you were to have stumbled on the camp of the hosts of the Sen Erainn at that very moment, you would have wondered what barbarous folk could have erected so many wooden idols in this grove.

I read a tale once when I was young. A very good one it was too. It was written by a Roman emperor of old, no less. His name was Cæsar Julius. He was a big man in his day, this Julius. He led his armies to the far corners of the known world, indulging his passion for the conquest of foreign peoples and the enslavement of their womenfolk.

They say he got as far as the west coast of the Cymru lands which the Saxons call Wales, and as far north as Orkney. He never made it to Ireland but not for the want of trying.

He was famous for many things. Most of all, though, our Julius was renowned for having a fondness for the drop.

He'd tasted, or I should say swallowed, wines from all the far-flung edges of his empire. He brewed his own beer while away on campaign to take his mind off the day-to-day business of subduing barbarians. And because he loathed the thought of having to go without a sup at bedtime he always had a few barrels in his tent discreetly disguised as a writing desk.

It so happened that once, while he was off teaching the Cymru the finer points of getting drunk, a ship washed up in that land after a mighty storm. And aboard that wrecked vessel was a barrel painted honey yellow with strange markings written on the side in red.

Well, all his soldiers knew how much the emperor loved a tipple, so the centurion who discovered the treasure presented it to Julius as a tribute. It had come from Ireland, he told old Julius. And it was a drink brewed from honey for which the Irish have always been famed.

Without much ceremony the emperor cracked the barrel then settled down to sample this exotic pleasure. I believe there was much merriment in the imperial tent that night. But Irish mead is incomparable to any other drink. Like the heady intoxication of infatuation, the honey brew is powerful strong. For though it's sweet it's also terrible treacherous.

Indeed, if you read the accounts I've perused, they report that the Emperor of the Romans got so drunk he had to postpone raping, pillaging and harassing the locals next day. He slept right through the whole thing.

A week later, when the barrel had worn off, he woke with a noise in his head like a legion marching on loose gravel. And he found himself facing a bit of a crisis.

While he'd been sleeping off the barrel of mead his men had started to whisper that perhaps the old boy had kissed farewell to his prime. Everyone knew Julius had fallen over dead piggly-soused after just one barrel of the stuff and that had never happened before.

Now there were only two conclusions his generals could come to. Either the drink was unbelievably strong, which it was, or old Julius just wasn't able to toss down the pots like he used to, which was equally true. The ordinary soldiers were saying he didn't have what it took to be emperor any more.

You have to wonder, don't you. I mean to say it's not surprising the ancient Romans lost their bloody empire. The main qualification for being emperor was an ability to get drunk without falling over whilst off on the far side of the known world putting strangers to the sword. It's not really a firm foundation for a lasting regime, is it?

Anyway, old Julius got wind of the discontent among his troops so he came up with a plan. He decided to invade Ireland in vengeance for the barrel of mead they'd inadvertently delivered to his tent.

He wrote a letter to the Senate in Rome declaring that such evil weapons were the mark of a savage people who must be brought under the heel of decency for their own good and for the future stability of the Empire. Why couldn't these foreigners face their enemies in the field instead of employing such poisonous tactics? The Irish had to be stopped before they infected the world with their tainted honey ale. Julius informed his people he intended to make the Irish into Roman citizens. Well, that is to say, any Irish who survived the invasion.

His legions were assembled. Ships were constructed to bear the fleet across the short stretch of sea to where the mead-making enemies of the civilised world were plotting the downfall of high Roman culture in their secretive brewing rooms.

It was round this time the Emperor Julius wrote his diatribe against the Druids. I don't know if you've read it but to me it sounds like he still had a touch of mead-head when he penned the thing.

He claimed the Druids sacrificed innocent victims to their bloodthirsty gods and goddesses. He claimed the Celts, of whom we Irish were reputedly the most barbaric of all, collected the heads of their enemies to hang upon our doorsteps. He said a lot more too but I won't bother repeating it. It's obvious his thoughts were clouded, to say the least.

The eve of the invasion drew nigh and in his wisdom Julius sent to Gaul for two thousand short throwing javelins with which to arm his soldiers. He'd heard the Irish had no such weapons since they preferred to fight at close quarters, hand to hand. Or worse, simply poison their enemies before the battle then slice off their heads as they slept off the drink.

That order was the downfall of his invasion. You see, for all the might of the legions of the Roman Empire, for all the lofty ideals of their society, for all the codified laws of their judiciary and the vision the emperor held of Roman superiority over all others, there was a detail Julius had overlooked. The Roman Empire was dogged by a fundamental failing.

When the ship arrived from Gaul in answer to the emperor's order, it contained two thousand short leather aprons. Yes, you heard me right. Aprons.

The scribe who had taken down the emperor's command was overworked and sleepy. He'd misspelled a word or two and scribbled the rest hastily. The man who read the order wasn't that well educated. So his interpretation of the scrawled words was somewhat freer than it might have otherwise been. He wrote it out again in a neater hand but the basic message was not quite right.

The master of stores who fulfilled the order was unfortunately drunk when he received it. I have not been able to ascertain whether mead was once again the culprit in this instance. But it matters not.

The Governor of Gaul, who had aspirations to the imperial wine cellar himself, read the resulting supply dispatch and could hardly stifle a smile. He was only too happy to embarrass dear old Julius. He countersigned the shipment and sent it on its way. Then the governor indulged in a bout of exuberant chuckling at the emperor's expense.

Of course it goes without saying that once the aprons arrived the invasion was cancelled. Julius saw the whole episode as a sign from the gods that Ireland was too barbaric to benefit from being brought into the Empire.

By the time old Julius got back to Rome the tale had expanded a little. The Irish mead had certainly been poisoned, it was said. But the gods had spared Julius. This proved he still had a right to call himself their lord.

So he got off lightly really. The Governor of Gaul wasn't so lucky when Julius realised his part in the whole debacle but I won't go into that.

The important thing is that Ireland was spared the ravages of Roman civilisation. And the mighty legions never discovered the virtues of Irish mead. Thus they were denied the daily experience of waking up in a pool of their collective vomit to groan at the sun as one.

Why did I tell you that story? I hear you ask.

Well, in many respects the Normans weren't that different from the Romans. You see, apart from inheriting the Roman system of government, laws, morals, prejudices and book-keeping practices, the Normans simply couldn't hold their drink.

And this was no more evident than in Wexford town. That's where Bishop Ollo the Benedictine was amassing a force of Hospitallers, adventurers and miscreants to sweep across Ireland to claim the riches of the land for himself.

It had taken him a few days to realise mead was the root cause of his warriors' sloth. But as soon as he worked that out he acted quickly. All the strong drink in Wexford was gathered up by his most loyal of knights. The barrels were stacked in a great pile at the market cross. And there, with great ceremony, Bishop Ollo set a torch to the liquor, thus starting a fierce blaze which lasted a full week, nearly destroyed the whole town and could be sniffed on the wind in England.

As the barrels exploded our bishop gave a rousing speech. He spoke of the glory of God and the rewards which awaited each and every soldier of the Cross. He promised the praise of Heaven. He invoked the wrath of Hell.

Our Ollo was a shrewd bugger, I'll give him that. He knew how to win the loyalty of his men. During the speech he noticed his warriors couldn't take their eyes off the burning gallons of evil honey brew. So he told them there was much more mead out there in the wild lands. He pointed west as a thousand pairs of eyes lifted from their mournful mead-ward gaze.

Out there in the untamed lands of the Gael, he told them, there was mead aplenty. It was the duty of every knight among them to do whatever they could to eradicate this scourge from the face of Ireland.

A thousand pair of eyes lit up. Bishop Ollo had inspired them all. As soon as he'd done with talking, his thirsty warriors set about getting ready to march off west to perform their Christian duty. Every man among them was determined to do whatever was required of him to save the heathen Irish from the ravages of this wicked drink. Even if they had to consume it all themselves.

This mighty force will come into the tale again later. For now it would do you well to bear in mind that while all the other events of this story were taking place, Ollo and his men had been marching north and west more or less in the direction of the settlement of the Killibegs where my people had their winter lodgings.

By Samhain Eve they were not far from that place. Thankfully, their initial encounter with the honey mead had slowed them down somewhat. Otherwise they might have crossed our path a lot sooner and this whole story would have had a very different ending. Very different indeed.

BEAUTIFUL HANDS

I t's time I spoke of the other players in this little saga. Do you remember Mirim of the desert country and her husband? You may recall she entered my tale in the company of Tom Curdle, who was none other than our dear Robert FitzWilliam travelling in disguise. Her other companion was likewise not all he appeared to be.

Shali, her mute manservant, the one who took greatest care of her, who kept watch through the night while she slumbered was, in truth, her husband, Alan. I've already told you the story of Alan de Harcourt. But his strand in the weave of this tale is an important one, so at the risk of boring you, I'll briefly tell some of it again.

Alan was one of those idealistic youths who sought adventure, fame and absolution from all sin by going off to the Holy Land to serve in the great crusade. His path eventually led him, as it did many like him, to the gates of the stronghold of the Knights of the Temple.

There he took vows, surrendered all his worldly wealth into the keeping of the order and commenced his career as a soldier of Christ. He already had some experience as a warrior. His father had trained him well and to reinforce his learning had often sent him off on expeditions to deal with brigands in Normandy.

He'd taken part in a great battle against the Bretons during one of their many insurrections against Norman rule in Brittany. And he wasn't a bad swordsman considering he'd only drawn breath a mere twenty-five summers on this Earth.

Alan had been a Templar for little over a year when he was commanded to go on a strange errand. With two other companions he set off toward the Oasis of Shali, known as Siwa in the Arabic tongue.

There they met a priest of the Orthodox faith, a Copt who lived in a monastery high in the eastern mountains. A quantity of gold was given over to this man in exchange for a manuscript written in a strange hand and an ancient language.

'Tis a curious fact that books should feature in so prominent a role in my tale. It strikes me as poetic that I was trained as a bookbinder and the greatest adventure of my life was brought about largely because of books. And all this in a country where the spoken word is held in much higher esteem than the written one. For Ireland has always been a land of learning but our wisdom is mostly preserved by storytellers not scribes.

I'll tell you something I've learned. You may pay good gold for a manuscript and read every word within but that doesn't guarantee you'll understand any of it. Listen to a storyteller, though, and you walk away with a treasure which cannot be weighed in any precious metal.

But I'm drifting off.

No sooner had their transaction been concluded than a terrible sandstorm descended upon the three knights of the Temple. Alan was lost in the wild sandy tempest, thirsty, disoriented and cut off from his companions.

He had the book in his possession but all else he owned, including his horse, was swallowed up by the hungry desert. He was close to succumbing to the sands himself when he stumbled upon a well and quenched his thirst. Then the winds died away suddenly, as they can in that part of the world, and our knight, surprised by what he thought was a vision of the

Madonna, collapsed into a dark troubled sleep.

When he awoke he found himself lying wrapped in fine linen sheets, watched over by a beautiful woman of the desert. Her speech was unknown to him, her face only vaguely familiar. But much more disturbing, Alan could not remember any detail of his own life. The desert had stolen away his memory.

The elders of the Shali Oasis knew the punishment for drinking from that well without the permission from the old woman who guarded it. They understood Alan's memories had been washed clean by the draught of water that had saved his life. No one held it against him that he hadn't formally requested a drink. He was a foreigner after all, and he did not speak their language.

So he was given clothes to replace the tattered rags ripped to shreds by the wind, then he was lodged with Mirim and her family who were given the task of taking care of him.

There his story might have ended. He might have been forgotten by time and the Templars altogether. He could have gone on living at the Shali Oasis for the rest of his days, as ignorant of his past as most of us are of our future. But that was not to be his fate.

A few months after he stumbled on the oasis a man came in out of the desert. He was an old man, a wise man, a hermit. He'd been a Templar knight himself once until his desire for solitude had overwhelmed him. He was taken to see our Alan straightaway. He was shown the book and the letters the young Templar had with him. The elders of Shali had taken these from Alan and kept them in a secret place. They were untrusting of the written word like all sensible people and like many folks they had no knowledge or need of such things. The old hermit knew when he read these documents that the young knight's life was in deadly danger.

He advised Alan to set off for Acre on the coast where he

could find a certain Templar by the name of William FitzWilliam. That man would take the book off his hands and ensure it fell into the care of folk who would not misuse it.

The problem was that Alan had already taken the name Shali by then. And what's more, he'd fallen in love with and married the woman who'd cared for him from the beginning – Mirim.

Templars are forbidden to marry, as I'm sure you know. And since Shali was happy with his new wife, he was reluctant to go off on such a dangerous adventure, risking his liberty and his life. not to mention that which gave him the most joy in life – his loving spouse.

The old hermit insisted that if he did not go, a great disaster would befall the people of Shali Oasis. The Grand Master of the Temple would be searching for this book. There was no doubt about it. It would be only a matter of time before Alan's existence came to the attention of the Templar spies.

He told Alan the grand master was a ruthless man with a distaste for the slightest hint of rebellion amongst his warrior-monks. He wouldn't just punish the young knight for deserting his duties. He would likely seek retribution from the entire oasis community as well.

You see, the book our Temple knight had in his possession was one of the most sought after in the Christian world. The Gospel of Thomas was considered heretical by some and authentic by others, but scholars of both camps desired to take a look at it. That's why it was worth a fortune.

It was rumoured the contents of that manuscript could shake the very foundation of the Pope's authority in Rome. One thing is certain: the book was already stained with blood.

A hundred years earlier a battle had been fought for its possession. And in like manner it had passed from one caretaker to another down the generations. The priest who'd sold it to Alan had murdered three of his brothers to thieve it.

Almost everyone who came to possess it, whether they knew its worth or not, suffered ill fortune or fell before the knives of others who coveted it. Few kept it in their possession long enough to read, much less understand, its contents. For the book was cursed. Or so the old hermit said.

He insisted there was only one way Alan had any chance of survival. That was to hand the book over to a man who knew what it was but who would not be tempted by its contents. And that's how William FitzWilliam came to be mentioned.

So, with the protection of his friends and new family in mind, Alan and Mirim, who refused to be left behind, set off for Acre. They made discreet enquiries about old Lord FitzWilliam. Plenty had heard of the old man but none could tell his whereabouts. That is until they chanced upon a fellow who took them to William's son, Robert.

Now our Robert was a loyal Templar at heart. But he had seen enough of the intrigues that plagued the order to know this book would cause a terrible stink. Robert was on his way home from the Holy Land. He'd been given an errand of his own to perform by the grand master of the order. He suggested Mirim and Alan accompany him. And he promised to keep silent about the manuscript.

'I desire to pass through the world unrecognised,' he told them. 'It will be easier for me to do so if I am in your company. I will take you to my father. He'll know what to do with the book.'

Of course, as a Templar, Robert should have handed them over to the grand master straightaway. But as I said, he'd seen enough to know there were darker forces at work within the Temple. And he was already beginning to change his view of the world, if you take my meaning.

So the three of them set off on the long voyage across the Middle-Sea to France. From there they travelled overland to the channel which they crossed to England. On the west coast of that country they eventually found a boatman who'd take them to Ireland where Robert's father lived.

All the while they were journeying they kept the secret of the book to themselves. In time they concocted a story about Alan being a mute servant named Shali to protect him if he was questioned. His accent and speech would have given him away immediately.

Along the way they heard rumours of a renewed Norman assault on the Gaelic lands of Ireland. They picked up stories about the wild people of that country. And most important of all they learned of a legendary well there which could restore sight to the blind, steady feet to the cripple and clear thought to those afflicted in the mind.

The moment she heard about that well Mirim knew her duty was clear. It was fate that had led them to Ireland in search of William FitzWilliam. In Ireland her husband could be cured of the malady of his misplaced memories. They must find this holy spring though the price might prove very high.

Mirim was a wonderful soul. I grew to admire her very much, you know. She was wise and selfless. She taught me a great deal about love and life. Mirim knew that if Alan's memory was restored to him she could well lose him. He might recall his vows to the Temple and decide to abandon her. But she wanted him to make that decision for himself. She knew, as I did not in those days, that love is a stronger force than you or I can comprehend. It cannot be held in a bottle nor imprisoned in any cage nor bound to any promises concocted in the fickle minds of mortals.

So it was that once Mirim and Alan handed over the book into the keeping of William FitzWilliam they immediately prepared to set off on their next great journey.

The well they sought was not of this world. The spring-waters of healing they had been seeking only bubble up from one place. It is a well beside a pool situated beyond the bounds of mortal knowing, across the Bridge over the Chasm, in the realms of the Otherworld.

Mirim and her husband waited by the stables within the rath of the Killibegs for Robert FitzWilliam to return. They could not have known that he would break his word to them or that he was already coming perilously close to catching up with his enemy, Guy d'Alville.

Alan had just finished unloading the cart and sorting through the gear they'd take with them on their journey to the Otherworld. No horses was the advice everyone had given them. So he'd repacked their belongings and wrapped everything to be left behind in waterproof oilskins. Old Father Clemens, the leader of our community, had offered to let them store their goods in the dry rooms of the huge underground storage cellars of the fortress.

You must understand no one ever expected to see either of them again. A journey to the Otherworld was no small undertaking. Those who set out rarely returned within living memory. A hundred summers might pass before such a traveller came back to visit hearth and home, either to find the hearth covered over with cobwebs or the home with a new housekeeper.

Clemens intended to say as much, to warn them of the dangers of their journey. He found the two of them seated on hay near their horses. Alan was softly strumming a lute. Out of his deep respect for music the old priest stood quietly aside to allow the spirit of the instrument to sing.

But as Alan strummed a most unexpected thing happened. It was unexpected because Clemens had rarely heard a woman's singing voice who was not Irish. Her song was in Latin.

'While I am sleeping you carry off all my pain and suffering, in your beautiful hands, your beautiful hands. While I am weeping you carry me like fragrant rosewater, in your beautiful hands, your beautiful hands.'

Then Mirim broke into a wailing wordless melody which followed the tune of her words but not too slavishly. When she came to the end of that part she sang the first verse again.

'While I am sleeping you carry off all my pain and suffering, in your beautiful hands, your beautiful hands.'

As Mirim pronounced that last word she drew the note out with all her breath so it lasted an eternity, or so it seemed to Clemens. She sat after the song had faded from her. Her dark eyes were firmly shut, her fine-boned hands clasped in her lap. In her mind's eye she was seeing a scene from her home at the oasis of Shali near the city of Alexandria in the east of the world. Her ears heard the gentle echoes of the night music which brought all the folk of the desert in from their hermitages.

Mystics, millers and musicians all mingled on those nights. For a shoemaker might be a fine drummer and give that skill to the gathering. A hunter might offer a fine voice for singing. A merchant might not contribute anything more than a steady clap. But all were joined together in the sacred unity of the music.

Mirim could envision the people all around the fire performing on various instruments – drums, rattles, indescribable string instruments from Ethiopia, the land of the lakes. In her imagination a flute player stepped forward from the crowd to play a few notes of an unforgettably sweet melody. Then something distracted her.

'Mirim!' her husband called out. 'Mirim!'

She shook her head, opened her eyes and looked directly at Alan.

'What's the matter?' she asked with genuine frustration at being interrupted.

Then she noticed another person seated beside her husband. It was Father Clemens.

'I hope you don't mind,' the old priest told her with a gentle bow of his head. 'I was listening to you sing that wonderful song. Does it come from your own country?'

'It's a song in the style of my country. But the words are mine. They are a gift to my dear husband. That is why they are in his language. I made the song soon after we first met and I sing it for him often.'

Clemens was obviously touched to the heart by her words.

'I have never heard such a voice as yours and I cannot hope to again on this side of heaven.'

Mirim bowed her head, politely lowering her eyes.

'If you come to my country you will hear many who sing better than I. Though be warned, it is said that the Oasis of Shali is situated just on this side of Hell.'

The old man caught the twinkle of mischief in her eyes.

'It would be a terrible pity if you went off to the Otherworld and did not return,' he told her. 'You would be sorely missed among us here. And not just for your singing voice. If only more pairs of youthful shoulders were able to bear the weight of such wisdom in these days. You have travelled far and suffered much. I'm sure you must have learned a great deal since you left your home.'

Alan placed the lute in its fine leather case shaped to fit the instrument perfectly.

'As long as Mirim and I are together,' he said, 'nothing else matters. We've travelled a long way hand in hand. This is merely another stage of that wayfaring ramble we have come to call our life.'

Clemens looked as though he was searching for the right words.

'Why have you come to us?' Miriam asked, noticing his discomfort. 'What is it you wish to say?'

Father Clemens put a hand to his brow and scratched softly. After a few moments he looked her squarely in the eye and said, 'The moon is high and twilight is fleeing. It is Samhain Oidche. It is the night our people call All Hallows Eve.'

'Why are you so worried, Father?' Mirim smiled. 'Would you have us be frightened by the road ahead? Wouldn't it be better to offer us words of encouragement than to offer us tales of warning?'

'It's reckless to go off in search of that other land,' he told her, an unexpected sudden sternness in his tone. 'There's no telling what may befall you once you venture beyond the knowledge of mortal kind.'

'Someone must have gone on before us,' Alan pointed out. 'Or else how would anyone have heard of the place? Somebody must have seen the well which we seek or we could not have been directed to it.'

'Not all that is spoken within a Gaelic hall should be taken so literally,' Clemens sighed. 'We are a people inclined to exaggeration, to boastfulness and to tampering with what Norman folk call the truth.'

That's true enough, if you don't mind me saying. But then, we Culdees have a different concept of truth from the Normans. They, like many other folk from Italy to India, are easily seduced by the glittering things of this world. I speak of gold, silver, fame, power, possessions. Folk who live close to the land or the sea are not so elated by gain nor so devastated by loss. They know the cycle of the seasons and so their vision of truth and falsity is not clouded by ambition, reputation, acquisition, acclaim or avarice.

When folk stray from the deeper truths, they adopt a certain insecurity in their dealings with others and are far too easily influenced by unsupported viewpoints. Thus many Norman people, for example, accept as truth anything they are told by anyone they are led to believe is more worthy than themselves.

Opinion is too often lauded as the truth among them. Many who are aware of this fact become unscrupulous liars for their own material gain. They know that most people have forgotten how to think for themselves. Their goals boil down to either gold or God and there is no room for anything in between. With that in mind, perhaps you may better understand the goings-on of the Norman folk who inhabit my tale.

'It was old William who told us of the Well of Many Blessings,' Alan pointed out. 'He's a Norman, isn't he? So perhaps we can more confidently take him at his word than any Gael.'

'The Normans are the worst of all!' the old priest snapped as he placed a hand on the man's shoulder. 'That's the trouble with all these bloody Norman mystics who wander round the countryside soaking up the folklore and music of the Gaels. Before too long they all end up thinking they know more about this country than we do.'

He let his hand drop away.

'You did not grow up in this country. You do not have our language. You cannot possibly understand our complex relationship with this land and the folk who inhabited it before the Gaels ever came here.'

Once again Clemens had struck the red circle on the target with those comments. The Irish weren't the first folk to inhabit this island. They won't be the last. Those who've gone before did not simply disappear or fall before the sword. For the most part they withdrew into the Otherworld. For they were the Old Ones whose understanding of the world was so much greater than ours.

They made treaty with our ancestors when the Gaels first set foot here. They still call this country their home and they are tied to it by sentimental and physical bonds. Some of them choose to live among us either in secret or openly. We still to

44

this day use their names for the mountains, valleys, hills and rivers.

Their presence is as strong as ever. But the complexities of their lives and existence are almost incomprehensible to the mortal kind. Their Otherworld is unfathomable to those who are born to taste death.

'Are you saying there is no well in the Otherworld which will restore my husband's recollections?' Mirim asked with sinking heart. 'Was it just an empty tale?'

Clemens saw the hope dimming in her eyes.

'There is no such thing as an empty tale,' the old priest countered. 'Every story has something to offer if one is willing to seek out its gift.' He didn't want her to give up all hope.

'I've heard of a spring named the Well of Many Blessings,' the priest admitted. 'I have seen it in my dreams if that means anything to you. I know a man who once travelled to the Otherworld. When he returned he told me how he'd once been afflicted in the same manner as your husband.'

'What happened to him?' the desert woman asked, excited again. 'Where is he? May I speak with him? Will he show us the way to the well?'

Clemens held up his hand to still her questions so he could go on with his story.

'My friend spent a long while seeking the whereabouts of the Well of Many Blessings in that uncanny country. When he found it he engaged the lady of the well in a game of skill. Three times he beat her. This earned him the right to battle the guardian of the well in a game of wits. He won. But that wasn't the end of it. After that he had to face another challenge of his warrior skill.'

Clemens paused.

'At last, after all these hardships, the lady of the well set him a quest to fulfil. And that proved the hardest of all things to complete. It was three summers before he'd filled the quest and returned to her to claim his prize, a cup of water from her bubbling well.'

'And what happened then?' Alan cut in.

'She let him drink,' Clemens shrugged.

'And?' Mirim urged.

'And his memory was restored to him.'

'Three years and a few tests is all it took to have his recollections back?' Alan asked. 'I have already been afflicted these three years past.'

Clemens solemnly nodded but then he shrugged his shoulders to show he wasn't sure if he agreed.

'Don't you think it is a small price to pay to have my life returned to me?' Alan pressed.

'There was another reckoning which had to be brought to account,' the priest declared solemnly. 'My friend had to find his way back home. For he not only wished to remember his loved ones, he wanted to embrace them. Fortunately for him the lady of the well was pleased with him. She led him home.'

Once again old Clemens paused. He wasn't sure how to break the news to them.

'By the time he returned to the mortal world all the folk he'd ever known were gone. The people who dwelled in his village did not recognise him. They had trouble understanding his speech. They treated him as a stranger in his own home. They shunned his company so that he wandered round like a lost calf. In the end my wife and I took him in.'

Clemens looked Alan directly in the eye.

'You see, he was granted his memories and a full recollection of all the dearest things in his life. But three hundred summers had passed since he'd travelled to the Otherworld. That is the nature of the place. All his kith and kin were dead or gone. Everyone he'd called to mind had turned to dust. And even his home had changed beyond recognition. The world did not in any way resemble that which he'd hoped to find.'

Mirim edged closer to her husband and took his hand in hers. Alan thought carefully before he replied.

'All my blood family and the friends of former days are little to me now,' he stated. 'And since I cannot bring any of their faces or names to mind, I cannot say whether they will mean any more to me when I am released from this enchantment.'

He looked at his wife lovingly. 'But if by chance I find myself in the same situation as your friend, I will have some comfort. For Mirim will stay by my side and travel with me. As I will with her. We made this promise to one another when we wed. Together we will face the challenges of the world. And if we must also face the dangers of the Otherworld to win our quest, then so be it. Once we have achieved our goal we will return together hand in hand as you see us now.'

'And what if the world has changed when you come back? What if three hundred winters fly by while you stray in the Faerie realm?' Clemens pressed. 'What then?'

'Mirim and I will be together,' Alan smiled. 'I may weep for my home and I may mourn for those who have long since passed away. But not the depth of the ocean, nor the height of the stars, nor the breadth of the mountainside, nor even the measure of the length of the Otherworld from end to end will keep me apart from my true love.'

He smiled, a tear welling in his eye.

'So tell me, wise, gentle priest, how will I suffer?'

Clemens touched the other man on the shoulder again to show he was struggling to find the words to answer. In the end he spoke a blessing over them both.

'If you must go, then may God go with you.'

Alan winked. 'From what I've heard, Father, God doesn't venture into the Otherworld very often. But if Robert FitzWilliam is to be our guide, then I am certain God will never be far away from us.'

'There is something else,' Clemens added with a cough of

embarrassment. 'I have a great favour to ask of you before you go, if your hearts are so set on that journey.'

'Ask what you will, Father,' Mirim replied. 'We will grant you anything within our power.'

'Stay here this night.'

Alan shot a glance at his wife.

'Stay here and lend us your strength in the fight that is to come,' Clemens begged. 'We are too few to fight off the Normans. Even if Sianan manages to hold off Aoife, we still have to face the Hospitallers who are marching from Wexford.'

Neither Mirim nor her husband spoke. They avoided the old man's gaze.

'You are a warrior,' the priest went on, pressing his point to Alan. 'You know how to fight. Your weapon arm would be greatly appreciated.'

'I have forgotten such things, Father,' he protested. 'If I ever knew them.'

'But you have your strength. And your wife is no stranger to the sword, I'll warrant.'

'I have lifted a blade once or twice,' Mirim admitted. 'In my country women are accounted equals to men in all things, as they are among the Culdees, I believe.'

'All I ask of you is one night,' Clemens repeated. 'One night of your lives. Stay until dawn. When the sun rises go on your way again with my blessings. But do not desert us in our time of desperate need.'

He drew them closer with a gesture of his hand. Then he spoke in a low voice.

'If my people see you depart at this time they may falter. They may doubt their strength. They will ask why you have chosen to leave them on the eve of battle. Their hearts will fail. But if you stay they will have the resolve to carry on.'

'Why do you choose to stand?' Alan asked. 'Why don't you order your people to disperse? Would it not be better to scatter before the hosts of your enemies than to face them at uncertain odds.'

'The odds are not so uncertain,' Clemens replied. 'We have a few little tricks in our storehouse yet. But if we disperse they will hunt us down one by one. Make no mistake about that. If we stand our story will go out to every clan-hold in this country. Others will follow our example. Though we may go down fighting, neither Aoife nor the Normans will win out.'

'You speak as though you expect defeat,' Mirim noted.

'If we disperse we will certainly be defeated. There is nothing in this world you can be more sure of. If we stand we have a chance.'

Mirim and Alan looked hard and long at one another, sharing a silent exchange. At last Alan spoke up.

'We will stay here till dawn,' he promised the old priest.

'But not a moment longer,' Mirim added firmly.

'Thank you!' Clemens gasped as he held them both close.

'Now assign us to our duties,' Alan told him. 'From what you've told us we shouldn't be standing here in the barn talking. We should be out there among the people helping to build the defences.'

Clemens stood back and smiled.

'May the road of your quest be paved with joy. May the house of your quest be a palace. And may the hearth of your quest banish the chill winds of despair.'

An Ounce of Persistence is Worth a Hundredweight of Skill

You'd better get used to it. There's more to this world than meets the eye. There are too many folk these days who'd have you believe there is no such thing as enchantments and the like.

Well here's the truth. It's the disenchanted ones who speak out the loudest against enchantment. Fools who laugh in the face of possibilities are impossible to bear. And people who proclaim that the secret of the creative realm is not given to mortals are really just terrified of what they might dream up if they called upon their God-given talents.

Or they're just lazy.

Enchantments or magic or whatever you will call them are a firm fact of life. Though you may not have a grasp of what I'm saying you certainly will by the end of this story. Mark me when I tell you, hand on heart, anyone can dream up their deepest desires and bring them to life.

For the moment let's put aside whatever objections you might like to raise. I have a cautionary tale for you. It's about a monk who attained to his desire, discovered his own gift for enchantment and performed what some would call a miracle. Though he could have mastered many more if he'd been bothered.

Before I ever went to the community of the Killibegs, before my twentieth summer had passed upon this Earth, I was a nun.

I studied the art of bookbinding in the Benedictine convent of Glastonbury. My brother Eriginas had taken me there when I was very young.

With great devotion to my craft I learned the stitches, glues and tooling techniques of my trade from the unsung mistresses of the scriptorium, the elder nuns. For although women were not permitted to write the holy words on vellum, we were allowed to participate in what the brethren monks considered dull, repetitive, demeaning labour.

To begin with, the life of the veil and service to God calmed my childish fears of eternal damnation. I loved my work, excelling in the gentle skill of binding pages. But I soon lost interest in the empty muttering of prayers and the endless slavery of the life of the cloth.

So I ran away. I was no more than nineteen when I decided I'd had enough. I knew I had to escape this cloistered world of bitter men and women or I would risk becoming bitter myself.

Now it just so happened that soon after I made my decision to escape a strange coincidence occurred. I was removed from the scriptorium and assigned to assist the abbess in her day-to-day duties. It was my honour to tidy her bedchamber, cook her meals, deliver her messages, clean her privy and attend to her every need.

She was a dour old cow that one. Hilde was her name and she was a severe Saxon woman who rarely smiled and never let her feelings show one way or the other. I guess she must have been quite beautiful when she was younger for her features were fine and she had a noble bearing about her.

I was by her side for three months. In that time I never once saw her remove her head covering. She wore the same long black shift that whole while without flinching at the stench of her own body odours. The Saxons are renowned for their uncouth ways.

But it was when it came to prayer that Abbess Hilde showed her true nature. She was an enthusiastic, some would say overzealous, indulger of the mumbling mutters. Morning noon and night she could be found beseeching the Lord to save her from this or forgive her for that.

She was utterly convinced she was the worst of all sinners. It's a mystery to me, with all that supplicating, when she could have had a free moment to break a single commandment.

And her voice! What a whining, nasal noise erupted from her lips! She's lucky she wasn't struck down for it. I used to imagine the choirs of the angels sitting up in Heaven with their hands over their ears willing her to stop. Truly, angels must have the patience of saints, I used to think.

Well it happened that every year the local lords and nobility made gifts to the abbey. And the first week I was with Hilde a strange present arrived at her chamber. Some knight who was setting off for the Holy Land to seek his fortune had a suit of riding clothes made for his son. The lad never got to wear them. He died of the fever before the last stitch was sewn. So the knight gave the suit to Hilde, begging that she say prayers for his son's soul in return.

I'll never forget the look of disgust on the old girl's face when she opened the linen wraps. She held up a pair of britches that would have fitted her perfectly, for she was, like me, no bigger than a boy of sixteen summers. She commanded me to stow the clothes in an iron-bound chest in the corner of Hilde's chamber. Then the abbess went off to catalogue her daily sins before the altar and pray earnestly for the knight's son.

I packed the clothes away while she was gone but could not resist examining the fine garments a little closer. The tunic was fine green velvet lined with grey linen. I'd never seen such beautiful workmanship. I'd never felt such soft cloth against my skin. I must have sat there for ages brushing my hand against the clothes, marvelling at the texture.

It was as I was sitting there that Sister Ortha came to the door.

Now Ortha was a good-hearted soul. She was considered reserved by some, but let me tell you that was all an act to keep tongues from wagging. She always smiled warmly when she met me. I reminded her of our homeland. She'd left Ireland to come to Glastonbury when she was twenty. She'd heard this abbey was a centre of learning and a place of renown. But she hadn't heard that women were not allowed to undertake the same tasks as men in England. She'd had no idea that learning and renown were not doled out to females as freely as they were in Ireland.

By then it was too late. The high walls of the abbey held her as surely as if she'd been a prisoner. Which of course, like me, she was.

'What are you doing?' she snapped in perfect Latin as she entered the chamber.

I shut the lid on the chest as I stood up. Then I shrugged. Ortha's eyes formed into slits. She stepped closer as she slipped into our native Gaelic language.

'How old are you?'

'Nineteen summers,' I replied, nervous lest we be caught not using Latin.

'Then it's about time I started your education. Where's the muttering one?'

'Hilde's gone to prayer.'

Ortha smiled. 'Then we've only got an hour.'

'For what?'

'Come with me.'

She turned sharply round on her heel and left the room. I didn't move. I knew what sort of trouble I'd be in if the abbess came back looking for me. Ortha poked her head around the door.

'Come on!'

And bless me! I was off after her with my heart pounding in my chest.

'Where are we going?' I whispered as I tried to keep pace with her.

'We're going home,' she told me.

Before I knew it we had stopped outside the stone storehouse where all the raw wool for spinning was kept. It being the season after the shearing, the room was full. It was Ortha's duty to watch over the store and keep all damp from the wool. We stood at the door for a moment as she looked me in the eye.

'You must promise not to speak a word of what I'm about to show you.'

I stared back blankly, trying to imagine what she was hiding in that room.

'Swear it!'

'I swear.'

'Then come in. This doorway leads to Ireland.'

I half expected that when she opened the oaken doors I'd see a vision of Wexford town before me or that I'd walk on fields of fresh green grass again and hear the voices of my native land.

But all I saw was wool. I was confused. I must have frowned deeply.

'You and I are going home,' Ortha told me. 'What do you think of that?'

I know my eyes lit up because that's usually what happens when my heart skips a beat with excitement. There was some mischief afoot, I could tell. And even today, though I be well into my ninetieth year, I love nothing so much as a bit of mischief.

'How?' I asked.

'First of all we're going to escape this monastery.'

I shook my head in disbelief. 'We'd never make it. How will we get through the gates without being stopped? Are we just going to walk right by Brother Anthony the gatekeeper?' I waved my hand at the imaginary Anthony. 'Sorry, Brother, we've had enough of living with all these rules. We're off home now. Goodbye!'

I didn't wait for her to reply. 'We'd both end up on our hands and knees scrubbing the abbot's kitchen for the rest of our miserable lives.'

'I've got it all planned,' Ortha hissed.

Then she grabbed the corner of a small wool bale and dragged it until the stitching loosened to reveal the contents. There was a bundle of linen like that I'd seen lining the boy's tunic. It was grey and it was beautiful.

'We'll make ourselves some clothes. Fine clothes befitting women of quality. Whatever's left we'll sell to pay our passage home.'

'How? We live in a nunnery. When do we have time to stitch clothes? As it is we're only allowed to sleep six hours a day.'

Ortha put a hand on my shoulder.

'Listen to me. That's six hours a day that belongs to us. We can give up half our sleeping hours to work on getting out of here. It might take us six months to finish the job but it's better than rotting in this dungeon for the rest of our natural lives.'

I thought about it.

'When do we start?' I asked her.

'You'll come here this evening when the abbess goes to sleep. Together we'll work through the night. That's how we'll do it every night. No one will notice what I'm doing since I'm assigned to rest here. But you will need a little help to keep the abbess off your back.'

Ortha reached into the bale and drew out a small leather parcel. Then she handed it to me.

'Take these herbs. Heat them in a little butter till the whole mixture turns green. Then mix a pinch into Hilde's evening meal or give it in a draught to her as a bedtime drink. No more than a pinch, mind you! She'll sleep so soundly and wake so refreshed she'll never notice you've been gone.'

'You have a knowledge of herbs!' I exclaimed in shock.

Such expertise was forbidden to women in the monastery.

'I know much that will come in handy to us on the road once we're free of this foul place.'

Free. The word hung in the air like a swirling cloud of glittering promises. But then a question arose in my mind.

'Why me?'

'I've seen you seated at mass,' Ortha whispered. 'Your thoughts are not on your holy duties. You have that look in your eye all exiles get when they think on their home. Am I wrong?'

I weighed up the risks. I let my doubts call out a warning to me deep in my quivering heart. And then I ignored them.

'What time do you want me here?'

'Midnight.'

Ortha was right. The green herbs put the abbess to sleep before the pious woman had even finished her prayers. For the silence alone I was truly thankful. Once I'd tucked the abbess under her threadbare covers I headed off to the wool store.

Along the way I tried to think of what I'd say if I was caught. The one thing that kept me going was the realisation that if I stayed on here at Glastonbury I'd have nothing much to look forward to. Even the abbess, after all she'd done for the community, had little more than a thin blanket to keep out the chill each night. What kind of a life was that?

That was the first night of many. In three months we'd finished a suit of clothes that fitted Ortha perfectly. Then we started work on a shift that would be my disguise. Until one evening when I opened the wool store door and heard sobbing.

It was Ortha. She looked up at me with tears in her eyes.

'I'm being sent to serve the bishop in Wells,' she cried. 'I have to leave in three days.'

The town of Wells where the bishop kept his palace was seven miles, no more, from Glastonbury. But it might well have been a hundred. All our work had come to nothing. We didn't have my clothes finished and we couldn't possibly complete the task in time.

'You must go without me,' I told Ortha. 'Make your escape and do not hesitate.'

'I can't do that! How far do you think I'd get on my own? We need one another if we're going to manage a horse and cart full of fine goods.'

I have to admit I was a little taken aback. In all the time we'd laboured together she'd never mentioned this part of her plan. I asked her what she was talking about and this is the explanation I got.

Her intention all along had been to wait until the rich noble ladies came to the convent as they did every Sunday to attend mass. There was one noblewoman in particular, Ortha called her the grey lady. She always dressed in simple grey linen to show her piety and she always brought her sister with her dressed the same.

After mass the two of them often sat to dine with the abbess in the great hall, though sometimes they took their meal in Hilde's private apartments. They were great patronesses of the abbey and the abbess always treated them with respect.

I for my part had waited upon the ladies in question each Sunday. Their names were Edwina and Eleanor. I knew they travelled in a cart in which they usually brought some gift or other, a bolt of fine fabric from the exotic east or a barrel of spices from even further east. And their manservant always left the cart unattended after mass while he sat down with the monastery servants to eat and drink his fill.

He was in the habit of unloading the cart at the very last minute, just before his mistresses were ready to depart. There was at least an hour in which someone posing as the ladies in grey could climb aboard the cart and leave.

'I was hoping we'd be lucky enough to find ourselves some worthy booty we could sell to fill our bellies and smooth our way over the Irish Sea,' she told me.

'*That* was your plan?' I hissed with disbelief. 'You thought we'd steal a horse and cart from under the noses of the abbess and her guests, then just ride out past the ever-watchful eye of Brother Anthony?'

'Can you come up with anything better?'

I could not. But in any case it wouldn't have mattered. Ortha would be gone in a week. This coming Sunday was our last chance to make good our escape.

'It's hopeless,' she declared. 'No one can help us. We're prisoners. We may as well lock ourselves in our cells and never come out.'

But before the words had even passed her lips a change came over her expression.

'What's the matter?' I enquired, noticing the strange twinkle in her eyes.

'Have you ever met Brother Neart?'

'I've never even heard of him. Is he Irish?'

She nodded. His name meant, One Who Has Power. It was an odd name for a monk, you understand.

'Come with me,' Ortha said, grabbing me by the sleeve. 'Neart will know what to do. He'll be able to help us. They say there's no problem he can't solve if he puts his mind to it.'

So I followed along after her, avoiding the night watch as they passed by bearing their halberds with lanterns dangling from the blades. We hid among the thorn bushes near the abbot's kitchen for a long while then made a dash up the slope toward the hill folk call the Tor.

Before we came to the apple orchards on the slope of the hill we found a ramshackle collection of huts. The sound of heavy sleepers drifted out of every simple cell but one.

'What if we wake the monks?' I whispered, having second thoughts about the wisdom of this midnight jaunt.

Ortha smiled a devilish grin.

'You're a naughty girl, you are!' she exclaimed. 'We haven't got time to be thinking about that sort of thing!'

'What sort of thing?' I asked innocently.

But she didn't reply. She held her fingers to her lips then dropped her voice to a whisper so low I could hardly make out what she was saying. We knelt down by the door of a hut that was silent within.

'Whatever happens don't show any surprise or shock whatsoever. Old Neart is easily offended and we don't want to put him off helping us. No matter what you see on the other side of this door, don't cry out.'

'What are we doing here?' I pressed.

'We've come to ask the advice of the wisest, most mystical monk in the whole abbey. Neart is a man of such piety there is no problem he cannot solve.'

I couldn't imagine that I could have dwelled in the monastery all these years and never heard of such a holy man. Surely if he was so wise he'd be the abbot.

But before I had a chance to make this point the door was opened and I was pushed inside. The door silently shut again as Ortha and I stood together hand in hand in the semi-darkness.

A candle on the bookshelf and a faint glow from a small hearth fire illumined a figure dressed in a long cloak and standing with head bowed toward the coals. He did not look around at us as the draft lifted the edge of his woollen wrap.

'Who's there?' an old man's weary voice enquired in perfect Latin without a trace of accent.

'It is Ortha,' my companion replied in Irish. 'And I've brought you another of our folk to meet. Her name is Binney.'

'Binney?' he asked. 'Are you the young sister of Eriginas?'

'I am.'

'Then you are welcome here,' he told me in a friendly tone. 'Your brother is one of the few folk who bother to visit me from time to time.'

Then a most remarkable thing happened. It's something that has stayed with me ever since. Even now if I close my eyes I can picture every detail of what took place. Neart turned around.

And as he did so I realised he wasn't standing up at all. His legs were crossed in a seated posture. His cloak flowed down around his body to drop to the floor. The old man was floating in midair.

My mouth must have dropped open wide because the next thing I knew Ortha was sticking her elbow into my ribs.

'Let her be,' Neart laughed. 'I seem to recall you fainted the first time you set eyes on me.'

Then the old man started to softly laugh. It wasn't a fully fledged guffaw nor was it an insincere cackle. It was the most beautiful sound I've ever heard. It was the kind of laugh that made you want to break out into a chorus of laughter along with him. To begin with I smiled.

Then Neart drifted over to a bookshelf, picked up the candle and moved closer. As the shadows fled before the little light, I could plainly see he was an old man. But his face was not etched with bitterness, pain or disappointment. His skin was traced by laughter lines, as if he'd been giggling his whole life long.

There was an aura of mischievous joy about him I'd only ever seen in a small child before. And I remember wishing I'd turn out just like that when I grew old. I don't think I've done too badly by the way.

'We need your help, Neart,' Sister Ortha told him. 'We both want to go home.'

'You are home,' he laughed.

'Home to Ireland.'

'But you have made vows to your vocation.'

'We don't like living here in the abbey.'

Neart shrugged his shoulders.

'Who among us truly does? It's a cold wet place. The food is awful. The heating is inadequate. The abbot is a surly fat man with no understanding of basic bodily ablutions. Nor do any of the Saxons.'

He sighed heavily then smiled again.

'But that's what comes of choosing to live among the foreigners. They're a race of savages, with small minds and smaller vision. We must put up with these inconveniences for the sake of our faith.'

I was still too shocked at the fact Neart was floating around before me as if by magic to take in much of what he said. I thought I must surely be dreaming. I rubbed my eyes again and again to clear them.

He floated closer to me when he noticed I was having trouble accepting the situation.

'What's the matter with you, child? Haven't you ever seen an old man levitating before?'

'No,' I replied.

He broke into a laugh again.

'Of course you haven't!'

Ortha stepped between us, pushing me back with her hand.

'Don't tease her,' she told the old man. 'We need your help. They're sending me to the bishop's palace in Wells. They're going to separate us.'

'You made a promise to uphold your vows to the Holy Mother Church,' the old man snapped, suddenly seeming to lose his patience. 'It's a bit late to be having a change of heart, don't you think?'

'Wouldn't you make some changes to your life if you could?' she countered.

Neart sighed, then smiled again. He laughed. He couldn't seem to go too long without laughing. His eyes twinkled with merriment as he spoke.

'It is within the power of all of us to change that which we do not wish to continue. It is an easy thing for any of us to alter that which has become unbearable. Why are you asking me for help? You should be seeking the solution to your problem within your own heart.'

'You're just a bitter old man!' Ortha spat. 'We're wasting our time asking for your help.'

'I'm very happy actually,' he corrected her. 'Very happy indeed. But I must agree with you. You are wasting your time here. Go back to your cells. Meditate. An answer will surely come to you if you pray hard enough.'

'Muttering Hilde hasn't found any answers,' Ortha shot back.

'An ounce of persistence is worth a hundredweight of skill,' he laughed.

She grabbed me by the arm and dragged me out the door before he could say another word. On the way back to the wool store I pestered her till she told me the story of Neart.

In his youth Neart had travelled from Ireland seeking knowledge. Like so many of our countrymen and women he ended up here at Glastonbury, a place famed for its learning. But like most he was disappointed.

He found a hive of literal-minded Saxons, rule-makers and regulation-keepers who had no interest in the deeper mysteries. And no desire to have any experience of the Holy Spirit beyond what they could read about. They were content to live their lives as empty thoughtless vessels married to the Benedictine laws.

This wasn't the life for Neart. So one day he asked his teacher, an old Saxon monk, what course he should undertake to gain direct experience of God. His teacher told him that the holiest of all holies was not meant for mere mortals to experience. It was beyond the capabilities of one such as him to attain such a sacred goal. He might as well try to learn to fly.

So, being a stubborn man who was also deeply unhappy living in the community of Glastonbury, Neart decided it was time to take his leave. Of course the abbot wouldn't let him go. As a punishment for attempting to throw off his vows, the old bugger ordered him to work longer hours.

Naturally that only inspired Neart to climb the monastery walls. He was caught time and again until at last the abbot ordered him to be locked within a cell in the dark depths of the crypt until he came to his senses.

Food was left for him through a slot in the door cunningly designed to prevent light reaching the law-breaker locked within the cell. But that didn't worry Neart. He was glad to be free of all those rules. In this place his thoughts were free to roam wheresoever they would go. After he had spent a long while imagining himself far away in his native country, his thoughts turned to his teacher's words.

'You might as well try to learn to fly.' That's what the old man had told him. So Neart set his mind to meditating; with all his heart he focused his attention to attaining that very goal.

He didn't come out of that cell in a week. He didn't emerge after two. A month passed. Still Neart refused to accede to the abbot's demand that he repent his wilful ways. Every evening the old man came to ask him if he'd changed his mind. But after six months Neart had not said a word to the father of his community.

This was no small embarrassment to the abbot. It was a direct challenge to his authority. But he ignored the advice of his peers and refused to release the Irish monk unless he promised to honour his vows. By then, however, Neart had lost all interest in the outside world.

Each day he ate his simple meal, pushed his refuse pot out

through the light-fast door and received a clean one. He drank the sweet waters of the holy well of Glastonbury from an earthenware jar and he thanked God for setting him this sacred challenge.

In this manner a remarkable forty years passed. At the end of that time three abbots of Glastonbury had gone to their eternal reward. Three kings had ruled over England. And three bishops had been buried in the crypt near to where Neart's cell was situated.

By that time a holy reputation had built up around him. Saint Neart, some called him. Simple folk who worked as servants left candles at the door to his cell hoping for some miraculous cure. But in all those forty years no one heard a word spoken by the monk who dwelled in the crypt.

Then one night the serving abbot went down to ask the customary question. This monk, who had been a mere novice when Neart entered his living tomb, pushed the steaming broth and oatbread through the door.

'Will you repent?' he asked, expecting that as usual there would be no response.

'I will,' came the answer.

'What?'

'I said I'm ready to accept your authority and return to the life of a holy brother,' Neart told him.

The abbot hastily ordered the cell to be opened. The sight that met his eyes was exactly the same as that which met mine when I went to visit Neart. The holy hermit of the crypt was floating round his cell with his long hair and beard flowing over his crossed legs.

And he was laughing. For he had learned to fly. He'd taught himself to float. By sheer force of will, through ardent meditation, he'd achieved what some would term the impossible. Unfortunately his old teacher was long dead so it was a bit too late to rub his nose in it.

There was another problem. Though Neart had learned to float about, he hadn't worked out how to stop this strange effect from taking hold of him. So he could be sitting quietly at table one second and drifting off toward the kitchen the next. This unsettled the younger monks, to say nothing of the lay folk who came to mass each day. The holy monk floating round the high arches inside the great cathedral distracted them from their devotions. Some stayed away from mass for fear he'd been possessed by dæmons.

So in the end he was ordered to remain in his small hut at the edge of the apple orchard. And because he'd promised to do as he was told, Neart did as he was told. He'd been in that hut for another forty years when I met him, so he was close to a hundred summers on this Earth. But he was still laughing. He saw the funny side of his situation.

For all his effort to escape the monastery, for all his concentration on his task of learning to levitate, he'd failed to achieve his original goal. He was as much a prisoner at the end of his life as he'd been in the beginning.

His stubbornness had cost him dearly and his desire to show up his old teacher had cost him even more. He would never leave the abbey. His fame would remain long after he had drawn his final breath, to be sure, but he was still a prisoner. It's a good thing he'd learned to laugh about it all.

Neart was the holy hermit who floated. You'll hear his miracles related the length and breadth of Christendom.

After she told me his story I left Ortha at the wool store then headed back to my cell to get some sleep. Floating Neart was in my thoughts the whole way. I realised he'd been able to achieve his incredible goal against all odds.

I was inspired by his holy example, so as I was passing Abbess Hilde's chamber on my way to my own room next door I thought I'd say a little prayer. I knelt down there in the corridor with the moonlight streaming through the window onto the cold marble paving before me.

I pictured Ortha and myself riding that cart to freedom headed west toward the coast to catch a boat home. And you know something? I noticed a change. I can't pinpoint what it was even today, but as I tell you about it a tingle passes through every muscle in my body. Something moved in my spirit. A miracle was set in motion.

I went straight to bed, with Neart's words echoing in my thoughts.

'An ounce of persistence is worth a hundredweight of skill.'

I lay down, concentrating all my thoughts on finding a solution to our problem. And do you know what? Just as my eyes were closing with exhaustion I remembered the suit of clothes the abbess had locked in a chest in the corner of her chamber.

My heart jumped a beat or two I can tell you. And I thanked Neart for his gift. He'd shown me there is *always* a solution to every problem. All it takes is persistence.

That's how we made our escape from the abbey. The next Sunday, while the grey lady and her sister sat with the abbess to dine, I dressed up as a lad and Ortha, clothed as my mother, took the reins of that cart. After confusing the gatekeeper completely, we were outside the walls of the abbey on the road west.

That wasn't the end of our adventures either. It was a long while before we managed to make our way to Ireland. By then Ortha had found herself a lad, fallen in love and abandoned all thoughts of the monastic life.

Her parting gift to me was a small bag of herbs wrapped tight.

'When you find the lad you love,' she told me, 'warm these herbs in butter till the whole mixture turns greenish. Then slip it in his broth.'

'I don't want a lad who's going to sleep all night!' I told her.

66

'He won't sleep,' she promised. 'These aren't the same herbs I gave you for Hilde. These are the magic spices of love which grow around the stone enclosure of the Well of the Goddess. They are known as the tincture of true love, the butter of the beloved and the instrument of infatuation.'

That's how I came to possess a very dangerous and treacherous secret. If it hadn't been for Ortha I never would have escaped the monastery. I never would have found my way to the Killibegs. I never would have become entangled in a web of confusion brought on by a love potion. I would never have tasted from the Well of the Goddess.

The Love Philtre

here was I? I'd just talked about Mirim and Alan and told of their decision to stay at the Killibegs for the night. Then I got on to the love potion.

You heard me. What's the matter with your ears anyway? Don't you understand what I'm talking about? I've a sense it's not your hearing that's the problem. It's your listening. I'm speaking about the love potion. This is my part of the tale.

It came to be that I sat in the house of healing at the Killibegs while Aoife was stitching together her plot to raise her status to goddess and the Slua Sen Erainn were marching down from the port at Gaillimh to challenge her. Within the walls of the rath where my kinfolk had decided to settle for the winter I waited by the side of unconscious Caoimhin.

He was out to it, recovering from the effects of a terrible poison administered to him by John Toothache, the servant of Bishop Ollo. I had no other thought on my mind at sunset that Samhain Eve than the giving of thanks for his miraculous recovery.

I'd taken a shine to the lad from the first instant I laid eyes on him. I had this notion that he and I were meant for one another and that he was the man I'd been praying for. So when he fell to the hand of a murderer I was sorely disappointed.

Cruel chance, I told myself, had intervened in my life yet again. Like the time that shepherd boy fell off the mountain after he'd declared his undying passion for me. Or the unfortunate occasion when that young fisherman rowed his curragh into the mouth of a whirlpool the morning after we'd shared a night of unbridled lip-tickling in his hut.

All they found of him was his oar, snapped cleanly in two, washed up high and dry on the beach. I still have half that oar hanging above my lintel to remind me not to go out in flimsy leather boats near treacherous whirlpools.

So I'm sure you can understand that when Caoimhin fainted from the effects of the poison and Sianan declared there was no hope for him, I wasn't surprised. I simply shrugged my shoulders and whispered, 'Bloody typical!' under my breath.

I begged Sianan to give him the Quicken Brew. Of course I did. And I wasn't just thinking of his wellbeing either. I knew his passing would make it nigh on impossible for me to attract an eligible mate. After the deaths of two suitors already, three if you count the lad who fell off his horse just as he was asking me to marry him, the young men of the Killibegs were beginning to become wary of me.

Sianan refused to give him the Brew. She told me immortality was a curse not a blessing and that she had promised never to administer the draught of healing to any mortal. But as I told you last night, a change of heart had come over her and she had relented. She didn't tell me, though. Oh how I wish she had!

I've always been fascinated by stories of the Quicken Brew. If you recall, it is the secret enchantment of the Danaan people who lived in Ireland before our folk came here. In their day the land was called Innisfail. They made this liquor to stave off death forever. It was their weapon against the invasion of the sons of Míl who were the ancestors of the Gaels.

You see, the Danaans were wise folk but they did not possess iron weapons. Their Druids foresaw a terrible slaughter for their folk. So they came up with the Brew. That way their warriors could fall to Gaelic swords but as soon as they fell they'd stand up again ready to go on fighting.

It worked a treat, as most Draoi-craft does. There was only one small problem. The mortal kind are meant to perish. It's the only way to refresh the spirit and so move on to greater things. Unless we are freed of the body we cannot hope to attain to other stages. You'll see what I'm on about soon enough.

Suffice to say that the Danaans and those of the Fir-Bolg who took the Quicken Brew were doomed to dwell forever in the casing of their flesh. Many of them gained great wisdom during their unending lives. A few chose to go to sleep. For in their dreams they were free to roam the realms of the Otherworld at will.

Of all the Gaels who ever lived in Ireland only two had been granted the Brew. They were the Fanaí called Mawn and Sianan. Some folk call them the Wanderers, but that title tells nothing of the extent of their travails.

Caoimhin wrote their tale down in a book which he named after them. He got the story of their early life from Mawn. But I will tell you now something of Sianan for she was known to me and I often spoke with her in later days about her life.

In the time when my tale took place Sianan had been dwelling at Dun Gur. She was the abbess of a small community of Culdees who chose the settled life rather than the nomadic existence my kin endured.

She'd lived there nearly eight hundred summers by then. She had been a child in the time of the one they call Saint Patrick. I'm not talking about that fraudulent invention touted by the Church fathers as Saint Patrick. I'm talking about the real Patrick. In fact his name was Patricius Sucatus and he wasn't so much a saint as yet another persistent cleric.

Sianan was already old when Guy d'Alville and his mercenary band chanced upon her settlement. And what a ruckus he caused. With typical Norman disregard for local customs he released the Natharaí worms who had been imprisoned in the well of Dun Gur since before anyone could remember. Soon enough his warriors were nothing more than undigested pulp lining the guts of two fat hungry beasts of the darkness. And Sianan was on the run to the Killibegs to warn us of the danger.

Along the way she and Martin, a former foot soldier who'd worked for Guy, discovered Aoife's plan to snuff out the fires of Samhain then set her Redcaps loose upon the land. Sianan made it here to the Killibegs just in time to nurse my Caoimhin with her Quicken Brew.

But as I said earlier I had no idea she'd used the Brew on him. I'd begged her to do so but she'd steadfastly refused. So how could I have expected she might have given in to my pleading? Believe me, I would have done everything differently if I'd known. I wouldn't have used the love potion for a start.

Well, it so happened that Sianan was called off to attend the council of chieftains who were making ready to defend the rath against Aoife and her Redcaps. I was left with Caoimhin in my care.

Before she departed Sianan told me that a miracle had occurred. Caoimhin would live, though he might take some time to recover fully. I was ecstatic. Not only was this beautiful lad going to be restored to me but my tally of deceased suitors would round out at only three. My run of ill fortune was ended!

I must have sat there a long while watching over him as I waited for him to wake. I offered copious thanks to Danu, Bride and all the Old Ones. I had just started addressing the saints when an idea entered my head. Was it just coincidence we had met. Wasn't it meant to be?

I had been a nun at myself, you recall. Caoimhin was a monk. And he wasn't just any mumbling monastic dressed in black. He'd been apprenticed to my brother, the master scribe,

Eriginas. So it was remarkable to me that he and I had never met.

There were other wondrous happenstances of course. For example, he'd been placed in the monastery after the death of his parents. No one asked him if he wanted to be a monk. I was talked into the nunnery by my brother. I was there against my will as well.

Another remarkable thing was that when he crossed my path I'd just finished calling down a solemn prayer for a companion in this life. I'd been feeling lonely. I was a fool of a girl in those days, I admit it. I truly thought I could find my peace with a soul-mate, if I could find one who'd live long enough to marry me. I didn't know, as I do now, that one only discovers one's true soul-friend when one is at peace within.

I was young and overcome by a sense of urgency. I didn't want to risk this one getting away from me as the others had. What if he woke up and didn't feel the same way about me as I'd convinced myself I felt about him?

As these questions boiled about in my brain an answer presented itself to me. Ortha's gift. I eagerly pulled out the little bundle of herbs from my tunic and sniffed at the contents, hoping they were still potent. That's what brought me to consider cooking them up in a little butter till the whole mixture was a deep green hue. And that's why I wondered whether I should stir the love philtre into Caoimhin's broth.

Now Ortha left me strict instructions for this potion. For the enchantment to work properly he had to take it with his food. And the very next person he looked upon when the butter began to digest would be the object of his love.

There was enough kick in those herbs, she'd told me, to win the lad of my choice over to my charms without too much effort. All I had to do was prepare the butter and the broth then wait for him to awake.

Call me an eedyit. Go ahead. I won't argue with you. I can

72

think of a few other things I'd like to call myself. I'm still embarrassed about it now and there's seventy summers or more have passed since I sat there beside him. As sure as my name is Binney that was almost the worst mistake I ever made in my life. Almost.

It's a hard thing for an old woman like myself to face up to but I was so smitten with him I must have lost what little wits I had. I don't know what came over me. I had merely to look at that lovely face to know he was the one for me.

He was good-looking. He was a scribe. He was youthful. He was in need of nurturing. And most important of all, he'd survived, as his three predecessors had not.

Actually, if you take into account that young fellow who single-handedly took on an entire Norman garrison armed only with a ferret, it was four. He was trying to impress me, I know. He was a show-off. That laddie was doomed from the start. And I'd only just met him so I suppose he can't really be termed a suitor in the strictest sense of the word.

If only I'd taken more careful note of the most important part of Ortha's instructions! She'd told me the potion would not take hold until the very moment it had digested.

I should have realised digestion periods vary greatly from person to person. I just didn't think of it at the time. I was too caught up in silly thoughts of what I believed to be love. For the moment, though, I tucked the little bag of herbs back into my sleeve and resisted the urge to use them.

Here's my advice. Don't trust a love potion into the keeping of a heart-sick young eedyit. Don't give the herbs of loving to a woman who has already outlived three young men. No good will come of it. As you'll see, no good came of my foolishness. Only trouble.

As Caoimhin slept, soothed by the healing properties of the Quicken Brew, a dream state descended upon him and transported him to another place. I've told you before he suffered from an affliction of the visionary kind. Often his dreams revealed to him glimpses of what was to come or of what was taking place in the very moment.

And that's how it was this time. Though his eyes were shut and he drew the breath low, Caoimhin's soul was wide awake. He was seated on the pebble shore of a dark pool. Trickling water spouted forth from the mouth of a carved stone head to ripple the surface of the pond.

The moon was bright and the air was balmy which should have struck him as unusual for it was Samhain Eve. At that season the warm days have fled. Trees whispered to one another on the slopes of the wooded hill behind him. But their talk wasn't malicious. It was welcoming. So Caoimhin lay back to take in the refreshing surroundings.

The sky above him was brimming with countless stars spread out upon the purple velvet of the night. Owls hooted in the far distance. All was peace. All was calm.

Then a thought struck the young monk. The last thing he could recall was drinking from the chalice at the holy feast of Killibegs. He remembered feeling ill. He knew he'd fallen over as his knees gave way under him. He'd heard someone declare that he'd been poisoned.

He took in a sharp breath before he asked the terrible question that had leaped into his mind.

'Am I dead?'

'Not dead,' a woman replied from behind him. 'Just a little lost.'

He was on his feet in a second. It took only another breath for him to spot the outline of a person standing in the shadows among the trees at the foot of the hill.

'Who are you? Where am I?'

'My name is Flidais,' the woman replied, stepping out from cover into the silver-blue moonlight. 'You are wandering in the land of dreams. But you are unusually awake for one of your kind.'

'Are you a dæmon?' he stuttered.

Flidais laughed. 'Some would call me that. But they'd be wrong. I am no different from you in some respects. But I am also unlike you in many others. I am the Huntress. I am the Queen of the Hunt.'

She smiled, showing a hint of some wicked thought. His heart raced. The woman's eyes were of a violet blue that would have inspired envy in the ocean. Her dark hair was tied up in braids which sat on the back of her head. Her clothes were practical as befits a huntress. And she moved like a cat, sleek and confident, ever awake to any sign of prey or predators.

'Come with me, young man. I have an eye for you. If you do as I command, great rewards await you.'

Caoimhin must have baulked. I know I would have if I'd been in his position. And I was a lot less pious in those days than he was, I can tell you. Anyway, he made no move when she held her hand out to him.

'I'm a monk. I'm sworn to God. I cannot go with you.'

In a blinding flash she'd covered the short distance between them. Such was her swiftness that Caoimhin took a sharp intake of breath in shock at the move. But before he could pull away Flidais brushed a gentle hand against his cheek.

That simple gesture calmed him completely.

'I'll come with you,' he conceded in dreamy obedience.

Of course he did. Who among the mortal kind has the will to refuse Flidais? Indeed, there's few among the Earth-born who can refuse the wiles of any of the immortals. But she is the eternal seductress. She is the everlasting goddess of sensual pleasures. She is the mistress of the hunt and the sovereign of all lovers. And she's a jealous one too.

The next thing he knew young Caoimhin was lying down upon a soft bed of linen overhung with a canopy of lace and flowers. He smelled the sweet scent of roses, the spice of exotic cinnamon and the taunting aroma of holy frankincense.

He closed his eyes as he sank into a bliss such as he'd never known before, surrendering to a joyous intensity which threatened to engulf him entirely in its sweet embrace. He felt a soft caress against his cheek as a hand swept his unruly hair away from his forehead.

Then Caoimhin found himself responding to the kisses. Before he knew what was happening he was overcome by a wave of unrestrained desire. Soon enough he lost all sense of time or of reality or of guilt, shame or hesitation.

As the wave of passion rose high to crash upon his shore Caoimhin stopped himself. Some thought had come into his mind. He told me later it was a picture of my face. And I'd like to believe him. But in those days I know he was still attached to the monastic life. I reckon he was just throwing out a line hoping I'd take the hook.

Whatever it was that brought him out of the trance of Flidais really doesn't matter. The end result was that he pushed her away so forcefully that she rolled off the bed and landed on the pebbles with a crunch.

Which just goes to show that even a goddess can be caught off guard. She was so surprised she lay on her back upon the rounded stones for a few breaths before she rose up. But when she did she was lifted on the strength of her fury.

Few had ever pushed this woman away. Few had ever dared refuse the Huntress. She wasn't about to let Caoimhin get away with this affront to her beauty. She was going to teach him a lesson. And that began with the telling of a story.

Before his unbelieving eyes Caoimhin witnessed a strange scene unfold. A youthful lad with dark hair stood before Flidais. Her hunter's garb was gone. Now she wore a long trailing black gown. She had her back to him so our Benedictine brother could look into the other lad's face.

He heard them speaking softly to one another, though he could not discern precisely what they were talking about. Then, without warning, Flidais stepped out of her gown to stand naked before the lad.

Caoimhin was so shocked at seeing the fine white skin of her backside that he immediately averted his eyes. Then he clearly heard the lad speak.

'I will not go with you,' he stated in a steady, determined tone. 'Sianan is waiting for me. She is my soul-friend. I am sworn to the service of my people and I may not tarry here with you. Though you were the most beautiful woman in the Otherworld, which I suspect you are, I could not stay. Though you may wish to hold my heart in thrall with your tender embraces and soothing touch, I must return to Sianan.'

Caoimhin heard the tenderness with which the lad spoke the name of his soul-friend and he marvelled that he was speaking of someone he knew.

'Very well,' Flidais proclaimed. 'There is but one fate which befits you, Mawn of the Fánaí. You will go to the depths of the Well of Many Blessings. You will dwell there until you've changed your mind. You will not go back to her while I still hold any desire for you. You will not see Sianan as long as you refuse to satisfy my longing. You will remain here my prisoner forever if need be.'

Then she smiled wryly.

'Unless I choose to release you, only my death will free you from this enchantment. And as I'm an immortal too, I wouldn't count on outliving me.'

'You can imprison my body,' he replied, 'but you will never cage my heart.'

'Foolish Mawn. The day will come when you won't be so haughty with me. I'm patient. I can wait a very long time.'

In the next breath the lad had disappeared. Caoimhin didn't need to be told where he'd gone to. Flidais was standing before him now dressed in her long flowing gown of black, high-necked to the collar with sleeves flaring outwards from her wrists to touch the ground beside her.

'What say you, Caoimhin?' she asked. 'Will you go to the bottom of the pool to join poor Mawn? Or will you submit to me?'

He never had the opportunity to reply, which was lucky considering what he probably would have said. As she finished speaking a strange winged creature resembling a diminutive mortal woman flew in between them. The creature would have stood no taller than Caoimhin's shinbone. She was dressed in a black gown almost identical to that which Flidais wore.

Her wings were like those of a dragonfly except they were entirely black. As the creature landed it turned to observe Caoimhin, smiling with a predatory grin which exposed tiny rows of pointed teeth. He was fascinated by the diminutive dæmon. But the creature showed no more than a fleeting interest in him.

'I have news!' the rasping little voice reported. 'Robert FitzWilliam is at the borders of our country. I've heard he's coming this way.'

'The young FitzWilliam!' Flidais cooed excitedly, gathering up her gown in one hand as she turned her gaze to Caoimhin once again.

'And the rebels are gathering for the feast!' the creature added. 'Will you come to them?'

'I will.'

Flidais turned to Caoimhin.

'You are dismissed,' she told him curtly. 'Leave this place before I change my mind. I have bigger fish to fry. You can't really compare with a man of Robert's standing, can you?'

In the next instant she turned to run off. And as she did so

Flidais faded from his vision like a cloud dissipating on the breeze. Our dear innocent Caoimhin stood there with his mouth gaping, left to ponder whether he was truly dead. Still undecided, he muttered a quick prayer to dispel the sinful thoughts which filled his monkish mind.

When that was done he knelt down to cross himself. But no sooner had his knees touched the pebbles than he heard a quiet chuckling.

'You're a very fortunate one, you are,' the familiar voice remarked.

'Gobann!' the young Benedictine exclaimed, recognising the deep resonant tones immediately. 'Where have you been? Why didn't you come with us to the Killibegs? So much has happened.'

Now I've told you about Gobann before. But he's a strange one this lad and difficult to explain. He'd been the Druid teacher of Sianan and Mawn who were proclaimed the Fánaí. And he was a renowned poet in his day.

At the battle of Dun Righ in Alba he lost his life just before his two students were separated from one another. You may scoff when I tell you his spirit had returned to the world. But the simple truth is we all leave this world with unfinished business. As I told you last night, Gobann had a few attachments left to resolve from his former life. That's why he'd come back.

By the time that last phrase was out of his mouth Caoimhin was up on his feet hugging the Druid like a long-lost friend. Which in some respects he was. The Druid's knotted locks came untied and fell about his face as he enveloped the lad in his raven-feather cloak.

'I was at the Killibegs,' Gobann replied as he stepped back from the embrace. 'I spoke with Sianan. But I'm not the sort to announce my arrival to everyone like some Norman lord riding the circuit of his lands to the accompaniment of trumpet blasts and herald-calls. I prefer to keep quiet about my presence. In that way I may observe folks without being constantly pestered.'

'Pestered?'

'We Druids are few and far between nowadays. But the demand for our services hasn't waned along with our numbers.'

'What services?'

'Don't you know anything?' Gobann shook his head with an odd mixture of amusement and sadness before he went on.

'The Draoi-craft is an ancient discipline,' he explained. 'We of the dwindling company of the Eolaí Draoi are practised in the sacred art of balance. A practitioner of the Draoi speaks with spirits, dances to the music of the Sidhe-folk, listens to the woodland and to the water, strikes the sparks of healing and above all may view those things which have yet to come.'

'You are talking about the visions.'

'Indeed I am, young Caoimhin,' Gobann told him as he placed a reassuring hand upon his shoulder. 'Did you know you are experiencing a vision right now?'

'What are you talking about?' the young man asked nervously.

The Druid's hand tightened on his shoulder.

'Don't be alarmed. At present your body is lying unconscious in the healing house at the Killibegs. You're wandering in the Land of Dreams. And you're very lucky Flidais lost interest in you. When her eye is fixed on something it's usually very difficult to shake her off.'

'So I'm having another of my visions,' Caoimhin stated solemnly with resignation. 'I believe you, Gobann. Though I would never have realised it if you hadn't pointed it out to me.'

He cast his eyes down to the ground before he went on.

'I wish I'd never been afflicted with this curse. I'm sure Eriginas would never have brought me under his wing if it hadn't been for my dream-sight. I know he wouldn't have bothered with me if I hadn't been of some value to him.'

'To some extent that's true,' Gobann conceded. 'Folk who lack your talent have no idea of the terrible price you pay for your visions. They only wish to be able to see into the future for their own gain. They cannot comprehend the awful responsibility which comes from such vision.'

'And what is this vision meant to tell me? What message am I to carry back to the Killibegs?'

'You must tell Sianan all about Mawn. You must let her know Flidais is keeping him captive at the bottom of that spring. Let her know also that Robert FitzWilliam is about to stray into the Otherworld of his own free will and that Flidais has set her eye upon him but that she's not the only one.'

'Why is it I rarely witness anything of my own future in these visions?' Caoimhin asked bitterly. 'If I'd had some forewarning I was going to be poisoned I might have been able to avoid it.'

'When you have more skill and practice you'll be able to focus your attention on anyone and anything. You're still learning the tricks and pitfalls for the moment.'

'Then teach me how to see into my own future,' the young monk demanded. 'I want to know something of myself and my destiny.'

Gobann swallowed hard. 'Be careful what you wish for,' he admonished the lad. 'You may not like what you see.'

'I don't often like what I see anyway,' Caoimhin laughed coldly. 'So why should it be any different just because I'm witnessing my own fate?'

'You've come a long way since I first spoke to you at Wexford town,' the Druid told him. 'You have all the hallmarks of a fine Druid.'

'I'm not a Druid!' Caoimhin insisted.

'No. Not by half,' Gobann smiled. 'But you will be one

81

day. Are you certain you wish to see something of your own future?'

'I am.'

'So be it,' the Druid shrugged. 'Just don't expect to understand everything presented to you.'

As he spoke that last word Gobann let his hand drop away from the young monk's shoulder. Then he turned, sweeping his arm around with a flourish to usher Caoimhin past him.

'Behold!'

The young man took a hesitant step forward and Gobann pushed a hand into his back firmly to urge him on. As Caoimhin turned to glance at his friend to thank him he saw the Druid had vanished. This startled him. Gobann had told him he was walking in the midst of a vision but everything seemed so solid, so real. He couldn't quite accept that this world of dreams was any less substantial than the world of dross and dreariness.

And that's a common mistake most people make. They think the Otherworld is no more significant than their daydreams. Of course these fools don't give much value to their daydreams either, which is where all the problems start. If you haven't got dreams, what have you got?

I ask you, is this world we seem to inhabit any more real than the Realm of Dreams? Are the mortal lands less ethereal? Is the Otherworld less substantial? Not in my experience. If you're wise you will not make any distinction between your dreams and the rest of your life. For whether you like to believe it or not, there is none to be found.

Anyway, as I was saying, after he recovered from the surprise at Gobann's disappearance, Caoimhin took a few tentative steps forward. Then as his confidence returned he walked boldly over to the spring. Where the water poured out through the mouth of a carved stone head there was a deep black pool.

Our lad leaned over, hoping to get a glimpse of Mawn

trapped in the depths of the water. But the blackness was so impenetrable he could see nothing but his own reflection. He didn't take much notice of himself staring back from the surface of the water. However, just as he was about to give up hope of glimpsing Mawn, a tiny sparkle caught his eye.

Caoimhin squinted. Then he blinked. Then he rubbed his eyes in disbelief.

He focused on his reflection in the pool. There was something very odd about it. What he saw was so strange he had to take a few deep breaths to calm himself.

His own eyes stared back at him, his face that showed an expression of disbelief. But his reflection was dressed in a deep red flowing winter cloak with the hood pulled back behind his neck in a fold of fine wool. Around his neck was a thick golden necklace made from one piece of metal such as he'd never seen before.

His fair hair was shoulder length and braided. He had the start of a thin goatee beard at his chin. Most remarkable of all a fine circlet of gold sat upon his head holding his hair within its grasp. A single red jewel was set in the circlet so it sat in the middle of his forehead. He didn't have a chance to question what he saw before his reflection faded away to be replaced by another scene.

In the next instant a tense drama played out before him. Caoimhin saw a field covered with snow. Upon that icy ground there stood a host of warriors arrayed for battle in long lines four or five ranks deep. Their banners of green and red cracked in the chill wind as they silently raised their shields. As one, the host sang a low solemn rhythmic warrior song.

The shields were lowered again and weapons were raised. There were swords and spears and axes lifted up. And there were terrible sickles mounted on long shafts. Caoimhin gasped with horror and dread at the sight of these folk with their wild painted faces, outlandish clothes and fearsome weaponry.

The gathered host gave out another low growl as the snow began to miraculously melt away. It was as if the sun had suddenly come out from behind a cloud and poured down the full force of its heat upon the battlefield. Arrows whistled away toward the mass of warriors but none found their mark. By some miracle all the shafts fell short.

In no time at all the snow was entirely gone, the sky was blue, the fresh green grass lay underfoot and the faces of the warriors shone with hope. With one voice again they raised up a mighty booming call as they surged forward into the fray.

The cry that was on their lips was made up of two words. But it took Caoimhin a few moments to understand exactly what they were saying. When he heard it clearly he nearly stopped breathing with shock. He reached down to the water to dash the vision into a thousand ripples.

Then he lay back on the pebbles beside the pool with the war cry still echoing in his head.

'King Caoimhin!' the warriors had shouted. 'King Caoimhin!'

Caoimhin lay still for a long while catching his breath. When at last he sat up the sweat was running down his face in streams. And it was all for the terror of his vision.

'I'm not made of the right stuff to be a king,' he whispered to himself.

'What are you doing wandering about without that staff I gave you?' Gobann asked.

The Druid was kneeling down by the water cupping his hands to take a drink. He half turned as he swallowed a mouthful of the cool refreshing liquid.

'Where did you go?' the monk asked. 'Did you see the host of warriors?'

The Druid shrugged.

'I saw them. I've seen much more. But you are not ready to witness such things. What little you have glimpsed may or may not come to pass. It all depends on whether you pass the tests.'

'Tests?'

'Did you expect to be elevated to the rank of Ollamh Eolaí Draoi without a testing? No one attains to that high office without they've earned it. A master of the Draoi knowledge must also have attributes of compassion, restraint, cunning, if called for, and patience. Until you have proved yourself you will continue to be tested.'

'Are you an Ollamh, master?'

Gobann nodded.

'I was once. Alas I have not practised the Draoi-craft these many winters past. I too am seeking to undergo the tests to be accounted among that shining company again. Don't be fooled by my raven-feather cloak. I'm allowed to wear that because I was once of high renown.'

'Will I wear the raven cloak or the circlet of the king?' Caoimhin enquired anxiously.

'Perhaps you will wear both. But not if you leave your staff behind when you go off wandering. I went to a lot of trouble to fashion that stick for you. It will come in very handy one day. So don't go anywhere without it.'

'You!' a gravelled voice shouted from behind the Druid. 'You there!'

Gobann turned around and stood up.

'Yes.'

'Did you ask whether you could drink from that pool?'

'I did not! I certainly don't have to ask my leave of you. I don't care how ugly you are. It takes more than a stone head to frighten me. I'm a bloody Eolaí Draoi!'

'All right! Don't get your tunic in a twist, old man. It's not me you'll have to answer to. It's Flidais. She calls this pool her home. This is the Well of Many Blessings.'

Gobann stooped to splash another handful of water to his face. As he did so Caoimhin caught a glimpse of the stone wellhead. It was a hideously carved creature with pursed lips out of which the spring poured.

'Don't do that!' the head screamed. 'You've no right to steal the holy waters.'

'Shut up!' the Druid replied. 'You're giving me a headache.'

'You'll be sorry for this!' the stone warned him.

'What are you going to do? Spit on me?'

Gobann turned his attention back to Caoimhin. But before he had a chance to speak the stone head sprayed him with water. Without hesitation the Druid picked up a pebble from the shore and hurled it with all his might at the head.

The pebble struck the well-head right between the eyes. It shrieked with shock and pain.

'Now shut up!' he commanded.

'Whatever you do you must never be intimidated by the likes of him and his ilk,' the Druid told Caoimhin, indicating over his shoulder toward the head with his thumb. 'Creatures like that are just spiteful and bitter from being trapped in their ugly forms for so long. They'll do anything to hold you back or interfere with your ambitions. Don't allow them to.'

Caoimhin nodded to show he understood.

'I must be off now,' Gobann told him. 'We won't meet for a while. I have every confidence in you, my lad. You've proved yourself to be worthy of my attention. From now on you must find your own way. I can't be of any assistance on the next part of your journey.'

'But Gobann …' the monk began.

'You've work to do,' the Druid interrupted. 'I've struck a bargain with Sianan. You are to lead her to this well so she can find Mawn. In exchange I will have the opportunity to spend a lifetime with the love of my heart.'

'I don't understand.'

'You don't have to,' Gobann soothed. 'Just do this thing I ask of you and I promise you peace and happiness for the rest of your days though they might last forever.'

He hugged the monk close to him again so that Caoimhin's nostrils were filled with the dusty odour of the raven feathers.

'Get yourself some rest,' the Druid advised. 'Binney is cooking up a broth for you. Eat your fill. Then make ready to embark on a great adventure. Though you might live forever you will always look back on these days as the most exciting of your life.'

Then Gobann simply melted away into the air.

'Come back and fight, you Druid bastard!' the stone head bellowed. 'I'm not afraid of you. Just because you wear the raven cloak doesn't mean you have the right to abuse folk like me. I'll teach you a lesson, you vicious bugger. Wait till Flidais hears about this outrage. We'll see who has the last laugh then.'

Caoimhin sat down heavily. An overpowering exhaustion struck him. He felt compelled to lie back and close his eyes. Soon enough the shouts of the well-head were distant and muffled. And in no time at all the pool, the pebbles and the Otherworld were completely shrouded in darkness.

Eolaí Draoi

B efore All Hallows Eve folk come from near and far to attend the festivities. But mortals are not the only folk abroad at that season. All those hungry spirits that inhabit the Earth and roam the far-flung lands also seek out the fires of Samhain.

For that is the time of the spirits. It is their festival. The Feast of Samhain heralds their merriment and the changing of their watch. On All Hallows Eve the Enticers and the Frighteners choose new hosts or join together as allies for the coming year.

Now it's worth mentioning here that you won't hear any of the clergy of Rome speak on these matters. They're either entirely ignorant of spirit matters or they choose to be. This knowledge is in danger of being lost forever.

So take careful note of all I have to say. You have only to gaze at the world around you armed with the knowledge I'll impart to see everything as it truly is. Not merely as it seems to be. Once I've revealed this secret it's up to you to keep this wisdom alive in the world.

You must believe me that if mortal kind forget what little we know about the Enticers and the Frighteners, those spirits will have free reign to do as they wish. All who walk upon this Earth will fall into their slavery. And then what a terrible world this would become!

Those dæmons already hold sway over much of this

existence. Imagine what would come to pass if no one remained to warn us of their ways. There must always be someone among the mortal kind who can speak reason when the burning words of the Enticer tempt us to break our vows.

There has to be somebody tempered by fear who can assuage the powerful terror a Frightener may induce in the unwary. Without knowing-folk among us, all the Earth-born are nothing more than cattle led on from one fright or pointless material desire to another.

The Frighteners feed off fear. That's why they're ever urging us off to war or into terror. They are the source of all distrust, hatred, malice, rage, anger and disgust. They foster uncertainty. They further insecurity. They feast on all these feelings.

Enticers are no better. When one of them latches onto you then you might as well kiss goodbye to every independent thought, word or deed. It takes a strong soul to resist their temptations, believe me.

They live off the excitement generated by lust, infatuation, longing and desire. Their wiles are many. Envy is their sharpest sword. Only love of the purest kind may defeat them. And even that will feed them if they manage to turn its course away from truth.

All of us have an Enticer or a Frightener on our backs. Most of the mortal kind live out their lives as little more than tools for these parasitic spirits.

Thankfully the vast majority of their kind are lesser beings content to carry on as they have always done, jumping from one poor soul to the other as their host wears out and dies. But there are those among their breed who aspire to greater feasts of fear or adoration.

They're the most cunning spirits of all. They are wiliest of all their folk. They might cling to a family generation after generation, passing down from father to son or mother to daughter in succession like some valued heirloom.

They end up accompanying a king, a potentate or a pope. Yes, you heard me right. Look carefully at any man who gives himself holy airs. At his shoulder you'll find either an Enticer or a Frightener.

And if you think popes are above such dæmonic acquaintance, you're not as intelligent as I thought you were. Look at all the wars, conflict, heresies, witch-hunts and woe the popes have conjured up since Emperor Constantine sanctioned the Holy Office in the fourth century.

Do you really believe all that trouble was the popes' doing alone? Don't wander down that path of reasoning. It won't get you anywhere. Why do you suppose none among the clergy speak of these matters? I'll tell you.

The last thing the Frighteners and Enticers want is everyone going about warning one another not to fall under their spells. Take my word, a pope, king or cardinal usually has an old and powerful spirit at his back. Such a dæmon daily feasts upon the fears and adoration of everyone who is subject to its host. Just as a knight pays homage to his lord and a lord in turn offers fealty to a king, so the lesser orders of these spirits surrender tithes unto their betters. So a king's Enticer gets a share of the love, if you can call it that, directed toward its host through the nobles and their serfs.

And do not be beguiled by all that talk of original sin. What a load of tainted tannery trimmings that is! It was the Frighteners and the Enticers came up with that story to keep us gullible mortals in our place.

Think about it.

If you're worried about committing sins it's just one short step to being *frightened* about committing sins. So if you finally do get round to overcoming your trepidation and indulge yourself in a so-called sin of the flesh and it turns out to be fun, there are two results.

First the sin becomes very attractive, largely because it's

considered a sin in the first place. That's the Enticer at work, leading you on to desire so it can feed off your obsession. Then once you've committed the sin a few times there's usually a sudden onset of guilt or shame. That's the sort of thing a Frightener likes to feed off. That's not to mention that rule-breakers, unconventional types and sinners are usually among the most attractive mortals ever born into a warm fleshy covering.

Let me tell you, the whole concept of sin is the single most powerful weapon the Enticers and the Frighteners have at their disposal. It's a trick to milk us of nourishment. Nothing more.

What can be done, I hear you ask? How can one such as yourself avoid the vile attention of such feeding spirits?

Well that isn't an easy question to answer. In one sense you can't avoid them. It's part and parcel of being mortal. These spirits hide behind a veil of appearances. Unless one is constantly vigilant it's hard to recognise their influence. In the old days before the coming of Christianity to Ireland it was the responsibility of the Druids to be mindful of such matters. The wise ones, the Eolaí Draoi of old, studied the ways of the Enticers and the Frighteners. Then they offered their advice to folk who had but a restricted vision of this world.

The Druids counselled kings no less than craftspeople. They cautioned chieftains and chambermaids alike about the consequences of their actions. Indeed, all the ancient tales are perfect illustrations of the terrible influence the feeding spirits have upon our lives. That's why the Druids learned those tales in the first place.

The Eolaí Draoi were wise indeed. But their days have passed and no Druids now walk beneath the sun or wear the clothing of clay. Their knowledge passed on to the Culdee folk who are my kin. And the Culdees have kept this wisdom sacred. Though to all outward appearances we are followers of the Christian myth.

Don't misunderstand me. I have great respect for the teachings of Christ. I have found immeasurable inspiration in that tale. But to every faith there are two strands of the tradition. Let us speak of the Christian tradition by way of an example. On the one hand there are those who literally believe every word read to them from the Gospels. They hear the stories of the Testaments as if they were an actual history. They do not understand the story of Christ has been changed over the generations to suit circumstances.

On the other hand there are those Christian folk who understand there are deeper truths hidden within the tales of their tradition. They don't mind whether Jesus rode a donkey or a dog. It could have as easily been porridge and hedgehog as it was loaves and fishes.

I can see you know little of these matters. Your vacant stare, raised eyebrows and general air of mockery give you away. I'll be willing to bet you've never even held a ferret by the scruff of the neck and waved at your enemy.

No matter how far-fetched my words may appear, I encourage you to try to digest everything I say. For this is an accurate retelling of the events of those days. Do not question me. But if you are tempted to challenge any detail of my tale, please feel free to keep quiet until I've finished the whole bloody story.

Now, listen carefully. This is the most challenging part of my narrative.

There's more to Enticers and Frighteners than you might think.

So here is another hurdle for you to mount with your mind.

There is no death. The body you recognise as yours is not you. The flesh you see in the calm watery reflection of the pond is merely an aspect of you. To use an expression the Druids once made much of: your body is a caterpillar.

As you become older and wiser your soul weaves your flesh

into a chrysalis. And after it releases the butterfly within, only a shell is left behind. The corpse is nothing more than an empty vestige of the soul which has burst forth. Observe a chrysalis abandoned by its butterfly. Just looking at that empty husk it's impossible to guess how beautiful the creature was that birthed from it.

You and I are at a certain stage in our cycle of life. It is a stage which may be repeated again and again until we've fed enough on the food of spirits to build a new chrysalis ready for the next transformation. Through each of our progressions our spirit is refined. Then at last we attain to unity with all things for spirit returns to spirit. The great One-Soul, too, will one day weave a chrysalis for itself and who knows what shape-shifted form that will take? It's beyond imagining.

When we leave our chrysalis at the end of our Earth-born sojourns we continue on as spirits for a time. And spirit needs nourishment in the same way the body does. All the while we dwell as spirits we feed off the emotions which derive from attraction and fear.

Yes, my dear. I'm sorry if this distresses you. It isn't easy to break the news. We mortals are doomed to transform one day into Enticers and Frighteners. It is our next stage. It is our destiny.

But do not despair. One day, having fed sufficiently, our spirit form will change into that of an Angelic Being and shed the chrysalis of the Enticers and the Frighteners. After that each one of us may graduate to deity status and from then on the refinements continue. So don't think the Enticers and Frighteners of my story don't know something of what it is to be mortal.

It just so happens that an Enticer may also have a frightful aspect. If you would consider the other edge of the sickle-blade for a moment, the most frightening Frightener is one who knows a few things about enticement.

Just as mortals are categorised by the Church into good folk or bad folk, so the spirits may also be identified. However, they may be classed according to whether their enchanting or terrifying side predominates.

Some will have fond memories of their existences. Others may bear some inexplicable grudge. They are no different from us in many ways. In common with mortals they may inhabit the Otherworld or this Earthly plain.

It was the terrible interference of the Danaan Druids which made a mess of all this order. By concocting the Quicken Brew they put a wedge in the cycle of existence. Those who tasted the Brew could not shed their flesh. They were doomed to walk forever in the clothing of clay. And though their spirits certainly matured with the passing ages, they could not move on to their next form.

What a terrible thing that is to contemplate. An eternity without hope of rest. An evermore without the promise of the turning seasons of life. There is no spring for them, only the monotonous weary passage of the years unbroken into the future.

Pity them. But save your deepest sympathy for those among the immortals who do not realise there is a way to change their fate. Aoife was one of them. She got it into her head to become a goddess. Which is well and good. There's nothing wrong with that ambition. It's just it's not that easy to achieve while you're still wrapped in a cloak of flesh. I'll grant you there have been one or two embodied souls down the ages who've managed to lift their status to that of deity. But they were few and far between.

Do you want me to give you a few moments to take all that in? I know it can be a bit difficult to grasp at first. Take your time. I'll go on when you're ready.

Dear, pious and true. Saintly some would have called him. Robert FitzWilliam was a holy legend in those days. Anyone who knew Robert felt the presence of the Holy Spirit about him. He was enfolded in a veil of beauty and courage. But there was a terrible secret about Robert which no one knew save himself.

The thing is, the younger FitzWilliam simply didn't share the high opinion everyone else seemed to have of him. He thought himself to be a slow, clumsy, sinful halfwit who always managed to make some mistake or other and cause more trouble than necessary.

That's what he told himself as he trudged on toward the forest. He cursed his own weakness of spirit, muttering a constant stream of self-criticism under his breath. For he knew he'd made an awful mistake in letting Guy go free.

Robert stopped in the middle of the cow path then knelt down to touch the earth with his hand. He removed his fine kidskin war gloves and stroked the surface of the ground with his fingers. He'd found what he was looking for. He checked ahead and behind him then lowered his gaze to where his fingertips touched the disturbed earth.

There was the unmistakeable outline of a footprint. The footprint of a man wearing heavy mail armour and carrying a burden. And these feet were shod in the leather boots of Guy d'Alville. Robert quietly thanked the Virgin that he'd discovered d'Alville's trail before dusk. Now there was a hope of finding the thief and dealing with him properly.

Robert FitzWilliam was a marvel. Indeed he was. I'm sure I told you as much about him last night when I spoke about the Well of Yearning. You may recall he was the son of the illustrious Lord William FitzWilliam. Despite being raised in a noble Norman household, he'd matured into a fine gentleman indeed.

But credit goes to him who deserves it. His father, old Lord

Will, was a shining example of knighthood. I often marvelled that a man born of barbarian Norman blood could appear so Gaelic in his nature.

The old man was courteous to everyone for he truly considered all men and women to be his equals. He honoured the traditions of our people though he did not necessarily understand them. And he practised the ideals of chivalry. So naturally his brother Norman knights tended to shun his company and call him names behind his back.

Enough about Lord Will. I was going to tell you about his son. Robert must have brought a proud tear to his father's eye when he gave his life over to the Order of the Temple. For there was no more prestigious vocation a warrior's progeny could adopt than that of a Poor Knight of Christ.

And to be sure old Will must have been doubly proud. His Robert was a truly pious man, not just an ambitious upstart with an eye on a high rank like so many others. As a youth he'd had many visions of the Blessèd Virgin herself. But he wouldn't have suited the priesthood. Robert was chiselled out of a different stone altogether. His ancestors had all been warriors.

So the life of the sword came just as comfortably to him as the vocations of prayer and contemplation. Not that he'd had much chance for any of the quieter pursuits since he'd taken the white habit and the red pilgrim's cross.

On his first sojourn to the Holy Land he was caught up in a terrible intrigue which I've heard tell involved the Holy Grail and the Ark of the Covenant no less. It was there he first met Guy d'Alville who was at that time a high-ranking official with the Hospitallers.

Well it so happened, as it does in stories such as this one, that fate decreed the two of them would become entwined with one another's destinies for a while. So they each ended up here in Ireland searching the other out. Guy had revenge on his mind. Robert was following the orders of his grand master in Rome.

All you need to remember is that Robert was sent to Ireland to track Guy down and kill him. And, as you'd know if you'd been listening last night, the two of them had faced each other down with drawn blades and murder in their thoughts. But Robert had failed to despatch his enemy when he'd had the chance. I can assure you it wasn't for a lack of skill. It was Robert's compassionate heart which spared Guy's life. Now he was tracking Guy down to put that mistake to rights. If only he'd known he was treading treacherous ground. For he had strayed close to one of those rare gates which lead into the Otherworld.

As Robert stood up he sniffed at the wind. Something prickled his senses. He slipped a hand over the hilt of his sword ready to draw the blade.

There was a sudden flutter of wings in the shadows and the unmistakeable clicking of a beak. Any other knight might have laughed off his nervousness at hearing a bird among the low branches. But Robert sensed something else.

Slowly and with as little sound as possible Robert drew his weapon from its polished black leather scabbard. In a few seconds he'd levelled it out in front of him ready to strike any enemy down with one blow.

There was another clicking as the shadow of a creature half as tall as a man shuffled out from under the shady branches of a low rowan tree. The young FitzWilliam lifted the sword above his head with the point still forward, ready to swing.

'Put that thing down!' a harsh grating screech of a voice demanded. 'If I was Guy d'Alville you wouldn't still be drawing breath. You'd have gasped your last when you bent down to look at the footprints.'

'Come out where I can see you,' Robert declared. 'I'll not speak with a shadow. I'll not greet you till I see your face.'

'It's a long while since anyone wished to look on my

features,' the voice cackled with amusement. 'Are you sure you want me to step out?'

'Do so immediately or I will cut you into a thousand pieces and leave strips of you hanging on the trees for the carrion-crows to nibble.'

'Very well!' the voice snapped, and the creature hopped forward. 'As I am a carrion creature myself I'll take your threat seriously.'

Robert swallowed hard when he discerned the shape of a huge raven of sparkling eye and twitching feather. He lowered the tip of his blade.

'Put that away!' the bird demanded. 'I refuse to converse with a man who's waving a flat piece of iron at me. I hold you in very high regard, Robert FitzWilliam, so have a care you don't slip in my estimation.'

'Lom Dubh,' the Norman sighed, speaking the raven's name as he took up the scabbard again and sheathed his sword. 'It's been many winters since we last spoke together.'

'It has indeed!' the bird chirped merrily as he hopped a little closer. 'I'm so proud of you, Master Robert. I've heard so many wonderful tales about you.'

The younger FitzWilliam sighed heavily and sat down on the grass beside the cow track.

'I've heard how you stormed a castle all by yourself to rescue a maiden. They say she was so grateful she insisted you spend the night in her arms. But of course you're too saintly for any of those shenanigans. You made a vow to the Order of the Temple that you would never lie with a woman again as long as you live. And being an honourable man you've stuck to your promise.'

The bird took a sharp swift breath to go on. But just as he did Robert removed the string of beads which always hung round his neck under his tunic. His fingers fumbled the tiny ruby-like jewels of glass one at a time.

'Is that the famous Rosary of the Venetian Merchant-King?' the raven sputtered with excitement. 'I've heard all about it!'

He hopped closer to get a better look at the hallowed object.

'The story goes that you rescued a merchant from the sack of the city of Acre and that he was so grateful he offered you anything it was within his power to give. You could've married his daughter, the most beautiful woman in the whole of Venice. You would've inherited all the merchant's gold and been a wealthy man yourself if you had. But you nobly declined his offer. The merchant wouldn't let your valour go unrewarded. He insisted on giving some gift to you to honour your courage and chivalry. So you told him that during the hard fight to save him your rosary had broken and the beads had been scattered and lost.'

The raven took a deep breath as his excitement built up to fever pitch.

'So the merchant removed those beads from his own neck. And they are worth a fortune by any standards, yet that means little to you for you are sworn to poverty and your oaths prevent you from looking on the rosary as anything more than a companion to your prayers.'

'That's enough!' Robert snapped. 'That story is simply not true. I don't know where you heard it but whoever told it to you was a bloody liar. I've never rescued a Venetian merchant, nor have I ever been offered a daughter or so much as a donkey in payment for any insignificant service I may have rendered.'

'So that's not the Rosary of the Venetian Merchant-King then?' the raven pouted, or as close to a pout as a raven can manage considering the length of the beaks they wear.

'It is not the Rosary of the Venetian.'

Lom Dubh shrugged his wings with disappointment.

'That's a shame. Well never mind. I'm sure those beads have been with you a long while. And I'm certain there's a magnificent story behind them.'

The bird sat in perfect silence with his head cocked to one side waiting. Robert noticed the strained silence only after a long interval had passed.

'Have you nothing more to say?' the raven asked. 'I was hoping you'd tell me the tale of those beads. Do they have anything to do with Guy d'Alville?'

That got Robert's attention.

'Have you seen Guy?'

'Yes.'

'Where?'

'I saw him at the Killibegs.'

'How is that possible?' Robert asked, incredulous that his quarry might have slipped by him unnoticed. 'Did he go back to the settlement? I must return immediately. He's a very dangerous man.'

'Calm down,' the raven cooed. 'I last saw him when I watched you challenge him at the Sword Dance. I haven't seen him since.'

The young FitzWilliam frowned. Then his face softened. 'It really is wonderful to see you again, Lom Dubh,' the knight said. 'We've not spoken since I first took ship to the Holy Land years ago.'

'It has been longer than that, my young master. You stopped seeking me out when you were fifteen summers on this Earth. You had already set off on your great soul-voyage even then. Talking ravens aren't appropriate company for those who devote themselves to the Cross.'

Robert smiled broadly.

'It is a treat to see you. But I have no time to talk with you, I'm afraid. I must track Guy down and do what should have been done this afternoon when we danced with blades in our hands.'

'It was an honourable thing you did,' Lom Dubh told him. 'To have granted him his life in that manner was the very epitome of the warrior way. My chest bursts with pride to think I have known you since you were a little child.'

'I hope you will not be insulted if I go on my way,' the Templar replied. 'But much depends on my finding Guy as soon as possible. I have work to do in the Otherworld. I must guard and guide two friends of mine upon their quest to find the Well of Many Blessings.'

'That's an honourable thing to do,' the raven observed. 'But the time may be approaching when you need to be your own guardian and guide for a while. Take the time to help others on their quests but do not forget your own.'

'I thank you for the advice, old friend. Might I ask a favour of you?'

'Of course, dear laddie. Ask away.'

'Would you watch over me and mine while we sojourn in the Land of Dreams? Do not let us stray from the path too often.'

The raven hesitated.

'Is it the Well of the Goddess which you seek?'

'It is.'

'It is not hard to find,' Lom Dubh promised. 'I have visited it many times. You will see many other marvels before you drink from that cup and be granted many blessings, I'm sure.'

'Let's go together then,' Robert smiled. 'I'll be glad of your company. For in the time since I've been away from Ireland it has slipped my mind that so many wonders are still in the world. Wonders such as you.'

'You are a kind and accepting man, to be sure,' Lom Dubh complimented him. 'There are many of your folk who wouldn't stint to call me a dæmon. Others of your race, bough-splitting bastards they are, would not baulk at condemning me to the eternal fires of Hell given half the chance. Bark-bending berserkers! Splinter scattering scoundrels! I despise the

THE WELL OF THE GODDESS

Normans with their bearded axes. I loathe their timber-getting ways and devious tree-stealing hearts.'

The raven bowed as best he could considering the shape of his body.

'You're not one of them, to be sure,' Lom Dubh pointed out. 'You're a good man with a healthy respect for all living things. You wouldn't hurt a leaf in any wooded grove. May Danu bless you, Robert.'

Robert smiled uncomfortably, then said, with some urgency, 'We must press on, my friend.'

'I won't come with you just yet,' the bird told him in a nervous manner. 'I'll fly off to tell Sianan how you're faring. I'm sure she'd like to know.'

There was obviously some pressing business Lom Dubh had to attend to, but Robert didn't want to pry.

'Very well,' he agreed. 'Let Sianan know where I am. Tell her I'm close to catching Guy d'Alville. As soon as I've recovered the books I'll return to the Killibegs. We'll deal with the Redcaps next. Then the Hospitallers, I suppose. After that's all done I intend to set out with Sianan to guide Mirim and Alan to their goal in the Otherworld.'

'It may already be too late for all that,' Lom Dubh told him. 'Sianan intends to confront Aoife in her lair in the Land of Dreams. She'd have a better chance with your sword arm to guard her.'

'What of the defence of the Killibegs?'

'You must follow your heart, dear Robert,' the raven replied in as serious a tone as he could muster with a raven-voice. 'Don't be swayed by what your head tells you is the right course. It's a mistake you mortals too often make. You become so obsessive about your destination you forget to enjoy the voyage.'

In the next breath Lom Dubh lifted his wings out wide to leap into the air.

'Farewell, Sir Robert!' he cawed as he rose into the air. 'Farewell.'

When the bird was gone the knight set off to follow the cow track again.

'I wish they wouldn't call me Sir Robert,' he muttered under his breath. 'I don't deserve their praise.'

What a humble fellow he was. But there's some folk, and I speak here of the uncouth Norman bastards, who would likely tell you the young FitzWilliam's show of mercy for Guy was unknightly. They'd probably tell you a successful warrior needs to be ruthless to survive. As I've said earlier, the Norman concept of chivalry leaves a lot to be desired.

Sadly, Robert, despite his piety and good-hearted compassion for others, had been brought up as a Norman in a Norman household. So it wasn't an easy thing for him to accept that perhaps this whole situation might have been a bit easier on him if he'd cut d'Alville's throat when he'd had the chance.

If he had, then Guy wouldn't have made off with the holy books that had been in the keeping of the folk of the Killibegs. And all this bother chasing along the cow tracks at dusk might have been avoided.

Poor Robert. If only he'd understood then that nothing in the world of mortals is ever simple. And if he'd known what the future held for Guy and himself he would've been proud, glad and thankful that d'Alville was not a corpse. Perhaps he would've even been delighted the holy books of Killibegs had been stolen just when they were.

An oak tree is an awesome creature. Take the time to really look at one when you next have the chance. Gnarled and twisted by the years, toughened with each passing snow season, an oak will weather all and wither not.

Yet it takes only a strong gust of wind to crack the back of such a wondrous woodland creature. And every oak tree knows it. That's why they stand so heavy on their ground, bracing themselves against every expected assault.

Oaks are a proud race, strong, defiant, almost arrogant, you might say. So Aoife could not have chosen a better form in which to trap our Guy d'Alville.

Shortly after the sun had set on All Hallows Eve, Guy of the Gnarled Branches stood perfectly still, trying to cultivate man-thoughts and deny the evidence of his oakness. In his fitful, bough-branch half-slumber he struggled to breathe. Now and then the nightmarish nature of his predicament brought a panic of strangling tightness in his throat. Or as near to a throat as a tree may know. He felt himself teetering between oak-awareness and mortal-sensation. He couldn't quite work out whether or not this was all a bizarre trick of the mind.

Though he put all his effort into rousing himself from the depths of his dream he could not rally himself enough to actually wake. Haven't you ever experienced that sensation? I have. It strikes terror into me whenever it happens.

There I'll be, half stirred from slumber in the middle of the night. I'll be vaguely aware that my chamber is shrouded in darkness. But my body will not move. My eyes will not open. Then the *other* dream takes hold of me. I'll dream that I've risen from my bed and started walking round.

That's what happened to this oak-man. In his sleeping vision Guy perceived a world he could never before have imagined. All about him here on the grassy hill near the edge of the forest many creatures danced and played. They were dressed in colourful costumes of odd yet striking designs.

These folk were not unlike most people he'd ever met,

except their faces were either incredibly ugly or breathtakingly beautiful. Some were pale, while others wore the leathery brown skin of toilers in the fields under the sun.

Every one of them was bounding ecstatically about. They seemed to have a great deal to be happy about. The dancers circled all about him, laughing and singing. Some were performing exuberant steps that Guy would have thought impossible to execute had he not seen it with his own eyes.

Though it was after sunset the air was bright with full moonlight. The world shone with a blue-silver sheen of beauty. All colours were more vibrant than he had ever seen them. All sounds were sweeter, more intense. There was a joy in everything that would have had him smiling broadly if he'd been able to get his mouth to move.

Then some warning sounded within Guy. He forced himself to remember that this was all merely a dream. You see, my dear one, he hadn't yet been able to fully grasp the fact that Aoife had changed him into an oak. He wasn't aware he was observing his surroundings through the finely tuned senses of a tree.

He reasoned this was all just a fancy of his sleeping mind. It was a dream such as he'd never had before, but a dream nonetheless. And as is the nature of these sleeping visions there were elements of the inexplicable layered over reminders of the everyday. For example, Guy could not explain how he was able to see everything happening around him all at once without turning his head. It was as if his eyes were able to focus in any direction. At the same time he noticed items on the ground before him which were very familiar. A leather satchel full of books had been left unguarded by his feet. He knew without question this satchel contained the books he'd stolen from the keeping of William FitzWilliam.

There were holy books among them and heretical works also. He'd intended to take them to Bishop Ollo or on to Rome where he might recoup some of his lost fortune and revitalise his reputation with the Pope. Strangely, though, now that he turned his attention to those manuscripts they didn't seem so important. The restoration of his reputation hardly seemed to be worth the effort of travelling to Rome.

Questions arose within his mind. What use was gold to him? What did he care what anyone thought of him? Why had he bothered thieving those heavy books? What worth were they to him?

A strange thought struck him. Trees don't read books. In that flash he realised he was an oak tree. With this quiet revelation he began to sense a strange contentment flooding in through leaf, root and branch.

Guy thought to himself, with an inward smile, that he could stand here for a thousand summers watching these merry folk go about their dancing, and it wouldn't matter to him if he never left this pleasant grassy clearing ever again. He glimpsed a vision of the future.

He saw himself as an ancient oak standing right where he was now at the edge of the forest. His life was draining out of him yet he was not frightened for the consequences nor concerned whether Hell or Heaven awaited him on the other side of life.

Guy sensed there was no death. He knew his great oaken body would fall and return in time to the soil which had nourished him throughout the ages. In turn his decaying timbers would enrich the Earth giving life again to some other tree or grass or bush.

If he'd had breath it would have been snatched away with his next realisation. He suddenly understood that by the time he passed away his acorns would have seeded an entire forest of descendants. His corpse would be their nourishment. That was how he'd go on living.

There was no sense in struggling against this fate. There was no point in striving to avoid it. This was life, unending, ever-changing and complete at every stage. His soul would one day fly forth from this splintery prison to a new and better existence in the beyond. And with that understanding Guy discovered, much to his surprise, that trees are among the wisest creatures born onto this Earth.

That's how the title Druid was reputed to have originated, you know. There's some folk who say it comes from the ancient words Dair-Eolas, which mean Oak Knowledge. I can't tell you for certain whether that's true or not. It makes sense to me though.

These ruminations granted Guy a calm such as he'd never known before. He was enjoying this new-found peace in the depths of his soul. So he only gradually became aware of the presence of a strange person standing very close to his wooden body.

This thin weedy fellow was dressed in a green and purple particoloured outfit which marked him as a jester who had spent time at the French court. He had little bells on the ends of his curly-toed shoes and a bag over his shoulder fully laden with the toys of his trade. The little man would have stood no higher than the waist of Guy d'Alville the Hospitaller knight, yet he was obviously a mortal. That was clear from the sparkle in his eyes.

Guy felt the desire to ask this fellow who he was and what he was doing here. But he still couldn't force his mouth to do his bidding. In a flash the little jester was seated close to d'Alville, leaning up against him.

'What have we here?' the weedy fellow laughed in his strange high-pitched voice, part man, part mocking woodland creature.

He didn't wait for Guy to answer.

'How the mighty have fallen,' he giggled, placing his shoulder bag down upon the ground at his side.

Then the jester's face turned from joy to malice and he gripped one of the oak's roots tightly. This got Guy's attention immediately. It was an uncomfortable feeling, similar to having a hand placed on his throat.

'Guy d'Alville, do you remember me?'

Once again the jester didn't wait for a reply.

'My name is Mugwort. I was a servant at the court of King Richard. I met you once in the Holy Land. You had me whipped for what you called insolence.'

Guy would have frowned in the effort of recalling the fellow if his eyebrows had consented to move. But they did not. Mugwort took his hand away from the root. Then he reached into his bag to bring out a small knife and a sharpening stone.

He went on speaking as he carefully began to hone the blade.

'I fell out of the king's favour after that,' the strange little man went on. 'When the king went back to England he left me behind to fend for myself. I suppose that was for the best since Richard ended up in the Holy Roman Emperor's prison. But it took me three years to work my passage home to England. Three years of hardship. Three years of hunger. Three years of my life you cost me.'

Mugwort laughed.

'I'm not a vengeful man myself,' he quickly added. 'I wouldn't have bothered to hunt you down to extract some little payment for the ills you caused me.'

The jester went on sharpening the knife, concentrating on the shiny razor edge of the tiny weapon.

'But since you've fallen into my hands and you're quite helpless, I think I'll make some small entertainment for myself.'

Suddenly he tossed the knife up into the air. He caught it by the hilt and quickly stabbed it deep into an oak root. Guy felt a great pain reverberate through his whole body.

'You're a tree, bold Guy,' Mugwort hummed. 'You can't

escape from me. You're a tree. Don't you see? You cannot flee.'

The rhyme wasn't his best, but it was effective.

'I'm not a tree,' d'Alville reminded himself. 'None of this is real. This is a dream.'

Mugwort's eyes lit up with delight as if he'd heard the inner voice of the oak-man.

'Didn't Aoife tell you? Don't you remember what she did to you?' Mugwort cried in a mirthful shrill. 'You're an oak tree, Guy. This is no dream. The Queen of the Night has made you one of her many timber-bodied Normans. That's what she does to our lot whenever she meets one of us.'

Mugwort removed the knife with a vicious twist before he went on.

'That is to say, if Aoife doesn't have a use for a Norman it's certain they'll end up as a tree. You must have really upset her. She had high hopes for you.'

Guy would have spat with disgust if he'd had lips and if he hadn't been flinching with pain at the bough-splitting he'd just received. Then he would have asked how it was that Mugwort hadn't been turned into a tree. Once again the jester went on as if he'd heard the thought. Which of course he had. You don't spend a lifetime learning the tricks of the troubadour trade without picking up a few unusual skills here and there.

'I entertain the queen,' he explained. 'I bring a ray of sunlight into her dreary life. I cause her to laugh. She giggles in my presence. She'd never make an oak out of me.'

Mugwort stuck the knife in again, this time with less force.

'Can you feel the cold iron splitting your timber, splintering your bark, piercing your bough-body?'

D'Alville suddenly knew with absolute certainty this was no dream. A panic started to spread through him. His leaves began to rustle, starting in the upper branches then spreading down through to the lowest. A tingling sensation engulfed him. And at that instant all the creatures dancing round about him stopped their wild reverie.

Mugwort removed the little knife, held it up to Guy's all-seeing gaze then smiled his wicked jester smile.

'Wake up, sir knight,' he cooed.

'Stop it!' someone protested.

Guy turned his attention to this interruption. It was another courtly performer dressed in yellow and black attire similar in design to Mugwort's.

'Leave him alone!' the entertainer whispered urgently. 'Isn't it enough that she has placed a punishment on him? We shouldn't interfere. No good will come of it.'

The jester stood up.

'I'm Aoife's favourite!' Mugwort asserted. 'Not you! I'll do as I wish and I won't have you preaching to me.'

'I'm not preaching. I'm merely pointing out that Guy is the queen's plaything. You should be careful.'

'I was here long before you, Feverfew!' the jester snapped. 'I've been loyal to Aoife through thick and thin. When you've spent three seasons in her service and managed to survive, then I'll hear what you have to say.'

'I was just offering some friendly advice,' the other entertainer protested. 'Don't take offence.'

Mugwort knelt down by the tree. As he did so he shifted the knife in his hand and drew it along the side of the root and up under the bark. In this manner he slowly peeled off a long thick strip. A deep satisfaction was visible on his face at the sound of splitting oak-skin. When the knife had done its work the jester lifted up the piece of separated bark to admire his handiwork.

'I lost a layer of skin to your whip-man,' Mugwort told the tree. 'I nearly died after my encounter with you. But don't worry, I have no intention of doing that much damage to you. I'm going to make you suffer little by little as the years go by. Every day I'm going to steal a bit of your bark to use as kindling at my hearth.'

Guy would have swallowed hard if he'd had a throat. I can't tell you what it felt like to be stripped of his bark but I imagine it was like having a thick strip of flesh slowly torn from my leg. In my imagination I can hear it tearing even as I tell you about it. It's an awful thing to contemplate. I'm sure I would have screamed.

It was at that moment Mugwort noticed the satchel of books lying at the foot of the tree where Guy had dropped them just before he'd been transformed into an oak.

'What have we here?' the jester hummed with delight.

In a flash he'd sheathed his knife, much to Guy's relief. Then he had the satchel open and was sorting through the contents. He discarded one and then another as if searching for something in particular. Until at last he opened a small manuscript bound in bright red leather. His face lit up with wonder and excitement.

Impatiently the jester leafed through the pages, stopping here and there to read a few words, to click his tongue with delight or take a sharp breath of disbelief. At last he slammed the book boards shut and stuffed the manuscript into his own shoulder bag. Then he replaced all the other books in the satchel and dropped the bag to the ground.

'What are you doing?' Feverfew asked. 'Are you stealing a book?'

'I wasn't the first to thieve it,' Mugwort retorted, throwing an accusing thumb at Guy. 'I'm merely saving it from destruction. If it's left here under the wind and weather it won't last long.'

'She'll have you for dinner if she finds out. You know how Aoife feels about us nicking what's rightfully hers.'

'She won't find out. Will she?' the jester answered back and there was real threat in his voice. He held up his little knife. 'You're not going to tell her, are you? What if I let slip to her about the way you mock her in her absence.'

Feverfew gulped loudly. 'It's just harmless fun,' he protested. 'I'd never say nothing that would intentionally upset the queen.'

'I'm still the leader of this troupe,' Mugwort pointed out. 'I make the decisions. I arrange the performances. This book may be valuable to us in our work. So for the sake of her entertainment I'm keeping it.'

'What book is it anyway?' Feverfew asked.

'That's my concern. It's not as if you can read anyway.'

'I like to look at pictures,' the other jester replied sulkily.

'Not these pictures,' Mugwort told him. 'This is the Book of Pictures.'

Feverfew gulped as his face drained of all colour.

'It's not!'

'It is.'

'Y-You mustn't keep it,' Feverfew stuttered. 'No good will come of it. It's a dangerous manuscript, it is. And well you know.'

'I'll decide that for myself, thank you.'

'There are alchemists of the highest degree and sorcerers of the lowest who'd shy away from that book. Why, it's said even Simon Magus the notorious dark master of the south refused a copy when it was offered to him. You're no more than a dabbler in the black arts, Mugwort. The Book of Signs and Sigils will destroy you.'

At the naming of the manuscript there was a tremendous clap of thunder that rolled through the ground like a mighty wave of Earth-anger. There were clouds in the sky and now they seemed to be gathering to a storm. The moon disappeared, plunging the scene into darkness.

All the folk who'd been dancing round the tree stirred with fright, muttering anxiously to one another. Mugwort had brief second thoughts about stealing the book. But he wasn't about to put it back in its case with the others. He had no intention of giving up this prize.

'Don't call it by name, you fool!' he spat.

By this time Feverfew wasn't listening. He was frantically sniffing at the wind and becoming more agitated by the minute.

'There's someone coming!' the jester hissed.

'Hide there within the oak until he's gone!' Mugwort commanded, pointing to a narrow gap in Guy's body. 'And cover your tracks! If you leave your footprints all round the tree the intruder might hunt you down. There's no room in Aoife's company for any more mortals like us.'

Feverfew would have objected but he knew Mugwort was absolutely right. This company of entertainers had grown too large of late. Another mortal would be another mouth to feed. So with a wave and a bow he assented to withdraw and had soon squeezed into the narrow split in d'Alville's trunk.

The dancing folk quickly followed after and were filling up the hollow space within in a flash. Only Mugwort stayed outside.

Once they were concealed he climbed to the highest branches with his bag over his shoulder. And when he'd found a spot where no one on the ground could see him, he slowly and with uncharacteristic reverence took out the Book of Signs and Sigils. Then, despite the poor light, he settled down to a close study of that famed and terrible work of enchantment.

The Picture Book

R obert was a handsome man. His copper red hair, though cropped short since he'd taken the disguise of a cheese maker, was of a wondrous lustre which once caused women to swoon. His broad shoulders and noble bearing were the talk of all the milkmaids at the Killibegs.

Even dressed as he was in the humble attire of a curd-crafter he cut a dashing, heart-fluttering figure. Many a lass lamented loudly what a terrible waste that he'd sworn himself to a life of chastity.

To be sure, our Robert had his admirers and they were many. But he would've scarce believed it if you'd told him he was the heart's desire of innumerable young women from Constantinople to the Killibegs. His humility was genuine if somewhat misguided.

As our lad stopped on the path to check the footprints he was following, a chill breeze caught his cheeks. He knelt down to touch the ground again in the shadow of a great spreading oak. Another clap of thunder rolled as if it were travelling through the ground beneath him. It was so powerful he felt it through the soles of his boots.

There was something unnerving about the way the branches of this great tree seemed to claw desperately at the air with their leaf tips. Robert's keen warrior instincts sensed a presence. Someone was watching him.

He put the kidskin glove of his sword hand to his teeth and tugged gently, getting ready to remove it if he needed to draw steel. What a fine glove it was. It was a gift to him from a sultan of the east, so I heard. Given as a token of deepest respect and friendship. Pearls were stitched into it. One for every Saracen whose life he'd spared.

But alas I've no inclination to tell that story now. Perhaps another time. The best thing about that fine glove was that there was another exactly the same as it on his other hand. Truly Robert was a man twice blessed in all things.

The blood beat loud in his ears as he spun around to stand up. He dropped the glove from his teeth to the ground and grasped his sword hilt. His senses reeled in a rush of skittish fright.

He scanned the immediate area, searching for the merest hint of movement. He narrowed his eyes till they were tiny slits. He sniffed the wind and strained to hear the slightest rustle in the underbrush which might betray the presence of another living soul.

Robert was certain someone was nearby yet he could sense no trace of a watcher. He'd come to a place where the cow path headed into a darkly wooded forest. Beyond the oak under which he was standing two other great trees overshadowed the entrance to the woods, creating a natural arch with their intertwined branches. This must be the place where Lom Dubh had agreed to meet him.

Though he was no coward, he dreaded the thought of having to follow Guy into that forest at night. And on this of all nights. For the evening was drawing on to Samhain and we all know what happens on Samhain Eve, don't we?

Well *do* you know what happens on Samhain Eve? What did your kinfolk teach you? Do you know nothing of the intricacies of God's marvellous creation?

On Samhain Eve the doorway between this world and the

Otherworld is thrown open. And the inhabitants of that strange land emerge to search for slaves, lovers, sport and entertainment among the mortal kind.

It chills my very bones to speak of it now. For there are countless tales of wretched folk who've found themselves enslaved by the terrible beauty of the Otherworld.

As I said, Robert was not usually of a cowardly bent but on this occasion his resolve faltered. He didn't want to venture into that wooded realm tonight. He bowed his head and covered his eyes for shame. He rubbed them hard, calling himself worthless and unworthy of God's grace, then knelt to pick up his glove, tucking it into his belt. He reached out to touch the footprints again. That's when he noticed something very strange indeed.

In less time than it takes me to tell you about it he was on his feet again with his father's sword flashing silver in the blue twilight. The footprints he'd been following inexplicably disappeared at the base of the mighty oak under which he stood. It was but a short distance from there to the entrance of the forest but no tracks covered that ground.

To Robert this could mean only one thing. Either Guy d'Alville was hiding himself up in the tree or the great bough was hollow. Our young Templar checked all around the roots of the oak. There were certainly no other tracks because Mugwort's companions had obliterated them when they'd hidden inside the hollow.

It was while he was searching for footprints that he discovered the satchel full of books lying behind a large root. Robert's heart lifted up with joy. He breathed deeply with relief and swiftly sheathed his sword to examine the manuscripts.

Of course he had no way of knowing there was one book missing. So as far as he was concerned this little part of the quest was ended. The thought crossed his mind that he no longer had to find Guy. Well he had no stomach for the chase.

He shouldered the bag with the strap across his chest, evenly distributing the weight over his body. As he stood up he once again sensed the presence of another person close by. He drew his blade, this time with a flourish that made the weapon ring against the iron bindings of the sheath.

'I know you're here somewhere hiding from me,' Robert stated defiantly.

There was no reply. Robert waited for a few seconds anyway just in case d'Alville decided to show himself. When a good interval had passed with only the sighing of the trees and the creaking of the oak to fill the silence, our young hero decided to take a closer look for his rival.

He walked round behind the oak, his blade pointed low and level ready to swing up in parry. There was a split in the side of the tree but Robert judged it too small for a man of Guy's height and girth to hide within.

He didn't hear the strange people muttering as they frantically withdrew into the depths of the hollow bough. Few mortals can discern the presence of such folk. Thus Robert concluded that his enemy must be concealed up among the branches.

In the next moment his suspicions were confirmed. From far above a single page of pearly vellum fluttered down through the leaves and landed gently at his feet.

I don't know who stitched the Book of Signs and Sigils together but I can say to you for certain they didn't do a very good job of it. No one has any pride in their workmanship any more. Good craftspeople are as rare as honest Normans these days.

If I'd done the bookbinding that manuscript wouldn't have fallen apart, I can tell you. If a job's worth doing it's worth doing well, I always say. Shoddy work gets my goat.

Anyway, Robert looked down at the page for a few seconds then back up into the tree.

'Come down, Guy,' he demanded. 'I know you're up there. The chase is finished. I have you. And I won't let you escape me again.'

Well our Robert waited a long time for Guy's reply. And as you must realise he would've waited a lot longer if circumstance hadn't intervened. He was sure the wily Hospitaller was hiding up in that oak tree. Of course he had no way of knowing d'Alville actually *was* the tree. I'm sure the possibility never even crossed his mind.

If he'd had any idea of the truth perhaps he wouldn't have sheathed his sword yet again and climbed up into the lower branches in search of his enemy. The tree groaned as only the rigging of a ship or the branches of a trespassed disgruntled bough can.

Robert sensed the malice in the breathy timber threat, so he jumped down straightaway. High above, Mugwort breathed a sigh of relief, grateful for the bitter enmity Guy still held for Robert. If it hadn't been for that the Templar might have ventured higher up and found him.

Luckily for the jester, all Robert's intuition told him to keep his feet planted firmly on the ground. He picked up the vellum to examine it. The clouds rolled away from the moon as he did so. There were a series of symbols scribed upon the page, each with a brief explanation in Latin. But Robert didn't pay too much attention to the vellum. He quickly folded it inside his tunic to keep it dry when the rain came down.

'What sort of a coward are you, Guy?' he called out.

And to his shock the tree seemed to reply in a voiceless hiss which ruffled leaves and snapped small twigs with each uncanny word.

'What sort of a coward are *you*?' it seemed to say.

Robert stepped back out from under the branches, unwilling to stand any longer in the moonlight shadow of this oak. To his shame he felt his pulse quicken and his palms sweat. He drew his blade once again.

Now with all that sheathing and unsheathing of sword-iron he was asking for trouble. He should have let the weapon be and waited till he really needed it. For a blade like Órán is best left unattended as much as possible. But Robert didn't know much about those matters then.

'Come down and face me like a man!' he called out. 'I'll wait here till dawn if I must. You can't stay up there forever.'

Now his sword was out of its scabbard again it gleamed brightly like a newly forged weapon, unblooded and untried, even though it certainly wasn't either. For the first time since his father had given the blade into his keeping, Robert sensed it was guiding him along a path of its own choosing.

Though he was certain Guy was hiding somewhere in that tree he turned his attention to the woods. The forest entrance beckoned to him to step beneath its arches and enter into the dark realm of forest night.

Well you might accuse Robert of timidity. That's easy to do while you're seated here at my fireside with a pet ferret to keep your lap warm. I'd like to know what you would have done if you'd been him standing there under that oak tree wondering what in the name of Saint Michael's Unkempt Beard was going on.

Our gentle knight wasn't going to pass through the gate into the woods if he could help it. Unseen threat was all about him and Robert FitzWilliam was beginning to succumb to fear. He swung his blade around in the air as if that futile gesture could dispel the terrors of Samhain Eve. He strode further from the looming shadow of the oak tree until he stood in the open under the stars and clouds.

Our hero's heart was still pounding but he couldn't decide which way to go. If he returned to the Killibegs without settling the score with Guy there was no telling what the evil bugger might get up to next. No telling what might happen if he climbed the tree either. He was certain there was something dæmonic waiting up therefore him.

At last Robert resolved to calm himself in the best way he knew how. He found himself a space of level ground on the path and prepared to launch into a deep meditative state. I know this might seem a strange thing to do in the circumstances but it was the best way he knew to offer a challenge to Guy.

In those days there were still some of the knightly class who took their profession seriously. There were still a few who understood that being a sword-bearer involved more than wearing a mail coat and riding through the land eyeing pretty maids with a view to a tumble in the hay.

There used to be a code of honour which governed the actions of men such as Robert. His kind are rare today. The knightly class have declined since the days of my tale. I doubt you'd be able to find one among them now who'd know how to clear his thoughts and focus his being as Robert could.

Our good knight knelt down, Órán laid across his knees. And in that position he prepared himself to perform the Sword Dance.

The Sword Dance isn't all that difficult to understand. The moves are simple enough and easily learned. It's the meditative state that goes along with the dance which is difficult to master. Our Robert sat on his knees for a long while, struggling to restrain his rambling thoughts.

The Sword Dance was his way of broadening his awareness of the world about him. All the unseen things that escaped his attention were suddenly apparent to his senses when he'd attained that trance-like state.

So he sank into quietness. And it was the first real chance he'd had in months to rest fully. Every waking moment he'd been looking after someone, off questing or expecting trouble. Robert sighed and relaxed further.

Thus our gentle knight breathed easy. A bit too easy perhaps. But he was suddenly weary of the matters that had been pressing in on him of late, of all the worries that had been thrust upon his shoulders. What if he were to abandon this warrior path entirely? What if he simply tossed the way of the weapon aside and joined a closed monastic community? What if he withdrew from all the troubles of the world?

He laughed a little at himself for entertaining such thoughts. Robert was, as I've told you, an honourable man. He might have had his doubts about his life now and then but he wasn't the kind to give in when a situation became uncomfortable.

He sighed to realise he was very tired in his soul. His devotion to his vocation as a warrior-monk had not granted him one ounce of peace. He didn't feel as if he had come any closer to God through wearing the red cross of the Templars. Neither had he found solace riding off at the head of armies or fulfilling the quests his grand master set him.

Robert's fingers tightened round the hilt of the sword. Then a strange thought entered his pious head. What if Robert FitzWilliam were to become a little more like Guy d'Alville?

The idea was such an unusual one he could hardly believe he'd thought of it all by himself. And truth to tell, he hadn't. You'll see what I mean shortly. How it got into his head isn't important right this minute. All you need to know is that once the concept took root in his mind he found it was not such an abhorrent idea after all.

His meditation lapsed into an undisciplined daydream. Robert began to imagine what it would be like to command a band of mercenaries. He imagined roaming the country with no other aim but to bring in booty and boost his own prestige. For that's what men like Guy d'Alville did. They claimed to have holy authority for their pillaging and looting but in fact they were nothing more than well-armed thieves set loose on a rampage of self-indulgent destruction and self-enrichment. Our noble lad couldn't stomach that idea. It was repugnant to him and at the same time utterly fascinating.

A picture formed in Robert's imagination. He saw himself as a lord with many territories under his sway. Loyal servants watched over his estates while he passed judgement on his subjects.

He would be a just ruler, he told himself. He wouldn't allow corruption or self-interest to sway his decisions. He would take care of those folk placed into his keeping. He wouldn't tax them unfairly. He'd see to all their needs. He'd be remembered as a wise and beloved lord. And when he was gone folk would recall the years of his lordship with a fond nostalgia.

His waking dream suddenly moved on to include an element which truly shocked him. He found himself asking what it would be like to be wealthy.

Now all his life young Robert had eschewed gold and material wealth in favour of his aspirations toward the cleansing of his spirit. He'd always considered that wealth hindered devotion and service to God.

Suddenly it hit him that this might not be entirely true. Perhaps it was possible, he reasoned, to be very rich in material goods and yet not be bound in slavery to those goods. It might be possible to use one's wealth in the service of others. After all, was it not true that the Pope himself dwelt in golden splendour? Did he not slumber within a fashionably adorned bedchamber lined with silks of great value? Was it not true the Church was wealthy beyond the imagination of even the richest king?

Who could accuse the Pope of impiety? He was quite an innocent, our Robert. He reasoned that if the cardinals could live surrounded by riches and still follow the Holy Writ, why should it not be possible for one such as himself to remain uncorrupted?

He was a good man with a well-meaning heart but he was a certain kind of fool for all that. He didn't know he could have counted the number of pious cardinals who'd ever lived on the fingers of one hand. He didn't know popes were nearly never chosen in recognition of their adherence to the Ten Commandments. They were picked for their ability to keep the papal coffers full.

In his innocence Robert was certain that even if he had gold in great store he'd be able to stay true to his ideals.

Before he knew what he was thinking Robert was beginning to wonder what it would be like to dress in fine clothes every day or sleep on sheets of embroidered linen and exotic eastern silk.

This line of speculation led Robert into a realm of possibilities that included a wife. A woman. A spouse. A person of the opposite gender with whom he might propagate in a carnal manner with a view to birthing offspring. That's how Robert would have put it. He was such an innocent really. As I was saying, he'd surely need someone to inherit the estates he'd built up.

The young Templar took a sharp breath then let it hiss out through his teeth. He was suddenly deeply ashamed of himself. If there'd been anyone else around, those thoughts would never have entered his head. But he was alone out here, or at least he liked to think he was. There was no one to overhear his musings or judge him.

So he continued to indulge in an alternative view of his life. And to his dismay he found he quite enjoyed the thought of a wife and family of his own. Quite aside from the company he yearned for, there was an aspect to this daydream that he'd struggled with all his life.

He loved women just as much as they loved him. Naturally, being the pious man he was, he didn't allow himself to examine this attraction too much. He'd sworn himself to chastity. There was no point denying it.

In truth it had been no easy matter to refuse all those advances from pretty, willing girls over the years. As he pondered the possibilities he hadn't pursued, he discovered he was working up quite a sweat in the britches department, if you take my meaning. So he turned his disciplined mind to other more mundane aspects of a lord's life.

Such an existence had been good enough for his own father, William FitzWilliam. After all, hadn't Lord Will come to Ireland with a band of his own mercenaries? Hadn't he taken his estates by force from the local Gaels then built a fine castle? Hadn't he married a beautiful woman, Robert's mother Eleanor? And then fathered two sons by her?

Old William had amassed a mighty fortune for a man who'd started out with little more than a sword and a suit of mail. He'd wooed and won a woman of high rank, a lady of renowned charm. He'd lived a happy life as a just administrator of his estates. He was well loved by those under his care.

No one could have accused Lord Will of impiety. He was a model of Christian virtue and charity. He was revered and admired by all who met him. And at the end of his life he'd found the opportunity to seek the contemplative existence of a hermit. Surely Heaven would not be barred to him simply because he'd once been a warrior, gathered gold to his purse and lain with a woman.

Robert seriously began to question why he'd undertaken this hard road as a Knight Templar. The vows of chastity, poverty and obedience he'd sworn suddenly seemed meaningless.

He asked himself what sort of a God required such strict adherence to rules and regulations. What God demanded chastity on the one hand yet ordered the murder of unbelievers and opponents on the other? Was it evil to bring life into the world? Was it less evil to take life away from one's so-called enemies?

It had been the Grand Master of the Temple who'd ordered Robert to eliminate Guy. The grand master claimed to speak with the authority of God for he was God's intermediary on Earth. But would God really condone murder? And if He did, was it right to bend to the will of such a god?

Another question formed in Robert's mind no less shocking than the rest yet profoundly unnerving. If God was really so powerful, omnipresent and good, why would He need to eliminate those who didn't follow his word? Could anyone, no matter how determined, present a threat to His plan for creation?

When Robert opened his eyes he looked at the world in a new way and with a fresh understanding. That's not to say he'd never considered the possibilities before. It's just that now he was beginning to yearn for them in earnest. And he wasn't feeling the slightest bit of guilt. I can tell you he wasn't going to blindly follow orders again. As sure as he'd seen the apparitions of the Virgin in his youth he knew he'd been granted a revelation that would change his life.

Without an ounce of shame Robert began plotting a way to release himself from the oath bonds he'd made to the Order of the Temple. He wanted his own castle. He wanted gold and wealth, fine weapons, exotic foods at table and the best of wines. He desired clothes of quality and shoes that didn't blister his feet the moment he put them on.

But most of all Robert found himself longing for a woman to share his life with. He wanted a wife to bring laughter into his dour existence, to herald light into the dark places of his heart and to be a mother to his children. Children who would carry on the proud FitzWilliam name into the future.

Trembling with inspiration Robert leaped to his feet and raised the sheathed sword above his head. He gave a great yell such as he might have done if he'd been charging into battle on his warhorse. His voice echoed against the forest wall of trees in front of him. And for a moment he thought he heard someone laughing at him.

His instincts took over. In an instant Robert had his sword held high. He threw aside the scabbard to take up the first posture of the Sword Dance. Every muscle tautened, each breath slowed a little more than the last.

The moon was high and bright, free of clinging clouds. A shadow flitted between the two trees that arched over the entrance to the woods. A muffled chuckle seemed to pass through the very soil beneath his feet. It wasn't loud or menacing but it was enough to set Robert's senses on edge. In the distance thunder rolled again. But there was no storm coming other than the one Aoife had cooked up. The thunder was just one of those ominous touches aspiring goddesses and old storytellers like to employ.

'Who's there?' Robert ventured. 'Is that you, Guy d'Alville? Come out so I can see your face.'

To his surprise a tall figure immediately stepped out from the shadows of the forest. The stranger was draped in a long cloak and hood. Even in the moonlight Robert could plainly discern the vibrant deep blue colour of the cloth. It must have been dazzlingly rich in the daylight.

The dye was indigo. Robert had seen garments coloured

with it many times on his journeys in the Holy Land. None could dye cloth like the folk of the east.

The figure walked slowly toward Robert, lifting both hands to remove the hood covering the face. The wrinkled fingers were fine, pale and elongated, with long fingernails on the first three of the left hand and the thumb of the right. These were the hands of neither a young person nor a warrior. No knight would keep his nails this long.

The veil fell back to reveal a pair of sparkling jewels full of enticement. Robert let his sword tip drop in astonishment. The moment he glimpsed those bright smiling eyes the stranger didn't seem as strange or tall or menacing as he had at first.

Before Robert stood a gentle, unassuming old man possessed of a welcoming heart and an enchanting manner. His long grey hair was tightly knotted in neat locks tied at the crown to keep them off his face.

'Who are you?' the Templar asked, open-mouthed.

The stranger avoided the question.

'Robert FitzWilliam is *your* name. Your father is William FitzWilliam. He and I have been fast friends and constant allies during the last fifty years. But alas his time is coming to an end. Soon you will fill his shoes. And I will ride beside you as I did beside Lord William.'

'If you were with my father all those years, how can it be we haven't met? I swear I have no recollection of you. Nor do I think he's ever made mention of one such as you in his tales.'

'Come with me,' the smiling old man offered, holding out the hand of friendship. His voice was warm and reassuring. 'We have much to discuss. I have a fireside waiting within the woods.'

Robert hesitated.

'Would you have me follow you into that forest on All Hallows Eve?'

'You're not worried, are you?' the old man retorted with the merest hint of a teasing tone. 'You're a Knight of the Temple. Surely you have nothing to fear from the dæmons of the night or the Faerie folk of old.'

'Are you one of them?'

The figure laughed good-naturedly. It was such a delightful mirthful sound that Robert felt immediately at ease. Indeed, he found himself smiling back at the old fellow, embarrassed at his foolishness for fearing a wayfarer from the forest.

'My name is Órán,' the stranger bowed.

'That's the name of my sword,' Robert gasped with renewed suspicion.

'In actual fact, that weapon was named after me,' Órán explained. 'It is merely a rod of iron forged into shape. I am made of something else entirely. Now if you'll come along we have a lot to discuss. We haven't much time. If we're going to work together there's one or two matters need to be settled.'

'I don't understand,' Robert replied, but his eyes twinkled with interest.

'You will, my son. You will.'

Órán approached with confidence. When he was standing beside the discarded scabbard he stooped easily to pick it up. He was surprisingly agile for one of seemingly advanced years. Before the knight could protest Órán slipped the leather sheath over the sword Robert held.

Then the old man took the Templar by the hand and led him past the gnarled oak. In a few moments they were crossing beneath the two arching trees which guarded the forest.

Robert looked back as he reached the leafy arch. Before he passed into the shadows of the woods the great oak tree where he'd thought Guy had been hiding flailed its branches around in impotent fury. A moment later a terrible menacing growl rent the air.

128

It was followed by a bone-tingling snarl such as Robert had only once before heard in his life. He grabbed Órán's hand tightly.

'If I didn't know better I'd say that was the hunting mew of a lion,' he stated in as calm a tone as he could muster.

Órán winked at the knight.

'Now what would a lion be doing wandering about the land of Ireland?' the stranger asked. 'They don't like cold, rain-soaked countries like this one. They prefer the dry, hot lands of the south.'

Another roar, less vicious than the earlier one, thrummed through the evening air. Robert's belly vibrated to his very bowels.

'I'm certain that's a lion,' he gulped.

Órán immediately stepped so close to Robert his nose almost touched the knight's cheek.

'That's no lion,' the stranger declared in a whisper. 'That's something far worse than any lion. That's a monster. An abomination. An evil-hearted, self-centred pit of delusion, manipulation and all-devouring greed.'

He turned his head sharply this way and that to check he hadn't been overheard.

'The creature bellowing those calls is the ugliest, vilest, most contemptible, most treacherous, least compassionate and above all the blood-thirstiest of any being it has been my misfortune to encounter during the span of my existence.'

'What breed of beast is this monster?' Robert hissed back urgently.

Then he noticed something very odd indeed. It felt to him as if the forest began to close in tightly, leaning over him to overhear the conversation. It was as if every leaf and twig and bough desired to hear the answer to his question.

Órán breathed in loudly through his teeth. 'I can't tell you. You wouldn't believe me.'

Then the old man grabbed Robert's hand again, trying to drag him along.

'If we wait here much longer you'll see for yourself with your own eyes what kind of hideous deformity is attached to that voice.'

'Then I'll wait.'

Órán grasped Robert's hand with such force and violence the Templar was almost thrown off balance. But the stranger didn't care. He was beginning to show signs of panic.

'There is no mortal who can look upon that creature and hope to live. If you stay you will surely not survive the encounter. I'm certainly not intending to linger here. I'm quite fond of the way my limbs remain attached when I walk around. I'm used to waking up in the morning to find my head firmly placed on my own shoulders, not rolling about on the ground for some Redcap to trip over.'

Robert resisted. His curiosity could be a powerful thing. After all, it had led him off on his adventures to the Holy Land, hadn't it? And it beckoned to him now to wait just a moment longer. But Órán was not going to have any of that.

'Listen, my lad,' the stranger hissed, 'I've been cultivating you for a goodly long while. I've got big plans for the two of us. Do you think I'm going to throw all that hard work away just to satisfy your curiosity?'

Robert smiled with excitement as if to say he didn't care. His eyes sparkled with a new-found sense of mischief. Órán began to lose his temper.

'All the times I could've deserted you! But I hung on to you, hoping for you, praying for you, doing everything I could to make sure you survived. I made certain you learned your lessons and moved on without any serious injuries. Don't I deserve some thanks? Isn't it high time you paid back a little of the tutoring you've been receiving at my hand?'

'I don't know what you mean,' Robert replied flatly.

'You and I really need to have a little chat, my boy. I'd better set your mind straight about a few things. I should've done it years ago but it wasn't easy convincing Old Will to give me up into your care. I had to inspire him to become a hermit in the end.'

'What are you talking about?' the Templar frowned.

'Come along with me and I'll tell you the whole tale,' Órán declared, the urgency clear in his voice. 'I'll tell you anything you want to know. I promise you I will. Just come along *now!*

'I'll come with you if you vow to show the roaring creature to me one day,' Robert replied.

'That one?' Órán raised his eyebrows. 'What makes you think I've been close enough to get a look?'

'You must have seen it,' Robert reasoned. 'Otherwise you wouldn't be so frightened of it.'

'I've seen what it can do! I've seen the remains of its prey. And yes, I've come face to face with it just once. That was enough.'

The stranger noticed Robert was still hesitating.

'I promise I'll take you to see the monster,' he promised grudgingly. 'But not today. And not tonight. This is a very bad time. It's after sunset on Samhain Oidche. The beasts of the Otherworld are at their most powerful at this time. And that one will tear you to shreds as soon as look at you on this night. We must run as far and as fast as we can!'

Mention of the Otherworld and Samhain Oidche dampened Robert's curiosity with spine-shivering speed.

'Lead on, Órán,' he conceded. 'Let's find a safe place where you can tell me everything I want to know.'

The stranger cocked his head in surprise.

'That was part of the bargain, wasn't it?' Robert demanded. 'If I go with you you'll tell me whatever it is I want to know. That is what you offered me, isn't it?'

'That's what I promised,' Órán admitted, realising he might have been tricked.

'Then let's not waste any time,' Robert smiled. 'I have so many questions. You couldn't have turned up at a better moment. I've been waiting to meet one of your kind for a long, long time.'

A Friendly Warning

At the same time Robert was passing under the two guardian trees into the forest the settlement of Killibegs was in uproar. We knew the Redcaps were planning to bring war and woe to our walls. We'd heard there were Hospitallers, Normans and mercenaries on the march from Wexford town with murder in their hearts and conquest on their minds.

So our people abandoned the festivities of Samhain. For the first time in living memory we broke with tradition. We laid aside the rituals of the season and looked to arming our folk for battle.

Naturally everyone was grim-faced and resigned. There would be no feasting or dancing. There'd be no drinking or carousing. There'd be no comfort this night for anyone while our future remained so desperate.

I sat beside Caoimhin as night drew its curtain of shadows around the world. After nightfall I rose to warm some broth for the boy. The fire needed building up so I stacked new timber to the coals.

And as I was doing that a bundle slipped from the sleeve of my tunic. What a different life I might have had if I'd only stuffed that package deeper into my clothes again and ignored it. How much suffering might have been avoided if only I'd put it straight back where it came from. If only I'd paid it no heed!

But I was a weak one in those days. I let my foolish wilfulness rule me. I allowed temptation to get the better of me.

My heart skipped a beat as I glanced across at Caoimhin sleeping peacefully. I made up my mind I wanted him at any cost. He was the lad for me. What a pair we'd make!

He was a scribe. I was a bookbinder. We'd be the talk of Christendom. We'd make such books as would be talked about in the great ancient monasteries of the east. We'd craft such masterpieces as hadn't been seen since the torching of the great library of Alexandria.

I must have spent too long in the wilds of the west. I'd clearly let my daydreams get the better of me. I'd surely lost all sense of restraint. But anyone who has experience the heady spinning dazzle of infatuation will understand what nonsense was galloping through my eedyit head. I was standing at the mouth of a dark perilous abyss without so much as a light to keep away the nasties of the night.

Before I could reason myself out of this impending disaster I'd fetched a mortice and pestle. I poured out a pinch of the dried herbs from the pouch and started working away at it. After a while I wondered whether the leaves and roots might have lost their potency since Ortha had given them to me. I didn't want young Caoimhin falling in love with me only half-heartedly.

I wanted him to surrender himself entirely to me. I was after his full attention. As if it were not foolish enough to be dabbling in this dark art, I did an even more foolish thing.

I emptied out almost the entire contents of the pouch and ground the ingredients down into a fine powder. Fortunately I saved enough in case I had a need of this Draoi-craft again one day. That was the only wise thing I did that evening. For if I'd used the whole contents of the pouch I would have regretted it with all my heart.

My reasoning was this. I'd mix the love potion into his

broth. But I'd only give him a little taste at first. I wanted him to fall in love with me, for certain. But I'd had enough experience of love-sick puppy-dog lads tumbling off mountain-sides and the like to know I didn't want him falling too madly in love. I wanted him to keep some of his senses, if only to preserve life and limb.

The butter was melted gently in a pan just as it had been explained to me. I lightly fried the ground-up powders. When the whole mix had changed colour slightly I poured it into the broth.

I wasn't thinking. In an instant I picked up a wooden spoon to taste the brew. It was almost to my lips when I realised my mistake. *I* didn't want to take the love potion. I didn't need it. It was meant to fire up the flames of Caoimhin's passion, not mine.

I returned the spoon to the pot, stirring all the while to make sure it was well mixed in. It was as I was doing this that the lad stirred in his sleep. He took a deep breath, stretched his arms above his head but did not awake. He was still wandering in the depths of a dream. And I could tell by the way his eyes flitted about under the lids that it was one of his visionary dreams which either spoke of the future or warned of the present.

Suddenly his eyes snapped open.

'Where am I?' he demanded. 'What happened?'

He turned his gaze to me and smiled with recognition.

'Sianan? Is that you? How did I come to be asleep?'

I have to say I was struck by a short stab of jealousy. Well, in truth it was a nagging jab. I'd noticed Sianan looking across at the lad in the great hall before he'd been poisoned. I'd seen him returning her unseemly interest. But how could he mistake me for her?

I politely explained to him he'd been poisoned by John Toothache and that at first we'd held no hope for his recovery. I arranged the furs of his bed so I didn't have to catch his eye.

Then I told him the healing craft of Abbess Sianan had saved his life.

'Abbess Sianan!' he gasped in shock. 'You're not Abbess Sianan. I must speak with her! Where is she?'

I hushed him as I lifted his head to place another straw pillow under him.

'Sit up,' I commanded. 'It's time you had a bite to eat.'

'Who are you?' he asked, still dazed.

'It's Binney,' I told him reassuringly. 'My name is Binney. Don't you remember me? I've been watching over you.'

'Where's Sianan?'

'She'll be back soon,' I replied tersely.

At the same time I dragged the bed furs up round his neck, perhaps a little too emphatically. I'm ashamed to say I was showing signs of jealousy. Me of all people. I haven't a jealous bone in my body. I didn't have in those days and I don't have now.

'I must talk with Sianan,' he told me, tugging on my tunic.

'That two-tongued temptress!' I spat. 'Why would you want to have anything to do with a woman like her? I thought you were intelligent and sensitive. But you're just like all the others. Half an hour after you've brushed the hay out of your hair you'll have forgotten how it came to be there. Why don't you row your boat out into the middle of a whirlpool now and be done with it?'

Perhaps I am capable of a touch of jealousy after all. But only now and then. I was beginning to sound more upset than could be justified under normal circumstances. So I coughed. Hard.

That roused Caoimhin from sleep. He sat up straight and looked into my eyes.

'Is there something wrong with you?' he asked with genuine concern.

'What are you implying?' I snapped.

'I hope you weren't poisoned too.'

'I wasn't,' I conceded with a strained smile. 'At least I haven't been poisoned in the same way you have.'

I was about to confess to him my feelings and admit I wanted him all for myself. I was going to tell him I'd been poisoned little by little at the hands of every lad who ever broke a promise to me or fell to his death off a horse after he'd asked me to marry him. I wanted to explain it was *their* fault I'd come over all protective and insecure. Not mine.

But Caoimhin's eyes lit up before I had the chance to speak.

'I must speak with Sianan,' he insisted. 'I've just this minute woken from a dream all about her!'

'Have you now?' I hissed as my mood instantly turned black again. 'Don't tell me the details! I don't want to hear what enchantments that ancient witch has put upon you! I don't want to know what thoughts and aspirations she's filled your foolish head with. But I'll tell you this much. If you go off with her you'll live to regret it. I've met your kind before. Let me fetch a ferret for you. When the Normans arrive you can face them down with it!'

'What on earth are you talking about?' he stammered.

The poor lad was obviously confused. But I didn't notice. I was fuming.

'I'm warning you that if you go off with Sianan you needn't bother showing your face round here again. I wouldn't care if you were a king with nine hundred warriors at your back. I wouldn't care if you inherited a thousand head of cattle. I wouldn't care if you owned your own castle tower along with all the silks and sables in the kingdom. If you go off with Sianan you deserve everything that comes to you afterwards.'

'Where would I be going with Sianan?' Caoimhin asked.

I took a sharp breath, closed my eyes for a brief moment and called myself an eedyit. What the bloody hell was I talking about? Why was my treacherous tongue so intent on telling the truth? I had to think quickly if I was going to cover up for my foolishness. Fortunately quick thinking's never been too much to ask of me.

'I was just warning you,' I told him in a calmer tone. 'Sometimes I get glimpses of the Sight. You know. The Faidh. If I'm caught up in a frenzy of the vision I just let the passions surge out of me and I say whatever needs to be said. And the Faidh warned me that you shouldn't go off with Sianan so I just blurted it out. I'm sorry. I didn't mean to make a fool of myself.'

'That's quite all right,' he cut in. 'I know exactly how it feels.'

'You do? You don't come across as a fool.'

'I've suffered from the visions all my life,' he corrected. 'I know how it is when the full passion of a vision overtakes you. Sometimes it's all I can do to force myself not to scream with agony, fear or joy. A few times I've been utterly overwhelmed. Once or twice I've issued a warning to a friend or companion without for a moment considering the consequences of the revelation.'

Caoimhin took my hand gently in his.

'I can't tell you how happy I am to finally have someone I can talk with about this. Someone who understands because she suffers the same as I do.'

I was a touch shocked. I hadn't expected my little lie to expose such a deep layer of emotion. Of course I'd never really suffered from the Sight in those days. I'd simply been thinking on my feet.

'I've just had a dream,' Caoimhin told me excitedly. 'I saw a dark pool and I met a talking stone.'

'Hush now,' I cooed. I didn't want anything interrupting my plan to feed him Ortha's love potion. 'You've been through a terrible ordeal. You must rest. Sianan is very busy, far too busy to be worried about you. I doubt she'll even be able to come to your bedside again this evening. You must try to eat.'

'I'm so hungry,' he exclaimed, 'I could eat that whole pot of broth!'

'You'll have just a little to begin with,' I told him sternly. 'You're not to eat too much. Your stomach may still be weak.'

As I ladled out a bowl of the steaming barley broth I tried not to shake with nervous energy. I didn't want the lad to suspect my intentions but all I could think of was what would happen the moment the potion took effect.

Caoimhin held the bowl on his chest with both hands and I spooned out a mouthful of the soup for him.

I don't know how I kept my hand steady but I didn't spill a drop. The spoon edged closer to his entrancing lips. His eyes met mine. In that instant I knew he'd surely fall under my spell.

But at that very second, just as he was slipping his head into my snare, just as he was about to surrender himself to me entirely, the door to the chamber opened. And in walked Sianan.

'Bloody typical,' I muttered under my breath. 'I knew she wouldn't leave him alone for too long. She's got her eye on him.'

'What did you say?' the lad asked me.

Before I could think of an appropriate answer Sianan had cut in.

'How is he? Is he awake?'

In a breath Caoimhin pushed aside the broth. He took the spoon from me, emptying the contents back into his bowl. Then he handed it to me.

'Sianan!' he called out with great excitement. 'I have news for you.'

Mugwort waited up in the oak tree formerly known as Guy. He stayed there still as a stone until Robert and his companion were swallowed up by the shadows of the forest. Then he went back to paging through the manuscript he'd snatched from d'Alville's satchel.

Let me tell you something by way of a friendly warning. I don't care whether you call it magic, enchantment, spell-casting, Draoi-craft or whatever, don't dabble in the Draoi! Unless you know exactly what you're doing you're going to end up in deep trouble.

I know of dedicated men and women who've devoted their entire lives to the practice of the magical craft. And even they make an utter bollocks of things with startling regularity. But if you haven't got any idea what you're up to then you're headed for certain disaster. Laugh if you like. All you young folk are the same. You think you know everything.

Bloody fools the lot of you. I speak from personal experience. I know what I'm talking about. I've seen the results of the thoughtless dabbling of folk who really don't know what they're getting themselves into.

The magical arts are fraught with dangers such as you can't begin to imagine. To be sure the rewards are potentially quite satisfying. But they don't outweigh the payment which must be exacted. I don't want you to get the idea you can cast a spell without having to pay a heavy price in return.

The wise practitioner of the Draoi-craft knows his own heart. The true Draoi-master understands that every enchantment is cast through the veil of his own being and is thus influenced by his or her own character, moods, experiences and prejudices.

Think of it this way. Each one of us is like an immense stained-glass window. The mystic sunlight of enchantment passes through the glass, changing hue to fall upon the cathedral floor in a mighty splash of colour. Each of us is a unique pattern in the panel, with our own individual shades of blue, yellow, green and red.

When a mortal casts magic of any kind it is like the sun passing through the window. The light is transformed. It may still illumine the dark places of the building but it is filtered through the window of the self.

So, for example, a warrior who takes up the magic arts is likely to be responsible for strong, brutal, ferocious spells. Even if he casts an incantation of love it will be tainted by the touch of his warrior self.

Bear this all in mind. It'll help you understand what became of Mugwort in the end. For he was a jester, a jongleur, though he would have denied it most vehemently; a travelling entertainer. He'd built his reputation on making people laugh and lifting the burden of everyday life from their shoulders.

As Mugwort sat up in the tree he studied the book intensely. This manuscript was more than merely a book of spells. It was a complete magical philosophy. You may have heard of the work. It was known as the Book of Signs and Sigils. Or simply the Book of Pictures to the uncouth. I'm sure I mentioned it to you last night when I was telling you about the satchel of books Caoimhin inherited from his teacher. For you see our young scribe also had a copy of this manuscript in his possession.

What was the book all about? How can I summarise such a complex subject? It would take many years of study for you to comprehend the nature of the sigils. But basically the theory goes like this. Anyone who has a wish, desire, whim or need can attain that which they yearn for simply by employing the techniques contained within that manuscript.

Each of us holds a certain mystical force within us. It is the force of creation. And in this respect we are somewhat like gods, though a great many folk would never guess it. Most of the time we mortals wander about in a stupor, unaware of the immense potential we each possess. That's because we have come to believe that our lives are beyond our ultimate control.

What a firkin full of fish feathers that is. I'll tell you the truth. You and I and everyone who walks in mortal flesh has the capability to create anything they desire in their lives. We also have the necessary skills to destroy anything which attracts our displeasure. Or *anyone* for that matter.

I only met him once and the occasion was far too brief for my liking. But it was Neart, the floating monk, who taught me that lesson.

The sigils are said to unlock our potential. I'm not enough of an expert in this field to explain to you how it happens. But it certainly works.

This is the method a sigil-caster uses to achieve his or her wishes. To begin with you must clearly visualise the object of your desire, whether it be the attainment of riches, the possession of the throne to a kingdom or the secret of making a good cheese. Once the vision is detailed clearly in your mind it's time to move on to the next stage.

Now you must write down a clear, concise statement of your wish. I'll give you an example. Here's my wish. It is my will that you listen to the remainder of my tale without interrupting me.

You will note that the statement is very clear and uncompromising. There's no use of negatives. If I'd said, 'It is my will that you not be distracted from my story,' it wouldn't work. For some reason I haven't been able to fathom, the process of creating a sigil cancels out all nots and nevers. So the result of the last statement would most certainly be that you *were* distracted from my tale.

Are you listening? Do try to concentrate. This is all very esoteric, I know, but it does have a bearing on the story, I promise you that.

The next step is to examine the written statement while crossing out all the repeated letters. Once that's done you end up with a tincture of intent. In this case the letters

ITSMYWLHAOUENRDFWP would represent the final tincture which will, with one more step, grant me my wish.

Now comes the interesting part. Redraw them into a little picture which incorporates each of the letters. The letter I is always a strong central one to anchor the rest on. Then the M and the A could be added to top and bottom of that for example with the other letters joined into the drawing as you see fit. Once that is done there are two methods to bring the spell to fruition.

Some versions of the manuscript advise that one forget the original wish completely by putting the Sigil away in a drawer for a while. Once a sufficient period has elapsed, take the parchment out then memorise or meditate upon the resulting Sigil picture until it is locked within your mind. Others prescribe setting fire to the parchment on which it is drawn.

I personally prefer the method Caoimhin's book prescribed. That is to hang the sigil somewhere about the house where it can be seen every day. It's still very important that the original wish be entirely forgotten and this is the most difficult part of the spell-cast.

I can't explain to you why it is so important. I couldn't begin to tell you how this whole process works. But I can assure you it does. Without a shadow of a doubt anyone who practises sigil-craft according to the traditions and prescribed rules will achieve their heart's desire.

Now for a further warning. If what I have told you about making sigils seems simple, then beware. As I told you earlier, magic, enchantments and Draoi-craft are subjects which require many years of study, experience and perfection to achieve the desired results. You can't simply read a book and expect to be a master of the sigils overnight. Just as you couldn't hope to achieve anything from following the method I have described to you until you'd made a thorough investigation of all the pitfalls and possibilities.

It's simply too dangerous to indulge in such folly. Undisciplined minds, immature practitioners and unfocused wishes often result in terrible consequences. That's why I've only told you enough about the sigils so you'll understand the theory of their application.

If you decide to go off experimenting with this practice don't blame me if things go wrong. You can't say I didn't warn you. Indeed Mugwort's tale should be a cautionary one to you. So I'd better get on with it.

As he sat there in the tree thumbing through the book the jester, like many a fool before him, got the thought into his head that the sigil-craft was a simple one, easily mastered. There didn't seem much to it at all.

Woe betide anyone who comes to such a hasty conclusion. For it's usually a result of greed or wanton wilfulness or worse. Sadly Master Mugwort was certainly a greedy wanton wilful eedyit of the worst kind.

He held a hope in his heart that would have been unthinkable to anyone but himself. This simple jester wanted to supplant his queen and rule in her place. Mugwort thought he had it in him to be King of the Night, Sovereign of the Dark Places and Lord of the Redcaps.

And he imagined this manuscript would help him attain those dreams. What severe silliness was he suffering from? What feeble reasoning ruled the roosting place of his mind? What a dangerous path to tread! What an interesting little tale.

As it happened Mugwort was no stranger to magic. He'd tried everything in his time. He'd followed a coven of witches round one winter hoping they'd teach him a thing or two. But he hadn't learned anything worth telling you about other than a few folk songs about the bonfires of the Inquisition to while the wintry nights away.

He'd once entered the service of a reputed magus from the Languedoc, eager to glean occult secrets. But his efforts had come to nothing when the Inquisition stoked a bonfire with his master. The great magus didn't turn out to be that skilled at his chosen profession after all. Nor for that matter have most of the witches they've burned in the last two hundred years.

Think about it for a moment, will you? If these folk were truly in league with Satan or suchlike, don't you imagine they'd have a trick or two up their sleeves when the executioner came to light the reeds around their feet?

Now, were was I? Oh yes. Mugwort quickly read through the first few pages of the book. And because he considered himself quite experienced in these matters he didn't heed the warnings or take a moment to consider the dangers.

He took a piece of charcoal from his tinderbox and scrawled a few words in the margin of one page. He wrote carefully in a neat monkish book-hand. This first sigil would be a test. He wasn't going to ask for too much to begin with. When he was done he read the sentence back to himself to decide whether it sounded right.

'It is my will that my audiences fall about in laughter at everything I do.'

Mugwort had always fancied himself as a wit. So he reckoned this spell wouldn't prove too difficult to attain. He meditated upon the letters and the wish for a long while, concentrating all his thoughts into this one narrow focus. Soon there was no other distraction to his mind but the wish within his spell.

A shape made up of all the letters began to form in his thoughts. He sketched a drawing of a few letters joined together. In less time than it takes to take in a dozen breaths he'd sketched his sigil, the distillation of his wish.

Now it so happened that the particular manuscript which had fallen into Mugwort's hands advised the practitioner to memorise this sigil before setting fire to it. So the jester sat there high in the tree committing the magic drawing to memory.

When he was certain he would be able to call up the shape to his mind at any time he desired, he removed the remaining contents of his brass tinderbox. Flint, iron and charcoaled cloth soon lay on his lap. He tore off the section of parchment on which he'd made his Sigil.

As he'd done countless times before he flicked the iron striker against his flint, expertly bringing three bright purple sparks to life. He struck again. Three more sparks. The third time the jester aimed his sparks with care toward the charred cloth square on his lap. Three more sparks shot out. One took hold, immediately catching the cloth so that it burst into flame.

Mugwort held the parchment scrap over the flame until it took with a crackle and a spit. Twenty breaths later the sigil had been consumed entirely. The parchment was no more than ash floating gently down toward the ground.

'She's coming!' Feverfew declared, shouting up to his companion.

Ash drifted earthward.

'What's he up to?' Feverfew frowned.

A heavy satchel suddenly crashed to the ground and Mugwort landed lightly right beside it.

'I'm about to give my greatest performance ever,' he explained excitedly. 'Watch and learn. I'll show you why Mugwort is a name spoken with hushed awe among the jesters of this world.'

'What have you done?' Feverfew giggled, already warming to the possibility of mischief.

But no answer was given. Before Mugwort could boast of his accomplishment the air was filled with the din of an unrelenting choir of bees. A great hive of creatures was winging its way toward this place.

'No time for idle chitchat,' Mugwort shot back. 'The queen is here. I must prepare to give my performance and you must warn the others we're about to be called on to entertain Aoife. Now go! Leave me to my preparations.'

Feverfew did as he was told but before he'd gathered the small band of travelling entertainers who were hanging about at the edge of the forest the swarm of noisy insects had alighted. The countless bees quickly coalesced into a form resembling that of a slender woman with long red hair and flowing clothes. Then, as her subjects gasped in awe, Aoife appeared before them dressed entirely in deep forest green.

All those who saw her instantly fell to their knees as if they could not bear to look on her shining countenance for more than a few seconds. Eyes downcast toward the grass in the bright moonlight, they trembled with anticipation.

Now some of these folk were mortals and some were of the immortal kind. But all of them had a healthy respect for the queen. They knew how she liked to be treated and they waited with genuine trepidation for her approval.

'It is well,' she began after a long silence had been observed. 'I've been looking forward to your entertainments this evening. This Samhain is a very special occasion. Before the sun rises I will have attained the rank of goddess. Tonight is to be a joyous celebration of my achievement. You may rise.'

The entertainers in the gathering stood up slowly, caps in hands, and Mugwort stepped forward.

'We are honoured by your presence, gracious lady,' he declared, removing his hat and sweeping it around behind him as he launched into a deep bow.

But as he did so his pointed hat flew out of his hand, up and behind him to catch on the branch of a tree and hang precariously. Mugwort stood up straight, deeply embarrassed. Then he quickly stretched up to retrieve the hat and what was left of his dignity.

He stood on his toes and reached his arm up as high as he could. But the hat was just beyond the touch of his wiggling fingers. He was beginning to feel a hot flush course through his body. This wasn't going to plan. He found a rock and struggled with its weight to place it on the ground directly under the hat.

Then he stood up on the stone, hoping he'd be able to reach the object of his desire. But the unstable rock rolled from beneath him and he tumbled clumsily to the ground. As he fell he thumped his knee against the stone so hard he screeched with pain.

By the time he'd stood up, the agony of the bruise was so great he began hopping about holding the knee close to his chest. His colleagues collectively gasped with horror. Then they laughed behind their hands, delighting in his misfortune.

The jester was off to a very bad start, nobody knew that better than him. But for the moment all Mugwort could do was grasp his knee and wish the pain would go away. When he noticed the laughter, however, he immediately forgot his agony.

He placed his foot on the ground with a wince of pain. Then he bowed low again. As he arose he noticed Aoife was laughing too.

'You fool!' she managed to gasp between guffaws. 'You bloody fool!'

For a second he didn't know whether she was displeased or not. Then it struck him that she was laughing uncontrollably. At him.

Now, as every jester will tell you, there is a vast difference between courting an audience that laughs *with* you in appreciation of your wit and enduring spectators who laugh *at* your unfortunate mistakes or failings. Mugwort was annoyed the queen was so entertained by his clumsiness. So he resolved to put his initial awkward fumbling behind him and get on with his performance.

'What else have you prepared for my feasting hall tonight?' she enquired.

'Your Majesty,' he declared, abandoning his hat to the branch with an upward glance. 'Your most gracious Majesty, Queen of the Night, Sovereign of the Dark Places, Ruler of the Redcaps. She who makes the forests to tremble with her voice and the seas to still with her beauty. Tonight the Magnificent Mugwort will entertain you.'

Aoife calmed her laughter as he spoke so that by the time he'd got his introduction over she'd settled down again. Feverfew brought her a folding wooden stool of beautiful workmanship. He flapped it out into shape then placed it solemnly down. Aoife regally took her seat with a little backhand flick of her wrist to dismiss him. Feverfew stepped back from her with a bow.

Mugwort watched all this as he bowed low yet again, sweeping his arm around behind him as before. But this time a loud tear could be heard as he reached the lowest part of the bow.

In fear of the worst Mugwort stood up, his hand searching behind him to locate the feared rip in the back of his britches. But the cloth that had torn was under the arm of his tunic.

When he found the tattered spot where the stitches had separated he touched it with disbelief. And then he heard the laughter again. Aoife was beside herself with amusement. Mugwort was beginning to become annoyed. He marshalled his talents, his stage craft and all his will. He was determined this was going to be the performance of his life despite the unfortunate start.

He opened his mouth to speak, ready to launch into his first story. But before he could say a word Aoife asked a question.

'What's in your satchel?'

'I beg your pardon, my lady?'

'What's in the travelling bag you have at your side?'

Mugwort glanced at the container which held all his worldly possessions, including his latest acquisition.

'Just a few trifles I've picked up here and there on my journeys,' he told her politely.

'Show me.'

Mugwort's tongue nearly stuck in his throat.

'But Your Majesty, I was just about to tell you the tale of the flying ferret.'

'Show me what's in your bag,' she insisted, the jovial tone rapidly disappearing from her voice. 'You may tell me the story another time.'

'It's a wonderful yarn,' he insisted.

But Mugwort could see she wasn't interested in the tale of the flying ferret. He wasn't keen to reveal the book to her. So it was fortunate there were plenty of other distractions in his bag he could entertain her with.

The jester picked up the bag from where it lay beside the tree. Then he carefully placed it down again on the ground in front of him. He bent low over it, untying the leather straps which held the flap closed against the weather. This took some time.

Mugwort always sealed his bag tightly. He was suspicious of the jealousy of other performers. He knew his colleagues would stop at nothing to learn what secrets he held in that satchel. So he made certain always to tie a secure knot.

'I won't be a moment,' he assured Aoife. 'I'm not myself today. Everything seems to be topsy-turvy and higgledy-piggledy.'

The queen giggled at his incompetence, but Mugwort was genuinely having trouble untying the knot. At last, after struggling with it for a long while, he relented and took his recently sharpened knife from his belt to slit the strap.

But as he ran the blade under the leather knot the whole weapon inexplicably collapsed. The blade dislodged from the hilt and the knife fell into two pieces on the ground.

The jester picked up the two broken sections of the knife,

trying to fit them back together again. But they wouldn't stay in place.

'I don't understand it,' he complained. 'I paid thruppence for that blade in Wexford town.'

Aoife was laughing again, her hand over her mouth.

'I can't work out what's going on,' he told her. 'I must be a little under the weather today. I was up late last night. I really should have got some more sleep but I was so nervous about performing for you today I simply couldn't get a wink.'

The queen burst out into uncontrollable fits of laughter. Mugwort was beginning to lose his confidence. Disconcerted, he sat down to concentrate on opening his bag.

Remarkably the leather strap relented straightaway. The knot simply fell open, almost of its own accord. Mugwort rummaged through the satchel, removing a few items to make his search easier.

'I have something here that will surely interest Your Majesty,' he declared.

Mugwort removed a crystal ball, placing it carefully on the grass before him.

'Not that,' he apologised. 'I'll show that to you later if you like. I've never really worked out how to use it.'

Beside the crystal ball he placed a collection of eating utensils, each one twice the size of anything ever seen in Ireland before. There was a spoon as long as a man's forearm with a bowl as wide as a warrior's hand and a three-pronged fork of the same dimensions. As Mugwort laid down these articles side by side he muttered to himself.

'I know it was in here this morning. I checked it.'

He stopped to stroke his pointed beard thoughtfully.

'I couldn't have left it down by the bridge, could I? I mean, I only had one jug of ale. Surely that wouldn't be enough to make me so forgetful.'

Aoife was coughing with laughter by now, though I can't for

the life of me tell you why, unless of course it was the influence of the sigil Mugwort had made. The situation doesn't seem all that funny to me.

Other items quickly joined those laid out on the grass. Out came a green glass vial with a cork stopper in it. Then a wooden cup. Then a small brightly coloured rainbow ball that kept rolling away every time Mugwort placed it on the ground.

It took him a long while to tame that ball. Every time he thought he'd found a stable spot for it the bloody thing would roll away again and he'd have to dive on it to stop it.

'I don't know what's happening to me!' he cried frantically. 'I can't find what I'm looking for. I must be overtired and nervous about performing for Your Majesty. That's it! I'm just suffering from the jitters.'

But the more he protested, the more Aoife laughed, until the tears ran down her face and she doubled up with cackling. And so they passed an hour in that fashion, Mugwort's panic raised to fever pitch with every mistake or fumbled trick.

He ended up choosing a feather, an acorn and a small velvet cushion. And being practised at the juggler's art he didn't make any blunders whatsoever when he tossed them up into the air. With a flourish he ended the juggling performance and swept his arm back to bow.

You'd think he'd have learned his lesson by then. As he bent forward he noticed the bag was open, revealing the cover of the book he'd plundered from Guy's satchel. He leant forward to drag the flap over it. But as he reached out for the leather he lost his balance and fell forward with a crash on top of all the many items he had laid so carefully on the grass. He yelped as he toppled.

He rolled around, reaching for his lute, then managed to bring himself miraculously to his feet as if he'd practised the manoeuvre a hundred times before. Once he was standing firm he strummed a sweet chord, broke two strings loudly in the process and took a deep breath ready to launch into song.

But he never got the chance. Aoife was standing in front of him with her hands firmly placed on her hips. She was looking down at the manuscript which had fallen out of his bag.

'What's that?' she asked him. 'Is it a book of tales?'

'No, Your Majesty,' he stuttered, fearing she would take the manuscript off him if she discovered its worth. 'It's nothing. Just a silly little thing I've been writing myself.'

He picked it up quickly but his hand slipped against the ancient spine. And as he lifted up the precious manuscript it disintegrated page by page before his eyes in a beautiful dance of falling parchment.

As the stitches gave way Mugwort was left with nothing but a pair of empty book boards in his hands. All about him were scattered the many pages of the Book of Signs and Sigils. And the queen was bent double with loud guffaws.

It was at that moment Mugwort noticed something very odd. Every one of the entertainers in his company was rolling around in fits of amusement. Some were screaming for him to stop. Others were simply too much out of breath to make anything but a small squeaking noise through their nostrils. At least one man, a famous fart-craftsman from the Moorish lands, had obviously lost consciousness.

'What's going on?' the jester asked in genuine confusion.

No one answered. Every word he spoke seemed to elicit uncontrollable guffaws from anyone who still had the wits to hear him.

'This isn't funny,' he stated in a terse voice.

But that only increased everyone's amusement.

'What's wrong with you all?' Mugwort shouted. 'I haven't said or done anything even mildly amusing yet. I told you, I'm not having a very good day.'

That brought a renewed round of screaming laughter to his audience.

'I've trained most of my life to tell stories and sing songs in the high troubadour tradition,' he went on. 'I'm an expert dancer, a magnificent musician and I'm possessed of a rare singing voice.'

The crowd were now leaning against one another, coughing and weeping with joy. Aoife had made her way over to the oak tree and had sat down among the roots. She placed her head in her lap and gasped with amusement.

'With the greatest respect, Your Majesty,' Mugwort protested, 'I don't think I've done anything to warrant your raucous laughter.'

The gathering echoed the phrase.

'He doesn't think he's done anything worth laughing about!' they cried to one another. 'He's the greatest jongleur in Christendom.'

'I'm not a jongleur,' Mugwort hissed, with contempt at the distinction. 'I'm a troubadour.'

No matter what he said, he was a jester and that's that. He wasn't fit to call himself a troubadour's privy seat. He just had airs and a high opinion of himself. But of course he couldn't see that. At his words the queen stood up, struggling to maintain some vestige of regal dignity.

'That's enough!' she declared with a hand held up to still him. 'I can't take any more.'

Mugwort decided the queen and his fellow entertainers must be mocking him.

'What are you laughing at?' the jester yelled.

They all screamed the phrase back at him and nearly collapsed laughing.

'It's just that I didn't get enough sleep last night,' he added in a soft voice.

'He didn't get enough sleep!'

He shook his head in confusion as his hat dislodged from the branch of the tree. Then, as if Mugwort had rehearsed the moment a thousand times before, it fell down from above and landed perfectly on his head.

The jester understood his craft well enough. He may not have been a troubadour but he'd learned a thing or two in his time. Rule number one for being a successful entertainer was never to let such a rare occurrence pass you by. With a flourish he removed the hat again then very carefully and discreetly bowed to the queen; not too low nor extravagantly, mind.

Aoife immediately put her two hands together in applause. Moments later the entire company were clapping as loud as they could.

'Brilliant!' Feverfew cried. 'Pure bloody genius! You're a comic master!'

But Mugwort still suspected he was being ridiculed. And he wasn't too happy that they'd all been more amused by his blunders than they'd ever been by his finer artistic accomplishments.

'I'm a humble troubadour,' he reminded them.

'You're a fine fool,' Aoife corrected him. 'I've never encountered such a simpleton. And it comes so naturally to you.'

'I'm a troubadour!' Mugwort told her with indignation. 'I trained with the great Giraut Riquier at the court of Acquitaine where Guilhelm the Ninth instituted the first assembly of troubadours. I have played for the King of Jerusalem and the crowned heads of every principality and kingdom in Christendom. I'm the greatest living exponent of the noble craft of storytelling, music and other distractions.'

'And you're the best clown I've ever seen,' Aoife added.

Mugwort was about to tell her he wasn't a bloody clown. And he wasn't a fool either. He was a master of his craft and she'd better bloody admit it. But he didn't get the chance.

'As a reward for your wonderful performance I am going to make you my personal entertainer. You'll travel with me everywhere after I'm named a goddess. And you will make me laugh.'

'But Your Majesty, who will take charge of your royal performers?'

'Let Feverfew do it,' she replied. 'He's got enough experience.'

'Thank you, Your Majesty,' Feverfew bowed.

'Wait!' Mugwort cut in. 'I'm in charge of the players.'

'Not any more,' Feverfew told him. 'Her Majesty wants you for other tasks. She's doing you a great honour. And you deserve it. That was the most hilarious fooling I've ever witnessed. It was so convincing I couldn't tell whether you were really being clumsy or just playing to the crowd.'

Mugwort rolled his eyes as a disturbing realisation struck him. The sigil he'd created had done its job very well. Everyone was utterly amused by him. But not because he was a skilled performer. They were laughing at his bungling stupidity.

By the time he'd come to this conclusion Queen Aoife's interest had moved on. She turned to look up toward the oak tree.

'Guy d'Alville,' she began, addressing the bough by name, 'have you learned your lesson, I wonder?'

There was no reply, only the rustling of the wind through the branches.

'You can remain in the form of a tree a while longer I think,' she decided.

Then Aoife turned to the rest of the company.

'It's Samhain Eve. Tonight I will achieve that which I have so long desired. So my dear entertainers, you will come to my feasting hall in the depths of the Redcap fortress. At midnight I expect you to have appropriate amusements ready. We are going to celebrate with a great masked ball. By sunrise I will be acclaimed a goddess throughout the four-fifths of Ireland.'

Meanwhile Mugwort had gathered up every page of his

book and stuffed them all into the book boards again. Before he had collected the rest of his things he felt a breeze rising. The breeze soon became a gust of wind and then a tunnel of swirling air filled with the buzzing drone of thousands of bees. Before he'd taken another breath he was swept up into the sky, clutching the precious Book of Pictures to his chest. And as he was carried high above the forest treetops tossed and turned by countless insects, he swore an oath to himself.

He uttered a determined vow that in future he'd be much more careful with the sigils.

When Mugwort regained his senses again he was lying propped up against the oak tree formerly known as Guy d'Alville. His satchel was by his side and his head ached as if he'd been hit hard on the back of it with a stone.

He leaned forward to rub the lump that was forming on his skull.

'By the putrid contents of Saint Michael's Unkempt Beard!' he squealed. 'What host of armed knights has been laying siege to my defences? What in the name of Saint Finbar's white pebbles was I drinking last night?'

There was a rustling noise nearby. Mugwort opened his eyes and slowly focused on his companion, Feverfew. The other jester was leafing through a pile of loose parchment pages. It took a few moments for Mugwort to understand what he was looking at. When he did his reaction was swift.

'Get your hands off that!' he barked as he sat forward. 'The Book of Pictures is mine!'

But the sudden movement brought a striking pain to his head, forcing him to sit back against the tree with a wince.

'I feel like I've had a cow catapulted into the back of my head,' Mugwort groaned.

'I'm just putting the pages back in order for you,' Feverfew explained. 'They scattered everywhere when Aoife let you fall to Earth. It's a very interesting book, isn't it?'

'I told you to leave it alone! It's mine.'

Then Mugwort touched a hand to his head to stifle the pain. 'What happened?'

'She dropped you from the treetops,' his companion explained. 'She shouted out that she wanted you to prepare another performance to be presented at midnight. Then she flew off laughing like a madwoman. You've done well for yourself. You keep up your fooling and there's no telling where you might end up.'

'Flat on my back up against a tree is the best I've managed so far,' Mugwort noted dryly.

'It can only get better,' his companion noted.

Mugwort gingerly felt the back of his head.

'Is there much of a crack? Did any of my brains spill out?'

Feverfew was laughing uproariously. 'Stop!' he shrieked. 'Stop! I can't take any more!'

The injured jester narrowed his eyes with contempt. Then he leaned forward to snatch the bundle of parchment pages out of Feverfew's fingers.

'Leave my things alone!' he snapped. 'Go off to rehearse your performance for this evening.'

'There's no sense in me bothering to do that,' his companion retorted sharply. 'Queen Aoife only wants to see you. She doesn't care about the rest of us. She won't notice if I'm not presenting my best face. I doubt she'll even care to witness my performance. I'm going to get myself well drunk on Redcap mead this evening. There's going to be a huge feast.'

Mugwort shook his head again as his thoughts began to clear.

'Aoife's coming back later to free Guy d'Alville from his enchantment,' Feverfew whispered.

'Why?'

'Because she says he's learned his lesson. She wants him to serve her as her consort and as the commander of her Redcaps.'

Mugwort swallowed hard as a quiet panic started to seize hold of him. Only a short while earlier he'd been stabbing his knife into Guy's bark and roots. He didn't want to think what the cruel Norman would do to him if he regained his manly form.

'Surely she's not going to let him off so lightly?' he postured. 'Guy isn't worthy of such mercy.'

'I think she has the eye for him,' Feverfew winked. 'If you know what I mean.'

The great tree rustled above him menacingly. Now Mugwort forgot the pain in the back of his head completely. He suddenly understood his life was in great danger. No matter how amusing Aoife considered him to be, Guy would have his revenge. No doubt about it. He hugged the pages of the manuscript to his chest. And an eloquent solution to his dilemma unexpectedly presented itself.

'Go away!' he bellowed at Feverfew.

'What?'

'Leave me alone!'

The other jester backed away in confusion at this sudden turn in Mugwort's mood.

'No need to be so pushy.'

'Bugger off!'

'All right,' Feverfew told him. 'Don't get your underbritches in a bind. I'm going.'

With that the offended jester removed himself to the company of the other players. They were gathered round a fire, drinking as they retold the tale of Mugwort's hilarious antics.

Our Mug blessed the bright moonlight as he searched

through the pages of his book till he found one with enough empty space for him to concoct a sigil on. Then he went about his task, secure in the knowledge that he had a special ability for this type of spell-working.

You'd think he'd have learned his lesson. But that's the danger with sigils. It's so easy to convince yourself you've got what you asked for and ignore the price you've had to pay. Mark my words well.

'I just have to remember to be precise,' he told himself under his breath as he scrawled a carefully worded statement on the parchment.

Once the wish was down in writing he read it aloud to ensure it sounded right. There was no room for ambiguity. No going back once the Sigil had been cast.

'It is my will that the spell Queen Aoife placed on Guy d'Alville never be broken nor annulled for all time and forever.'

The tree above him creaked with malice, shaking all its leaves in a fury of desperation.

Mugwort stood up to get away from Guy. But he soon enough remembered d'Alville was powerless to do anything to stop him. Mugwort sniggered at the impotence of the mighty oak. Then he did a little dance of satisfaction, but only a little one as his head was still very sore.

He returned to his seat by the tree to concentrate on the wish with all his mind. At last, when an appropriate sigil shape had formed in his mind, he made a quick sketch of it with the charcoal stick from his tinderbox. Then he sat before the drawing for a long time, soaking in the form of it so that he'd remember it for all time. Above him the oak tree groaned in angry protest.

Mugwort sniggered again.

'Hush, O Lord of Leaves. O King of Acorns. Be still. You can do nothing and nothing can save you now.'

In a few moments the jester had the sign committed to

memory. Then he had his flint and steel ready in his hands. Before you could have said, 'Mind the sparks don't get in your eyes,' he had a blazing piece of charcoal cloth in his fingers and he was touching it to the corner of the parchment he'd marked his sigil on.

The whole thing immediately sputtered into a brightly flaming spectacle and was consumed in a matter of moments, much to Mugwort's surprise. He hadn't expected it to burn so quickly.

When there was left nothing but ash he dropped the last corner of parchment from his fingers. It burned out at his feet with a slow orange glow. Then Mugwort brushed his hands together contentedly and leaned back in satisfaction against the tree. He was already gloating.

And here's a warning to you. Don't be a gloater, my dear one. Don't indulge in the gloats. Not even now and then. A gloater never gloats very long, they say. And he who gloats will profit little from his gloatiness.

Mugwort shouldn't have gloated. Not only is it bad manners, it's often premature. As it most certainly was in this case.

For as the jester leaned back, instead of a huge oaken trunk to rest his back against, he encountered a knight's leather riding boots. Mugwort's hand reached round behind him. He was too afraid to look.

His fingers fumbled the toes then found their way up to the noble shins. There the leather was scraped and a large piece had been cut out of the boot just below the right knee. Kidskin britches had been tucked into the boots. And the lower edge of a mail coat brushed against the back of his hand just there.

'Who is it?' the jester asked himself.

But he knew who was standing behind him. Do you?

There's a very important rule to remember when performing the Draoi-craft of sigils. I've already told you this rule must never be broken. Never say never. Do not say not. If you do, the enchantment will turn out the opposite way you want it to.

I don't know why this is. So don't bother asking me.

Because Mugwort skimmed over the warnings in the book he didn't know his spell would do exactly what he did not want it to. He didn't understand his wish would actually free d'Alville from Aoife's enchantment.

'Stand up, you miserable wretch!' the Norman lord demanded as his heavy hand came down upon the jester's shoulder. 'I'm going to take the greatest pleasure in giving you a damn good caning. You've ruined my boots. The last man who ruined a pair of my boots ended up replacing the leather out of his own hide.'

Mugwort didn't need to turn round. He didn't have to check the identity of his assailant. When he heard that voice, it was enough to confirm his worst fears. In that terrible moment he didn't consider pleading for his life as he might have done with any other nobleman.

This was Guy d'Alville. The only hope remaining to him was to run as fast as he could and pray the knight wasn't in a mood to chase him. So Mugwort slipped out from under the Norman's grasp, crawled a distance of a dozen footsteps as quickly as he possibly could, then got to his feet and sprinted.

In the rush he left his precious book and his bag of valuables behind. He would have to do without them. To have stopped would surely have cost him his life. Before he disappeared into the woods he glanced across to see his companions were rolling about on the grass with laughter. But he was in too much of a hurry to address that particular indignity.

It took a few moments for Guy to realise he was having trouble pursuing the jester. Then it took a few more for him to notice his feet and legs were numb. By the time he'd managed to put one foot before the other and stagger after Mugwort, the jester had disappeared completely into the darkness of the forest.

And that was how Guy d'Alville came to be wandering in the Otherworld. When the feeling returned to his legs he followed Mugwort into that realm, unwittingly and without any understanding of what terrible fate awaited him there. It was a fate so awful indeed that I'm not going to tell you about it until later on.

It's interesting to note that Mugwort felt nothing unusual as he crossed into the Otherworld. He wasn't a particularly sensitive individual. But Guy noticed a difference the very instant he passed between the two intertwined oaks. The air was strange. It was charged with a buzzing brightness of tingling textures, sounds and sights.

Guy found he was suddenly attuned to an unusually high level of awareness. It was as if he'd abruptly been granted all the senses of a predatory beast. You see, Guy was a naturally sensitive man, though he rarely let on to anyone about it. Be open to the intuition, he used to say, but don't give your opponent any clue you have it in the first place.

He may have been a sensitive individual but he was just a bloody Norman. And most of those ignorant bastards wouldn't recognise an Otherworldly experience if it snatched them by the arm and dragged them screaming to the bottom of a moat.

So although colours, sights and sounds were suddenly more intense to him, the Norman convinced himself he was just feeling a little out of sorts after his ordeal. He put it all down to the bright moonlight, the closely growing trees and the abundance of night creatures dwelling within this forest.

Guy trudged on down a well-worn path, recalling that Robert FitzWilliam had gone off into these woods earlier that evening.

'Maybe I'll be blessed to find that bastard too!' Guy spat under his breath.

His knees were very sore and stiff after standing still for so long. And he had a terrible crick in his neck. But his strength was returning to him with every step.

'Where are you, Mugwort?' he bellowed with all the force of his noble knightly voice. 'Just wait till I get my hands on you. I won't just kill you. I'll slice you up into long strips then wrap you round the trunk of an oak. You bloody bark-splitter! Tree-killer! Bough-slicer!'

Guy stopped in his tracks suddenly. He listened carefully to the echoes of his own voice.

'Did I say that?' he asked himself in surprise.

Then he laughed a little at his own foolishness. After a few more hasty unintelligible mutters he continued down the path in silence, alert to the presence of any fugitive jesters or renegade Templars. But Mugwort had slipped by Guy. And Robert was already a long way off.

It's worth noting that d'Alville's senses were so overwhelmed and muddled he didn't even notice when he nearly stood on Mugwort hiding amongst a mound of fallen leaves. He strode on ever further into the woods. And before long his footsteps had faded from the jester's ears entirely. So, with a deep sigh of relief, Mugwort made his way back to the spot where Guy had stood to retrieve his possessions.

CRIGINAS ThE SCRIBE

Sianan strode across the room to where Caoimhin lay. I stood up, embarrassed that I was so obviously blushing with indignation. I was upset the lad had called for her. I was miffed she suddenly had all his attention. But I was absolutely fuming that I hadn't been able to feed him his soup. For the bowl in my hands held the untried love broth of my dear friend Ortha.

'I know where Mawn is being held!' the lad told her. 'I've seen the place with my own eyes!'

Sianan cast a questioning glance at me. She knew he hadn't woken since the attempt to poison him. I shrugged as if I didn't know what was going on.

'I saw Mawn,' he insisted. 'I looked into the spring where he's being kept prisoner. Flidais showed me a vision of Mawn refusing her advances. She told me all about him.'

'Flidais?' Sianan gasped. 'You've spoken with Flidais?'

'I've been to her spring. The one where she has Mawn as her prisoner. It is called the Well of Many Blessings.'

Sianan could hardly believe her ears. Nearly eight hundred summers had come and gone since she'd last seen Mawn. He was her soul-friend, her Anamchara. He had been intended as her companion through the long ages of their lives.

Sianan and Mawn were of the Fanaí. Together they'd been granted the Quicken Brew, bestowed upon them by the

Danaans and the Druids of the Gaels. Their eternal role in life was to have been to protect and preserve the lore and law of their people forevermore. They were to have been the King and Queen of Storytellers, the reigning duet of harpers and guardians of the old ways.

But their life together had barely begun when they were parted after a terrible battle. Since that day their ways had never crossed again. How she yearned to hear his voice. How she longed to have him by her side to still the endless loneliness of her immortality.

Sianan knew the Redcaps were massing against the Killibegs. She understood the Culdees needed every sword arm they could muster to their defence. She feared there was also a great force of Knights Hospitaller riding north from Wexford town bent on the destruction of these folk whom Rome saw as heretical. She'd already decided to stay to fight with us.

She'd dismissed the possibility of confronting Aoife with a Draoi-poem. There were some who thought that the best hope. But Sianan thought it wiser to wake the ancient Goddess Danu from her sleep and beg her intervention.

'Can you lead me to the spring?' she asked in a soft tone, striving to still her excitement.

'It is in the Land of Dreams,' Caoimhin answered hesitantly. 'In the place where I journey when the visions come on me.'

'You have the Sight?'

'I've always had it.'

'Then it is well I was the one who tended you after your poisoning. For I would pay any price to know where Mawn is and how I might find him.'

I rolled my eyes. She's already got a lad trapped in a spring somewhere and here she's looking to thieve mine off me.

'Are you well enough to travel?'

'I'm feeling remarkably rested for one who's recovering from a poisoning,' Caoimhin noted. 'Give me a turning of the sand glass and I'll be ready to go.'

'You may have half that time,' Sianan replied. 'We must also seek out Aoife and try to bring an end to her ambitions. If that fails we'll call on Danu. You and I will be very busy this night. The sooner we are about our business the better. Make certain you have something to eat before you leave. It's unwise to travel to the Otherworld on an empty stomach.'

'Are we really going to that place?' the lad asked wide-eyed.

'We are.'

'How do you know to look for Mawn's prison there?'

'Flidais doesn't enter into the land of mortals very often. If she has Mawn in captivity it will certainly be somewhere within the boundaries of that part of the Otherworld to which she lays claim.'

Sianan turned to leave.

'I'll be back for you shortly. You must be ready to go. This may be the best chance I ever have of finding my friend.'

Then she was gone. I retrieved the bowl of broth. I only had half an hour. I decided I wasn't going to waste another moment. I pushed Caoimhin back against his pillow, filled the spoon and placed it at his mouth.

'Hurry up and get this meal into you,' I told him. 'You'll need your strength.'

He swallowed the soup and I instantly breathed easier.

'What's all this about Flidais anyway?' I asked him, relaxing a little now I knew my love broth would be about its work within him.

'She told me she's the Goddess of the Hunt,' he explained. 'She tried to convince me to stay with her. She's a wicked woman I'm sure. There's no telling what she had in mind for me.'

'I can imagine what might have crossed her thoughts,' I replied cynically.

I filled his mouth with soup again and whispered under my breath to myself: 'Just what I need. Another one chasing after him.'

Then there was a fresh spoonful at his lips before he'd had a chance to swallow the previous one.

'Eat up, my dear,' I told him. 'This broth will do you good. I promise.'

When time drew close to Sianan's return he hadn't shown any of the usual symptoms of lovesickness. I was beginning to despair of Ortha's potion. I'd fed enough of it to poor Caoimhin to turn a horse to amorous thoughts, yet he seemed unaffected.

He was rearranging the books in his satchel with his back to me when he suddenly turned around to look at me. He was all very serious as young men are wont to be when they're love-struck. He stared into my eyes for a few moments with the hint of a tear welling up in each one so that the firelight caught the sparkle. He sighed deeply, searching for the right words.

My heart skipped a few beats. He was so beautiful. It was plain some profound realisation had struck him. I tried to pretend I didn't know what was going on. Then he stood up and stepped closer to where I was sitting by the fire. I couldn't bear the suspense any longer. I had to say something.

'Are you going to lug those books along with you?'

Caoimhin half turned to glimpse the satchel over his shoulder. Then he nodded without speaking.

'Will you read me a page from the *Leabhar Fál*?' I asked.

Again he nodded and he turned to retrieve the book. Soon he had a page open at random. He read it silently to himself at first. Then he spoke the words aloud.

'The first sip of broth is always the tastiest.'

He looked up to catch my eye. 'I have something important to ask you.'

'Yes.'

He took a deep breath before he spoke.

'Do you know anyone who plays the harp?'

I must have stared blankly back at him. I was still pondering the coincidence of that wise little saying he'd read out from the Book of Destiny.

'Does anyone at the Killibegs play the harp?' he repeated. 'I have a great desire to learn to play that instrument. I was wondering whether you might know of anyone who could teach me.'

'Sianan is a renowned harper,' I replied. The words were already out of my mouth before I had the wit to bite my tongue.

'Sianan?' he asked as his eyes lit up. 'That's a strange thing, isn't it? Ever since I first saw her I've felt a strong affinity with her. It's almost as if I've known her all my life.'

'I see,' I said, rolling my eyes. 'Bloody typical.'

'I know she's a strange one,' Caoimhin went on. 'I've heard she's an immortal, though I find that very hard to believe. Her huge eyes are unlike any I've ever seen before. But apart from that she seems no different from anyone else. Is such a thing possible? Do you believe she's an immortal?'

'Of course she is! Didn't you hear old Clemens talk about her at the council? He's known her since he was a boy and his grandparents knew her in their time. She hasn't changed at all in the last six generations at least.'

'There's an odd beauty about her,' he went on dreamily.

That was about all I could take. The love potion had obviously failed me and this conversation was beginning to grate on my nerves.

'I'm sure you'll both be happy together in the Otherworld,' I snapped. 'But here's a warning you'd better take heed of. Whatever you may think of Sianan, be sure to be wary of her. She's not like us. She's lived over seven hundred and fifty summers, some say. And whether her heart is true or not, she has no allegiance to any but her own kind. All the immortals are like that. Don't be cajoled. Don't be sweet-talked into anything you don't truly desire. And if ever you change your mind, I'll be here waiting for your return.'

'Why don't you come with us?' he suggested excitedly. 'I'm sure Sianan wouldn't mind.'

'I'm sure she would.'

'Let's ask her when she returns.'

Well it was just as he said those words that Sianan pulled back the cowhide which covered the door and entered the chamber.

'What is it you'd ask of me?' she said, looking from one to the other of us with interest.

'Binney would like to come along with us.'

'No,' she answered tersely. 'It'll be difficult enough for me to keep an eye on you, Caoimhin. I can't be playing nursemaid to two mortals in that place.'

I knew it. I knew it all along. Sianan wanted to get my lad alone in the Otherworld where she could work her enchantments upon him without interruption.

'She wouldn't be any trouble,' Caoimhin protested. 'I'm sure the two of us wouldn't slow you down.'

'It's the eve of Samhain,' Sianan shot back, her strange eyes flashing with urgency. 'It's not a time for mortals to be wandering about in the Otherworld.'

'But you're taking me along with you.'

'You are a special case.'

'Why's that?'

Sianan hesitated. Then she dropped her eyes away from his toward the fire before she spoke.

'You have the Sight. You've been granted the sacred vision.'

'So has Binney!' he exclaimed. 'She's told me all about it. She also has the Sight.'

Sianan frowned and turned sharply to search my face.

170

'Is it true? Do you suffer from the Faidh?'

And do you know something? Even though I was mighty upset she was taking my Caoimhin off to the Otherworld, I looked back into those dark wide eyes of hers and I couldn't lie.

'Not that I'm aware of,' I told her and lowered my head in shame.

She smiled in a smug manner, as if to say her suspicions had been confirmed. Then she turned to Caoimhin. He frowned in confusion.

'We must leave immediately. I've explained the situation to Clemens and his people. They've given us their blessing on this journey. There's no time to lose. If we manage to find Mawn quickly we might be able to return in time to give our aid to the people of the Killibegs.'

'Mirim and Alan are going with you, aren't they?' I asked.

'They will remain here to help with the defence of the Killibegs.'

'What about Binney?' Caoimhin pleaded.

'She's needed here. It's best Binney remain with her kin-folk where she can lend her hand to the defence of the settlement.'

Sianan placed a hand on his shoulder.

'Are you ready to go?'

He nodded sullenly and faced me with a deep sorrow in his expression.

'I'll go fetch us some oatcakes and ale for the journey,' Sianan declared. 'I won't be gone long. When I return we will be leaving. Do try to find yourself some other clothes to wear. A black monk's habit is not very practical for travelling.'

'I don't have any other clothes,' he protested. 'I've never dressed in anything but the black.'

But Sianan was already gone.

His eyes were wet with emotion as he gently took my hand.

'I know why you lied to her,' he said. 'I know why you didn't

171

tell her about the Sight. I'm always careful who I reveal it to. I'm sorry if I embarrassed you.'

'That's quite all right,' I reassured him.

'Do you have any clothes I could wear?'

'I have a cap to keep your head warm,' I offered.

I pulled out my own grey linen coif. It was a simple close-fitting cap with flaps to cover the ears and long strands to secure it under the chin. It was a style favoured by both men and women in those days as an undercap. Norman nobles used to wear them to keep their greasy unwashed hair away from their expensive silk or embroidered hats. Ordinary folk wore them in the fervent hope of one day being able to afford such fine hats as needed protection from their hair.

'I wish you could come with us,' he told me as he took the cap from me. 'You're such a good friend to have looked after me the way you did. May I take some of your broth with me to drink while I walk?'

He picked up a skin from the fireside and began ladling the soup into the vessel. I put a hand on his.

'I think you've had enough broth. You should eat oatcakes on the road. They won't weigh you down quite so much.'

By this time I'd given up hope the love potion would do its job at all.

'But it's such a nourishing soup,' he countered. 'And I'll think of you each time I take a sip.'

I laughed at the compliment and relented. I reckoned if the broth hadn't done its trick thus far, it wasn't likely to. What harm could there be in letting him take it with him?

'Very well. Since you have flattered me, and if it would make you happy, then please take some broth.'

'It would please me greatly,' he said softly.

He finished filling the skin with soup. That done, he placed the stopper hard into the neck of the vessel to seal it.

'I must go,' Caoimhin told me as he stood up to shoulder his book satchel and wrap a simple grey cloak around his shoulders. 'Sianan will be waiting.'

'I wish I could go with you,' I sighed.

'So do I,' he nodded.

Then Sianan's voice was raised outside.

'Caoimhin! Get a move on, will you? We've a long journey ahead of us and it's already after nightfall. We mustn't waste a moment if we're to find Mawn.'

Caoimhin pushed past me to the door, still clutching the skin full of broth. He stopped there at the cowhide and hesitated. Then he turned to face me.

'Binney?' he whispered.

'Yes,' I replied moving closer, my heart beating in my throat, for I could sense some change had come over him suddenly.

Our eyes met in that second. Before I knew what was happening his lips were pressed against mine. Perhaps his chance encounter with Flidais had inspired him. I didn't care.

He dropped the skin of broth and his arms were about me in a passionate embrace. I nearly fainted with the ecstatic joy of it all. Even though I'd fixed the love potion myself, I wasn't really prepared for the consequences.

Sianan called out again but I only half heard her voice in the background. Caoimhin must have caught her words, though, because he suddenly pushed me away.

'Goodbye Binney,' he gasped as he brushed a lock of my flame-red hair from my eyes. 'I'm sorry.'

And then he was gone, leaving me all weak-kneed and wobbly. I was so shocked I stood there for a long while with my jaw wide open wondering what had happened. When eventually I came to my senses I gathered up a few things, including my satchel, a skin full of ale, some oatcakes and a cloak to keep out the chill.

I'd made a terrible decision, you see. It was one that would haunt me for the rest of my days but I had no inkling of that then. You see, my dear, I was determined to follow Sianan and Caoimhin into the Otherworld.

I set my mind to the task of tailing them and promised myself I would not let her get her immortal hands on him. I made for the door and as I did so I picked up the skin full of broth Caoimhin had dropped.

I don't know what was in my mind when I pushed the strap over my shoulder. It must have slipped my mind that I'd tainted it with the love brew. All I could think of was that old warning we were given as children. My grandmother used to tell me this all the time.

'If you find yourself wandering in the Otherworld, don't eat of the food or drink of the drink of that place. For those who do so are trapped forever in that country and may never return.'

The broth would serve me well if I got hungry, I thought. I wish I'd taken cheese instead.

Outside the air was chilly. I wrapped my cloak tight about my body as I silently prayed with all my heart that no one challenged me at the gates to the rath. Fortune cloaked me in her veil at that hour for everyone was in such a rush to attend to the laying in of food that they paid no heed to me. There had, as yet, been no sentries posted at the battlements.

Torches had been placed at various intervals around the open space within the walls. But there were wide gaps between them, so it was a simple matter for me to slip around in the shadows until I came near to the gates. There I found my way was blocked.

Caoimhin and Sianan had been stopped as they were

leaving. I recognised the Breton warrior Martin who had been with Sianan on her arrival to the Killibegs. His red-haired Sotar dog was yelping enthusiastically by Sianan's side. I crept close until I could hear what was being said and though the moon was high I found a place under the walls where the shadows were deep.

'Take him with you,' Martin was insisting. 'I'd rather he went along with you. If the Redcaps come there's no telling what they'll do to him.'

'But he's your companion,' Sianan countered. 'How could I take him from your side?'

'He adores you!' the Breton pointed out. 'I'm sure you'll break his puppy-dog heart if you go through that gate without him. And I'd feel better if I knew he was with you. I owe you my life. If you won't accept my sword arm at your side, at the very least take my dog with you.'

Sianan was silent for a few moments.

'You don't owe me anything,' she insisted. 'And no harm will come to me. I'm a Fanaí.'

'What about the young master?' Martin asked. 'You're not going to tell me he's an immortal, are you? Not with the crown of his head shaved like a monk and those black Benedictine robes.'

Sianan glanced at Caoimhin who was wearing my grey linen cap tied under his chin.

'We aren't likely to stand in need of any aid,' she replied.

'I'll be deeply offended if you leave Oat-Beer behind,' Martin shot back. 'And I don't doubt he'll pine for you as well.'

There was an uncomfortable silence as Sianan rolled her eyes.

'Very well,' she relented at last.

And as she spoke those words the red dog fairly jumped for joy, chasing his own tail in circles and giving jubilant yelps.

'All right!' Sianan told him sternly and waved a finger of

authority. 'If you're going to come along with me you'll have to learn to behave yourself. Such antics won't endear you to the folk of the Otherworld.'

Oat-Beer planted his backside down firmly on the ground, still shivering with excitement and barely holding back his cries. But he was obviously determined not to do anything that might raise another reprimand from his beloved Sianan.

'I swear it's as if he understands every word we speak,' Martin laughed. 'Take care of him, won't you?'

'I promise I will,' Sianan assured the Breton. 'Goodbye.'

Then, without any further words, she, Oat-Beer and Caoimhin were gone down the path toward the stream. I waited till Martin had moved on back to his work digging a trench within the gates. Then I was off after the three of them as fast and as silently as I could manage.

It wasn't a difficult matter to slip out of the fort. No one would have expected me to want to leave the hearth of my kith and kin. And likely as not I wouldn't be missed until someone called at the house of healing seeking some cure for sleepiness at the watch.

I must have been an awful kind of person in those days. I almost find it impossible to believe I could have acted so selfishly. To have abandoned my people in their time of need all for the sickness of my heart! I'm ashamed of course.

The worst of it is that everyone would have been saved a whole lot of trouble if I had stayed behind. Not the least of all me. For I've spent a lifetime paying for my foolishness and my dabbling in matters I should have left well alone. That decision to follow them into the Otherworld set a new course and bearing for my soul-voyage.

In any case it will all become clear as my story unfolds. Nothing can be done to mend the damage now, except that you listen well and take heed of the warnings woven into my story.

They crossed the stream a short while later and I was close behind. I had a notion they'd be heading for the forest entrance. For in those days it was notorious as a spot where the Otherworld might be encountered.

My heart beat loud in my throat. And though the night was cold I sweated under my cloak, panting with the effort of keeping up with Sianan and Caoimhin. By the holy farthings of Finbar, they set a cracking pace!

I never thought to question at the time just how Caoimhin might have performed such a feat. Having only just recovered from a poison draught delivered to him a few hours earlier one might have expected him to be less energetic. The trouble is I had no idea then that Sianan had slipped him a taste of the Quicken Brew.

So on they strode toward their goal and I was keeping as close as I could behind them. Now, it started to strike me that there were many things I'd been told about the Otherworld as a youngster which would probably be worth recalling to mind before I crossed the borders to that country.

First and foremost every storyteller always gave a special emphasis to one rule. Never under any circumstances should a mortal eat the food of the Faerie lands nor taste the drink neither. To do so most certainly makes any return home to the mortal lands impossible.

I patted the skin full of broth I'd brought. Then I touched the skin full of ale. I must say I was reassured.

I'd heard many tales of the Otherworld, and I was deeply frustrated that this was the only hard and fast rule I could recall. There must have been others, I told myself. I began to have second thoughts about the wisdom of traipsing off into the Land of Dreams without any idea what I was in for.

I somehow reassured myself I'd be all right if I kept my thoughts clear and made sure Caoimhin and Sianan never strayed from my sight. But there remained a nagging doubt in the back of my mind.

In my youth I was very adept at ignoring such doubts. I could push them away or pretend they didn't really exist at all if they interfered with the object of my desire. These days I listen to my instincts a little more carefully and weigh up the consequences of my actions with keen attention to the balance of the scales. So would you if you'd been through what I have.

The journey to the edge of the woods passed by in this manner. There I was all the way alternating between doubting the wisdom of this adventure and dodging to keep out of sight of Sianan's sharp Fanaí eyes.

To be sure I was certain she'd looked back over her shoulder once or twice directly at me. I could have sworn she knew I was following her. But as she made no move to dissuade me from my path I came to believe she approved of what I was doing.

Oat-Beer may have been a hunting dog with a nose for danger but he certainly never caught scent of me. It was only when we came closer to the edge of the woods that he stopped to sniff the air. Then he ran off ahead, barking wildly and wagging his tail exuberantly.

Sianan stopped there for a long while waiting for his return. For certain she'd sensed some danger ahead on the path. I had no way of knowing Oat-Beer had been drawn in by Feverfew and his band of entertainers.

They must have dispersed quite quickly at the sound of barking for when the dog returned he was silent. That's when Sianan deemed it safe to journey on. She doubled their pace when they took off again. And that caught me entirely by surprise.

By the time I got to within sight of the forest gate I was puffing and panting. I arrived in time to see Caoimhin glance back before he disappeared into the shadowy woods.

I thought I'd lost him. And then another concern struck me.

I was now out alone on Samhain Oidche, the night when the hosts of the Faerie folk ride out from their strong places in search of mortal slaves. Queen Aoife might be abroad this evening or any of her Redcaps. What would happen to me if they caught me all alone?

I suddenly remembered one of the other warnings the storytellers always emphasise. If you must travel at night, never go out on Samhain Eve and never ever stray near to the places where the Faerie people dwell.

But it was too late to turn back now. I sprinted toward the cover of the forest gate overhung with two great intertwining oaks. I vaguely recall crossing a patch of soil that had been stripped of grass but I couldn't have guessed that this was where Guy had been standing in the shape of a tree.

Everything was such a blur of reeling fright in those last few moments before I passed into the Otherworld and beyond the knowledge of mortals. But if those seconds are not clear in my recollections, all that happened afterwards is as lucid to my mind as if it had taken place yesterday. Just as any vivid dream may be.

The shadows of the two ancient overhanging trees veiled the entrance to the Faerie woods. I stood for the briefest hesitant breath under that pair of oaks. Then I lunged into the darkness of the forest, determined to catch up with Sianan and Caoimhin.

I immediately noticed it wasn't nearly as dark under the cover of the forest canopy as it had been in the open. I recall being very surprised at this but the strange light nevertheless emboldened me. I think I would have been terrified beyond imagining if I'd found it was dark within the woods.

I don't know why it is I never thought to bring a rush-light or a torch with me when I left the Killibegs. Perhaps it was the bright full moon up in the sky or perhaps because I hadn't seen Sianan and Caoimhin carrying anything to illuminate their way.

The light in the forest was silvery blue, just like the luminescence of the full moon. Everything seemed to glow with the force of it. I'd just become accustomed to this Other-worldly light when I came to a crossroads. There the road divided into three. There were no signposts and there was certainly no way for me to discover which path Sianan and Caoimhin had taken.

I hadn't considered I might lose them so soon after we crossed the borders of the dream country. I searched for any sign of tracks in the path but the road was paved over with cobbles.

The next thing I knew I'd fallen into a mild panic. That immediately progressed into a sense of despair and loss. Then I told myself I was a fool to have ventured off in this fashion in the first place. Little did I realise the Otherworld was already digging its claws into me.

In desperation I decided to call out in the hope Caoimhin, Sianan or even Oat-Beer might hear me. My voice cracked as I announced to all the varied denizens of the Land of Dreaming that I was hopelessly lost.

My voice had not yet died off in the distance when the forest erupted in a cacophony of bird calls and animal cries such as I had never heard before. I have to say that I was a bit of a night wanderer myself. This wasn't the first time I'd been out alone in a woodland by moonlight. But I'd never heard half those cries before.

That chorus of creatures went on for a long while as I stood there at the crossroads unwilling and unable to make a decision about which path to take. My instincts were ablaze with a thousand tiny details of my surroundings.

I recall being fascinated by a short squat bush with foliage of the deepest green and berries of the brightest red. I would have dearly loved to have tasted one of those fruits for they looked so delightfully sweet dangling heavily there upon their branches.

I hadn't so much as reached out to pluck a dainty berry from the bush when an immense sadness welled up in me. I don't know where it came from but this terrible emotion took me completely by surprise.

Before I knew what was happening I was curled up on the ground, weeping my heart out for the loss of Sianan, Caoimhin and Oat-Beer. I wept for Father Clemens. I wept for Ortha. I wept for the loss of everyone who had ever been dear to me at any time in my life.

And strangely enough I even wept for my brother, the harsh and unfeeling Eriginas who had stolen me away to Glastonbury Abbey when I was but a child. I'd never had any feelings for him. I'd spent most of my early life deeply resenting him. But now he was dead I felt I'd lost the dearest of friends.

Mortals beware! If you go off adventuring into that land, mind you keep a weather eye upon your emotions. For in that realm every taste, scent, touch, memory, vision and sound is intensified a thousandfold.

And most important of all, in that place heartfelt emotion has a frightening way of coming to life. Who's to say why my brother's face came to my mind just then. Perhaps it was some premonition. I suppose it was my first real tangible experience of the Sight.

For as the weeping left me and I sat up again there was a figure seated by the roadside. He had a cowl of Benedictine black over his head. I immediately thought Caoimhin had returned to me.

But the black of my young monk's robe had not faded so much. This man was older. It was apparent he'd been a member of the order for many years. When I realised I knew who he must be I spoke his name.

'Eriginas.'

He looked up and drew the cowl from his face. There was an uncharacteristic smile there on my brother's thin lips and a sparkle in his bright blue eyes I'd never noticed in life.

'You don't seem to be too alarmed to meet me,' he noted with a hint of surprise. 'I was quite stunned when they told me you were here. So I thought I'd better come to make my apologies while I have the chance. It's not every day one has the opportunity to express remorse.'

'Remorse?' I stuttered.

'I'm sorry I stole you away with me when I went off to Glastonbury,' he soothed.

There was genuine feeling in his expression. I could hardly believe my ears.

'It was wrong of me to have taken you against your will. I should have been more considerate of your wishes. Can you find it in your heart to forgive me?'

I nodded. I was dumbstruck. Speech had left me entirely.

'Good!' he stated with a slap of his thigh. 'That's very good.'

He stood up, brushed down his monkish habit and spoke again.

'Well I'll be off.'

'What?'

'I promised I'd spend the evening teaching the finer points of book illumination to a group of the more enthusiastic novices. The moonlight is marvellous, isn't it?'

He looked skyward with his hands on his hips.

'I can't recall a night as bright as this one in all my winters,' he told me. 'So I'd best make the most of it. Will we see you at mass tomorrow?'

I was confused to say the least. Caoimhin had told me he'd been present at the passing of Eriginas. Yet here was my departed brother in the flesh inviting me to sing the holy office.

'Is there a church nearby?' I asked him.

He looked at me as if I were mad.

'In the City of God there are countless churches,' he laughed. 'But I return to the Abbey of Our Lady time and again. I prefer the chapel there. It's the holiest place I ever visited. You're welcome to come with me. We have so much to talk about, you and I.'

I was still rather shocked by this strange turn of events. I suspected this was some sort of Faerie trick meant to disorient me or drive me to distraction. Yet I couldn't be absolutely certain.

There was one question which jumped to mind and it wouldn't wait. I knew if this were truly Eriginas before me and not some tricksy dæmon it would show as soon as I asked it.

'Have you seen Caoimhin?'

'My goodness yes!' the old scribe replied. 'I saw him wander off down that road.'

He pointed at the left-hand path which descended toward a staircase cut into the road then disappeared out of sight.

'Strange that he didn't hear me calling out to him. But there are many inexplicable things here,' the old monk winked.

'I must find Caoimhin,' I told him. 'Perhaps you and I will have a chance to talk again on my way home.'

'Home?' he smiled throwing his arms wide with palms outstretched. 'You are home.'

'I must go now.'

'As you wish. I hope that lad is still looking after my books.'

'He is.'

'Farewell then.'

A thought struck me.

'Where does this road lead?'

'Down. I've been there a few times. It isn't the most pleasant of journeys but the destination more than makes up for any inconvenience you may experience. Don't take any notice of the knight who guards the bridge. He's an old fool. He thinks he's still off on some quest or other.'

'You didn't answer my question,' I noted.

'It's rude to ask questions.'

'I would be very glad of a guide,' I ventured, not wishing to offend him further by requesting his help.

'I'm sure you would.'

Then my brother slapped his thighs again.

'Well, it's been very nice catching up with you. We must do it again sometime. I really should be off now. I don't want to keep my young students waiting. Goodbye.'

With that he turned on his heel and skipped lightly off down the path which forked to the right. He was singing a nonsense song in full voice and bowing to the trees as he passed them. I shook my head as I watched him go. But when he simply vanished from my view after he'd walked no more than a dozen steps, my jaw dropped wide open.

The Lack of a Friend

A s I set off down the left-hand path Robert FitzWilliam sat silently staring into the flames of a little fire, watching a duck roasting on a spit. Once in a while he looked up to glance at Órán, who had seated himself in a place on the opposite side of the blaze. But he couldn't bear to look at him for long.

Our knight was utterly speechless. Well not utterly. But he must have seemed that way. There were a few things he would've liked to say if he hadn't been a very polite and respectful man at heart.

You see, he'd just been listening to Órán give a full account of himself. And this unusual fellow had offered a few very surprising revelations.

Now I'll tell you Órán's story. As you should know by now there are two tribes of spirits which inhabit the world of mortals and the worlds beyond. They're not the only kind of spirits. They're just two of the tribes. There's more spirits out there than you or I could shake a ferret at, believe me.

As I've told you before, a Frightener feeds off fear. Every emotion connected to fear – terror, fright, panic, distress, revulsion, anger, rage, disappointment, dread – is nourishment for a Frightener spirit.

An Enticer lives for the taste of love, admiration, infatuation, desire, longing, yearning, worship, laughter, joy or heart-rending nostalgia for an unresolved and unrequited love. But these spirits also feast on satisfaction, ambition, self-indulgence, drunkenness, avarice, vanity, gluttony and the mindless pursuit of whatever material pleasures may be had in this world or the Other.

In order to feed properly, Frighteners and Enticers must attach themselves to their host so they can soak up the raw emotions or reactions as soon as they bubble up to the surface. Some spend their existence hopping from one host to another. These spirits are generally the weaker ones who haven't been that successful in finding prime quarry for their hunt. As a consequence of all this jumping about, most of these minor Frighteners and Enticers don't progress beyond a fairly weak stage of existence for a long, long time.

That's not to say that they can't play a huge part in the life of their victim. In fact there isn't a person living who could honestly claim these spirits don't play an important role in their day-to-day life.

We've become accustomed to them. They're so much a part of our lives that we don't even notice them any more.

I'm sure most people these days would probably say I'm mad for believing all this. But it isn't a matter of faith for me. It's the ways things are. I may be mad, and to be sure I've been accused of worse things, but I'd rather be mad than the helpless unknowing string puppet of a nasty, hungry parasitic spirit that considers me the same way most folk think of cattle.

The likes of you and I are lucky if we're burdened with such minor troublemakers. Let me tell you there are Enticers and Frighteners much more powerful than the simple feeders we have with us. And they're much more demanding too.

These are the ancestral spirits. I've heard it said that they are the most ancient of all their kind and have become so powerful because they've had a long time to gather their strength. I'm not sure that's the whole story though. All I know for certain is that it's the Frighteners and Enticers attached to certain venerable family lines that are the most dangerous in existence. They have their sights set on the longer cycles of which the mortal can only imagine.

These Frighteners and Enticers require a lot of food and usually attach themselves to folk who have followers, admirers and henchmen who can also be fed off.

Every spirit-feeder dreams of one day setting their king, queen or pope upon a throne from which they'll be worshipped or feared according to the leanings of the feeding spirit. Adoration or revulsion on such a massive scale is the richest source of nourishment for an Enticer or a Frightener.

Now it's no easy matter to place a man, woman or a cardinal upon the throne. Such an enterprise may take years, indeed generations, to bear fruit. It may sometimes seem as if some upstart from the farm has walked into the kingdom to run things, as simple as that. But the truth is his Frightener or Enticer has likely been working toward this result for up to six generations, perhaps three hundred years. No one just walks in off the farm to be crowned king by popular acclaim. It just doesn't happen.

You've probably guessed by now that Órán was one of those powerful spirits who stays with a blood line for a long time. He'd been with the FitzWilliam family since the days of Lord William's father who sailed to conquer England with the Duke of Normandy's fleet.

It was at that time he took up residence in the sword Robert now cradled by his side at the fire. Our knight brushed the leather scabbard with his fingertips as he considered everything that had been told to him.

His red stubble of his hair looked as if it were aflame in the firelight. His bright eyes sparkled with intelligence and generosity. A truly good man is easy enough to spot if you know what to look for.

Robert glanced up from the flames at the stranger who had led him into the forest, lit this fire and told him the disturbing tale. It was unfathomable to him that such an ordinary-looking man could in fact be a terrible Frightener. I don't want you to think Robert didn't know something of these creatures. He'd done a bit of reading on the subject and he'd grown up in a part of Ireland where the Culdees still had an influence. He knew there was more to the world than his grand master or the Church let on about. Still, he wasn't entirely comfortable either. It's one thing to read about Frighteners but quite another matter to be sitting opposite one.

Órán's eyes were soft and boyish but there was more than a hint of the fox about them. The spirit had chosen a strange form to present himself in. He was a grey-bearded old man with short hair. His deep blue cloak was unfashionably tattered, though the colour was as vibrant as if it had just been lifted from a dyeing vat in Jerusalem. His shoes were very basic foot coverings topped with leather leggings which wrapped shin and calf up to the knee.

Robert frowned. Then Órán answered the question he knew the knight was itching to ask.

'I chose this form because I didn't want to frighten you,' he explained. 'There's nothing I can do about it. I'm a Frightener. Some folk don't take kindly to me. I don't want you getting all upset and attracting some other spirit onto my turf. I told you before. I've been cultivating you for a long time.'

Órán smiled.

'I know you respect authority. You listen to your elders. I admire that in a young man.'

'You claim to be an ancestral spirit who has been plotting, scheming and working for three generations to foster these qualities in me. Is that correct?' Robert asked.

'That's correct.'

'And why would you have put in so much effort? To what

end could you possibly have been manipulating the destiny of my grandfathers, my father and myself?'

'I have a surprise for you,' the spirit replied with a wink.

'I am sworn to the Order of the Temple,' Robert cut in. 'I will not break my vows. You cannot tempt me.'

'I know that!' Órán snapped. 'You ended up incorruptible because that's how I wanted you. I created you. I may be a Frightener but I want folks to genuinely love you. How can they truly adore you if you're not a perfect paradigm of honourable behaviour?'

He was a sly one old Órán. He was one of those Frighteners who had come to understand the power of enticement also. He knew that if he was going to get a really good feeding out of his host then it would be best if Robert's people loved him.

There is no fear so all-powerful as the fear of loss.

'Be gone, dæmon!' Robert growled. 'I'll have none of you.'

'We can do this two ways …' Órán shot back. But he calmed his tone before he went on. 'I'm offering to work with you in partnership. A partnership of equals where you can achieve anything you care to imagine.'

Robert laughed before he answered.

'In return for feeding your craving for a feast on the emotions of your victims? In return for feeding on me?'

The spirit looked away, avoiding the gaze of the young Templar.

'You're mistaken if you imagine you can avoid such a union,' he said with an odd weariness of tone. 'We are insepar-able. I am tied to you as surely and as strongly as you are tied to me. We might as well work together for our common good.'

Robert tightened his fingers around the scabbard.

'I have long suspected there was something odd about my father's sword. I noticed how much this blade changed him. Whenever he removed it from its sheath he was bathed in an unearthly, fearful light. The effect intrigued me. So I did some reading on the subject of enchanted weapons. I listened to the storytellers' tales of such things. I was seventeen when I realised my father was already too old to fulfil the aspirations any Frightener might have for him.'

The Templar smiled at Órán as the spirit turned to face him again.

'I guessed what you had planned for me. That's why I ran off to join the Templars. That's the reason I turned to the Church to save me from your clutches. It's why I've avoided the world of temptation and the flesh as much as humanly possible.'

'And what do you imagine I have planned for you?' Órán inquired.

'You intend me to rise to the high-kingship of Ireland,' the knight answered immediately with a wry, cynical smile. 'And from thence you have a path plotted which likely leads me to London. From there to Paris, I suppose.'

The spirit threw his hands together in mock applause.

'You're very clever,' Órán said with a hint of sarcasm. 'But you're not wise enough to avoid what I have planned. You will do as I say whether you like it or not.'

'What makes you think I don't wish to be King of England, Ireland and France?' Robert countered. 'I'd be a very good king.'

The spirit took up the roasting spit to hand it to his guest.

'So you'll do as I command?'

'I can't say I ever thought of myself as worthy of kingship,' Robert told him. 'But after witnessing the excesses of King Richard and the weakness of his brother John, perhaps a breath of fresh air would do some good in London. But I'm not made to be a monarch.'

'You are and you will be. It is your destiny. And I am the instrument of your destiny. You will do as I tell you and rise to be a man of power, influence and prosperity. You will be respected by many and, most importantly, feared by all.'

'That doesn't sound like a partnership of equals,' Robert pointed out. 'I refuse to become an empty puppet for your schemes. Either we work together or not at all.'

'In the end you can't refuse.'

The Templar took a bite from the roasted duck. He spent a long while chewing the flesh and staring into the fire. When at last he spoke his tone rang of finality.

'I have friends who need my help. I must return the holy books which were stolen from the Killibegs. Then I will escort some folk into the Otherworld in search of a well. I won't have any part of your plan until you've helped me achieve those aims.'

Órán spat out a great lump of wet phlegm as he stood up.

'Don't presume to dictate terms to me, young man. It might have been all right for Alexander but he was twice the warrior you are. And he honoured his agreement with me.'

'Here are my terms,' the knight stated coldly. 'You will help me fend off the attack of Aoife and her Redcaps. You will help me rout the Hospitallers who are also descending on that settlement.'

He took a bite of the food then went on.

'When that is done you will help me find my way through the Otherworld,' Robert pressed. 'If you further aid me in finding the Well of Many Blessings, I'll willingly work with you toward your aims.'

The spirit laughed. 'I'll not do anything to help you unless you make a solemn pledge to me.'

'I cannot make an oath which in any way contravenes the one I swore when I joined the Templar Order.'

Órán laughed again, this time louder and longer.

'You are no longer a Templar,' he declared. 'You've already given up that life. Do you think I cannot see your heart?'

'I am a true Knight of the Temple,' Robert protested, though he had already begun to have serious doubts about that vocation.

'Do you suppose you'd have gone to the Templars without me to lead you there? Do you imagine that anything you've done, experienced or learned in this life would have come to you without my intervention?'

Órán considered the statement for a second then hastily added, 'Except for that awful business in the Holy Land with Guy. That wasn't my doing at all. I lost track of you for a while. I think I may have been preoccupied with your brother at that time.'

'My brother went mad, declared me dead and tried to take over our father's estates in my absence. Did you have something to do with that?'

'Of course I did. I had to test you. I had to know whether you'd measure up to the challenges ahead. And you did splendidly. You rode home in triumph to champion the people of your father's estates against the tyranny of your brother's hand. It was marvellous.'

'My family suffered terrible upheavals in the course of that incident,' Robert noted coldly. 'If I had not measured up, would you have disposed of me?'

'Of course not! That terrible tragedy could have been avoided if your fool of a brother had curbed his appetite for power and his cravings for a certain Irish woman. I blame that bloody Enticer he picked up. Enticers always go too far. Who could have foretold it would all come to such an end? I for one was certainly surprised. It took me a long while to get over the whole episode.'

Órán was speaking about events which can be read in Caoimhin's rendering of the Tale of the Tilecutter's Penny. I haven't the time or the inclination to present it all to you now. It's a long story and would distract me from the thread of this account.

Robert considered the Frightener's words for a moment. He decided it didn't matter what had happened in the past. Those days were gone and nothing could bring his brother back. He had more pressing concerns. His friends needed help if they were going to survive Aoife's onslaught.

'Lead me to the Otherworld,' the Templar repeated. 'I'll consider your terms once you guide me and my two companions to a certain well. One of them wishes to be healed of an affliction at that place. I have promised to guard him and his wife on their journey there.'

Robert took a deep breath before he went on.

'But before I set out with them on that adventure I have anoher duty to perform. I must help defend the Killibegs from the Redcaps of Aoife.'

'You'll do as I tell you or you can rot for all I care. I've put a lot of effort into you. I'm not going to walk away from the feasting table just as the servants are laying out the best meat knives. If you won't work with me you'll find yourself in deep trouble.'

'Show me the way to the Well of Many Blessings which is to be found in the Otherworld.'

Órán laughed again. Then he passed a hand over the fire. In response the flames died down low.

'If you reckon you don't need me then you can find the bloody well yourself. You've already crossed into the Otherworld. Hadn't you noticed?'

Robert took in a sharp breath of shock. He would've reached out to grab the stranger but the flames of the cooking fire rose high again so he had to shield his face.

Órán laughed.

'Calm yourself. You couldn't harm me if you tried. I've been around a long time. I know how to look after myself.'

The Templar sat back from the unnatural brightness of the fire, still shielding his face from the searing heat. Gradually the flames died down again. Robert dropped his hands so he could look the Frightener in the eyes.

'You cannot fight me,' Órán advised.

'I will not follow you,' Robert declared. 'I will not help you. I will not yield to your demands. I am a man of honour. I am promised to the Order of the Temple. And I have seen what trouble your kind can cause. I don't wish to be any part of such strife.'

'Yet you have ambitions beyond the order?' Órán smiled.

'I will achieve those ambitions by honest means or not at all. Certainly I will not ally myself with a Frightener.'

'Is that your final word?'

'It is. You will go hungry.'

The spirit allowed a smirk to form upon his old-man lips.

'We'll see. I've waited three hundred years for this feed. I can wait a few more hours. You'll come to me in the end. You'll see wisdom in walking through the world with my will to watch over you. Where once you were stubborn you will be contrite. No one has ever refused me.'

'I refuse you.'

'You say that now,' the Frightener laughed with a dismissive gesture of his hand.

'I'll find the well without your help.'

Órán laughed and stood up, patting the dust from his clothes. As he did Robert made a stinging promise.

'I'll shake you off as easily as you shake the dirt from your trousers.'

The spirit's expression turned sour. 'I wish you good fortune on your quest,' he hissed. 'But all the luck in the world won't help you if I do not lend you a hand. There is no hunger like the lack of a friend.'

In the next instant the fire went out and Órán was gone. Our Robert was left sitting there in the dark Forest of Enchantment and Uncouth Things without light, warmth or a way out. He had no idea where to turn or what path led on to his goal.

Worst of all he had no hope of returning to the Killibegs or to Mirim and Alan. He'd promised to help defend the settlement and now he could not honour that oath either.

There were strange noises in the night. The breeze was icy and full of a palpable malice for all beings that were not native to this country. Robert sat for a long while wondering what he should do. And though he was a brave man he shuddered to have been left stranded entirely on his own in the Otherworld.

Now it wouldn't be absolutely true to say that Robert was alone in the Otherworld. That's just how he felt. By that time Sianan, Caoimhin, Oat-Beer and myself were also wandering about in the Realm of Faerie. So was his old adversary, Guy d'Alville. The place was positively crowded with foolish mortals clumsily stomping about.

I've told you before that time passes differently in the Otherworld. For some the days appear to fly by in a blur of colour and music. For others the moments drag on as if they've each been weighted down with a large lump of lead. Thus it was that Guy by now felt as if he had been wandering aimlessly for hours. He was also beginning to worry that if this went on much longer he would likely starve to death.

He had no weapon, no bow, no arrows and no flint for making fire. His throat was swollen with thirst. His vision was blurred. His feet ached. When he decided to sit down upon a large flat rock at the side of the road he was surprised at how glad he was of the rest.

'I'm getting old,' he told himself.

There was a time he would have been able to walk all day long without breaking into a sweat. In his youth he could've gone for days without food or drink. He'd endured such hardships that even pain wasn't a pain to him.

The Norman sighed with exhaustion. He'd been through quite an ordeal since Robert FitzWilliam spared his life at the Killibegs.

He thought about the whole situation for a moment before he pin-pointed the exact second when things had started to go wrong for him. It was when Abbess Sianan interfered in his sacking of her monastic community at Lough Gur.

'She's a devil and no mistake,' he cursed under his breath when he thought of her huge, unearthly eyes.

One thing had led to another after that as they often do in stories such as this one. Guy had ignored her warnings about the two serpent-worms dwelling at the bottom of the well at Lough Gur.

When they emerged he and his warriors were quite unprepared for the consequences. He'd lost a hundred men-at-arms to those monsters.

'Fighting men are expensive,' he grumbled as he leaned forward to rub his calves.

Suddenly the Norman realised he was having a conversation with himself. Now that really worried him. He had to admit to himself that perhaps, just perhaps, he was losing touch with his former level-headed calm.

In other words he suspected he might be losing his mind. But let me tell you, as one who knows from first-hand experience, that's what a journey in the Otherworld will do to you. It's a very confusing place, you know. Not run of the mill at all. The Faerie realm will challenge everything you know about the world.

Just then d'Alville heard a sound in the forest he hadn't noticed earlier. It was the bright splashing song of a stream. Somewhere nearby there was water.

His parched throat commanded him to stand up. Though

the rest of his body complained, it was his thirst that won the argument. In a very short while he'd pushed his way through a stubborn blackberry hedge and found the source of the sweet sound.

There before him was the bend of a small river with a sandy beach and the brightest, clearest water he could ever recall having seen in his life. He breathed a sigh of joy as he cleared his way through the bush and felt his boots sink into the sand.

He staggered toward the water's edge like a man lost in the desert who has suddenly stumbled on an oasis. When his boots touched the cool water he let his knees bend under him, fell face forward into the stream and drank his fill. When his belly could take no more he rolled over onto his back and lay there staring up at the silver fullness of the moon in the night sky.

For the first time in his entire life Guy d'Alville let go of his petty vengeances. He threw off the shackles of his contempt and anger at the world. He ignored the nagging call of his ambition. And he was content.

So content, indeed, he composed a poem.

'If I were an oak tree,' he began, 'I'd stand here beside this sandy bank all day long. I'd squeeze my roots down into the soggy soil at the very edge of the grass over there and I'd make this my home through the long winter nights and the hot summer days. And whether it snowed, or rained, whether fire or flood, I'd stand here by my river. In time this watercourse and I would know each other quite well. Maybe we'd call one another friend. As long as I have this river for my companion I could want for nothing more.'

Guy d'Alville sighed after reciting this poem. It wasn't that bad a composition either when you consider it'd probably been years since he'd bothered to compose anything at all. Apart from drunken declamatory descriptions of his war exploits.

As he sat up in the running water his warrior instincts

suddenly sounded an alert. With a wild splash he was on his feet, ready to make for cover. But it was too late.

Nearby he could hear a strange sound. It was like a washer-woman slapping out her wet linen shift upon the rocks at the water's side. For a brief moment he thought that's just what it was. Then a figure emerged from the shadows and he was slowly slapping his hands together in applause.

'That was a fine poem,' the fellow declared in an impossibly deep and commanding voice.

As he approached, Guy could see the fellow was dressed in tight clothing which hugged his muscular body. The clothes were darkest purple in this moonlight. His boots were black, as were his pouches, belts and other accoutrements, everything but his shirt, of which only the sleeves were visible beneath his tunic.

It was a deep green, of a shade Guy had never encountered before in his life. Straightaway he admired the colour. And in a return to his old self he decided he'd acquire that shirt if the opportunity presented itself.

'My name is Eterscél,' the stranger bowed. 'May I be so bold as to ask you what a mortal is doing wandering about in the night forests of Queen Aoife on Samhain Eve? This part of the country is her royal domain. On the morrow when she's proclaimed a goddess, all the Otherworld will be hers. Don't you realise there's some danger involved in such pursuits?'

Guy bowed politely, having gauged the fellow was a head taller than himself and difficult to overpower in a contest of strength.

'I'm only too painfully aware of the dangers involved,' the Norman replied. 'Indeed, I've even had a taste of Aoife's wrath.'

'Have you now? I'm surprised she allowed you your liberty then. You must be a rare one.'

'Perhaps I am rarer than you imagine. She did not grant me my freedom,' Guy smiled. 'I took it.'

It was a small lie but it was enough to impress the stranger.

'What did you say?' Eterscél laughed, only half believing him. 'No one escapes from Aoife unless she wishes it.'

'I'm willing to wager she is not even yet aware that I am gone,' d'Alville told him.

'How is that possible? Either you are a boastful man or a liar.'

'I am neither,' the Norman shot back. 'You need a lesson in respect for your betters.'

'And you would give it to me?' Eterscél scoffed. 'Be careful. You may find yourself in deeper trouble than you can imagine.'

'Give me a weapon and I'll surely teach you a lesson in good manners,' Guy told him calmly. 'I've had men beaten to death for offering me less insult. But an affront such as the one you've offered me should be dealt with personally.'

'Where have you come from?' Eterscél enquired eagerly, seeing a spark of character in Guy that he admired and a shadow of arrogance he thought he might be able to exploit. 'How is it you have not crossed my path before?'

'I'm a warrior. I've spent the greater part of my life in battle. Unless you were my enemy or my servant it is unlikely our paths would have crossed.'

'And what did Aoife want with you then?'

'She wanted me for her consort.'

Eterscél could see the Norman was telling the truth. His expression began to turn from scepticism to excitement.

'Then why did she imprison you?'

'I decided she wasn't good enough for me,' d'Alville replied tersely. 'She's not ambitious enough for my liking.'

The stranger laughed. 'Are you ambitious then?'

'I am.'

'How ambitious are you?'

'What have you got to offer me?'

Guy was a perceptive man. He knew the smell of adventure on the wind. Not to mention potential riches as well. It was obvious to him this Eterscél was no wandering peasant. He was someone who'd likely be a good ally.

Let's face it. Right at that time Guy needed all the help he could get his hands on. He knew it wouldn't be long before Aoife discovered he was missing. Then he'd be in trouble unless he had someone to stand by him. One friend on his side was better than none.

'I'm a Frightener spirit,' Eterscél explained.

He told Guy all about his need to feed on the fear of others and his willingness to work with his host toward a common goal. Well I suppose the whole thing must have struck d'Alville as incredible at first. But after encountering giant worms, talking ravens, an immortal abbess, an aspiring goddess and an army of Redcaps, Eterscél's tale probably didn't seem too far-fetched. Which, I'm sure you realise, it wasn't.

'I've been attached to a poor old knight for a long, long while now,' Eterscél told him. 'He's past it but I still haven't managed to find anyone suitable as a replacement. You may be just the man I've been looking for.'

'Don't flatter yourself,' Guy snarled. 'What are your credentials? What experience have you had?'

'I was once aligned with Charlemagne,' Eterscél declared. 'He wouldn't have achieved anything if it weren't for me.'

'And what did he achieve?' Guy shot back.

'Everyone has heard of Charlemagne!'

'But did his empire outlast him?' d'Alville countered. 'Not for long. I don't want to rush into any alliances unless I can be sure you're made of the right stuff. If I must enter into a partnership I'd prefer to do so with a spirit I can depend on. Someone with a proven history of successes.'

'I'm one of the oldest and most experienced of my race!' Eterscél replied defensively.

'If that is so, why have you remained with an old knight who's past it for so long?'

'I had big plans for him,' the spirit shrugged. 'He was going to be the first of many in his family line. I intended to pass my way down from father to son for a few generations until I'd fostered one who would be capable of fulfilling my designs.'

'So what went wrong?'

'He was sent here to Ireland. He managed to attract Aoife's attention. And like so many of his kind he came close to being turned into a tree. He wasn't like the others of his people though. The queen granted him the opportunity to work for her as a guardian. He's done a good job, too, down the years. I'm quite proud of him really.'

D'Alville scowled.

'Doesn't sound like you're a very good judge of character.'

'I hold a certain loyalty toward him,' Eterscél explained. 'I should've passed over to his son but I never got the chance. I've been trapped here too, you know.'

'So,' Guy smiled, understanding now why this spirit was so interested in him, 'I could be your only chance of escape from this place?'

'Not my only chance. Just the best chance I've encountered in a long while.'

Eterscél clasped his hands in front of him as he spoke again.

'We could be very good together.'

'Possibly,' d'Alville conceded. 'But before I make any sort of commitment to this alliance you'll have to give me some evidence of your abilities.'

'What would you like to see?'

'You're a Frightener, aren't you?' Guy shrugged.

Eterscél nodded.

'Then go ahead. Do your worst. Show me what you're made of.'

'What do you mean?'

201

Guy's eyes showed a little of their mischievous sparkle as he placed a firm hand on the Frightener's shoulder.

'Let's see if you have it in you to frighten me.'

The Sword of Myself

terscél smiled at Guy's challenge. He couldn't believe the silly mortal was serious. Did he really imagine it would be difficult for a Frightener to terrorise a mere man?

'I've been doing this for some time,' he warned the Norman. 'I'm very good at it. So I'll start off with something mild.'

'Do your worst,' d'Alville shrugged, unconcerned.

Guy's calm nonchalance rattled old Eterscél a bit, I can tell you. So he decided he'd give him a real fright after all. He knew there was one thing that absolutely terrified your average Norman. He closed his eyes to concentrate, raised his arms high in the air then began to mumble a low dirge-like incantation.

'Lord of the Eternal Darkness,' he sang. 'Fallen One of the Everlasting Abyss. Keeper of the Flames of Hell. I summon thee!'

Over the surface of the stream a great cloud of mist rolled in around Eterscél, enveloping him entirely in its eerie embrace. The rolling bank of fog gradually coalesced into a column of seemingly solid form, changing colour from a greyish white through to a deep purple then to a dark blood-red.

In the midst of this column the shape of a man emerged standing with feet apart and arms folded. Guy watched with fascination as the mist lifted to reveal the creature within.

'Behold!' Eterscél declared. 'Your worst nightmare!'

'I've never been bothered by nightmares,' Guy informed him coldly.

'You will be by this one! I've summoned forth the Prince of Darkness himself! Make ready to meet Satan!'

The naked figure stepped forward and it was immediately apparent he was exactly as the priests described him. Two large goat horns protruded from the side of his head swirling skyward in symmetrical spiralling twists. The head and face of this creature were also that of a goat but the eyes were something else entirely. They burned bright red with an intensity of hate impossible to describe. Thick hair covered most of his huge muscular body.

Satan opened his mouth to speak, revealing rows of tiny vicious teeth and a forked snake's tongue of vivid red.

'I have come for you!' the booming voice declared. 'You will return to my kitchen and sup with me on the souls of your kindred.'

Guy put a hand to his mouth. Eterscél grinned, certain he'd set the horrors on him.

The Devil took a step forward and Guy noticed the creature had the hooves of a goat and a long swishing tail with an arrowlike point on the end of it. But there were other parts of the dæmon exposed to d'Alville's sight which were much more impressive. So I've been told.

Guy could not help but notice that Satan was more than generously endowed in certain parts of the body. How shall I put it? It would've taken a team of four horses to haul his plough, if you take my meaning. The hammer had not been made that could have driven that chisel. It was evident that Saint Patrick had not successfully driven all the snakes out of Ireland.

D'Alville stared in utter disbelief at this effigy of evil, his eyes wide and his jaw slack. Then he started to laugh. Soon he was laughing so hard he was bent over double with the exertion of it all.

He sat down to laugh. He lay on his back to laugh. When at last the spasm passed he looked up to Eterscél and laughed again. The Devil had already disappeared.

'You'll have to do better than that!' he guffawed.

'What was wrong with my Satan? I'll have you know I've scared a dozen men to death with that apparition.'

'I don't believe in Satan,' Guy shrugged.

'This isn't going to be as easy as I imagined,' the spirit admitted. 'But I love a challenge.'

'Would you like to try again?' Guy offered. 'Or is that the best you can do?'

'That?' Eterscél retorted in a bit of a fluster. 'Satan was just a warm-up. I think I have something for you that will invoke more than a passing twinge.'

Suddenly Guy felt the ground pitch under him. He put out his hands to steady himself against this unexpected movement. It was then he realised the sand beneath him had been transformed into timbers. The timbers of a ship.

A great wave rolled over the top of him, drenching him and nearly washing him away with the force and weight of its fury. When the monster was gone Guy shook out his hair and tasted salt. His nose was full of seawater and it stung the back of his throat.

The world had grown dark. There was lightning cracking across the sky above him in giant spearhead bolts of splintering rage. The very ocean rumbled with the thunderous voice of the storm as the ship tipped forward to ride down an immense trough toward an incoming wave as tall and broad as a mountain.

Guy was on his feet in a breath, making his way toward the bow, steadying himself as he went. At the bowsprit he found himself a hempen rope as thick as his wrists. In a flash he'd leaped out onto the sprit and commenced lashing himself to the timbers at the furthest point forward of the tiny vessel.

The ruinous mass of seawater dwarfed the tiny ship as it hurtled faster and faster through the deep trough which led the wave. Then moments before the vessel reached the lowest point of the mountain the wave crest broke in a showering eruption of white water and salt.

Guy finished securing himself to the bowsprit just as the first foaming edges of the wave crashed down across the ship. The angry sea tore sail and rope, smashed timber and twisted the rigging from the masts like a petulant child indulging in a tantrum of destruction.

And all the while Guy d'Alville screamed his lungs out until he was hoarse from the effort. He yelled and whooped and bellowed. He writhed about within the rope enclosure he'd made for himself, only pausing for a rest when he needed to take a huge breath before being swallowed up entirely by the waters.

Eterscél smiled with satisfaction, certain he'd achieved what he'd set out to do. As another mass of water rumbled in toward the ship he took careful note of Guy's expression. The wave crests engulfed the vessel in a foaming orgy of salt and sea and d'Alville completely disappeared beneath the white water.

When the bow emerged again Guy shook the water from his hair, coughed the excess from his lungs then screamed again. It was then Eterscél noticed something quite disturbing. Guy wasn't shrieking with terror. He was bellowing with joy.

In an instant the ship, the raging ocean and the storm were gone. Guy lay once again flat on his back in the sand by the edge of the little river. He was breathing deeply in great gasps of heaving excitement.

He sat up after a few moments, shook his head and screamed again in appreciation.

'That was magnificent! Let's do it again! Just once more!'

'Perhaps another time,' Eterscél muttered. 'Did you not experience the slightest measure of fear?'

'I've been through worse storms than that,' Guy laughed. 'And in any case, I knew it was something you'd conjured for me. It wasn't real. What's there to be frightened of?'

'Don't you quiver to think upon your death?' the spirit asked incredulously. 'Aren't you frightened by the unknown? Doesn't the loneliness of the cold grave concern you?'

Guy considered those questions briefly then replied with absolute honesty.

'No.'

'There must be some experience able to make you squirm. In the whole of creation there has to be something which strikes terror into your heart even if only for the briefest instant.'

Guy shrugged and stood up, brushing the sand off his britches and tunic.

'I'll make an agreement with you,' d'Alville offered. 'On the day when you successfully frighten me we will be equals in our partnership. Until that time I will guide and direct our course. You'll get the feeding you require. I'll make sure of that. But I'll be the one making the decisions.'

'Ridiculous!' Eterscél snapped. 'I've been around a lot longer than you. You're no more than a silly playful kitten compared to me. I won't submit to a mortal.'

'That's a pity. You're not a bad Frightener. I mean, if I had been anyone else you might have scared the bowel waters out of me. But as it is I'm just not easily frightened. I don't know why it is. I've been this way as long as I can remember.'

'You can't be frightened?' the spirit repeated in disbelief. 'How is such a thing possible?'

Guy placed a hand on the spirit's shoulder.

'I don't want to brag,' he began, which wasn't strictly true as Guy loved to boast. 'I don't want you to think I'm being big-headed either. But the fact is you couldn't find a better partner for your purposes than a man who can't be touched by fear. You're not bad at what you do. I'll grant you that. You have an impressive skill and I'm sure, given the right circumstances, your craftsmanship could really make an impression on some folk.'

Eterscél frowned, unsure whether Guy was talking down to him or simply trying to be friendly and complimentary.

'Listen to me,' the Norman went on. 'I believe you and I could form a mutually beneficial alliance that would reap untold rewards for us both. But until you can satisfy me that you have what it takes to really live up to your part of the bargain, I insist on remaining the dominant partner in this relationship.'

The spirit was a little taken aback. No mortal had ever spoken to him like this before. He was still taking this all in.

'That's not to say,' added d'Alville, 'that sometime in the future you won't prove to be worthy of an equal status within the alliance. But bear with me. I have but one life in which to achieve my ambitions and make my mark. You, on the other hand, have the leisure of limitless seasons in which to try different approaches or waste time clinging to a decrepit old knight who has been set to guard some silly bridge. Is that what you want to do until the next opportunity comes along?'

There's no doubting it. Guy was a masterful manipulator. He knew everyone had a weakness. Once he understood their vulnerability, anyone could become his tool. Even a Frightener spirit such as Eterscél.

But you see, this Frightener was a rather accomplished manipulator himself. He'd been around. I mean to say, any spirit that could have attached himself to the back of a king such as Charlemagne must have had a measure of nous about him. Eterscél bit his tongue and decided he would allow this arrogant Norman to believe he was in control of the relationship.

Frighteners and Enticers alike love the Normans. You ask any feeding spirit and they'll agree. Indeed among their kind they have a saying which just about sums up the situation.

'Arrogance makes for an easy meal.'

'So I've presented my position,' Guy went on. 'That's how I see things. Now I'd like to know what you have to offer this alliance.'

Eterscél smiled, relishing the opportunity to talk about himself. You understand that he wasn't an arrogant spirit himself. It was just that so few folk were ever willing to listen to his experiences. Mortals were always far more interested in the results of his work.

'I have been dwelling within a sword these three hundred years past,' the spirit told him. 'It's a blade of rare strength forged of a fine metal, almost unbreakable. I offer you that sword and my services if you promise to feed me the fear of others. I'm an old spirit. I've learned a trick or two.'

'What sort of tricks?'

'I shared the Emperor Charlemagne with an Enticer spirit,' Eterscél admitted. 'How we used to feast in those days! That spirit taught me all about enticement. I've never had a chance to put what I learned from her to the test, but I'm sure I could raise a rapture of adoration round you if I put my mind to it.'

'That's a very interesting proposal,' Guy hummed. 'Could you really convince folk to love me?'

'It's a simple enough matter.'

'I haven't found it to be so in my experience,' the Norman confided.

'But you're not a spirit,' the Frightener winked. 'You're just a mortal.'

'But I'm unlike any mortal you'll ever meet.'

Then Guy took Eterscél by the hand to seal the contract between them.

'Here are my terms. First. I will be the dominant partner in this alliance and plot our course into the future until such time as you are able to frighten me.'

'Agreed,' Eterscél answered without hesitation.

'In all other respects we will be equals,' Guy added.

'Agreed.'

But the Frightener wasn't really intending to let that happen. He allowed the Norman to continue.

'I promise to see you are well fed with fear as long as you continue to work with me for the advancement of my designs.'

'Agreed.'

Then Eterscél asked the obvious question.

'What *are* your designs?'

'I intend to be High-King of Ireland to begin with,' the knight told him. 'After we've achieved that we'll review the situation, discuss what we've learned and set more ambitious goals.'

'You're a remarkable man, for a mortal,' the spirit enthused. He understood exactly how to use flattery. 'I feel like a whole new chapter of my life has just begun. It's as if I've washed off the taint of the last hundred years.'

Then another thought crossed Eterscél's mind.

'I don't know your name,' he laughed. 'We've been here chatting away for ages. I've even agreed a contract with you and you haven't told me who you are.'

'I am known east and west as Guy d'Alville,' the Norman replied.

And as the name sounded to the Frightener's ears, Eterscél placed a hand on his comrade's shoulder to speak.

'Truly this alliance will serve us both well. For there is an omen in your name which confirms for me that we will sweep across this Earth like a cloud of terror.'

'What omen?'

'No words of mine would explain that to you. The omen must be shown to you.'

Guy looked into the Frightener's eyes and thought he perceived the slightest glint of delight mixed with a greater portion of mischievous glee.

'Then show me,' the Norman demanded.

'Let us go to retrieve the Sword of Myself,' Eterscél told him. 'All will be revealed to you then.'

He placed an arm over Guy's shoulder to lead him away, adding, 'Have you ever thought of changing your name? I mean to say, d'Alville doesn't exactly strike terror into the heart. I don't wish to cause offence, you understand, but we need a good strong name for you. A name that will have everyone in awe of you.'

Suddenly he stopped walking and held up a finger.

'I have it! I have the perfect name for you! Guy Stronghold. Or simply Stronghold.'

The Norman spoke the new name a few times under his breath. Then he nodded slowly. 'You're right. It sounds better than d'Alville.'

'Guy Stronghold,' the Norman repeated with more enthusiasm. 'Stronghold.'

I suppose Guy must have been speaking with Eterscél at the same time I was hurrying off down the stairs at the top of the left-hand path. I still had high hopes of finding Sianan and Caoimhin, and sure enough I hadn't gone far when I encountered a traveller's resting seat carved of stone. Upon that seat lay an oatcake that had certainly been baked in the ovens of the Killibegs. There was a cross cut into the dough before it had been baked and I recognised the style of it. Without a doubt it had been made by Derbáil the wife of Clemens.

I picked up the cake and held it close to my cheek. It was warm. Sianan and Caoimhin could not be too far ahead of me. A sudden hunger struck me. So I stuffed the dry cake into my mouth. It was delicious. As soon as I had finished chewing I was off as fast as my legs could carry me down along the cobbles of the descending spiral path.

I must have gone a thousand paces before I had to stop to rest and catch my breath. I was sweating and panting hard. The uneven cobbles were difficult to negotiate without falling over. My feet were sore.

I leaned against a birch tree by the side of the path and there among the roots lay another Killibegs oatcake. I thought to myself that was a strange thing. How would another oatcake come to be lying here?

I picked it up to examine it. It was still warm as if it had been baked only a short while ago. Once again a sudden hunger overwhelmed me. I smelled the sweetness of the cake. It would've been a waste not to eat it fresh and steaming.

So I shoved it into my mouth and chewed. It was a good while before I was ready to head off again. But I decided a rest wouldn't hurt me. It was obvious that Sianan and Caoimhin had stopped twice so far. They couldn't be too far ahead.

When I started off again, my pace was a little more sedate. I don't know why but I felt as if it really wouldn't hurt to take my time and enjoy this whole experience. After all, it isn't every day you have the opportunity to wander about in the Land of Dreams, is it? I was beginning to relax.

The trees in this part of the forest were evenly spaced, as if they'd been planted by some thoughtful hand. The space between them had been cleared of leaves so although it was autumn in the world beyond there was no sign of the season to be seen here.

Lush grass spread across the forest floor to either side of the road and a bubbling stream could be heard making its way through the woods, though I must have walked another thousand steps before I caught a glimpse of it.

It meandered its way through the trees to my left, gradually coming closer to the cobbles. I wondered how long it would be before I reached a crossing. And just as I had that thought a bridge came into view ahead of me. It was an elegant wooden construction curved in a great arch to span the river. Its posts were carved with fantastic creatures that could have leaped from the pages of an illuminated manuscript like the Gospels of Kells.

Bright moonlight drenched the crossing in a bluish bath of soft luminescence. No dream could have been more beautiful, no scene from the ancient tales so enthralling. I had to stop in my tracks to take it all in. I must have been a good hundred paces from the bridge.

Now you can imagine my surprise when I stepped out to walk on and my toes kicked an oatcake lying on the ground at my feet. At first I thought I must've dropped one from my satchel. But as I picked it up I realised it was still warm.

I knew Sianan had gone to the ovens to pick up her load of cakes before she left with Caoimhin. But I was a little surprised the oatcake had managed to stay warm this long. I was so hungry I'd taken a bite from it before I even stopped to consider the strange coincidence. I was chewing away at it merrily, reassured that Sianan and Caoimhin couldn't be too far off, blissfully ignorant of the danger I'd placed myself in.

When I did think about how odd it was that these cakes just kept appearing before me, I shrugged it off and put the whole experience down to chance. With the cake finished, I thought to myself that a mouthful of broth wouldn't hurt to wash it down. So I uncorked the skin and drank my fill of the brew, never considering for a moment that it might cause any harm to me.

What was I thinking? I can't explain my foolishness. I can't even imagine what must have taken hold of me in those moments. Rash. Stupid. Thoughtless. Eedyit.

In a few seconds I'd gulped down the broth loaded with love potion and I was headed off toward the bridge with a spring in my step and a whistle on my lips. I was actually beginning to enjoy this little adventure.

I could see there was a fine flat patch of grass on the opposite bank of the river which looked like a good place to rest for a while. I was suddenly remarkably sleepy.

The bridge must have measured thirty steps across from bank to bank. On this side of the river there was a quaint stone roundhouse with a neatly thatched roof. The aged brown wooden door was shut.

I considered the possibility this house had been placed here for the benefit of travellers. Then it struck me that Sianan and Caoimhin might be inside taking a rest. So I went up to the door and knocked loudly.

'Go away!' an old man shouted back. 'It's my day of rest. I don't challenge anyone again until full moon.'

I looked to the sky. It was my opinion the moon was full. And I told him so.

There was a loud rattling of chains and bolts being drawn back. Then a balding grey-haired old man who stood about my height poked his head out into the moonlight. He appeared to be dressed in a long grey linen nightgown and little else.

He looked past me toward the sky. He squinted at the moon. He frowned.

'Blast! I've slept in again! How did that happen?'

The door slammed again. Before I could draw a breath the door swung open wide. The same little old man stood there in a full coat of mail, sporting a huge antique Norman kite shield strapped to his left arm. His tunic was wine red, cut to knee-length in an archaic style. He wasn't what I would have called fashionably dressed.

The old knight's helm was rusty and of a design not generally seen upon the heads of the nobility these days. But it was his sword which really attracted my attention. He held it upturned in his left hand in the manner of a Gaelic warrior. It was still wrapped in its beautiful black leather scabbard. And it was the longest, narrowest sword I've ever seen, before or since.

'What do you want?' the aged knight shouted.

'I'm following after two friends of mine,' I explained.

'What?' he screamed. 'Speak up. It won't do to whisper, you know.'

I coughed to clear my throat, realising the old man must be a little hard of hearing. Then I raised my voice to be sure he could hear.

'I'm looking for two friends of mine who must have passed this way.'

'There's no need to yell!' he bellowed. 'I'm not deaf!'

Then the old man frowned. 'No one would dare to cross over without leave from the Keeper of the Bridge,' he stated. 'Would they?'

'I don't know what you mean.'

'I'm the Keeper of the Bridge.' He thumped his chest with his right hand to emphasise his identity. 'Anyone who passes by must ask and gain my leave to do so.'

'My name's Binney,' I offered.

'I don't care who you are. If you're after crossing my bridge you're obliged to request my consent. And the way things are going with you so far, I'm not sure I'll be in a mood to consider such a supplication when you finally get around to expressing it in a suitably polite manner.'

I opened my mouth to ask him his name but he declaimed over the top of me.

'Lady Aoife, Queen of the Night, has charged me to keep this bridge against all who would use it without leave. Only her Redcaps are allowed to pass and even they must ask me nicely.'

He squinted again to observe my features closely.

'You're no Redcap,' he stated confidently.

'No. I'm not,' I admitted as there was no sense pretending otherwise. 'I'm a mortal.'

The old man's eyes lit up. He grabbed my arm and looked this way and that.

'Quickly!' he stammered with urgency. 'Get inside my guardhouse before anyone sees you.'

He'd dragged me to the door and slammed it behind me before I could object. For an old bugger he was remarkably strong.

'What's the matter?' I asked.

'Be quiet! You're in great danger!' he hissed. 'I have to find a place to hide you.'

'Why? What's the matter?'

He leaned hard against the door with his back as he put down his sword and shrugged the shield off his arm.

'How did you come to be in this country?' he demanded to know.

'I followed two friends of mine who have come here in search of a holy well.'

I almost let slip about Sianan's plan to thwart Aoife's plans but I bit my tongue just in time.

'You fool!' he shouted. 'Didn't anyone ever warn you about the dangers of wandering in the Otherworld? Are you mad? Do you want to end up staring at the pointy end of Aoife's vengeance stick?'

But he really wasn't after an answer to any of those questions. He already had a hand to his mouth and was muttering quietly to himself, debating a solution to this dilemma.

'I can't send her out there again,' he muttered. 'It's simply too dangerous. The Redcaps will find her and then they'll take her off to Aoife. No. No. That's too awful to contemplate.'

The poor fellow seemed to me to have a touch of the moon

about him, as we used to say. I could tell he wasn't quite right in the head. I'd seen it before. There is one class of people who suffer from this malady more commonly than any others.

Hermits.

And I'd already known a few hermits at that stage of my life. I've known many more since. They're a strange breed. I've always found them difficult to fathom. With all the loneliness already in the world, why would anyone go out of their way to avoid their fellow mortals? What possesses a man or woman to leave their loving hearthside to go off in search of solitude? I know many of them have never known the joy of a loving hearth. That's true of two-thirds of hermits. I'll grant you that.

But of the one-third who have always been happy in the company of others it must be a terrible ordeal. They're the ones who go mad with the solitude, you know. It's the hermits who've never been alone before who experience the most loneliness and suffer the greatest pain as a result of it.

The old knight stood away from the door.

'I'm forgetting my good manners,' he told me very formally, his voice still unnecessarily raised. 'I invite you to take a seat by the fire.'

I quickly surveyed the interior of the little hut. It was a typical Gaelic home with a central fireplace and wooden benches set out around it. A space had been left for the knight's sleeping furs which he hastily gathered up into a pile.

'Please excuse the mess. I haven't had a visitor for a very long while,' he stammered in embarrassment.

A black iron pot of stew was bubbling away in the coals. All around the ceiling were hung various pieces of mail armour, bows, quivers full of arrows, tunics, helms, shields and saddles. There were swords, lances and fine engraved knives. A dozen elegant war-sickles set on long poles were leaning together in a stack. I'd never seen weapons like those before. The shadowy rafters held other articles as well. A great white horn with silver mouthpiece and intricately jewelled mounts was strung up by a leather strap from the wall. And I counted at least a dozen brightly coloured banners arrayed in a fine display around the door.

'You haven't told me your name,' I reminded my host.

'Yes I have,' he asserted.

'You told me you were known as the Knight of the Bridge.'

'That's right. That's my name.'

'But you must have another name,' I ventured. 'A family name or a first name. Something a little less formal.'

The old man sat down on the bench beside me and pointed to his shield which leaned against the wall by the door.

'Do you recognise the livery painted on that armour?'

I looked carefully. The shield was painted dark green. Emblazoned across it from top to bottom was a stylised white horse rearing up on its hind legs. Three flames of white were pouring out of its mouth and its one visible eye was red. I was no expert in heraldry. That was a purely Norman preoccupation.

'I'm sorry. I don't know very much about Norman families.'

'Norman families!' he shouted with excitement. 'Yes. Of course. My family is Norman! It's all coming back to me now. King William Rufus sent me here to Ireland.'

In that instant he reminded me of old Lord William FitzWilliam, the Norman who had spent three winters near the Killibegs living as a hermit.

'William Rufus has been dead for a hundred years,' I stated in disbelief.

'Dead? Then who sits on the throne of England?'

'King John,' I told him. 'He's the brother of Richard Lionheart and they're both the sons of King Henry, the second of that name. Of course they're all from the Plantagenet line that has ruled England since the wars fifty years ago. The line of William Rufus took a turn for the worse after he was ritually slain in the New Forest as part of some pagan sacrifice. At least that's what I heard. Then Henry the first of that name reigned for a long while. But after that there was a civil anarchy as the terrible reign of King Stephen began.'

My two greatest interests suddenly had an opportunity for expression. I'd always had a love for history and a predilection for any gossip that might have subsequently arisen from those historical events. I was fortunate to have been born during a time when the two often overlapped with a startling and most satisfying frequency.

It was a well-known fact in those days that William Rufus had indeed been slain in a pagan Norman ritual to ensure the continuation of their dominion over England. The Normans were the descendants of Viking raiders from the north who'd settled in northern Gaul three hundred years before the telling of my tale.

They were the same feared and brutal Norsemen who'd come to Ireland at that time. But in our country they'd been driven out by the famous High-King Brian Borumh. However, they had gained a much stronger foothold in France. So much so that the region was renamed Normandy.

King William the Bastard, Duke of Normandy, the man who conquered England, was no Christian. Though it goes without saying he never openly declared the fact. Let me remind you that his father's name was Robert the Devil. That's not an easily earned epithet.

So it shouldn't be surprising to you that Duke William practised the pagan ways of his Norse ancestors while retaining a thin cloak of Christianity. As often as he was ever seen at mass he was known to have attended the heathen rites. And those heathen rites often involved blood sacrifice.

Now I know you've heard me speak ill of the Normans before. I don't want you to arrive at the conclusion that I have any prejudice against their folk. But it has to be plain even to the unbiased observer that they're among the most degenerate, brutal, treacherous folk who walk upon the soil of God's Blessed Earth. They're a blight. A pox. A fungus growing on the white wheat bread of civilisation.

I've heard that the gods of their people required a sacrifice every seven years. And that sacrifice had to be in the person of none other than the king himself, or a willing substitute.

King William of the Conquest reigned for twenty-one years. That is to say he sat upon the throne of England for three periods of seven years before his sudden and mysterious death. He'd found two substitutes to take his place as the sacrificial Divine King during his reign. Though the names of both men are lost to us, their families were doubtless compensated for the loss with titles and lands. His third season came around as he was attacking a rebel town in Normandy. That's when he was struck down. He lived long enough to pass the kingdom on to William Rufus, his son. William Rufus ruled for two seven year periods before his most mysterious death.

Rufus is remembered for many evil deeds. His reign was marred by terrible bloodshed. When it came around to his time to be sacrificed he died in a most unusual manner.

On the night before the pagan summer festival of his people which some call Lammas, Rufus had retired to his estates in the New Forest, a hunting retreat created for him through the confiscation of many villages, churches and private holdings. He stayed up all night talking with his chamberlains, so the story goes. At dawn he went about settling his affairs, paying all debts, insuring the succession of his son Henry was secure and even granting a handful of titles to deserving and loyal servants.

He ate a hearty meal and drank much more than usual. When he called for the hunt late in the day his chamberlains had already laid out his clothes. He was dressing himself when a blacksmith presented six new quarrels for the king's crossbow. Rufus had commanded they be made especially. They were tipped with unusually sharp arrowheads.

The king handed two of them to the Master of the Hunt, Sir Walter Tyrell, and is reported to have said, 'It is best that the sharpest arrows be given to one who knows how to deal deadly strokes.'

Then a letter came to the king from a Benedictine abbot which stated that one of his monks had suffered a terrible dream. In his dream the monk had witnessed the death of Rufus while out hunting. The king is reported to have laughed loudly and joked that too much ale brings on the strangest visions. Then he awarded a costly gift to the monk.

Later that evening the news came that King William Rufus was dead. He'd been killed in a hunting accident, shot through the head by a quarrel launched from the crossbow of the Master of the Hunt, Sir Walter Tyrell.

His body was taken on a circuit round the kingdom to be shown to the peasantry. The Earl of Cornwall reported the news to the royal heir by telling a story that he had been wandering in the New Forest and had come upon a huge goat with the king's body slumped over its back.

The earl claimed he asked the goat what he was doing. And the goat replied, 'I am taking him down to the Devil for judgement.'

It makes my skin crawl just to speak of it. That a king should willingly submit to death at the hands of his master of the hunt all for a pagan sacrifice is too horrible to contemplate. They're all barbarians the bloody Normans.

Henry the First of that name, the son of Rufus, ruled for thirty-five years. That is to say five periods of seven. And if you think the heathen brutality of the Norman sacrifice ended with him you'd have to be forgetting the murder of Thomas Becket, Archbishop of Canterbury, who was slain in substitution for King Henry the Second.

The Normans were and always will be a bloodthirsty people. No matter how much we Irish may teach them the ways of civilised folk. They're greedy for power, for land and for slaves to fill their coffers. Just look what they've done to the forests in the short while they've lived in Ireland.

It's right that so many folk still call them the Norman Devils. So I'm sure you can imagine I didn't feel entirely comfortable in the presence of this old knight surrounded by his many trophies of war. I was certain he was at least a little mad. I had no idea what he was capable of.

Which brings me back to my tale.

The old knight shook his head, ignoring what I'd told him about King John and his ancestors.

'King William Rufus will be most displeased with me,' he sighed. 'I should've been back at the White Tower in London months ago. I'd be there now if I hadn't landed myself in this spot of trouble.'

'What trouble is that?' I asked, intrigued.

The old knight looked a little perplexed.

'I don't rightly recall,' he admitted vaguely. 'All I know is I must guard this bridge until some valiant warrior comes along who can defeat me in knightly combat. I'm under an enchantment, you know.'

He winked at me as he suddenly recalled his predicament. 'That's it! I'm under an enchantment.'

'Who placed you under this enchantment?'

He put out a thumb and jerked it over his shoulder behind him.

'She did! Queen Aoife.'

He sighed deeply.

'I didn't imagine so much time would go by before a worthy knight presented himself to me.'

He gestured toward the trophies hanging from the ceiling.

'But as you can see, every knight who has confronted me in

222

combat so far has fallen to my sword. It's unusual. I thought I was well past my prime. But young men who've lived less than a third the tally of my winters buckle under my blows like grass before the scythe.'

Once again he sighed with the weight of the seasons.

'I've often considered yielding to my opponents, though that would be the unchivalrous thing to do. Such is my desire to be free of this curse. I'm not fond of this bridge-house. The trouble is, whenever I've made up my mind to relinquish the field, I always get caught up in the fight and before I know it I've forgotten I'd intended to concede.'

He laughed a little at himself and placed a finger to his temple.

'I must have lost my mind,' he admitted. 'There's so much I can't recall. If I were freed tomorrow I wouldn't know the road home. Perhaps it's best I stay here. Who'd want an old fool like me hanging about the castle getting under everyone's feet?'

I was softening to him now. He didn't seem as dangerous as some of his kind. Before I had the opportunity to offer the old man any reassurance he sat up straight, his ear cocked toward the door.

'Someone's coming!' he shouted. 'The enemy approaches. I must do my duty!'

He was up on his feet after a brief struggle with his unwilling knees. Then he had his shield shouldered and his sword couched in his arm again ready to offer the challenge. He was just taking a deep breath when I reached his side.

'If it is a challenger you must try to let him win,' I reminded the old boy. 'Otherwise you'll never escape this enchantment.'

He stopped for a second with his hand on the iron door-catch ready to pull it open.

'I must remember,' he repeated.

Then he swung the great wooden door open and stepped out to defend the bridge. I stayed behind the door, peeking through the half-open crack, unwilling to be seen after all his dire warnings about being found by Aoife or her Redcaps.

Outside by the bridge a tall man stood in the blue moonlight. His short cropped hair shone as if it was woven out of tiny strands of silver. His pointed beard marked him as being of Norman nobility, even though the style of his tunic was rather dated and a little too long about the knee.

All his outer clothes were darkest purple. His gloves and boots were black. But his shirt was a vibrant forest green.

His eyes were much like Sianan's. They were large and the colour was an unearthly blue. His skin seemed grey in this light. Clearly this fellow was no mortal. But it was not until I heard his deep resonant voice that I was certain he was a spirit being. His first words were cheerful.

'Greetings, old man! I've come to have a little chat with you.'

'Be gone!' the knight growled. 'I have no time to speak with you. You left me here. You promised you'd return. But you never did.'

'In truth I never left you,' the spirit laughed. 'But the time is fast approaching when indeed I must leave you to your fate.'

'Is the enchantment ended then?'

'It will be soon enough.'

'Your name is Eterscél,' the old knight recalled.

'Very good!' the Frightener declared. 'That's right. I'm Eterscél the Eternal One.'

The spirit approached the old warrior and laid a friendly hand on his shoulder. 'This burden will soon be lifted from you.'

'Has Aoife forgiven me then?'

'No. It's simply time to pass your sword into the hands of another.'

The old knight swallowed hard. 'What if I don't want to surrender my sword?'

Eterscél smiled indulgently.

'My dear fellow. Your time is up. Your usefulness is at an end. Now you must embark upon the journey to your home.'

'I don't have a home!' the old knight spat. 'King William Rufus is dead these hundred years past. The world is changed. You've kept me a prisoner beyond the natural span of my years.'

The stranger tightened his grip on the old man's shoulder so that the knight flinched with pain.

'Who told you that?' Eterscél hissed. 'Who have you been talking to?'

'A traveller,' the knight lied. 'Just a warrior. He told me these things as he was dying.'

Eterscél narrowed his eyes, sniffed the air then pushed the old knight roughly away.

'You can't deceive me!'

In that moment the air all around the bridge-house was chilled. Instead of a bright moonlit sparkle the whole area was shadowed in a foreboding purple. Eterscél glowed with an inner luminescence.

The Frightener stepped closer to the knight. He slowly removed a glove of finely stitched kidskin. He calmly tucked it into his black waist belt.

Then in a flash so fast I didn't catch even a glimpse of the move, he had his bare pale hand clasped tight about the old knight's throat. And he was squeezing hard.

'You have come to the end of your days in my company,' Eterscél declared. 'I've found a new man to take me on. He's a tough fellow too, a better warrior than you'll ever be. At last I'll be out in the world again, not trapped here in this backwater waiting for stray challengers to offer their blades in combat.'

He tightened his grip and the old knight gasped for air.

'How long have I waited for this day?' Eterscél whispered, teasing his victim. 'No more feeding off the fear of wanderers and wayfarers. No more hiding behind a forgetful old has-been!'

Suddenly he released his grip and threw the knight backwards into the grass. The old man landed awkwardly. his hand clutched to his throat, coughing violently. I've never been able to stomach violence. Throughout my life whenever I've been confronted by the slightest brutality my bowels have always turned to water.

So when I started to feel sick just at that moment I put it down to a reaction to the ill treatment I was witnessing. I leaned against the door, my head spinning as I struggled not to throw up the contents of my stomach. Next thing I knew I'd slumped down to my knees. The interior of the roundhouse seemed to distort wildly. My head was spinning to be sure but it felt as if it was the walls that were turning not me.

The old knight's trophies were transformed before my unbelieving eyes into countless deformed shapes or pale reflections of the hideous long-dead faces of their former owners. It crossed my mind that perhaps it had been very unwise to eat those oatcakes I'd found upon the path. The first rule for travellers in the Otherworld is not to eat of the food of the Dream Country. The Faerie realm is a dangerous place. Many are lulled by the wonders and the beauty they find there.

'Eedyit,' I called myself.

Then just as suddenly as the gut pain and the spinning had begun, the spasm lifted from me. I breathed easier. The interior of the roundhouse regained some semblance of an ordinary guard's chamber inhabited by an old knight.

I dragged myself to my feet, my knees still a little wobbly. Then I leaned against the door to look out through the crack again.

I'll never forget what I saw in that moment for it changed the course of my life. And if you'd told me a few days beforehand that things were going to turn out the way they did, I'd have likely laughed in your face. And called you a bloody liar as well.

But that's the way with these things. That's how the

seductive treachery of the magical arts comes back to knock you off your feet when you least expect it. I warned you about it. Don't dabble with enchantments, I said. Well if only someone had been there to warn me.

The next thing I saw, the thing which utterly transformed my life, was the figure of Guy d'Alville. Yes, you heard me. That bloody Norman bastard was striding purposefully down the road toward the old knight. And there was murder in his keen, unflinching eye.

I don't think I'd ever seen such grim determined rage in a man, nor in a beast neither for that matter. And do you know something? If it hadn't been for my own foolishness I'd have stayed put there in the roundhouse and not come out until d'Alville had passed by.

I'm ashamed to say that it was at that very instant that the love potion took effect on me. Just enough time had passed for the broth to begin to digest within my stomach. Perhaps my unexpected nausea had been caused in part by it. I'll never know for certain.

All I can tell you with any surety is that I looked at Guy d'Alville and fell head over heels passionately and completely in love with him. I wasn't merely besotted with the bastard. I was speechless with awe, infatuation and giddy worship for him. The love philtre had worked its enchantment on me.

As he marched down the road I found I could not restrain myself. I ran out from behind the door to the roundhouse, my heart beating like the wings of a dragonfly. All thoughts of Caoimhin were instantly banished from my mind. There was now only one focus of my life. And that was Guy d'Alville.

I'm going to wait till you've stopped sniggering before I go on if you don't mind. I must say, this self-satisfied smugness doesn't suit you at all.

As I was saying, I emerged from the roundhouse as the old knight managed to rise to his feet to face the challenge from this new adversary. He struggled to draw his sword from its black scabbard but the blade was stuck fast and wouldn't budge.

Guy stepped straight up to him, punched him hard in the face and knocked him off his feet. As the old boy fell d'Alville snatched his sword from him, then easily drew it from the sheath with a flourish.

'I'll relieve you of that burden if you please,' Guy commented.

He swung the weapon round his head. The blade whistled as it flew. Eterscél whooped for joy and leaped high in the air.

'At last! At last, I've found a way out of this terrible place. At last I'll feast again as I did in the old days.'

The Frightener stepped close to Guy to whisper in his ear.

'You must end it now. You must bring the life of this miserable wretch to a close. Take off his head, my dear friend Stronghold.'

Guy grinned broadly. He'd never held a blade so perfectly balanced, so deadly, so beautifully crafted. He lifted the weapon ready to strike a downward blow as the old knight bared his neck in submission.

'Make it clean,' the old man begged. 'Make it quick.'

D'Alville grunted with delight as he prepared to bring the weapon down with all his force. But just as he moved to swing I dived at him and threw my arms about his chest. His blow was deflected and the sword swept wide of its mark to ring on the stones of the path.

I wasn't making some futile attempt to put off the old knight's execution. I wasn't interested in justice or a fair deal for him either. All my attention was on Guy, the object of my desire and the fulfilment of my heart's dearest dream.

I had my arms wrapped round him and my blushing cheek pressed to his manly chest as quick as any blushing cheek was ever pressed to any manly chest. He almost dropped the wondrous sword in shock. I think that was the last thing he expected to happen.

Of course he didn't let go of the blade. That would have been a very un-Norman thing to do. Somehow Guy managed to push me away from him until he held me at sword point. He must have been astounded. His jaw was wide open. I swear to you that if a monk had floated by it couldn't have shocked him more.

'Who the bloody hell are you?' he bellowed.

'I'm Binney,' I gasped full of girlish excitement, and a twinge of disappointment that he didn't recognise me. 'Don't you remember me? I sat across from you in the great hall at the Killibegs. I passed the ale around in wooden cups.'

His eyes narrowed down to slits.

'You're a servant?' he laughed.

'No. I'm a noblewoman of the Killibegs,' I replied, indignant and proud.

'You're little more than a girl,' he scoffed. 'What makes you think I'd have noticed you?'

Well, my eyes were full of tears by the time he'd finished that sentence. And the next thing I knew the Knight of the Bridge was at my side with his arm around my shoulders, patting my hair.

'There, there,' he soothed. 'Don't cry, my dear. This brute isn't good enough for the likes of you. You're a gentlewoman of a noble house. This thug isn't fit to clean out your stables.'

'Watch your tongue, old fool!' d'Alville spat. 'Or I'll cut it out.'

'Will that be before or after you've cut off my head?' the aged knight laughed. 'Don't waste your breath with idle threats. I'm not afraid of you. You haven't a chivalrous bone in your body, you wretch. You dress for war but you're no warrior. A knight who holds no respect for womankind isn't worth the mud that's caked on his boots.'

'Shut up!'

The knight stepped in front of me. His cheek was bleeding where d'Alville had punched him. But he wasn't about to submit now. He stood before Guy, his eyes fixed firm, his determination shining clear.

'I've faced better men than you!' the chivalrous old fellow shouted. 'I'll not bow down to have my head taken off by an ignorant brute who has no respect for others. If you want to blood my neck you'll do it with me standing face to face and eye to eye with you. I'm not afraid of your kind.'

'Prepare to meet your end,' d'Alville laughed. 'Have you anything else to say before I cut you down?'

'What's your name?' the old knight spat. 'I want to carry your fame to the gates of Hell so they'll be ready to receive your soul when the day comes.'

'I am Guy d'Alville. I was a master of the Hospital. I am of lordly rank though I hold no title. And one day soon I'll be High-King of Ireland.'

The old man's face turned pale as cream skimmed fresh from the milk as he heard that name. He swallowed hard and frowned; a memory returned to him like a ghostly apparition of the past.

'You're not Guy d'Alville!' the knight cut back with a nervous laugh.

'What are you talking about, you old fool? Don't you think I know who I am?'

'That's my name,' the old man managed to stutter after a few moments. 'I'm Guy d'Alville.'

Love and War

s I think back on the situation it must have been quite a sight and I'll wager there hadn't been that much excitement at the bridge for a good while. I stood at the point of Guy's blade. Eterscél watched from a dozen paces distant. The old knight was quivering in his boots as his memory returned to him.

'What are you talking about?' the younger Guy spat. 'How can you have the same name as myself? I come from a noble family. My great-grandfather was a loyal servant to the king. My kin are renowned in verse and story as a breed above the rest.'

'I see the resemblance in your features,' the old knight marvelled. 'You are of my blood.'

D'Alville stepped back a pace, lowering the point of his sword. I took a pace closer and he immediately raised the blade again to warn me back.

The younger Guy scrutinised the old man's face.

'It's strange,' Guy admitted. 'In some ways you remind me of my grandfather.'

'What was his name?' the knight pressed.

'William Rufus d'Alville,' Guy replied.

'I named him after the king,' the old man sighed. 'So His Majesty must have honoured the agreement. Did my son live an honourable life?'

231

Guy turned deathly pale as Eterscél stepped forward to intervene.

'It's just a coincidence,' the spirit told his new host. 'Don't believe anything this old bugger says. He's addled in the head. You must kill him.'

'That it should come to this!' the old Guy d'Alville cried, and there were tears rolling down his cheeks. 'That my own great-grandson should turn out to be such an unchivalrous blaggard. That the progeny of my loins should bear such bitter fruit.'

'He's not your great-grandson,' Eterscél cut in crossly. 'There must be countless d'Alvilles running around in the world. It's a very common name.'

The old man turned his attention to the spirit.

'You found my great-grandson,' he whispered in shock. 'But you've turned him into a bastard.'

'That was none of my doing,' Eterscél protested. 'He was a bastard before I met him. Ask anyone he's ever robbed, murdered or dealt indecently with.'

That was enough for the older Guy.

'So you admit it! He is my great-grandson.'

Eterscél threw up his hands, realising he'd been tricked. He could see there was no sense in denying the truth.

'Yes! For all the difference it makes to this situation. He is your kith and kin. And he seems to have inherited many of your characteristics. That's why I've decided to adopt him and discard you.'

'We may share a name,' the old knight noted, 'but that is the full extent of the resemblance.'

He turned again to Guy, raising a finger of scorn.

'Who do you think you are? What right do you claim to the destruction of my family name? How dare you desecrate the memory and reputation of your ancestors? You're an impudent, arrogant, uncultured brute who lacks any semblance of conscience. You look on your opponents with contempt. You treat women worse than you'd treat a horse. You swagger about as if being born by accident into the nobility gives you licence to behave with reckless, careless cruelty.'

Guy d'Alville opened his mouth to protest, but the old Guy didn't pause for breath.

'I worked damn hard to establish our family reputation for chivalry and fair play! I was known throughout the kingdom as an honest, trustworthy and respectful individual. The king relied on me. He sent me as emissary to Scotland and to the court of France. He trusted me to negotiate treaties and agreements. I was his most respected counsellor.'

'My great-grandfather disappeared without a trace while on a mission to Ireland a hundred years ago,' Guy replied flatly. 'The king granted his wife and child monies and lands in compensation for their loss. My grandfather turned the king's gift into a warrior reputation. It's true I shared a name with my great-grandfather, but apart from that we could not have been more different.'

'What do you mean?'

'He was a fool,' Guy shot back. That's when he realised this certainly must be his ancestor. 'King William Rufus used you as a diversion. You were sent to Ireland to parley with the Irish kings to make them think the king's intentions were peaceful. Meanwhile Rufus landed a small force near Dublin to catch the Irish by surprise. The enemy had somehow been forewarned of the expedition and lay in wait for the landing. They slaughtered the noble Norman warriors to a man.'

'What?' the old knight gasped in horror.

'Some said it was my great-grandfather who betrayed the invasion,' Guy went on. 'For a long while your wife and son were held under close guard in the White Tower while Rufus made up his mind what to do with them. But word came to the king that my ancestor had vanished without trace within a week of his arrival in Ireland. Apparently you hadn't even met with the Irish kings. Rufus must have known you didn't have an inkling of the planned invasion. You were a fool. That's why you'd been chosen for this task.'

'No,' the old man cried, his eyes wide. 'It can't be.'

'In time Rufus restored my great-grandmother to her liberty, endowing her with lands and gold. Then he conferred a knighthood on my grandfather and, in time, a minor lordship.'

'And what of the title?' the old man asked as another memory suddenly returned to him. 'The king promised I would be awarded the name Lord Stronghold upon my return from Ireland in recognition of my loyalty to him.'

'Stronghold?' Guy repeated, glancing quickly at Eterscél. 'I've heard that name before. But there was no such title instituted in my family.'

Well this much is true, whether you want to accept it or not. Guy d'Alville's great-grandfather had indeed vanished soon after he arrived in Ireland. But the fact is he'd strayed into the Otherworld after he'd been noticed by Queen Aoife. Now he must have been about the first Norman she ever encountered. She certainly wasn't in the regular habit of turning his kind into oak trees at that stage. So she granted him the gift of Eterscél embodied in a sword and set him to guarding her bridge.

What chance, if chance it was, that brought them together here must have truly astounded the younger Guy. I recall that as the full impact of everything hit him he sheathed his sword again. But he added a warning to me as he put it away.

'Don't come near me or I'll slit your throat.'

'I told you, that's no way to speak to a lady,' his great-grandfather insisted.

Guy stepped back and gave a little grunt.

'Was that a hint of fear I just sensed in you?' Eterscél interrupted in a flash.

'It was not!' Guy snapped. 'It was confusion. I just need to sit down to rest a little. Ever since I landed in this country I've been constantly confronted by the strange, the grotesque and the inconceivable. So I'll thank you to leave me be till I've had a chance to think this through.'

With that he strode over toward the bridge, found himself a seat on the carved rail and stared down into the gently flowing water with his back to us.

'I'll get him to apologise,' the old man assured me. 'Though I can't tell what it is you see in him,' he added.

'Everything I've ever wished for,' I gushed in reply. 'That's what I see in him.'

'What is going on here?' Eterscél moaned, throwing up his arms in despair. 'Is that a love philtre I see in your eyes?'

'It is love,' I replied. 'If only I could harvest a tincture of it to carry with me always.'

That's the sort of rubbish you can be prone to talking when you've supped a love potion.

'It is a love philtre,' Eterscél nodded. 'This complicates matters slightly.'

'It's time for you to reap what you have sowed,' the old man told the spirit. 'I'm sure you and he will be very happy together. He's as arrogant as you are indelicate. You were never renowned for your talents at subtlety. Why else would Aoife have imprisoned you within that sword and given you over into my keeping? You must have mightily offended her.'

'It was you who was given into *my* keeping!' the spirit shouted, letting his temper get the better of him. 'The queen got upset because I refused to bow to her will. I did not support her ambition to become a goddess. I've got better things to do with my time. I'm a Frightener, not one to be a servant to a wilful girlish halfwit who just so happens to be immortal.'

'Watch what you say,' the old man taunted. 'You wouldn't want her to hear you calling her names, would you?'

Eterscél took a sharp breath and his eyes twitched this way and that. A flash of fear sparked across his eyes. When he realised he'd been tricked he turned on the old knight again.

'You think you're so clever, don't you?' the spirit noted in a deliberately subdued tone.

'I know you well enough to strike fear into your heart,' old Guy shrugged. 'We've been together a long time.'

'I wouldn't be coming over too smug if I were you, decrepit one!' he warned. 'Your days are over. You're finished. Your great-grandson is going to cut off your head and add it to the trophies you've collected in your time here.'

'No he's not.'

'You old fool!' Eterscél shrieked with delight. 'Don't you see? I've no need of you any more. I'm free! The king is dead! Long live the king!'

Then the spirit raised himself up off the ground just like a floating monk and glided over toward the older Guy with his arms flung wide.

'Your descendant and I are going to rule Ireland together, bringing her people to their knees with our skill. I'll feed like I never have before and Guy will supply me all my needs. Who knows? Maybe we'll grow tired of Ireland and take ourselves off to England or France.'

The older d'Alville laughed.

'You're the fool if you think you can achieve any of that without me.'

Eterscél dropped to the ground beside the knight, close enough so that his nose almost touched the old man's.

'I'm telling you I don't need you.'

'Yes you do. You may rely on fear to subjugate the Irish people. But if my great-grandson doesn't have a certain measure of charm about him and is not outwardly chivalrous, you will both face a long period of warring and intrigue. You'll

236

have to live with the possibility that your positions may be snatched away at any moment.'

There's no doubt about it, the old boy was right.

'Go on,' the Frightener insisted, showing a hint of interest now.

'If, however, young Guy presents an image of knightly virtue and is loved by his people, they will willingly lay down their lives for him without you having to lift a finger. They will defend him. They will worship him.'

'I'm a Frightener. I can't digest such morsels. The food of enticement is unpalatable to me. I need fear.'

'If the Irish worship Guy as their High-King, they will be perfect instruments of fear. Fear imposed on other peoples. Can you imagine the potential for feasting?'

'Fear on a grand scale,' the Frightener half whispered in awe. 'It'd be like the good old days. Charlemagne was a great provider.'

Eterscél took a sharp step backwards and a distrusting scowl formed on his face.

'What's in this for you?'

'Spare my life. I hadn't finished living it when we met so I'd appreciate having the opportunity to squeeze some more of it out. I'll teach the young knight all about chivalry, respect and the responsibilities of a king. With a bit of effort, and some diligence on his part, he might turn out to be worth more to you than you could have imagined.'

'Why should I trust you?' the spirit asked.

'He's arrogant enough to believe that he's in control of you for the moment. But if you don't keep him distracted with improving himself he'll soon realise you're the one who gives the orders. Once he works out you've been misleading him he'll certainly rebel against your authority. Wouldn't it be easier if he never discovered the truth? Wouldn't it be better if you never had to face a mutiny from your crew?'

'I'm the master of this ship,' Eterscél hissed under his breath so the younger Guy would not hear him. 'I'm the one with my hand on the tiller, not him.'

Then the spirit smiled wryly.

'How did you guess I'd allowed him to think he was in charge?'

'I've come to know you very well, my dear Eterscél,' the old man explained with a wink. 'And I think I despise arrogance almost as much as you do.'

The old knight opened his palms to the Frightener in a gesture that indicated he had nothing to hide.

'What do you say? Will we work together?'

'As equals?' Eterscél asked.

'How could I ever hope to be an equal to you? I'm a mere mortal. You're a Frightener spirit of the ancient days. It's just not possible.'

The old man paused.

'No. I will not be your equal. But I won't be your slave either. I wish to earn my freedom and my life. I'll work wonders for you with that one and willingly, too, if you promise to grant me my liberty. I'm not quite ready to die.'

Eterscél put a hand to his chin as he weighed up the offer.

'What about her?'

The spirit pointed to me.

'I love Guy d'Alville!' I insisted, in the full throes of the stupor of lovesickness. 'I won't leave his side now that I've found him at last. He is my knight. He is the lord of my heart. And I will be his lady.'

Both of them winced. I must have been pretty far gone by that stage. I wasn't at all concerned that there was a Frightener spirit in front of me questioning whether or not I should be permitted to live. You see, that's the way with some spells.

When a love potion is first administered it can be a powerful

238

thing. I'm told this is a peculiarity of that class of enchantment. But as time goes by, as season follows season, the original fire of the love philtre loses the heat of burning urgency. It gradually dulls to brightly glowing embers but never fades entirely. Not until the object of desire has passed away from this Earth does the fire go out forever.

'Many a great love ended in war,' old Guy noted. 'Many a great war was fought for love.'

'What are you talking about?' I asked.

'Love and war aren't all that dissimilar,' he sighed. 'Not when it comes down to it.'

The old knight took me by the arm when he noticed I was about to burst into tears.

'I'm sure I don't know what you see in that uncouth vagabond,' he soothed. 'But if you're so struck with him then you must help me teach him how to be a chivalrous, gallant, generous and worthy knight. Your love might just be the salve which cures his arrogance and brutality.'

Then the knight turned to Eterscél. 'She's Irish,' he pointed out. 'If the native Gaels see one of their own kind so devoted to young Guy they will surely soften their objections to his Norman origins. We need this young woman. Her presence at his side could save you a lot of trouble in winning over the people to adoration of their new High-King.'

'I had no idea you were so clever!' the Frightener declared. 'I'm almost sorry I didn't take more notice of you in the early days.'

'Do we have a bargain?' the old man pressed, ignoring the flattery.

'You will have your life and freedom if you teach your great-grandson how to behave like a true knight.'

'And what about me?' I cut in.

'You'll be his wife and his queen,' Eterscél declared.

'And his name shall be Guy Stronghold,' the old man added.

'Though in time folk will simply call him Stronghold and his name will pass thus into legend.'

'Stronghold of the Strongarm,' the Frightener chimed in. 'Stronghold of the Shining Sword. Stronghold, the Earl of Graces, the Prince of Gallantry and the Lord of Women's Hearts.'

'Stronghold War-Counsel,' the old knight stated solemnly. 'Stronghold of the Keep. Stronghold Fire-Eyes.'

And I can tell you those names did come to be used for Guy in time. It was a long, long time, of course. But folk did come to respect him in his later years. They called him other fine names as well. Stronghold of the Silent Vigil. Stronghold of the Sacred Gold. Stronghold of the Dancing Blades. Stronghold of the Shining Mail Coat. Stronghold of the Unquestioned Virtue.

And every one of those epithets is a story in itself. What a pity I don't have the inclination to tell you any of them right now. If you're good to me I might share one short story with you after this tale is ended. But I'm not making any promises.

Our Robert wasn't one to be left sitting in the dark for long. While Guy was confronting his gallant ancestor the younger FitzWilliam set off in search of a way back to the Killibegs. And he drove all thoughts of Órán from his mind so he could concentrate on his duty to his friends.

Now the Otherworld differs in many respects from this waking realm in which we strive, starve and struggle day to day. In the Land of Dreams the traveller is no less likely to encounter that which he fears the most. It's just that in the Otherworld his fears are likely to be manifest in more potent forms.

And as for desires? You may take my word for it that whatsoever you desire will be offered up to you in that place until you can no longer summon the strength or will to refuse. Thereafter you will take your fill of those desires until you cannot face them without feeling queasy.

As for Robert? Well he had no idea that his deepest wishes, his most secret thoughts would ever have the chance to bloom. If he had I'm sure he would have stayed put there in the forest where Órán had left him and would never have ventured forth into that wild untamed world of the spirits.

It was a long trudge through the tangled undergrowth before Robert glimpsed a tower upon a hilltop in the distance, lit in the pale moonlight so that it seemed to be cast of white stone. This peculiar building immediately intrigued him, drawing him away from the direction his instinct told him would lead back to the Killibegs.

Briars and blackberry bushes blocked the way but our gallant adventurer would not be put off. He gradually cut a way through them, his blade ringing with every blow. It was hard work so it was not long before he had to stop to take a breather. He sheathed the sword and sat upon a patch of ground he'd swept clean of any thorns.

He put his face in his hands and shut his eyes. When he'd caught his breath he raised his head. It was then he noticed for the first time that the bushes were fully laden with the sweetest-looking purple fruit. Each blackberry was begging to be broken off and bitten in two.

He plucked one. It stained his fingers wine red where he touched it. Robert brought it to his mouth. All thoughts of the terrible consequences to be had from eating the fruit of the Otherworld were forgotten. He was driven on by nothing more than a grumbling empty stomach and the urgent need to fill it.

Fortunately Robert had learned a thing or two while he'd

been training with the Templars. One of the many habits he'd become accustomed to was to thank his God for each and every morsel of nourishment.

'In the name of the Father,' he intoned as he stared at the berry with hungry eyes. 'In the name of the Son. And in the name of the Holy Ghost.'

And as he spoke those words the berry crumbled to dust before his disbelieving gaze. Immediately Robert was reminded that all which he might perceive in the Otherworld was of no consequence whatsoever. This place was known as the Realm of Dreaming. And for good reason.

Now I don't want you to get the notion into your head that this knight's invocation of the Holy Trinity held any intrinsic power over the blackberries of the Otherworld. It did not. It takes more than a few mumbled words to make an impression on anything or anyone in that place. Or indeed in this world either.

Everyone may see the Otherworld for what it really is if they find a way to do so. For everything in that realm is an illusion worth no more than its weight in dust. Robert glimpsed that truth through his prayer of thanks, just as one who meditates on this world may realise the waking world is no less an illusion than the dreaming.

I don't wish to wax esoteric with you. I can guess you have little interest in such matters. You're wanting a good tale. So I'll see you're not disappointed.

It was his good fortune that Robert had also learned the skill of fasting in his time among the Templars. Since the food of the Otherworld was worthless to him and he carried no provisions, his skill at ignoring his grumbling belly would certainly come in handy now.

Robert stood up to return to his task of cutting a way through the blackberry forest. He drew his sword and slashed at the bushes which blocked his path. A terrible cry tore through the air. It was a shriek of agony tailing off into a wailing keen of pain.

His plain unbleached cheese maker's tunic was sprayed with damp purple. His sword was dripping with blackberry blood.

Horrified, Robert stepped back to wipe splashes of fluid from his face with his sleeve. As he was doing that a most remarkable thing happened. The bushes cleared a path for him, falling back to line a cobbled road. They yielded to the advancing enemy. They cast down their thorny weapons in surrender.

The forest of prickly bushes was no longer an obstacle to him. For the first time he could clearly see the tower ahead of him on the path. It was tall and round, built of shining white stone and completely surrounded by a moat of sparkling waters.

Robert knew without question that his destiny and all his dreams would find expression somewhere in the secret chambers of that tower. So he did not hesitate, not for the briefest breath of a moment. He sheathed his sword again and set off toward his goal, his heart full of hope and his head spinning with it as well.

Now he could better see the tower he marvelled at its construction. It was taller than any he'd ever encountered. And it was as slender as a sapling, elegantly decorated with smaller towers which jutted out here and there from the main structure. Each of these was topped with a red-cone roof cut from shingles of timber shaped with care and smoothed to perfection. Set against the white stones of the magnificent structure these red points stood out in sharp contrast. At the very summit of the tower there was a flat space encircled by battlements. An immense green standard was cracking in the wind, terminating in two points which draped down over the tower halfway to the ground.

Robert had never seen anything like it. Not even in the east where the Saracens had constructed the most magnificent palaces of marble and coloured glass. Now and then he had to stop on his path not so much to catch his breath as to stare at the structure in wonder and excitement.

His feet measured out four thousand steps before he came to the end of that road. It petered out into a track then disappeared completely at the very edge of a wide ditch filled with water. That was when Robert noticed the blackberry bushes had been closing in behind him all along the way.

Not that he entertained any thoughts of returning. That was the furthest thing from his mind. It simply confirmed for him in that odd way in which dreams often do that he must go forward into the tower.

The moat was deep, dark and wide, so Robert was loathe to swim across if the bridge would not come down for him. As he looked up with awe at the tower his neck began to ache almost as much as his heart.

It was at that moment his attention was drawn to a swishing motion in the water. The moon had been swallowed up by cloud but the Templar could still discern ripples over the surface of the moat. He put a hand to the hilt of his sword, ready to draw it at the first sign of danger.

The waters rippled again; now here, now there. The moat was alive with creatures too big to be any fish Robert had ever heard tell of, except in the depths of the wide open ocean. He took two paces back, unwilling to take his eyes off the water in case whatever lurked beneath the surface should rush out to snatch him.

The moon emerged from behind a cloud for a brief instant. Pale cream-coloured shapes were revealed moving gracefully beneath the rippling blackness of the moat. Little bubbles erupted to trail along the water behind these creatures. In that instant the moon was lost again.

Robert waited patiently until the great silver disk in the sky peeped out from behind the clouds again. His body shook as he caught a glimpse of one of the underwater creatures in the full moonlight.

She was a maiden with long golden hair who flitted by, rolling gracefully over to flirtatiously catch his glance. Her long flowing cream gown swayed like seaweed in the tide. She had a mischievous smile and eyes of the deepest violet. Her lips were a paler shade of that same colour and her skin was almost grey in the moonlight. Robert caught his breath. He thought she was beautiful.

Intrigued, he stepped close to the water's edge, though he didn't take his hand from the hilt of his sword. As he knelt down on the grassy verge his eyes widened with wonder. There were others of her kind swimming around beneath the moat, flitting this way and that. Every one of them was gracefully rolling, diving and floating as they tried to get a look at him.

They were all so similar to the one he'd first seen Robert couldn't tell them apart. But they were moving quite swiftly, so that's understandable. And he was probably not in the mind to notice such details.

One of the moat-maidens gradually moved closer to him, lying on her back with her legs close to the bank so she could look into his eyes. The knight was enthralled by her weird beauty and her gentle smile. She swirled her arms about to keep herself afloat, her long cream gown caught close around her body.

Robert leaned closer to touch the surface of the water. He'd never seen a sight like this in his life before. He could hardly believe his eyes. As the ripples of his touch spread out across the moat all the other maidens swam in to float alongside their sister.

There were nine of them, each a princess of beauty in her own right, every one of them a shapely temptation to sensual pleasure. Robert touched the water again and the nine sisters locked their violet eyes upon him.

Emboldened, he cautiously placed his fingers into the water. The first maiden reached out her pale grey hand to reciprocate the touch, but Robert withdrew with a splash of instinctual fright. The moat-maidens laughed in their silent way.

Robert smiled back at them. He relaxed his grip on the hilt of his sword and placed his weapon hand in the water, reaching out to touch the moat-maiden he'd first laid eyes upon. She turned over in the dark and ran her fingers under his palm. He immediately withdrew his hand with a shiver of delight.

When the maid rolled back again her gown clung tightly to her body, revealing the outline of her breasts and the enticing form of her hips. Robert leaned in closer, his face now directly over the surface of the water so he could better take in her beauty.

She turned her body again and her feet touched bottom. Then she slowly stood up, her gaze locked with his. Her head broke the surface and she closed her eyes for a moment and took in a deep breath.

When she opened them again they were focused entirely on his. Robert was transfixed. It was as if a spell had been cast over him. He couldn't move. The other moat-maidens turned around in the water one by one and rose up beside their sister. And every one of the nine stared at Robert with adoration and desire.

The knight retreated back onto the bank, resisting an overwhelming temptation to slip beneath the waters with them and swim away to their home. His heart beat so fast that his chest heaved with the effort to breathe and his head thumped with the steady rhythmic flow of blood.

The first maiden held out her hand to be helped from the water. Her gown slipped away from her shoulder enticingly, revealing the pale grey flesh beneath. Her lips parted but no sound came from them. Her eyes begged him to lend a hand.

And Robert was a perfect example of the chivalrous knight. So he reached out to help her. Her fingers traced along the palm of his hand as he did so. Then she lightly touched the tips of his fingers, exploring the skin on every side.

He'd never known such rapture, such abandonment to pleasure. The tiny hairs across the back of his arm shivered as the moat-maiden brought her long fingers round to his wrist. She slowly crept her way up the inside of his arm and he closed his eyes for a moment to take in the sensation.

When he opened them again she was smiling at him, her fingernails gradually digging into his flesh, teasing, tormenting, tantalising. In the next breath she'd clasped her fingers tightly round his arm, still smiling sweetly.

Then suddenly she wrenched his arm hard down toward the water. Robert resisted, reluctant to enter the dark foreboding moat. The maiden smiled sweetly still but he shook his head firmly, letting her know he would not venture into her watery home.

She shrugged. Then she tugged a little harder. And when he did not give in to her insistence the maiden gripped him tighter. Her nails gouged his flesh as he squirmed to release her grip.

Suddenly her face transformed completely. The moat-maid hissed as she bared her hideous teeth. They were two rows of greenish, bracken fangs, sharpened into tiny points and dripping with stringy saliva. Robert would have screamed with terror but his throat was dry and he was too shocked to utter even a cry.

He hauled back away from the moat but the monster growled, dragging him closer to the edge with what seemed to be the strength of two full-grown men. He slipped on the grass at the verge and his knees slid into the water. There was nothing for him to hold on to.

The maiden stopped her pulling for a second to smile again, her teeth hidden behind her pale blue lips. Robert thought for a second she was going to let him go after all. But she wasn't about to allow this lad to escape her clutches so easily.

In a flash her sisters lunged toward him, each one grabbing at his clothes or arms or legs as he was hauled headlong into the water. He managed to take a deep breath but it was all over in seconds and the world was a blur of swaying reeds and hideous rejoicing grins.

For the first time he heard their weird wailing underwater song. It was sorrowful and sweet, piercing and yet lulling at the same time. The music was a dirge of the dark water and the depths and he realised it was his requiem also.

Down, down they dragged him into the darkness of the moat. Deep, deep they took him until he thought he could hold his breath no longer and would surely drown. And when at last his lungs were fit to burst he cursed his foolishness. He cursed his weak will. He cursed his wayward eye and then he bid farewell to life.

That was the moment his fingers brushed against the scabbard of his sword. With renewed strength, buoyed by desperation, he wrenched himself free, his tunic tearing across the chest in the process. His right hand found the hilt and without hesitation he drew the blade.

The unsheathed weapon shone in the darkness of the depths so that the moat-maids cowered and covered their eyes to hide from the cold iron of death. The one who'd grabbed him first swam close to bare her teeth again as her eyes flashed to bloody red.

Then suddenly they were all gone, swimming off in a frenzy of bubbles and tangled reeds. Robert struggled to the surface, making toward the bright moonlight above. His wet clothes dragged him back, slowing his progress. But at least it wasn't the fingers of those monstrous maids that slowed him.

His head broke the surface and he devoured the sweet air of life. When he'd filled his lungs a few times he made his way as quickly as he could to the bank. He crawled out of the water and as far from the edge as he could. Poor Robert was sucking down great gulps of air, heaving half with fright and half from sheer exertion.

He rolled shivering onto his back but not before he judged he was far enough from the bank to be safe. There he lay for a long while to recover, his senses on alert for any ripple, splash or bubble. When he'd at last caught his breath he sat up to stare into the moat and look upon the tower with renewed suspicion. Then he sheathed his sword again. He kissed the hilt in thanks.

'What is this place?' he asked under his breath as his eyes strayed to the tower again.

You can't blame him for talking to himself in that particular situation. He wasn't mad. Not by any measure. I don't know your feelings on the matter but I find there's nothing so calming as the sound of my own voice. Especially after you've been dragged down to the depths to be drowned by moat-maidens and only just escaped with your life.

As Robert spoke, countless amber lights erupted at the long arrow slits and broad arched windows of the tower. The most glorious music struck up. It was a dance as light and merry as anything he'd ever heard.

Robert's whole being was awash with joy to hear that melody. He felt all the cares and troubles of the waking world drop away from him. The moat-maidens were forgotten like some dark dream banished with the light of morning.

He stood up, feeling so light it was as if he were lifted up off his feet and could have glided over the moat to enter the white fortress at the window of his choosing.

But he looked at the waters and he was loath to approach them. As Robert stood there longing to enter the tower the drawbridge lowered down to his feet with the heavy clanking turn of pulleys and chains. It came to rest with a thump and Robert thought it was the most inviting crash he'd ever heard.

His first foot was on the bridge in a flash and at precisely the same moment from high up in the tower he heard voices raised in merriment and laughter. He looked upward to the battlements where a great fire erupted into life. There were many shadowy folk dancing round the flames to the melody of harps and the beat of earthy sonorous drums.

For a long while he stood there and simply stared skyward full of awe. He wanted to go up and join in the fun. Yet he baulked as the moat waters swirled and bubbled beneath him. He wasn't willing to risk that the creatures dwelling within the tower were more vicious than those inhabiting the moat.

He might have stayed there on the bridge all night if it hadn't moved under him, the great timbers creaking and the chains rattling as the whole thing began to close again. Robert made a hasty decision. He ran forward to the portcullis into the broad courtyard beyond. Behind him the bridge pulled up tight to the walls and the great latticed gate fell with a crash, blocking off all exit. There was silence except for the sweet music from above.

Before him was a single wide stone staircase leading to a broad arched open doorway. He could still hear the merry music high above in the tower. But it was much more rhythmic now. He paused again, unwilling to enter this castle without some assurance of his safety.

And then it struck him that he'd once heard a tale about a place such as this. His heart was so wild with ecstatic jubilation he thought it fit to burst. Every pore of his skin tingled with expectation. Every tiny hair upon his body quivered. His eyes were filled with beauty. The very air was alive with bright rich colour. He was sure he'd been guided to this tower in reward for his steadfast adherence to the code of the Temple.

I'll explain something of why he might have thought this way. You see, it would have been impossible in those days for a young man such as Robert to have become a Templar knight, journeyed to the Holy Land on crusade and fought for the Cross without hearing something of the legendary Grail. Indeed he'd listened to fireside stories concerning the Holy Vessel long before he'd sworn his life to the Temple.

I don't think it would be an exaggeration to say that it was those stories, spread by troubadours from the southern lands, which fuelled his romantic notions of the Order of the Temple. Now when I talk of troubadours I'm not speaking about Mugwort and his ilk. Mugwort wouldn't have been worthy of addressing a troubadour's boot-lick. The real troubadours were the finest of poets, the most delicate of storytellers, the most gifted of musicians and among the most canny liars, thieves, innovators and opportunists Christendom has ever known.

A hundred years or so before the telling of my tale a poet from the southern lands of Languedoc told a tale about the Holy Vessel of the Grail. And it was a fine story too. Full of adventures and knightly quests, love forlorn and mystical wells.

In that regard it wasn't so much different from the story I'm telling you now. Except of course that my tale is true and that story was a load of old leech leavings. In fact the whole story of the Grail was picked up in Ireland then turned into a new tale by the so-called poet of the French persuasion who claimed to have invented it. I've forgotten what he was called. I've never been very good with foreign names, especially French and Saxon ones. He came from Troyes though, I believe.

He lifted the entire saga from an Irish poet and failed to give the fellow credit where it was due. Now I don't mind that one bit. Good luck to him, I say. The whole Grail myth is not a bad little chinwag either. What I object to is that while he left in all the parts about adventuring, questing, jousting and fulfilling vows, he left out the dancing, the drinking, the carousing and anything else that might have been any real fun.

And a couple of generations later the whole of Christendom was seething with young knights bearing a very distorted view of life on their proud manly shoulders. They mostly spent their time searching for their true love in deserted forests or rescuing maidens who really just wanted to be left to their tapestry stitching, thank you very much.

I know of one poor fellow who spent his whole life seeking to do battle with a dragon. In the end, of course, he married one. But that's another story. It does prove the truth of the old Irish saying though. Be careful what you search for. You may find it.

And don't get me started on the whole foolish notion of courtly love. That rubbish evolved from those fanciful and inaccurate renderings of the old Irish stories. It makes my blood ice over to think about it.

What's the bloody use of passion, infatuation and adoration if it's all unrequited and only expressed through mournful songs? What sort of a life is it for any young man to be off riding round the countryside searching for some mythical cup of dubious provenance, said to be guarded by an impotent, wounded Fisher-King and his subservient daughters? That's not to mention the recurring appearance of scantily clad maidens bearing decapitated heads on silver platters through the dining hall after supper.

It's all well and good to be off gallivanting about the countryside kissing hags or jousting with your half-brother. But where does that leave all the young maids who are looking for a husband?

I'll tell you. It leaves them to while away the years in front of their bloody tapestries waiting for a less-than-usually-deluded knight to ride up to rescue them from the drudgery of sitting in front of their bloody tapestries. Small wonder it is so many young women turn to the nunnery for solace.

It's an acknowledged fact that the only young women who ever get rescued are the ones who live in tall white towers in the midst of enchanted blackberry forests. Where is a young noblewoman going to get her hands on one of those?

Which takes us back to Robert. He turned to look toward the closed drawbridge, silent now as the stones of the tower. Then he turned again to the stairs and the door above. As he did so he glimpsed a young woman with long dark hair peeping her head around the corner of the doorway, her face half in darkness.

She placed her hand against the stones. Her fingers were long, elegant and milky white. Robert heard her laugh.

'Come in, Sir Knight,' she giggled mischievously in a high-pitched musical voice. 'We have a fine feast prepared for you. And we cannot start until you join us.'

Then she slipped back into the shadows. Robert heard her steps as she climbed the stairs hidden behind the door. And then he was off after her like a flash with thoughts of the Holy Grail filling his imagination.

You see what I mean? That's what this silly legend of the Grail has done to the minds of all the young noblemen. He should have been indulging a little fantasy about what he was going to do with that girl when he got his hands on her. Instead all he could think of was a stupid bloody cup!

It's madness! I reckon the troubadours should be brought to account for all of this. Burn them at the stake, I say. Pile them up and set them afire. The world would be a better place.

Full of delusions, and with never a thought that the last fair maiden he'd encountered had a mind to drown him, Robert passed through the arched doorway. Beyond it was a small antechamber where a torch had been placed in an iron wall-mount. He knew without being told that this had been left for him.

That's how it always happens in those tiresome, predictable

troubadour romances. There's always a torch waiting for the young knight so he can find his way in the darkness. So, without the slightest suspicion this light might be part of an elaborate trap, Robert snatched it up. With the torch held high before him he commenced his climb up along the narrow spiral stairs to the top.

Robert lost count of the steps or the minutes and indeed abandoned all sense of passing time during that ascent. But at some point he stopped to rest and leaned hard against the wall. That's when he realised this tower was not made of white stone at all.

As he stared at the wall opposite him he noticed a flicker of torchlight as if the centre of the stone held a flame. But it was not so. When he looked carefully he could see figures moving about in other parts of the tower. The whole building was constructed from a frosty, semitransparent glass.

He ran his hands over the cold smooth surface of the walls, pressing his cheek against the glass as he did so. He could just make out a chamber behind the strange wall. There was a huge canopied bed draped with rich red velvets and adorned with fine white furs. The room was dark but the light of Robert's torch was enough to throw a little illumination on the interior.

His attention was caught by a movement as the door to the room swung open. Someone carrying a lantern had entered this chamber. He could make out the form and clothing of a black-haired woman dressed in a long white flowing robe.

As he calmed his breath three attendant maidens also clad in white entered the room carrying lighted candles. They sang a wordless song that was echoed in the sweet merry voice of a flute from high above on the battlements.

The attendants placed their lights at intervals about the chamber. One of them came close to Robert and though the walls of glass separated her from him he could plainly see the deep green of her eyes and the ruby red of her lips. She

CAISEAL MÓR

turned to him with a smile before she returned to attend her
lady. Then the young knight noticed the noblewoman's robes
were also quite transparent. And beneath them she was naked.

He stepped back against the outer wall of the staircase in
shock as the three attendants picked up baskets and converged
upon their mistress. They circled round her a few times,
spreading rose petals. Robert thought they must be dancing by
the manner in which they stepped in close to her. But as they
retreated again each attendant held a piece of cloth which she
drew carefully into her basket

The woman in the centre was as naked as the day she quit
her mother's womb. Her long dark locks fell behind her in a
robe of hair. And though the walls were frosted glass Robert
could glimpse enough of her form for his imagination to fill in
the remaining details.

His jaw dropped open and he tried to tear his gaze away
from her. But it was to no avail. His eyes would not do as he
commanded.

She must have known he was looking at her. She must have
been taunting him. Her dark red lips parted as she spoke some
words which he could not hear. She opened her arms wide,
inviting him into her embrace as she stepped forward to the
wall.

The closer she moved, the clearer she appeared. His eyes met
hers then followed down the line of her neck to her shoulders.
Somehow he dared to take in the welcoming rounds of her
breasts and the gentle flowing outline of her hips. By which
time she was pressed up against the glass and that was all he
could take.

Abruptly he turned away. His palms were clammy and his
breathing short and shallow. Before he had the chance to
consider what might have stirred such terrible fear in him he'd
hurried on up the stairs without so much as a glance
backwards.

But now he was in no great hurry to reach the top. For he suspected he'd been led on to this place against his will and better judgement. Who can understand the mind of a Templar? You'd have thought he'd learned his lesson from the moat-maidens. But no.

I blame the fact that he had very little experience with women. Knights of the Temple, as you probably realise, are sworn to stay away from the female kind. Which begs the question: what drives anyone to the life of celibacy?

It is an unnatural state, that's what it is. Those priests who would teach you that the bliss of bodily union is an experience to be feared are the most evil bastards of all. For they are stealing from folk the gifts which God has granted.

And worst of all, they claim to be doing this in the name of God. They make me so angry. I can't help getting worked up about it. But then I was a convent girl for a while. Perhaps I haven't put that experience completely behind me even now.

Poor misguided Robert. He'd lived such a chaste life. He had no idea what perils or pleasures awaited him within the circle of a girl's arms. And it wasn't for the want of willing women who would have worked their wiles on him, given half the chance. But he was as stubborn as a storyteller who insists on employing alliteration at every turn. He'd sworn himself to the Temple. He was a Knight of the Cross. He wasn't allowed to have fun. And that was that.

If you'd asked him why, he would have told you he was following the fine examples set for him by the Master of the Temple and His Holiness the Pope. I'm sure you know what I think of all that sort of talk.

It's not that I hold anything against the papacy in general. I think the popes do a fine job enforcing the laws of Mother Church and generally bringing misery into every Christian household as they are expected to do. I just don't see why the world needs an aged, supposedly celibate potentate on the throne of a rich kingdom which taxes its inhabitants a tenth of their earnings, forbids them to indulge in any activities that might result in a smile, then burns them at the stake for having more than a passing interest in collecting exotic toads.

That's not to mention the rather dubious assertion that the Bishop of Rome is infallible because God has chosen him to sit on the apostolic throne of Saint Peter. Surely God must work in mysterious ways. In my lifetime two popes have been poisoned, the third collapsed and died from shock and the fourth turned out to be a woman.

But it's this whole matter of celibacy that gets my goat. For a start, everyone knows the popes aren't inclined to take much notice of that restriction. I call to your attention that within the papal palace there are innumerable chambers dedicated to visiting dignitaries, most of which are linked by hidden passages. The fact that whenever these visiting dignitaries take up residence in the palace, prostitutes in the city become as rare as a fartless cow should be a clue to the extent of the hypocrisy one may encounter in Rome. But there are other glaring instances recorded in the history books which better illustrate my contention.

Still, I won't go into all that now. I've a story to tell. But I'm sure you can see why the Church Fathers fell in love with the legend of the Holy Grail. It was a perfect piece of distraction for full-blooded young men with too much energy and an otherwise healthy interest in pretty females.

The troubadour romances teach that the only way to achieve the Grail is through abstinence. That is to say, only the chaste man will ever have a chance of fulfilling his quest. Let's forget for a moment that women don't even qualify to take part in the Grail quest. What does celibacy achieve? Why did the Church begin insisting on it for all its servants? Well I'll tell you.

First of all, the rule of clerical celibacy was introduced about the same time as the Grail romances were being invented.

That's a pretty coincidence, isn't it? The Church Fathers were extremely worried that priests, nuns and monks were leaving their property to their children and spouses upon their deaths. Sometimes the inventory of these goods included property the Church could rightfully have claimed if the law had allowed. So the real thrust of the celibacy laws was to bring immense amounts of wealth into the coffers of Rome. If a priest wasn't allowed to marry he could have no legitimate offspring and hence no heirs. So his property immediately passed to the Church on his death.

In the convent a system was introduced to marry nuns to Christ. If they did fall from grace and bear children, those children remained the property of God and not of the man who had seduced the holy wife.

And what a change it made! Within the past three generations the Church has become incredibly wealthy. This single policy alone has guaranteed the papal coffers will never be empty. Assertions that this practice was instituted in the ancient Church are just a laughable attempt to silence critics. I myself have seen the forged documents purporting to attest to the great age of these rules. They're no more than a hundred years old.

At first the celibacy rulings were intended only to stop clergy from marrying. Everyone expected the servants of God to go on sowing their wild oats through the week. The Church merely encouraged its servants spend Sunday praying for a crop failure. Then a few fanatics got in on the whole business and before anyone knew what was happening all clergy were forbidden from so much as speaking to a grain merchant, let alone spreading the seed, if you take my meaning.

Poor Robert was one of that generation who were too young to recall the days of clerical marriage and yet so influenced by the Grail romances he didn't even question the wisdom of enforced celibacy. So as he climbed the stairs to that tower, trembling with excitement with every step, he had no idea what he was walking into.

His ascent was long and arduous. There were many floors he passed by on his way to the top. And now he knew the stones to be transparent he couldn't help but snatch a glance at every one as he went by. Most were chambers shrouded in the dark and deserted. But now and then he came upon a room where some little drama or banal daily ritual was being played out beyond his hearing yet within his power to witness. He must have been close to the top when he had to rest again.

He leaned on his sword, clutching his parched throat. Before him he could see a chamber lit by the soft glow of one candle. A grey old man was seated at a scribe's sloping desk with his back to him. His long hair was matted into thick locks which fell across his back. The fellow was writing furiously, dipping his stylus into the inkwell time and again as he scribbled. Suddenly Robert felt a stab of fear in his heart. He clutched the hilt of his sword.

The old scribe turned as if he'd that moment become aware of Robert's presence. And the young knight felt his every muscle turn to water as he looked into those familiar weary eyes. He lurched forward to lean against the thick glass walls.

The old man spoke. But Robert could not hear a word he said. Nor would he have been able to take that much notice if he could. He was so shocked at seeing himself seated in that room he simply could not have taken in anything that would have been said to him.

As he leaned there with his left palm flat against the glass and his right still grasping the hilt of his sword, his older self arose from his seat. With that movement the years fell away from him. His hair turned from the white-grey of age to youthful red again. His beard fell out in great clumps to reveal the clean-shaven chin of a young man. Then the long red hair also fell out, leaving only a short crop across his crown. All the while his other self stared back at him wearing a wistful smile and a peaceful demeanour. Our Rob was entranced.

The door to the chamber swung open and a woman entered. Her hair was as red as his, though it was long enough to reach the floor behind her as she walked. By her dark green gown and rich jewel-encrusted collar Robert guessed she was the lady of this tower. The black-haired woman he'd seen earlier must have been her maidservant.

The other Robert took the lady's hand without searching for it as she stood behind him. She hugged him close to her. Then a young girl and a younger boy entered the chamber. Robert knew they were his children born of this gorgeous red-haired lady of the tower.

He swallowed hard and closed his eyes, refusing to accept the possibility of such happiness in his future. When he dared to open them again the woman was gone, the children were gone and the old man had returned to his scribe's desk to continue his work. His hair was long and grey again and his back was arched with the years.

Robert moved back from the wall and the merry music floated down to him from the rooftop battlements. He was in two minds now whether to press on to the top or to turn and run back down the stairs and flee this place forever.

It was the old man who made up his mind for him. The scribe turned in his seat to stare directly into Robert's eyes. Then he smiled. And it was the most genuine, the most contented, the most sincere and joyous smile Robert had ever seen on the face of a living creature.

The old man lifted a hand to wave him on toward the battlements. Then he nodded and returned to his labour. Robert swallowed hard again, once more clutching his throat with thirst. Yet he went on to the top.

Three steps on he came to an abrupt halt again. A figure cloaked and cowled in blue was standing on the stairs blocking his way. Robert looked up into the face lit by the flicker of his torch. The light sputtered out just at that moment but Robert found he could still make out the details of the face. A soft white glow emanated from within the glass blocks of the tower and illuminated his surroundings.

'You don't need that torch any more,' the figure informed him and Robert dropped the dead light.

'Get out of my way, Órán,' he commanded. 'I'm going up to the battlements.'

'If you go that way your life will be changed forever,' the spirit warned with an odd hint of regret in his voice. 'And your soul-voyage will take you to ports you could hardly dream of now.'

'Is this your doing?' Robert barked. 'Is this a trick to turn me to your will?'

But the Frightener shook his head and pulled the cowl away from his face.

'I have not raised this tower. This whole edifice is of your own making. It came from you. It became you. It is you. You have explored the stairs but in your haste to reach the top you have rushed by chambers wherein you would have learned much that might have aided you in your quest.'

'What are you talking about?'

'Your quest!' the spirit spat with impatience. 'Your bloody quest! What's the matter with your hearing? How many times does it have to be repeated before it gets into your impenetrable skull? I'm talking about your quest!'

Robert didn't want to admit that he knew what the Frightener was on about.

'Could it be you didn't realise what was happening to you?' Órán asked with renewed interest. 'Is that possible in one such as you? Surely not. Surely one who has been steeped in the Grail legend wouldn't miss all the obvious clues set out before him on the platter. Would he?'

Órán's eyes glowed red but there was neither hatred nor anger nor any malice whatsoever in them. The glow was more related to his impatient hunger.

'How long will I have to wait before I feed again?' the spirit snapped. 'I've been patient long enough! Your bloody father hasn't done anything interesting in years. How am I supposed to feed off a holy hermit who isn't moved by either fear or enticement any more? Tell me that!'

And it was true. You see, the fact of the matter was that William FitzWilliam had become a hermit for a very specific reason. He'd done it to starve the spirit out of his sword and free himself from Órán forever.

Old William always knew there was something about that weapon that was unearthly. But it had been lucky for his father before him and had served him well. Swords are expensive items and quality workmanship is rare. Robert's father had never been wealthy enough that he could have considered discarding it for a new one. So William had kept it by his side.

Lord William had been present at the battle of Hattin in the Holy Land. It had been his first major fight. And during that battle he'd realised the power which lay behind his sword. I won't tell you about Hattin yet in detail for that comes into the circle of my tale later and it's best left till William tells of it.

Enough to say that the old lord awoke to the existence of Enticer spirits and of Frighteners also. He was naturally appalled that such an item had fallen to his possession. But as I said he was loathe to part with it because he was too poor to replace it.

He took counsel from many folk in this matter. But it was the Order of the Knights Templar that provided the answer. William took his dilemma to the master of the order in the Holy Land and asked his advice. Now it would be fair to say that the Master of the Temple knew something of such matters. He was rumoured to be a necromancer, a dabbler in disreputable dealings with spirits of the dead.

He saw the worth of the blade as soon as William demonstrated its power to him. The master convinced Old Will to take on the white mantle of the Knights Templar. First, though, Lord William set off home for Ireland to settle the matter of his estates and the inheritance.

But as the months wore on and the dusty miles passed beneath his feet on the homeward journey, Will came to understand that yet another terrible dilemma was facing him. If he took his vows to the Temple and this spirit within the blade were employed for the order, how could anyone be certain it would abide by a Christian moral code?

Do not these spirits have their own laws of behaviour? What if that was against God's Writ? What if the spirit of the sword guided him away from the path of righteousness? All these questions coursed through William's mind as he made his way back from the Holy Land with Órán in his possession.

So he eventually arrived home and settled his affairs. Then he withdrew into a monastery. Why? Well it was because he'd made a decision about the creature. He'd decided to starve it out. In truth that's the only way to deal with these spirits. Banish fear from your life and you will bring hunger to the heart of a Frightener. Quell anger, stifle terror, dispel doubt and you will leave him empty-bellied also. Banish bitterness, forget regret and a Frightener will not stay with you long. So the monastery is a good place to start if you're going to achieve your freedom.

Will, however, imagined he could drive the spirit out if he devoted his life to God. But he was wrong. For the way of the Cistercian monks is the way of Rome. And the way of Rome is the way of fear.

It didn't take long for William FitzWilliam to realise the only real hope he held of ever parting with Órán was to take up the life of a hermit separated from other folk. That's why he'd come to the Killibegs. He'd been seeking a place where he could defeat his own fear and keep Órán away from all other mortals. Without anyone to feed off, the spirit would slowly starve. In time it would flee.

It's true. Órán did go hungry. Once when he was desperate he even showed himself to William. They sat up one night by the fire chatting together and swapping stories of the old days. But Órán did not withdraw. He arranged for William's son to take possession of the blade in which he dwelt.

Why did William so willingly hand over Órán? That's a good question. The simple answer is that over a long period the Frightener brought the old man to a state of confusion. So he was hardly aware of what was happening or of the likely consequences when he passed the weapon on to his son. That was why old Will seemed so confused when I first met him and when Robert returned.

The fight with Guy had replenished Órán to some degree. He'd feasted on fear and uncertainty before and during the contest of arms. But it hadn't been nearly enough to keep him going for long. It was understandable the spirit might now be annoyed Robert was about to embark on a similar voyage to that of his father.

But Frighteners are tricky ones, my dear. They don't always tell their hosts the truth. And in this case Órán was telling a particularly stinky lie, as you'll see. But there was something else at work here. All Frighteners and Enticers use confusion to get what they want from their victims.

I've already told you that Lord William was subjected to terrible confusion by Órán which ended with the old knight handing the sword over to his son. For our Rob this was just the beginning of a period of terrible confusion. Many of the strange things he does as my story progresses can be explained by the influence of this spirit.

'So now you're going to devote yourself to some high-minded holy quest, are you?' the Frightener grunted contemptuously.

'I don't know what you're talking about!' Robert threw back.

'Yes you do! You've been longing for this all your life. At the top of those stairs out on the battlements is a lady who will allot to you your quest. Then you'll ride off in pursuit of it and everlasting glory.'

Órán paused to calm his speech. He didn't want to be misunderstood.

'Quests aren't renowned as plentiful sources of food for my kind. The only fear anyone ever suffers during a quest is fear of boredom. I want something I can get my teeth into!'

'It's too late to stop me now,' Robert shrugged.

'I know that! Why do you imagine I'm so upset? Stupid boy!'

'I'm not a boy,' the knight replied firmly. 'I'm a Knight of the Temple.'

'You're a child! You claim to be seeking the spiritual path but how do you explain taking up arms? That's not a very spiritual thing to do, is it? Like everything that ever came out of Rome you're rotten to the core, my dear Robert.'

The Frightener lifted a hand with the first finger extended. For the briefest moment the Templar thought Órán was going to strike him down with some curse. But the spirit turned the nail of his finger to the wall of glass at his side.

Then, with a series of furious and excruciating screeching scratches, he carved two words into the frosted glass. When he'd finished he underlined the first one slowly, drawing out the awful sound to the very last. Robert was still shuddering from the screeching nail as Órán began his explanation.

'The first word I've put up here is the Latin word for love. Amor. It signifies not merely the love of one being for another but all the many facets of love. Passion and compassion are the two extremes, but every expression in between is also love. Without love we are nothing. Even we Frighteners rely on the love you mortals have for one another and for yourselves. Fear of loss is born of love. Without love there would be no fear for me to feed on.'

Órán paused and the thirsty knight swallowed painfully.

'Love is all,' the spirit went on. 'Love is sacred. In all its many forms and in every shade or size, love is the holiest of all things for it is within all things. Even within me.'

Robert clutched his throat again, his tongue swelling with desperate thirst. The Frightener put his fingernail along the glass, eliciting a tiny squeak which got the Templar's attention once again.

'Turn the word Amor around and then you read the word, Roma,' Órán noted, underscoring the name with pleasure at the grating scratch of his nail. 'Roma is the Latin word we use when we speak of Rome in all its glory. Is it not remarkable that one should be the exact opposite of the other?'

Robert nodded his head. Of course it was remarkable. Any fool could have seen that. But did it mean that Rome was a force opposed to love? The Templar felt beads of sweat break out all over his body. He was faint with thirst and yet his body insisted on evicting more precious moisture. The Frightener took silent note of the knight's condition before he went on.

'Roma signifies all which is corrupt on this Earth. It points toward everything that would attempt to diminish or vanquish love. But love cannot be so easily defeated. So the dark servants of Roma have woven a spell around the people they've enslaved. They turn the love of simple folk for one another and for their God to the service of a few clerics.'

'What are you talking about, you fiend?' Robert gasped.

It was obvious he was having real trouble accepting all that Órán was revealing to him.

'You've soaked up too many troubadour tales and far too

much of what the priests told you was piety. But that wasn't piety. God has gifted you with mortality so that you will seize this opportunity to revel in His gifts. But you have fallen to the false doctrine and would deny the joy of life.'

Now Robert may not have entirely understood what Órán was on about. But I do. For it accords very closely with the way in which we Culdees explain the wonder of creation.

A venerable holy man who'd travelled extensively in the east once told me the tale of the origins of mortal people and where the idea of Satan first cropped up. The story goes that God created man and woman and then commanded all the angels of Heaven to bow down to this new innovation. But Lucifer, who was God's favourite, would not do any such thing. He refused.

You see, Lucifer loved God so much he could not bring himself to bow down to any other. So God punished Lucifer by banishing him for a time from the Garden. Not long. Just long enough to give the angel time to do a bit of thinking. When he returned Lucifer had certainly done some thinking. He came back with a new view of the situation.

There is an old adage that there is no raging storm as fierce as that which was born of being scorned. Lucifer felt scorned. So he gathered one-third of the angels of Heaven to him. He told them that God had been too generous. It was wrong, he determined, for mortals to know such passion and delight in their lives. The angels were not granted such carnal pleasures. Why should the mortal kind know such bliss?

He took his objections before the throne of God, backed up by the angels who had given him their ears. And God was angered at what he heard. He called in the archangels and all the hosts of Heaven to battle with the rebels who dared question the mind and purpose of the Almighty.

Some say that the war was quick and soon ended. Some say Lucifer and his angels were banished to Hell forever to suffer the fires and torments of that realm. Others reckon he was set the task of dealing punishment out to sinners. But that's not true.

The war goes on to this day. Lucifer and his host are still in rebellion. But they do not fight in open battle with the Heavenly Hosts. They seek to undermine God's gifts to the mortal kind. They go about the business of souring any sweetness granted to those born of the clay.

And how do they do that? They spread guilt, false doctrines and the tyranny of the rule book. How many folk these days dance for God when they worship their creator? How many bite into the fruits He provides with thanks and praise in their hearts?

Does anyone think to thank God when they are attracted to another mortal or when they are lifted up on their first unfettered rush of passion? Our senses are gifted to us in recognition and in gratitude for our service. What service?

In merely living our lives we are fulfilling God's purpose. And for that reason we are entitled to the rewards the Creator has bestowed upon us.

So you know what I say to the rules and all the regulations that keep us apart from God? You know what I say to those black demure priests who stifle the senses God granted them to enjoy? You know what I say to those who tell me that lust is of the Devil or that there are six other deadly sins besides?

Bollocks. That's what I say. But I seem to have strayed again. Please forgive me.

Órán was trying to explain to Robert that he was misguided. The Frightener was pointing out that our knight was walking the wrong path. It's better to surrender to the experience of life than it is to give in to the temptation to avoid it. And a quest, as Órán understood it, was just an elaborate way to squirm out of involvement in the real joys of life.

'If you go onto the battlements you'll never have any chance of living the life you yearn for,' the Frightener told him. 'If you accept the quest you'll bring me to my knees with hunger until you've fulfilled it!'

'What are you to me?' Robert hissed. 'You're nothing but a vile, self-interested brigand. You hold no allegiance to anyone but yourself. You rob whoever crosses your path. You feed on the unwary and you toss their shrivelled corpses aside when you're finished with them.'

'It is not all so one-sided, you know,' the spirit protested. 'In return my host has experiences which bring out the full-bodied flavour of life. How can anyone possibly say they've tasted the wine of living if they've never sniffed the heady aroma of fear?'

'Get out of my way!' the Templar growled. 'I'm beginning to lose patience with you.'

Órán stepped back to allow the knight to pass but couldn't resist one more plea.

'If you take on this quest, I beg you to fulfil it quickly!'

But Robert had already pushed past to round the final bend in the long slow spiral stairs. And then he was out on the battlements. The music immediately ceased and all the gathering in that place stood perfectly motionless with their eyes on the intruder.

The knight was surprised by what he saw. A great carpet of dark red was laid upon the stones exposed to the evening sky. It easily measured ten paces along each side and was decorated with the most intricate spiral designs woven in a slightly brighter shade of red.

All around the edges of this floor cover were pillows so those who were resting from the dance could watch their companions in comfort. Above these seating places were draped silks of yellow and orange which wafted in the breeze. The whole scene reminded Robert of a rich merchant's house in the Holy Land. A bonfire was set on the opposite side of the battlement. It had burned low now, though Robert could still feel the heat of it on his face.

High above, the moon slipped from behind a cloud again so the battlement was also lit with silver light. It was then the Templar noticed that every one of the dancers, musicians and other attendants on the rooftop was a woman.

He bowed awkwardly.

'I beg your pardon, ladies, for this intrusion,' he stuttered.

'Were you invited?' a stern matronly voice inquired.

Robert looked up but he could not tell which of the women had asked the question.

'I was compelled to come here to this place,' he explained truthfully. 'I could not have resisted the enticement if a host of warriors had stood guard to hold me off. Indeed, the nine moat-maidens would have had me but I fought them off.'

'Did you not find them appealing?'

'I was drawn to them with the same force as I am drawn toward the grave.'

'That's a good answer,' another woman commented.

As she spoke the gathering parted to allow her to step forward. The woman had long red hair which almost touched the ground as she walked. Her robes were of green and they matched her eyes for vibrancy. She was fair of complexion and fine-boned. And she had an unearthly yet intriguing air about her.

'What do you seek, Robert FitzWilliam, Knight of the Temple?' she asked.

Robert could not bring himself to speak. He was struck dumb by the beauty of the lady who stood before him. Of course he recognised her. She was the woman he'd seen standing with his older self on the lower floor. Was she to be the mother of his children?

'Forgive me, my lady,' he began, bowing again. 'I do not know your name. Yet I have seen your face before.'

'Have you?'

'Indeed. You have haunted my dreams on the climb up to

this battlement and I believe my destiny may be somehow entwined with yours.'

The woman laughed and a giggle of amusement passed through the assembly.

'You're a flatterer,' she noted. 'But you'd best be careful what you say. You have come to the Tower of Glass. No man leaves this battlement unless he accepts the quest which is given into his hands by me.'

She stepped closer, though she was still ten paces away at the edge of the carpet.

'Not many make it this far. You must be an exceptional one.'

'I am but a humble knight.'

'Will you take on the quest?'

'I will.'

'Then put up your sword,' she advised him. 'For it is considered impolite among my people to carry a weapon among the feast-goers.'

He bent down onto one knee, placed the sword on the carpet in front of him and lowered his eyes to the floor.

'I am yours to command, lady. I will do whatever you ask. I will complete what tasks you set me.'

He sensed her crossing the carpet toward him. He longed to look up at her though he dared not raise his eyes to her beauty. Fear gripped him. What was he doing? Was this not madness? To bow before a woman of the Otherworld was perilous indeed.

'What do you seek?' she asked him.

'I seek the Grail.'

'Do you thirst?'

'My throat is as dry as the sands of the desert.'

And it was.

'Lift your face.'

Torn between fear and longing he raised his eyes to meet hers. The lady held a great silver cup in both her hands. The vessel was richly encrusted with jewels, patterned all about with knot-work twists of golden wire. Robert recognised the cup immediately.

It was the Grail.

Now everyone has their own ideas about the Grail these days. Some hold that it was the cup from which Christ toasted the Last Supper. But that tale is a very recent attempt by the clergy to claim the legend for themselves. Others say it symbolises the bloody sacrifice of Christ. They reckon he who drinks of the Grail Cup shares the suffering of Our Lord and so diminishes His pain. For Christ said as he dangled by the nails, 'If it be Thy will, Father, let this cup pass from me.'

There are a few who, having studied the deeper mysteries of creation, understand that the Cup of the Grail represents an awareness of a great mystery. I speak of the doctrine which cannot be taught. If you don't know what I'm talking about no words of mine can explain it.

I will say this though. Those who earn the right to drink from the cup are the ones who have found the answer to all things. They are forbidden to pass the cup to anyone else.

Robert's understanding of the Grail was a little different since he'd swallowed all that troubadour nonsense. He almost had it right. He thought, as many still do, that to merely taste of the wine from the cup would grant him enlightenment, understanding, peace and all his desires.

So when he saw the woman holding what he understood to be the Holy Vessel of the Grail he anticipated he was about to receive a reward for his many years of devoted service to God and the Temple. This was what he'd been hoping for. In his understanding few knights were worthy of such reward. If only he'd listened to a few good Gaelic tales instead of those silly romances.

'Who are you, my lady?' he managed to whisper. 'What is your name?'

The air was full of countless whispers as everyone on the battlements commenced speaking at the same moment.

'Are you the Queen of Heaven?' he asked.

'I am not the Queen of Heaven,' she laughed as she offered him the cup. 'Do you thirst?'

He nodded.

'Then drink your fill. For you have earned this honour. Many reach the moat of the Tower of Glass. Some climb the stairs. But few ever reach the battlements alive. This is your reward.'

He took the vessel from her with great reverence and looked into its shining bowl of silver. The cup was filled with a fine golden liquid which emitted a sweet exotic aroma made up of many herbs. Robert raised the holy vessel to his lips and drank deep of the refreshing honey mead. And that was how he broke the strict rule that everyone must be aware of who ventures to the Otherworld.

Do not drink of the drink nor eat of the food of that place. At the time it didn't cross his mind that he'd broken the prohibition. He told himself this was the Grail. It was a different matter from the blackberries.

Immediately Robert FitzWilliam noticed a change in his body. His throat burned with the gold liquor and that warmth gradually spread throughout his entire being. He had attained his goal. He had reached to the highest aspiration of the knightly class. He could do no wrong.

Now you and I both know this cup, though richly decorated and finely wrought, was not the Grail Cup of legend. I'm sure I don't have to state that for you but I thought I'd better just in case you were confused.

However, to Robert, whose head was swimming with notions of chivalry and knightly romance, there was no question. He had achieved the highest reward. He was worthy. His virtue was above reproach. His place in Heaven was assured.

Soon all would be revealed to him and his life would change utterly and forever. Órán had been right. This was the turning point in the soul-voyage of Robert FitzWilliam. So you can't blame him if he started to think a little highly of himself. It was only natural considering what he'd come to expect of this moment.

He handed the cup back to the lady and repeated his question.

'What is your name?'

'I am called the Queen of the Night. My name is Aoife.'

She passed the cup to one of her attendants then offered her hand to Robert.

'Arise Sir Robert.'

Now it would be true to say that Robert was more than a little shocked to discover this woman was the person everyone at the Killibegs was so frightened of. Of course he'd been struck by her glamour, that air the Faerie kind have about them when they appear before mortals. He could only see her fair side.

An attendant stepped forward with a shining coat of mail. Another held a gambeson, the padded tunic worn beneath the mail to cushion the armour against the body. Robert slipped off his torn cheese maker's tunic and put on the gambeson. Then he lifted his arms to take the mail coat.

He got to his feet as another attendant stepped forward with a white tunic draped over her arms. She unfolded the garment before Robert then slipped it over his new coat of mail. A red cross was emblazoned across the left breast of the garment. This was the tunic of a Templar knight.

Aoife hummed merrily to herself as she wrapped a fine leather belt about his waist. On the belt was hung a leather bottle.

'You're quite handsome,' the queen commented. 'I'm looking forward to this.'

What happened next was against nature and near

unbelievable to Robert. In less time than it takes to draw a single breath his hair lengthened and his beard grew. In less time than it takes to say, 'I wish I'd brought a razor with me,' his hair was as long as it had been before he'd left the Holy Land. His beard was full and curly.

'That's better!' Aoife smiled with a wink. 'Now you truly look the part. Are you ready for your quest?'

'I am,' he replied solemnly.

A flat-topped helm was brought forward. Robert had never seen such headgear before in his life. It was deep enough to cover his head to the shoulders and it was fronted by a plate which swung down to protect his face. The plate was fashioned to look like a monstrous creature with long slits for eyes and a sparrow beak for a nose.

A fine padded coif was placed on his head, fastened securely beneath the chin, then the helm was slipped over the top. Aoife lifted the face plate so she could look her knight in the eye.

'Here is your quest. Are you ready to receive it?'

'I am.'

'You will seek out Flidais, the Goddess of the Hunt. And when you have tracked her down you will put an end to her forever. I would have her head.'

'I will do as you command,' Robert replied, compliantly. 'Where will I seek her?'

And you may well ask yourself what was going through his head. Here he is being asked to murder a woman in cold blood and he just nods his head. Well partly it was Órán's doing. The Frightener had led him here knowing that Aoife would want him for her consort once she saw what he was made of. And partly Robert simply accepted the quest must be of a holy nature no matter how gruesome the act it might involve.

'Clever boy! Always ask questions. It will save you a terrible lot of trouble. You will find her at my feasting hall before midnight. I believe she has a little surprise arranged for me. Go to her and finish her before she has a chance to deliver her gift to me.'

'As you so command, my queen,' he promised.

'Have you no thought of reward?' Aoife asked him.

Robert was lost for words for a few moments. He stuttered a little when he did finally think of an answer.

'I have tasted of the Grail Cup which many seek and few find. That is enough reward.'

'Silly lad,' the queen giggled indulgently as she touched a finger under his chin. 'I think I'm going to enjoy having you around. I'm sure you and Guy d'Alville will get on splendidly.'

Robert's face flushed with surprise at the mention of his rival.

'D'Alville is my enemy. I've come to this place to put an end to him.'

Aoife raised her eyebrows but the gesture was a mocking one.

'You? You think you can defeat my Guy?'

She took a step back then sauntered around behind the knight, taking her time to observe every detail of him carefully.

'Perhaps you would be better suited than him for the role of consort,' she decided as she stood in front of Robert again. 'Do you think you'd be up to the task? Would you make a fine war-leader? Would you be my king in all but name?'

Robert knelt down again immediately to grasp his sword again. He lifted up the cross of the hilt before Aoife to receive her blessing.

'I have been a true knight,' he told her. 'I have kept my vows. I have honoured the grand master of my order. I have guarded my chastity and maintained my poverty in obedience to the Cistercian Rule which governs the Temple. But I would discard all those promises and that former life entirely if you would so command me.'

Don't drink the drink of the Otherworld, my dear. And

when it seems your daydreams are coming true at last, be sure you question whether they've turned out to be everything you hoped for. Of course you can't avoid being deluded by a spirit now and then so I won't bother warning you about that.

Our Rob could only think of his quest in terms of all he'd heard in the troubadour romances. He had no idea how wrong the troubadours could be.

'Then arise,' she whispered, taken aback by his impassioned declaration. 'You need not face Guy d'Alville. I have imprisoned him in a place where he will remain at my whim. His torment will be eternal, I can assure you.'

'Is it true what they say of you?' he asked. 'Is it true you aspire to becoming a goddess?'

'Where did you hear that?' she snapped. 'Who's been talking to you?'

'The folk of the Killibegs expect you to come upon them this night with the full force of your Redcaps. Will you truly attack those defenceless people?'

'They're not defenceless! They have weapons and warriors among them. Hush and don't concern yourself with such matters,' she cooed. 'You're a mortal. You cannot possibly understand my motives. Perhaps one day you will. Go and fetch me the head of Flidais on a long spear pole. Then we'll talk a little more.'

'Spare the Killibegs. I beg you.'

Aoife blinked in amazement at his request.

'Do you know who you're talking to? I'm the Queen of the Night.'

'I'm not afraid of you, my lady,' he replied. 'Do with me as you will. But spare the folk of Killibegs.'

'I need them as a sacrifice to my cause,' the queen explained petulantly.

Well I've told you enough about Aoife's ambition already for you to know what she had in mind. And Robert had heard the same story at the council at the Killibegs. He had another question for her. And it wasn't what she expected to hear.

'Will you be a just goddess?'

'What do you mean?'

'Once you've been proclaimed goddess by the people, will you treat them well? Will you protect their interests? Will you answer their prayers?'

He'd struck on a very interesting issue for Aoife. It's one thing to aspire to the title of goddess and all the privileges which follow on from that. It's quite another matter to live up to the responsibilities which accompany the office.

'I will be a servant to the people of Ireland,' she replied. 'I pledge myself to them in service. I will be a just goddess. I will not be a harsh, vindictive or petty deity. I will end suffering in this land. And I will drive the foreigners from these shores if they will not change their ways. Only those who respect the ways of the forest and of my people will remain.'

'If you truly pledge these things with all your heart, that leaves one question unanswered,' Robert went on, emboldened and suddenly suspicious.

He was no fool for all the delusion he was suffering from. Now and then a nagging doubt will surface in his mind as the story goes on.

'What is that?'

'Why would you wish to bring hardship, suffering or death to any of the folk of the Killibegs? They of all the Irish are among the last of the Culdees of these islands. They would be your greatest advocates. They are of the few who still believe in you and your kind.'

That last comment was a bit of a shock to Aoife. So much so she could hardly comprehend what Robert was on about. For the sake of the tale I'll tell you why she had trouble.

Our Aoife had spent the last thousand winters planning this leap onto the throne of a goddess. In those far-off days of the past all the folk of Ireland worshipped, venerated or at least held respect for the gods and goddesses of the land. But things had changed in Ireland since then. A foreign faith had landed on these shores. Slowly but surely the Christian doctrine had supplanted the old ways. Even though the wise Druids had understood the need to preserve their wisdom within the new teachings, a change had still taken place.

Bridey of the Holy Fire, Goddess of Fertility and Having Fun, was turned into Saint Bridget by the Christians. A legend arose purporting that she had been the nursemaid to Christ. That was obviously a barrel-load of bulls' backsides.

Sadly, however, it only took three generations for the story to stick. Soon enough Saint Bridget of the Virginal Vows, Chaste Bridget of the Everlasting Purity, replaced Bridey of the Joyous Rut and Bridey of the Sacred Flames of Passion.

Goddesses went out of fashion after the coming of the Christians. Only we Culdees, who stay firm to the precepts of the Christian doctrine yet preserve the ways of our ancestors, still know anything about such matters.

Aoife laughed nervously. 'What are you talking about, you poor man? Have you lost your wits? Did you drink too deep from the holy mead cup? What do you mean when you say the Culdees are among the few folk remaining who believe in me?'

'In future whenever you have any dealings with the Irish they will explain your existence in terms of the Christian myth. Only the Culdees remember the truth. And they are being hunted down as heretics. Their time is not long. You will disappear with them.'

Aoife's face reddened with rage as she turned to her attendants.

'Is he speaking the truth?' the queen bellowed.

All the women fell back before her fury with heads bowed. The secret was out. The devastating truth they'd all feared would emerge had finally been dragged into the open. None dared to speak nor even raise their eyes to Aoife. For the queen that was answer enough. You might ask yourself how such a thing could have escaped her attention. But the answer is simple. She'd been so attentive to her desire to become a goddess that she had lost touch with the people of Ireland. It's a common problem with deities.

'Why was I not told of this?' she shrieked.

There was stunned, frightened silence.

'Bring me my brother!' she cried. 'Summon Lom Dubh of the Long Beak. Let him answer to me for this outrage!'

She spun around to face Robert again and her eyes burned with ice-cold ire.

'If you're lying to me I will bring down such suffering upon you as you cannot even begin to imagine. If there is one word of untruth in what you've told me you'll spend the rest of eternity in a dungeon of this tower with naught but the moss on the walls for company.'

'I am telling the truth,' the knight replied calmly. 'I am a Templar. I am sworn to truth.'

She stepped up to him, grasping him roughly by the chin as she searched his eyes to discover any hint of deception. There was none.

'If you have misled me I will visit torments on you and your kin to the seventh generation. I am no mere mortal. I am Aoife. I am immortal. I am a Queen of the Fir-Bolg Redcaps. And I will be a goddess.'

The knight stared back at her unflinching.

'I am Robert FitzWilliam, son of William, bearer of Órán the Frightener. Until tonight I was a Knight of the Temple. From now on and for the rest of my life I am sworn to the service of Aoife, Queen of the Night, who is my goddess.'

'For the rest of your life?' Aoife shot back, her eyebrow raised with interest. 'Be careful what you promise, young man. The rest of your life could turn out to be a very, very long time indeed.'

With that two attendants stepped forward to usher him back to the stairs. They led him down to the drawbridge which opened as they approached. Robert crossed the bridge, constantly looking back hoping to catch a glimpse of Aoife. A great raven flew in to land on the battlements as the knight reached the other side of the moat bridge.

Then as he stepped onto the other shore, the battlements, the drawbridge and every vestige of the tower vanished completely. All that remained was a grassy island in the middle of a wide moat.

Our young Templar knight did not tarry there long. He lifted the leather bottle that had been belted at his waist and removed the tight-fitting cork with an audible twist.

Robert sniffed the contents with a shrug then drank deep to quench his thirst. In one draught he emptied the bottle of its sweet fresh water. So it was with disappointment he replaced the cork. To his surprise the bottle immediately felt heavy again. It had refilled.

'What a fine gift!' the knight exclaimed.

Perhaps, he thought to himself, some enchantments aren't so bad after all.

A Cow in the Garden

'd better tell you what became of Sianan and Caoimhin while Robert was dallying within the Tower of Glass and I was off falling under the reckless spell of my own love philtre.

I've never quite forgiven myself for the intrusive part I played in Caoimhin's life. For he had fallen victim to my love potion also but his suffering was all the more than mine. There is a saying that absence makes the heart grow fonder. That must be doubly so when there's a love enchantment involved.

As he and Sianan made their swift way into the Otherworld, Caoimhin regretted leaving me more and more. Sianan was dropping oatcakes here and there by the side of the road as they journeyed but her young companion didn't even notice until they'd reached the bridge old Guy had been commanded to guard.

Of course the knight was still asleep when they passed by. I hadn't yet stumbled on his roundhouse to wake him. But it was as they crossed to the other side of the river that Caoimhin first noticed Sianan placing a cake by the side of the path.

She had to push Oat-Beer away or he would've snatched the tasty morsel and swallowed the delicacy in a flash.

'Stay!' she commanded him in a low voice.

He barked his objections. So she placed a hand firmly on his muzzle to hold his mouth shut.

'You must be quiet,' she begged. 'The Redcaps will hear you and then we'll be in for a fine bother.'

She reached into her bag to bring out another cake. He sat still and quiet until she presented him with it. Then he ran off ahead of them down the path, enjoying this jaunt immensely.

'Why did you leave that cake there?' Caoimhin asked Sianan.

'They're just little reminders for me,' she explained. 'It's a very easy matter to become lost in the Otherworld. There are many paths and they're all very similar. If I leave these cakes lying about on the road we've taken there's a better chance we'll be able to find our way out again when the time is right.'

'And what if some creature comes along and eats them?'

'The denizens of the Faerie realms have no interest in food from our world.'

'Why not?'

'Once you've tasted the food of the Otherworld all else is plain and unsatisfying,' she explained.

Then she noticed something strange about the young monk. His face had suddenly turned pale and his eyes were filled with watery wells ready to erupt into tears. He was shaking slightly.

'What's the matter with you?' she asked. 'Are you sick?'

He shook his head.

'I was just thinking how much I miss Binney,' he replied.

'Binney?' Sianan shot back in confusion. 'You just met her. Why are you pining after her all of a sudden? Have you taken a love philtre?'

She laughed as she added that last question but even as she spoke she realised there might be a hint of truth in it. Her expression turned serious. She pushed his head back to look into his eyes.

'Poke out your tongue,' she ordered.

He did as he was told. Sianan looked at the yellowing scum

that coated his mouth and there was little doubt in her mind.

'That silly girl!' she cursed under her breath. 'What has she done? As if we haven't enough to think about. As if there aren't already too many irons in this fire.'

'Don't speak ill of her,' Caoimhin pleaded. 'She's wonderful really. She means well, even though it may not always seem that way.'

'Shut up, you silly boy!' Sianan snapped back. 'You're under an enchantment. You've no idea what you're taking about. Binney has slipped you a love potion.'

'I don't believe you!' he scoffed. 'She's a kind, generous soul with a heart of gold. She wouldn't do such a thing. It would run counter to her morals.'

'Her morals?' Sianan laughed. 'What have morals got to do with it? Anyone who'd use a love potion to get the attention of another person would have to be a dishonest, manipulative and untrustworthy person. Binney is clearly not any of those things.'

Sianan slapped him hard across the face with the flat of her hand. A red welt spread across his cheek.

'Wake up!' Sianan hissed. 'I need your help. I can't be babysitting a love-sick youth. I simply can't be distracted.'

He put a hand to his face to soothe the stinging.

'I'm sorry,' he said softly.

Instantly Sianan felt remorse for having been so harsh.

'That's all right,' she relented. 'It's my fault. I've long ago forgotten what it is to be in love with another. Whether it be true love or whether it be love inspired by a philtre of enchantment, I have no right to reprimand you.'

Caoimhin dropped his hand away from his cheek.

'I'm sorry,' he repeated. 'I can't give my aid to one who would slander my true love. You will have to find Mawn on your own.'

'What?'

'I refuse to accompany you any further.'

Sianan took him roughly by the arm and lowered her voice to a threatening rasp. 'The Redcaps are mustering to march on Ireland. Aoife is close to achieving her goals. Many lives will be lost and much blood spilled if we don't get a move on! We must find Aoife and deal with her. Then we'll have the leisure to find Mawn. But until then we must cooperate with one another. The fate of the Killibegs is in our hands.'

Sianan realised she'd struck a persuasive line of reasoning.

'Binney is waiting for you at the Killibegs,' she went on. 'If we work together we can save her and all her people from certain disaster. If we do not press on immediately they will be slaughtered. Her fate is in your hands. You must cooperate with me.'

The young man's eyes widened as he understood how high the stakes were.

'I'm sorry I spoke ill of Binney,' Sianan conceded. 'I'm weary and short-tempered. I didn't mean to speak so of the woman you love. I feel certain the Well of Many Blessings is not that much further along this path. I've heard rumours here and there that it is on past the bridge. Once we reach the well you must have a drink to dispel this enchantment that has come upon you.'

The monk shrugged his shoulders petulantly.

'Please forgive me, Caoimhin. I only have your best interests at heart.'

'Very well,' he replied. 'I will forgive you. I will work at your side to save the Killibegs and to help you find Mawn.'

Then he turned sharply and marched off down the path after Oat-Beer.

'Bloody love potions!' Sianan whispered under her breath the moment he was out of earshot. 'Bloody Binney! Wait till I get my hands on her.'

Just ahead of her the monk was already straying from the

path. She watched him kneel down and it was then she broke into a sprint to catch up to him.

'You must not stray from the road!' Sianan warned him tersely. 'It's dangerous. You'll become lost.'

'I was just looking at this strange beautiful bloom,' he told her.

As Sianan reached his side she looked down with horror. A dark purple flower resembling a rose was opening before her eyes. Caoimhin reached out to pluck it from the small bush but her hand caught his before he had the chance to touch it.

'Don't pick the flowers,' she warned him. 'Especially not anything that looks as sinister as that one. There are many traps and pitfalls in this realm. Stay by my side. Do not stray from my sight. And if you can manage to curb your curiosity you may have a hope of seeing your true love again.'

But the trouble was, Caoimhin was suffering under the enchantment of a love potion. And Sianan knew well enough what that means. Such Draoi-craft can easily cause the best intentioned person to forget a promise or be tempted from their path. So she shouldn't have been surprised at what came to pass.

They must have walked at their fast pace another hundred steps along the path past the bridge when Sianan stopped to lay a hand against Caoimhin's chest, bringing him to a halt. He stood beside her and they listened together. There was only one thing that could have made such a terrible racket.

'Redcaps,' she said. 'A whole troop of them.'

She dragged her young companion down behind a ditch at the side of the road with Oat-Beer following close behind. Then they crawled together into the bushes where they could observe the path without being spotted themselves.

In silence they waited, the dog crouched between them as the noise gradually intensified. A few minutes passed before the first Redcaps appeared on the path. These were the scouts who had been sent ahead of the column to ensure the road was free of ambush.

They'd run by before Caoimhin could get a good look at them. But he didn't have to wait long to get his first real look at the dreaded Redcaps he'd heard so much about. A great company of them suddenly appeared on the road marching nine abreast at a fast pace. There was barely room for them to pass by on the narrow path.

They were a grim, silent bunch. No songs of war for these warriors of the Otherworld. No joyous stirring chants extolling former battle glories. The only sounds to be heard were the rattle of their weapons and the tinkle of their armour clanking away in time with their marching step.

Caoimhin could hardly believe his eyes. He thought they were the ugliest creatures he'd ever seen. From their bright blood-red caps to their leather tunics and britches, they were hideous to look on.

'These are from the far north-west,' Sianan told him in a whisper. 'I can tell by the dark brown of their clothing.'

But Caoimhin wasn't interested in the subtle cultural differences between one band of these folk and another. He was astounded at their repulsive faces and the long matted knots of hair which sprang out from under their caps.

And most of all he was fascinated by the huge polished sickles they each carried at their shoulder.

'Are they going to the harvest?' he asked Sianan as quietly as he could manage.

'Indeed,' she replied with bitterness in her tone. 'A harvest of blood for the dyeing of their caps. They don't strike the blades of those sickles to the wheat stalk. It is to the necks of mortals those edges will be thrust.'

As she spoke a bellowed command passed down the ranks in a language Caoimhin could not understand. The entire company halted abruptly then stood perfectly still.

'We're in trouble,' Sianan whispered. 'They're going to take a rest here for a while. You must remain perfectly still. Do you understand?'

But Caoimhin didn't have a chance to reply. In the next breath another order was barked and the whole company turned to the right with snap precision. Every warrior waited for a count of three then they collapsed where they stood.

A great hullabaloo of chitchat and grumbling took place until another command was yelled out at them. Then their voices dropped to a much lower level. Caoimhin estimated there must have been three hundred warriors in view.

All of a sudden a narrow path was cleared through the throng of resting Redcaps. They scattered to the sides of the road to get out of the way of a two-wheeled chariot hauled by a single horse.

Caoimhin was fascinated. He'd read all about chariots in accounts of the ancient wars of Greece and Rome. He never expected to see one.

'Look at that!' he hissed.

'Be quiet!' Sianan warned him. 'You must be perfectly quiet.'

The chariot stopped a short distance away. The driver hauled in on the reins as his passenger jumped down from the back carrying an archaic-looking sword of polished iron. The hilt was narrow and the blade broad. It was unlike anything Caoimhin had ever seen before.

The Redcap who'd leaped down from the chariot walked amongst his brethren making conversation. Caoimhin decided he must be a chieftain of high rank because his warriors touched their hands to their brows when he addressed them personally. He'd laugh with a warrior here or place a hand of reassurance upon the shoulder of another there, until in that manner he'd passed through all the fighters in that area.

Then he strode forward to where the chariot waited for him, bellowed a command and mounted the vehicle. His warriors stood up wearily to form their ranks again. The chieftain raised his sword in the air then yelled another command.

The great mass of warriors moved off again, headed toward the bridge. Caoimhin estimated that near a thousand must have passed by before the wagons of the supply train and the blacksmiths passed on.

'They're going to war,' Sianan told him. 'I've never seen so many in one place. Aoife must have called on all the hosts of the Redcaps for this task. She's taking no chances.'

The abbess raised herself up a little to look on up the road in the direction from which the Redcaps had come.

'Stay here,' she commanded sternly. 'I'm going to scout ahead for a bit to make sure the road is clear.'

Before Caoimhin could protest at being left alone, she and her ever-faithful friend Oat-Beer were gone. Their footsteps faded quickly while he lay wondering when they'd be back and hoping it would be soon.

Caoimhin was cold and the ground was very damp. So he shifted about where he lay, trying to keep warm. But it was to no avail. He was beginning to really wish he'd stayed behind with me by the fire in the house of healing at the Killibegs. Of course if he had stayed there it would've saved us both a lot of bother.

The minutes dragged on so Caoimhin opened his book satchel and removed the *Leabhar Fál*, the Book of Destiny. Perhaps, he thought, the manuscript might offer him some clue as to how this adventure would turn out. He stood the book on its spine and let it fall open. He lifted the manuscript to read the words upon the page.

'Everyone can be pleasant until a cow invades their garden.'

He frowned. It didn't make much sense to him. He didn't

have an opportunity to speculate either. Just then he heard a noise on the road. He breathed easier, thinking it must be Sianan returning from her scouting mission. But it wasn't the abbess he heard. It was the company of Redcaps returning with the chariot at the lead.

In his hand the chieftain of the chariot was holding a cake from the Killibegs. They had been discovered and now the hosts of the Redcaps would be looking for them. Caoimhin realised that Sianan would probably not be returning to find him.

He stuffed the book back in its bag. As soon as that was done he rolled over to stand up, hoping to make a run for it. But something stuck hard into his back and caught on his monkish habit. He spun round sharply to release himself from what he assumed must be the grip of a wayward branch.

But it was not a tree that had caught him. It was the point of a Redcap's sickle. The creature grunted a warning in a strange language Caoimhin could not fathom. But the inference was clear.

The Benedictine monk raised his hands in the air and swallowed hard to cope with the stench of the unwashed warrior. Once more he wished he'd stayed behind with me at the Killibegs.

He opened his mouth to speak, to protest that he was an innocent caught up in the intrigues of others and that all he wanted was to return to his beloved. But before he'd uttered a single word the Redcap clenched a fist and threw his punch directly at our young monk.

And that was the last thing Caoimhin remembered for a long, long while.

Sianan, on the other hand, had gone quite a long way ahead on her jaunt. She was also wishing Caoimhin had stayed behind with me. He was proving to be quite a burden. It wasn't going to get any easier. She understood well enough some folk can be fairly out of sorts after they've tasted a love philtre.

About a thousand steps from where Caoimhin lay in hiding she came upon a long steep slope which led into a glade. At the bottom a dark pool was surrounded by the stones of the cliff face which bordered it on three sides. Trees grew up along the slope at intervals but a straight narrow path led directly to the pebbles by the water's edge.

Her heart beat faster at the possibility this might be the place where Mawn was being held captive. Oat-Beer could sense her excitement. He was crouching down beside her, whining with anticipation. Everything was a game to him as it is to all his breed.

A hundred thousand thoughts passed through Sianan's head. She didn't want to rush down to the pool in case there were Redcaps about. There was also the likelihood of a guardian of the spring being present.

That's something else I should have told you about the Otherworld. All the springs and wells have guardians assigned to them. Don't ask me why. I couldn't tell you. It seems to me that in every tale I've ever heard the guardian of the spring serves no other purpose than to make life as difficult as possible for the hero by setting impossible quests or demanding ridiculous observances.

All her instincts told her this was the place where she'd find Mawn. And if it was the spring then she realised she hadn't needed Caoimhin's help at all. It had been a simple matter to locate it without his aid.

However, it must be said, Sianan had a sense something was amiss. Her finely tuned instincts had awakened to danger. She was beginning to feel very nervous, though she could not immediately discern why that should be. Some intuition was nagging at her. She tried to calm herself so she could think clearly. It had been a long time since she'd felt so flustered and jittery.

'What is wrong with me?' she asked herself aloud.

Oat-Beer barked an answer. Then he was off down to the spring as fast as his long spindly legs could carry him. Sianan wasn't quick enough to grab him and she didn't dare call out in case she attracted unwelcome attention.

It was just as the red dog disappeared from her view that she realised why she was feeling so nervous. And it struck her like a slap in the face. The scouting Redcaps they'd encountered earlier were bound to find the cakes she'd left behind on the path!

What a fool she'd been! She called herself an eedyit, I'm sure, as I would have done if I'd been in her position. But of course it was too late to berate herself. She knew Caoimhin would be in great danger if the Redcaps came back searching for the folk who'd dropped the cakes.

She was torn. Down there at the spring was Oat-Beer and imprisoned beneath the waters she felt certain she'd find her long-lost Mawn. On the other hand she knew it was her fault Caoimhin had been placed in this terrible danger.

The dog would be all right, she reasoned. He'd find that she was gone and either track her scent until he found her or wait till she returned. Mawn would have to remain imprisoned a while longer too. She'd already waited nearly eight hundred years or so, an hour longer wouldn't be too much to bear.

So with no small amount of regret she abandoned Oat-Beer and made her way as swiftly and as silently as she could back toward the spot where she'd left Caoimhin. And all along the way she prayed that he was safe.

Of course, as I'm sure you understand, by that stage he was

already in the custody of the Redcap chieftain of the chariot. So he was certainly not what you'd call safe.

Caoimhin awoke long afterwards to find his hands bound tightly behind his back and his feet strapped together. He was lying on his side staring into a small fire. His head was sore and his lips were swollen where the Redcap warrior had punched him.

He tasted a little blood and tested his lip with his tongue. There was a nasty cut on his lower lip but he still had all his teeth. And for that he was grateful.

Smoke from the fire blew into his face so he coughed and turned his head away. It was then he noticed he was lying in front of a squatting Redcap. Caoimhin twisted around to look at the warrior but he'd hardly moved when he was slapped on the back of the head.

He didn't understand the Redcap's speech but he got the gist of what the warrior wanted him to do. Lie still and be quiet. So the young Benedictine looked into the fire for a while. Until he noticed there were other Redcaps seated all around it just out of the light.

None of them were speaking. Their ugly brutish faces were grim and sullen. Here and there one or two of them chewed on some morsel of food. Occasionally one of their number would grunt as a wineskin was passed to him. None of them seemed to savour the contents though. Caoimhin got the impression they had no choice but to drink of its unpalatable contents. Perhaps, he thought, there was nothing else available.

At length one of the warriors took up his sickle and a

sharpening stone. But he'd only run it along the finely honed edge a few times before his companions raised a howl against him and he put it down again.

Our Caoimhin could tell something was very wrong here. The Redcaps had a reputation for brutality unmatched even by the Normans. But these fellows didn't seem capable of cruelty. They weren't a happy bunch at all but they weren't the bloodthirsty brutes they'd been painted to be. Something must have happened since he'd seen them on the march to put them in this mood.

Careful to make sure none of the warriors noticed him, Caoimhin began to scrutinise them one by one. Directly opposite him sat a particularly large Redcap who seemed more sullen than the others. His head was big and ugly. Thick strands of dark brown hair locked together in great fat knots cascaded out from underneath his blood-red cap.

His eyes were dark pools of pale moonlight set in two bloodshot slabs of ivory. His skin was roughened, by weather or battle or sadness Caoimhin could not guess. His teeth were sharpened to points. They gleamed white.

But it was the warrior's face that was most unusual. He'd never seen such facial decoration before. Tiny red dots made patterns across the Redcap's nose and cheeks, flowing down in spirals to his neck and disappearing beneath his fine hide tunic.

His clothes were hard-wearing leather: a long-sleeved tunic coupled with a pair of loose-fitting trousers gathered below the knee then strapped close to the calf muscles. A great wide belt held the tunic close to his body and supported various small satchels, pouches and leather bottles.

A long curved knife housed in a rich red-brown leather sheath was stuck through the belt. The hilt of the knife was carved of fine white bone bound with leather strips and set with a jewel. Every one of the Redcaps had one of these knives and all of them were the same except for the nature of the carving or the colour of the jewel.

This Redcap wore a long beard plaited together into one strand. This was tucked firmly into his belt. His moustache was also long and drooped in two great falls until it reached his chest.

His hands were large and callused as might be expected of a warrior. But his boots were beautifully made with soles of hardened leather attached to the body of the shoe with fine iron nails. The shoes themselves were decorated with intricate hammered designs which echoed the fine red dots upon the warrior's face. And they were laced about the top of the foot so that they must have been very comfortable for long journeys.

As Caoimhin was admiring the boots a commotion stirred nearby. All the Redcaps turned to see what the fuss was all about. A few of them stood up. There was a general grumbling and muttering of curse-like phrases.

The next thing Caoimhin knew the Redcaps fell back out of the way to let one of their number closer to the fire. It was the chieftain who'd been riding on the chariot. He immediately squatted down beside the large warrior Caoimhin had been observing and stared into the flames.

Abruptly all the Redcaps broke into a deluge of talk. It was plain they were demanding answers. The chieftain waited till their rage had calmed a little and then spoke in a confident, unhurried tone.

Caoimhin had no idea what was being said. But he understood well enough that whatever the chieftain was talking about it was not to the liking of his warriors. Once or twice their chief pointed at their prisoner and the Redcaps made it clear they were enraged at whatever he'd said. The monk was beginning to become extremely worried.

What were they going to do with him? Was he to be

punished for straying into their realm? He considered speaking up but quickly changed his mind when the conversation turned to heated grunts. It began to look as though things were about to go very, very badly for him.

At last the large warrior stood up, looked down at Caoimhin and drew his thumb across his own throat. The other Redcaps howled with approval but their chieftain shut them up.

He got to his feet, speaking in soothing tones until the Redcap resumed his seat by the fire. Then the chieftain looked down at Caoimhin and shook his head.

Then, to our lad's horror, the chieftain drew the knife from his belt. He held it up with the blade pointing toward the moon. He intoned what sounded to Caoimhin like a vow.

All the young monk could think of in that time of peril was me. I was flattered when I found out. But the truth was he was still in a muddle after taking the love potion. He wondered whether I'd miss him and what it might have been like had we been married.

Then he made a solemn promise to himself that if ever he escaped this terrible situation he'd honour me and love me and discard his vows to the Benedictine order forever. Which just goes to prove that Ortha's love philtre hadn't diminished in strength with age after all.

No thoughts of Sianan came into his head for she had abandoned him. He wasn't none too happy with her to be sure. He considered it entirely her fault he'd been captured. And he had no mind for mumbling any prayers either. It wouldn't have done him any good if he had.

Without warning two warriors grabbed him from behind and lifted him to his feet. The Redcap chieftain spoke a few more words directed at the prisoner, then he stepped around the fire to stand right beside Caoimhin with his knife drawn and held firm, ready to strike.

The monk did not flinch. He wanted to face his end with dignity. Ah, he was a brave one was our Caoimhin.

The chieftain shouted something and his warriors cheered. Then he raised the knife again.

Before Caoimhin could cry out with fear the Redcap war-leader grabbed hold of his hands and drew the knife up through the leather straps which bound them. Caoimhin watched in astonishment as the chieftain bent down to cut the bindings at his feet.

The warrior straightened and held his knife high again to the resounding cheers of his fellow Redcaps. Before our young monk had even realised he was free the chieftain leaned in close and spoke to him in Gaelic.

'You free. Go,' he nodded with a smile. 'Go home now.'

'I don't understand,' Caoimhin protested.

'Go!' the chieftain insisted, making a gesture with a flick of his knife. 'No danger here for you. You go home now!'

Then he turned back to his warriors to accept their adulation once again.

'I don't know the way home,' Caoimhin cut in. 'Why have you set me free? I thought you were all brutal killers bent on destruction.'

The entire assembly fell silent, staring with stung outrage at the Benedictine monk. But it was the chieftain who replied.

'You watch your speaking,' he stated in twisted Gaelic. 'You lucky boy. Don't say bad thing about pretty Redcap. Redcaps angry to be called names. Not wish mortal kind fight with us.'

'But Queen Aoife is amassing her armies ready to strike at the Killibegs.'

Every one of the warriors ducked when they heard Aoife's name, as if she were waiting in the trees to swoop down on them. A few mumbled under their breath. Many swallowed hard in fear.

'You know her?' the chieftain pressed. 'You know queen?'

'No.'

There was a noticeable relief on the faces of the warriors as they looked from one to another, shaking their heads and smiling. Caoimhin was beginning to become very confused.

'Don't you want to hurt me? I was wandering about in your country without permission.'

'We not hurt you. You wander home.'

'I can't go home,' Caoimhin repeated. 'I don't know the way.'

The chieftain shrugged to his warriors to show he neither understood nor cared what the monk had said. He placed his fingers inside his lips to make a loud whistle. It sounded just like the half-gurgled shriek of a raven.

Then the Redcaps were picking up their packs and kicking the fire as they made ready to leave. Their former prisoner was bewildered.

'You can't just leave me here!' he shrieked. 'I don't know where I am.'

The chieftain came back and placed an arm over his shoulder in a friendly gesture.

'We not to hurt you,' he explained with a fatherly nod. 'Redcap men go now to war. Redcap men fight. We not hurt mortals. You go home. Lucky boy.'

'If you're going to war, who are you going to fight?'

Then the chieftain didn't answer but instead patted Caoimhin on the back and added one more word of well-wishing.

'Luck.'

While he'd been speaking his warriors had formed ranks on the road. The chieftain mounted his chariot and, with another whistle, urged his warriors on. They stepped out singing a song which, though unintelligible to Caoimhin, was obviously something warlike.

Our young monk then found himself in a terrible dilemma.

What was he to do? How was he to find his way home to me if he had no idea where he was? What would become of him?

He was filled with a profound longing to see me again. If he wanted to get back to me, he had little choice but to follow the Redcaps. Surely they'd be able to lead him back to the Killibegs. Weren't they part of the forces Aoife was massing to attack the Culdee settlement?

One way or another, he reasoned, this war party would lead him home to me eventually.

Caoimhin didn't know how lucky he was to have been picked up by the Redcaps. He'd find that out later. Sianan, on the other hand, wasn't very lucky at all. She'd followed the road back to where she'd left the young Benedictine. He was, of course, gone by the time she arrived.

She had no way of knowing with certainty that he'd been taken by Redcaps but there were a few signs which pointed to that. A piece of Killibegs bread had been flattened into the grass by the road. The spot where Caoimhin had been hiding was flattened by the tramp of many feet. And there was a strong odour about the place which reminded her of the underground lair of the Redcaps she and Oat-Beer had encountered before their arrival at the Killibegs.

She resolved to find Caoimhin. He was her responsibility. She reasoned it was very likely the warriors would take their captive straight to Aoife. So if Sianan managed to track them down, they'd lead her directly to the Queen of the Night.

Sianan knew well enough she couldn't follow such a trail without help. Even though the Redcap tracks were clear now, there was no telling where they might take him once they all went their separate ways within their fortress. How would she find Caoimhin's tracks among that mass of warrior feet? Oat-Beer would have to lend his nose to this enterprise.

And let me tell you it was a daunting prospect for her to face the Redcaps alone. She suddenly felt quite frightened. She thought that Oat-Beer would certainly be a good companion in the underground home of the enemy. As soon as the realisation struck her, she was off back to where she'd left her friend the red-haired Sotar.

Sianan sensed there were no more Redcaps on the road but she kept her eyes and ears open as she flitted through the moonlit forest to the spring. It wasn't really that far to travel but her watchfulness slowed her down.

When she approached the spring this time she didn't wait in the shadows to observe whether anyone was waiting to ambush her. She bounded down the path through the trees until she reached the place where the woods gave way to the pebbles.

It wasn't till she stepped out into the clearing that she realised there was a man standing at the pool. By then it was already too late to do anything about it. Her presence had been felt.

In the moonlight of the Otherworld the stranger seemed incredibly tall, though he was probably just above the average height of an Irishman in those days. His hair was copper-red and long, tied back behind his head to keep it out of his face.

His tunic was earthy brown, as were his britches and his shoes, though they were slightly darker. As Sianan wondered whether he'd heard her approaching he knelt down to splash a little water on his face. Then he spoke.

'Where did you go off to? I've been waiting here for ages. I thought I'd lost you.'

Sianan frowned. There was something very familiar about that voice. Was this Mawn? She asked herself that question knowing full well the hair of her long-lost soul-friend had always been black.

'I'm sorry,' she replied politely at last. 'I don't believe we've met.'

The stranger stood up from the waterside and turned around. His eyes were dark brown like chestnuts and his nose was long and hooked. Once again Sianan was struck by a twinge of recognition though she still couldn't quite place him.

'Don't you know me?' he asked with a hint of desperation in his voice. 'Have I changed that much since you were away?'

Sianan caught her breath.

'Is that you, Mawn?'

The stranger lifted his eyes to the sky and howled.

'She's forgotten me!'

Sianan had to take a step back as he bellowed again.

'She thinks my name is Mawn!'

'Who are you?' she whispered, utterly mystified now.

'I drank from the pool,' he whined. 'I was thirsty after all that running through the forest. I drank the waters and I turned into a Two-Leg. What am I to do? I want my old self back. But no matter how much I drink from the waters of this cursed pool, nothing happens. Am I trapped in this gangly great torso forevermore? I want my dog body back!'

'Oat-Beer!' Sianan gasped in wonder. 'Is that you?'

'Of course it's me!' he snapped. 'Who else would it be? Didn't you come back looking for me?'

'I did,' she assured him. 'I just didn't expect to find you like this.'

'The waters of this pool are enchanted,' he whined. 'I've been changed. And I don't like it.'

'This must be the Well of Many Blessings,' Sianan concluded. 'This is the spring Alan and Mirim are searching for.

301

Perhaps we'll find my companion Mawn imprisoned beneath the waters.'

'Of course this is the Well of Many Blessings!' a rough voice scoffed. 'Are you stupid? Have you never heard of Flidais? This is her well.'

'Are you the guardian of the well?' Sianan asked.

'I am.'

'Greetings to you,' she bowed.

'That makes a nice change,' the stone head noted. 'Most folk I encounter these days are so rude. You may drink of my waters whenever you like. Your kind are welcome here.'

'Is this the well where Flidais has entrapped Mawn?'

'It is.'

'Is this the well known for its healing and revitalising properties?'

'It is.'

'Are you under an enchantment yourself?'

'I am,' the stone head responded mournfully.

'Never mind about him!' Oat-Beer cried. 'What about me? Look at what a state I'm in. I'm a Two-Legs.'

Indeed it is often said of the Otherworld that it is the Land of Transformations. Some folk have to wait until they've departed their mortal flesh before they take on another form. But those who travel to the Otherworld, whether they be man or beast, risk that transformation without an intervening death.

I know what you're thinking. She's off on one of her little heretical rants again. Well and so I am. We Culdees live our lives according to simple principles. The main tenet of our existence is the knowledge that every soul returns life after life to new forms. So though I might be a cackling old woman now, my soul could just as easily inhabit a ferret body in my next life. Which is not something I'm particularly happy about I can tell you.

302

If it's all too complicated for you to comprehend, don't fret. All you need to understand is that Oat-Beer, the red Sotar dog, drank of the waters of the Well of Many Blessings and before he'd finished swallowing he'd become Oat-Beer the man.

Of course Oat-Beer was disgruntled at this development, to say the least. He'd lost two legs though he'd gained two arms. He'd exchanged two feet for a pair of hands. And he was having a little trouble moving about in this new form without losing his balance or tripping over. All round it must have been a distressing experience.

'Where did you find those clothes?' Sianan asked him.

'Flidais gave them to me.'

'You've spoken with Flidais? You've seen the Goddess of the Hunt?'

Oat-Beer nodded with excitement and Sianan caught a glimpse of his former self in the enthusiasm of the gesture.

'She's very nice too,' he told her. 'I expected her to be much more horsy after all that hunting she gets tangled up with. But she was really quite a feminine creature with a wit as sharp as a whippet. I could have talked to her all night if she hadn't been in such a hurry to gather her warrior host together.'

'I wouldn't let her hear you say that,' the stone head advised. 'It fairly gets on her goat that everyone expects her to be horsy.'

Sianan ignored the stone head. 'Why is the Huntress gathering her warriors?'

'For war,' Oat-Beer replied, before he realised he'd stated the obvious. So he went on to explain. 'Apparently she's going to face Aoife down sometime this evening. Of course Aoife isn't expecting a rebellion in the Otherworld so the victory will probably go to Flidais.'

'A surprise attack!' Sianan gasped. 'While Aoife's busy putting out the Need-Fire and preparing to bring battle to the

Killibegs, Flidais is going to lead an open rebellion against her!'

She paused for a moment. 'This could save us the trouble of confronting Aoife with Draoi-craft! This could be the end of the Queen of the Night.'

'So what should we do?' Oat-Beer asked.

'We must find Aoife. Wherever she is, we'll find Caoimhin as well, I feel sure of that.'

'The queen will be at her feasting hall. That's where Flidais and her Redcap rebels are going to ambush her.'

'Oat-Beer!' Sianan exclaimed with relief. 'This is wonderful!'

Suddenly, though, she was torn between her duty to the Culdee folk of the Killibegs and loyalty to her soul-friend Mawn, not to mention feeling responsible for Caoimhin. She glanced down at the waters of the spring with longing.

'Mawn will have to wait,' she decided aloud. 'We must hurry to Aoife's hall. Where will we find it?'

'Within the Redcap city. We've been there before, though we were only walking through the store rooms which are in a place between the worlds.'

'But Oat-Beer, how do we find our way to Aoife's feasting hall?'

'We follow some Redcaps,' he shrugged. 'That's where they are amassing for the attack.'

Then he thought for a moment before he added, 'Would you mind calling me by another name? It's just that Oat-Beer doesn't seem to suit me any more.'

'Of course I wouldn't mind. What would you like me to call you while you're walking in this form?' One thing I'll say about our Sianan. She was always an accepting soul. I don't know many folk who would've been able to carry on such a conversation with a man who had been a dog. I'm certain her long span of years on this Earth had granted her a special kind of wisdom.

'Whenever I've imagined what it would be like to be a man I've always thought Tóraí would suit me well enough.'

Sianan pronounced the name slowly as she examined his face to see if they matched.

'Toh-ree. It's a good name for you.'

'It's an old word. It means the seeker,' he told her. 'Or the pursuer.'

'Or the outlaw,' Sianan added with a hint of warning. 'It can also imply a thief. It's what we nicknamed the Saxon savages in the old days.'

'I like it,' he told her. 'I'll be known as Tóraí Tairngire until I change back into my dog self.'

'Toh-ree Tah-eerun-gee-ree,' Sianan repeated. 'Tóraí the Seer.'

She looked at her red-haired friend with a squint of scrutiny.

'*Are* you a Seer?'

'Flidais told me the Sight would be my gift as long as I walk about as a man. Once I become a dog again I won't retain the art of seeing.'

'That's a fine gift you've been given!' Sianan nodded. 'May it bring you nothing but joy. Will you change back to a dog eventually?'

'I will,' he replied. 'Flidais told me the enchantment would disappear at dawn or when I cross back into the waking world. I'm relieved to know it. I've often wondered what it would be like to have the body, speech and wits of a man, but to be perfectly honest I'd just as soon be a dog.'

A thought struck Sianan. 'If you've been granted the gifts of a Seer you won't have any trouble finding your way to Aoife's feasting chamber.'

Tóraí closed his eyes tight to concentrate. When he opened them again he smiled.

'That was easy,' he shrugged, impressed with his new

ability. 'Let's follow the path back to the bridge. The Redcap city is not far from there.'

'Tell me something else,' she cut in. 'Is Mawn really imprisoned within the depths of this pool?'

'He is,' Tóraí nodded without hesitation. 'There are two ways to release him. Either Flidais agrees to let him go or ...' He hesitated.

'Or?'

'The bonds of his imprisonment will break if Flidais should happen to perish,' he told her.

'That's not very likely,' Sianan laughed. 'She's the Goddess of the Hunt.'

'Robert FitzWilliam is on his way to kill her even as we speak,' Tóraí told her. 'I can see him in my mind's eye. He's been set a quest to fulfil. It involves cutting off the head of Flidais. If he succeeds it will certainly end her long life.'

'Why would Robert be seeking to murder Flidais?'

'The quest was set to him and he is bound to follow it to the end.'

'Did Aoife put him up to it?' Sianan sighed with resignation.

'She did.'

'But Flidais is raising a rebellion against the Queen of the Night. We don't want anything to interfere with that plan. The Goddess of the Hunt might just put an end to Aoife's ambitions. If Robert gets to her before we do we'll have to rely on Draoi-enchantments to defeat her.'

She grabbed Tóraí's sleeve.

'Can you see what will happen? Is the future clear for you or is it only the present moment you can scry?'

He shook his head slowly in disappointment.

'I can only see what has already come to pass,' he admitted. 'Nothing of the future.'

Then he added, 'We'd best be off to find Flidais.'

Sianan looked down into the pool, offering a silent farewell to Mawn. She picked up a pebble and tossed it in. When the last ripple had died away she stood up again. By then Tóraí had already run off down the road ahead of her. So she tore herself away from Mawn's pool to follow on after him.

A funny thing happened to Tóraí then. He was almost out of sight of Sianan when he realised what he was doing. He'd briefly lapsed into his old dog ways.

He stopped scratching his ear and realised that he'd been sniffing a tree with a view to emptying his bladder across it. He shook himself, determined to act as a man as long as he was walking in a man's body. Tóraí went round behind the tree out of sight. And when he emerged he waited patiently for his companion to catch up. As soon as she was alongside him he coughed nervously.

'Do you mind if I walk along with you?' he asked.

'Not at all,' Sianan replied. 'It would be a pleasure to talk with you as we travel.'

'Really?' he asked with a small tear of joy welling in his eye. 'You'd like to talk with me?'

'This is a rare and wonderful opportunity to get to know you better,' she told him. 'And we only have a short while before you change back into your true form.'

'May I ask a question?' he ventured shyly.

'Yes, Tóraí, of course you may. And you don't need to enquire whether you may ask me something. Just go ahead and ask. You're a man now. We're equals in all things.'

He thought about that and stood a little taller, pushing his shoulders back. It dawned on him that there might be some good points about having shed his dog body.

'I told you I'd imagined myself as a man and had even come up with a name for myself.'

'Yes,' Sianan replied, wondering where this line of

questioning was headed.

'In the past whenever you've been daydreaming about being a dog, what name did you choose for yourself?'

The abbess opened her mouth to speak, but then realised that her answer might offend him. In all her long life Sianan had never once wondered what it would be like to be a dog.

'If I were a dog I'd just like to be called Sianan,' she sputtered, mildly embarrassed. 'I'm used to that name.'

The reply seemed to satisfy the newly two-legged Seer. But his question had certainly given Sianan a different perspective on things, I can tell you.

The Broken Nose

G uy the Younger sat on the bridge staring down into the steadily rushing waters of the river, his feet dangling over the edge. He looked remarkably like a young lad lost in his musings about the world.

His great-grandfather, Guy the Elder, nudged me in the arm.

'Go over to him. He is in need of comfort.'

I nodded enthusiastically and did as I was told. Guy the Elder returned to his discussion with Órán. I managed to slow my pace from a skip to a moderate walk before I reached the bridge. I didn't want to startle the poor man.

'Go away,' the Norman whined without taking his eyes off the water. 'I want to be left alone.'

'How are you, my lord?' I stammered.

'Go away!' he insisted.

'What do you see in the waters, my lord?' I inquired.

He didn't reply.

'My lord?'

I approached as quietly as I could. His eyes were glassy. His expression empty. He was concentrating on something he'd seen in the river.

'What is it, my lord?'

He still didn't reply. You see, Guy the Younger had drifted into a little trance. It had been a day and a night since he'd rested in Aoife's chambers. He was hungry and his body was very tired.

But on top of all that he was confused. Very confused. Before he'd set sail for Ireland he'd been warned about the place. Seasoned hands on the ship across had told stories of giants and ancient ever-living denizens of the forest. He hadn't taken much notice at the time. But he was starting to feel as if their tall tales weren't that tall after all. He'd met giant worms and immortals. His great-grandfather had turned up from the dead to join forces with a dæmon to bring him to the throne of the High-Kingship of Ireland. A strange woman had declared her passionate love for him. (The truth is I'm not that strange once you get to know me. But at that stage he didn't. So I can forgive him.) And finally he'd been given a new name. Guy Stronghold. He said the name over and over as he sat there on the bridge. I was starting to get a little worried for him.

'Don't be concerned for that one!' Órán shouted. 'He'll be his old self in no time. He just needs a breather so it can all sink in.'

I turned back to Guy.

'My lord? Would you like a drink?'

'By all the saints,' he replied as he closed his eyes. 'I wish we had some.'

I'd meant water of course. He had a mind for something stronger.

'Go away.'

I sat down three paces behind him on the bridge because I was totally infatuated with him. Like a loyal servant I waited. Guy said nothing more to me but I wanted to be there when he came to his senses, gathered me up in his arms and spoke romantic drivel in my ear. I was that far gone.

In the meanwhile d'Alville struggled to think of himself as Stronghold. The name echoed in his head as if it had haunted him all his life, lurking in the crypt of his heart like a ghostly presence. He stared down at the dark waters rushing beneath the bridge.

The high bright moon reflected in the rippling swirling river as Guy repeated his new name in his thoughts. It wasn't long before the change started to take place. If you consider all he'd been through, it wasn't remarkable his transformation had begun now in earnest.

We of the Culdee folk used to refer to this first awakening of the soul as the Ruathar. But it was also known as the Onset. It takes many forms, each as unique as the individual undergoing the change. For Guy the Onset was taking the form of a vision.

As he stared down into the shimmering waters of the river the moonlight was clothed in various shapes before his eyes. At first these forms were either flashes of a scene or a face. But then Guy sighed out a deep breath and the Onset visions overcame him in earnest. The light on the water revealed a battlefield. He could see down from on high as a raven might see all the world spread out before him.

It was night and all the world was bathed as it was now in the moon's unwavering glow. In the distance Guy glimpsed fires, lanterns and flashes of reflected moonlight. So he willed the raven to fly him down toward them.

A hill came into view It was the rath where the people of the Killibegs had settled for the winter. The fires were all around the hill marking the encampment of an enemy host. Within the rath there were no fires. Warriors dressed in furs and long cloaks stood close together in twos and threes on the battlements to keep warm.

Women and children wrapped themselves in winter wools as they huddled within the stone houses of the settlement. Guy marvelled that he could see behind walls. He was amazed that he merely had to turn his attention to some detail and everything about it would be revealed.

To test this ability he concentrated on the tower of the rath.

Immediately he was able to see within to the place where he'd sat at council with the elders of the Killibegs and the chieftains of the Gael.

The hall was empty now except for one old man dressed in mail and a long white surcoat. He had straggly grey hair and a whitening beard. Instantly Guy knew this was William FitzWilliam, the father of Robert.

He realised, with some surprise, that he could look into the old man's heart. And when he did it almost took his breath away. For he saw the whole of Lord William's life. To begin with Guy saw Will when he was but twenty.

Our William was renowned for his chivalrous nature when he was a younger man. He'd fought with honour for King Henry and been rewarded for his valour with lands in Ireland. When he first arrived with his wife there were other Norman lords already occupying the land granted to William by the king. He had to fight them off, build his first humble timber fort, win over the Gaels who lived nearby and establish himself as a lord with authority to dispense the king's justice. It took him ten years, but through all the hardship William never once despaired that he would succeed.

Many Norman lords in those days certainly came to Ireland only thinking to rob the people through harsh taxes and theft. But not William. He'd been sent by King Henry because the king knew he could depend on him to do his best for the people placed under his care and keep the rogue lords in check.

All of which he did.

Guy could see William was a truly chivalrous man. He cared for those less fortunate than himself. He did not judge as barbarous the customs of the Irish simply because he didn't understand them.

He always sought out the best attributes in anyone he came into contact with. He offered encouragement. He fostered cooperation. He listened to the stories of other people's lives for clues to the riddle of his own.

William FitzWilliam saw to it that no one within his jurisdiction ever went hungry or lacked fuel for their hearth fire. His Irish chamberlain was also his trusted friend. His household servants were adopted into his family. They were not servants at all really. They worked for their lord out of a genuine love and concern for his wellbeing.

What a man he'd been! And as if he hadn't done enough good in the world, he wanted to do more. After the death of his beloved wife Eleanor, William went off to the Holy Land to offer his life to the service of the crusade.

His acts of bravery and battle craft earned him the indebtedness of both noble and knockabout. His friends had no doubt they could trust him. His enemies were of the same mind. He was an exemplary knight and a true nobleman.

Guy's vision focused on this old man seated in the hall of Killibegs. He was weary, hungry and cold. But he was not despondent. There was a light in his eyes as he sat there before the cold lifeless hearth. He leaned on a sword. It was point down and his hands clasped about the cross of the hilt. He was praying silently; his eyes wide open. Now this struck Guy as a little strange. But then he realised what William was expressing.

It is still heresy to speak of this even in these days so I'll be brief.

Guy had witnessed William's understanding of the oneness of all things. Guy, the tough, battle-hardened thug that he was, saw with clarity that he and William were not two but one. They were both expressions of the same God in two of His manifestations. This was the truth which the Culdees no less than the Cathars of the south had preserved in their secret doctrines.

Guy suddenly saw his own life as petty, cruel and pointless. He was ashamed to compare it with the exemplary existence of

William FitzWilliam. To be sure there once was a time in Guy's life when he would have looked on the old knight with contempt. But he regarded old Will with new eyes. Now he could see the value of a life well lived. Now he wanted to change.

The nature of his vision shifted at that moment. In his sight Lord William arose from his prayer, put on his old-style conical helm then went to the door. He was on his way to the battlements.

As he opened the door the wind howled in, scattering countless tiny flakes of wafting snow. The entire rath was enveloped in an unexpected snow storm. After he struggled to close the doors Will had to wrap his cloak tightly about him so it wouldn't be torn off by the wind.

Guy could see the whole rath again. Warriors were seated beneath the walls and around the gate, awaiting the enemy assault. William went round to every man or woman under arms and spoke to each with a smile on his face.

Such was the strength of his character and the charisma of his personality that everyone he greeted was left uplifted in their spirits. Lord Will gave all the defenders the confidence that they could hold the rath despite overwhelming odds.

Guy had to admire that. He followed on after the old warrior as he climbed the battlements to look out over the gathered enemy. Dawn was still a long way off. The world was dark, though the full moon was bright enough to give the clouds a strong glow.

Lord William spoke to himself as he looked on the foes assembled before the fortification.

'I should have kept quiet,' he whispered. 'I should have told the people to run. I shouldn't have boasted that I could lead them to victory. Many a man has had his nose broken by his own flapping tongue. I'm about to have mine well and truly punched.'

Guy turned his attention to the enemy. The Norman found he had no trouble seeing whatever it was he wished to focus on even in the thick fall of snow. This is the nature of such visions.

A pair of battle standards cracked in the icy wind. Guy recognised them well enough. The first was the banner of the Order of the Hospital under which he'd fought so many times in the past. The other was the yellow standard of Ollo the Benedictine.

The snowfall ceased as trumpets sounded within the Hospitaller camp. Then other horns, deeper and more menacing, answered in the distance. In the far-off fields to the south Guy could see another force approaching. They were running as fast as they could while still managing to maintain a strict military formation. He'd seen them before. They were Aoife's Redcaps.

A second blast of a horn brought his attention to yet another host of warriors. Their numbers were so great Guy could not estimate how many made up their force. They were warriors not unlike the Redcaps and they were hurrying along in the same neat formation from the north.

It looked certain they would converge on the rath at the same time as those from the south. The fortress would be assailed from two directions. The Culdees were hopelessly outnumbered.

Guy sensed that William understood this only too well. But the old man didn't let a hint of doubt show on his face. He drew his sword as he offered words of encouragement to those around him. In contrast to old Will's calm, Guy started to panic. His heart raced as he felt the overwhelming urge to help this noble warrior save his people from a terrible fate.

The army of the Knights of the Hospital had formed into their ranks of foot soldiers and mounted men. Archers stepped forward at the foot of the hill awaiting the command to loose their deadly shafts toward the fortification.

Bishop Ollo rode up and down behind the ranks, shouting curses, threats and damnation at each and every warrior who stood waiting to assault the rath. His words were fire.

'The heretics will burn!' Ollo bellowed. 'You are the Knights of Christ! This is the Great Crusade. Do not suffer any of the evil-doers to live. This is our country now. The time of the mystics is ended.'

Guy swallowed hard as he waited for the knights to advance. But they did not. They stood their ground, chanting prayers in Latin, soliciting the support of their god in defeating these heretics.

The Redcaps were closing in both north and south. Was this an unholy alliance between Church and Aoife? To Guy's mind there was no other explanation for Ollo holding back his attack.

He understood these Otherworld warriors were immortals. There was only one way to put any of them in the grave. And that was to separate head from shoulders at the neck. Wound them in any other manner and they would simply stand up to fight again in moments, magically healed by the Quicken Brew.

These two forces would easily overwhelm the defences. There was no sense in waiting on the battlements for certain death. William's warriors had to find a narrow place to defend where the Redcaps could only face his folk one or two at a time.

The great hall was the answer. It had been built as a Norman defence. Only a few warriors could pass through the main doors at a time. A small company waiting within could hold off an entire army if the walls of the building held.

The next flash that came to Guy was a funeral pyre such as might have been indulged in by the pagan Norsemen who were his ancestors. A great mound of precious timber as tall as a haystack had been prepared.

Atop this pyre, on a flat space, lay the body of a man dressed

316

in the white robes of the Templar Knights. His long grey hair had been laid out around his head in a great fan. His hands were on the hilt of the upturned sword that lay upon his breast. All that needed to be done was for a torch to be put to the timber.

This was the funeral pyre of William FitzWilliam. The vision was warning Guy that the old lord would die if he stood to fight the Redcaps on the battlements.

Next he saw the lord on the fortress wall again.

'You must hide from the enemy!' Guy told William and for a second it seemed as if the old lord had heard the warning.

He hesitated. He observed the approaching forces. But he did not call his warriors to withdraw within the hall.

'You must make for cover before the Redcaps arrive,' Guy insisted. 'They will be here soon. You must hide!'

Just then Guy felt a hand at his shoulder. It was me. I'd heard him say those words though he'd spoken them within his vision. And soon after I'd heard the word 'Redcaps' I heard the tramp of many feet approaching down the road.

Guy woke from his vision instantly, heard the marching feet then turned to me. As he looked me deeply in the eye I saw a beauty in his face I'd never noticed before. Truly with each passing moment I was falling deeper and deeper in love with him. Truly, though I could not have known it, a great change was coming over him.

'Take cover!' he told me, shaking me lightly by the shoulders. 'The Redcaps are coming down the road. We must hide beneath the bridge.'

With those words he got the attention of his great-grandfather and Órán. The two of them joined us crouching ankle-deep in water while we waited for the hosts of the Redcaps to pass. Guy's face was pale, though I'm sure it wasn't fear that had struck him. I found out much later it was a change of heart.

Caoimhin walked as fast as his feet would carry him, following on after the warriors. Before long he started to lose sight of the Redcaps so he picked up his pace to a run to catch them. However, it wasn't long before he was beginning to tire. He crossed the bridge just tailing their company.

Of course old Guy, his son, Eterscél and I were hiding beneath the bridge as they passed. It was only after they'd gone by that I dared look out, and that's when I saw Caoimhin tagging along behind the warriors.

I opened my mouth to call out but Guy the Younger put his hand over my mouth and dragged me back beneath the bridge.

'Don't be a fool!' he hissed. 'Be quiet!'

So Caoimhin stumbled by without guessing for a moment I was hiding there. And it was just as well. Heavens knows, it would have been a right mix-up if he'd seen me. He'd have been following me around like a lost ferret while I swooned after Guy. And who knows, if he had seen me perhaps he would never have encountered Srón and then . . .

I almost jumped ahead of myself then. Do forgive me. Each part of the story must be told in its proper place.

Caoimhin followed on after the Redcaps for a long way once they'd crossed the bridge. But when he came to a crossroads he had to stop for a few moments to make sure he was following the right tracks. By the time he'd worked out which path to take, the warriors were way ahead. He hitched up his long Benedictine robes again and ran as fast as he could. But he could no longer hear the jingle of their war gear nor the steady tramp of their feet.

At length the forest became much closer and the moonlight was stifled by thick cloud. There was still just enough light to see by but Caoimhin couldn't make out any Redcap footprints in the mud by the road.

He began to become concerned he might have lost the band of warriors. So he halted to catch his breath. The sounds of the forest were everywhere. Owls hooted wildly in the woods. The leaves of many trees whispered on the breeze.

Suddenly Caoimhin sensed he was not alone.

Just ahead of him he noticed two figures. One was standing perfectly still in the shadows of a tree. The other was lying down on the side of the road. He froze.

'Who's there?' he ventured after a while. 'Why don't you come out into the light?'

Neither offered any reply. Caoimhin summoned his courage and took a few steps closer. The stranger didn't move, not even as Caoimhin came within five paces of him. But by then the young monk had realised why. It wasn't a living breathing creature at all. It was a crude pagan idol carved of wood.

He ran his fingers over the fine workmanship, marvelling at the artistry. He'd never seen anything like it. It was about the same size as a man, but its features were not realistically interpreted. The face was long and narrow with huge eyes and a thin nose. The pointed chin was sharpened to a tip. The mouth was distorted into an oval as if the god within were crying out in anguish. The figure had a long tail like a herring.

But it was only wood.

Emboldened, Caoimhin approached the other idol standing closer to the trees. It, too, was a strangely executed representation but there was clearly no life in the piece. Caoimhin had to laugh a little at how jittery he'd become.

However, his amusement was short-lived because suddenly a great weight crashed down upon him from above and he fell forward with the force of it. As he landed the wind was knocked out of him so it was all he could to roll over to fend off any further attacks. When he did turn over he was surprised at what he saw. It was the Redcap chieftain.

'Why do you follow Redcaps?' he asked with a long bony finger pointed directly in the young monk's face. His words were stilted and considered, as if he hadn't spoken the Gaelic language in a long, long while. 'Why? Do you work for Aoife?'

Caoimhin shook his head.

'Whatever gave you that idea? I'm following you because you're going to the Killibegs to attack. I want to find my way back there.'

The Redcap chieftain leaned closer as his chariot rattled onto the scene.

'We're not going to Killibegs. We're going to Aoife's hall. We are Redcaps of Flidais. We fight against Aoife.'

The charioteer called out urgently to his chieftain but the Redcap was concentrating on Caoimhin.

'If you're not going to the Killibegs, how will I get back there?' the monk cried in disappointment. 'Aoife is planning a huge assault on the rath. They'll need every hand. My true love is there. I must not abandon her.'

The chieftain laid a friendly hand upon the monk's shoulder to calm him. Then he peered closely at him, trying to decide whether or not he could trust him.

'Are you an enemy of Aoife?'

Caoimhin nodded and the Redcap seemed to come to a decision.

'Aoife is not going to attack your people. Soon Aoife will be gone.'

The chieftain punched his palm to emphasise his meaning. The monk's eyes widened with wonder as the Redcap charioteer hissed at his war-leader. The chieftain ignored him.

'You go home now,' the Redcap told him. 'We go to war.'

'How do I get home?' the young monk pleaded. 'What road do I take?'

The chieftain sat back to consider the question. But in the end he had to admit he didn't know the answer for certain. With a shrug he drew his knife from his belt to draw a rough map in the mud at the roadside.

'Follow this path back to crossroads. Turn right. At next crossroads turn left. Then go into dark forest. A gate is there. It maybe take you home.'

'Thank you,' Caoimhin offered sincerely. 'Farewell and good luck. If you succeed you will save the lives of everyone at the Killibegs.'

'Goodbye.'

Then the charioteer yelled something sharp in the Redcap language and the chieftain leaped onto the back of the war-cart. In the next breath the charioteer had called to the horses and they were off down the road. The chieftain waved at him. And Caoimhin never saw him again.

The monk squatted there on the roadside staring after them until they'd disappeared from view. Then he sat back and crawled over to a nearby ancient yew and sat down against the trunk among the roots. He was tired but not too tired to give in. A short rest was all he needed, he told himself. A short rest and he'd be all right to go home.

His legs ached and he was terribly cold. But the moon emerged then from the clouds that had been intermittently shrouding it all evening. The light was bright enough to read by. So Caoimhin slipped his satchel over his shoulder, untied the leather straps and took out the Book of Destiny.

He closed his eyes to clear his mind. Then he asked the book a question. What should he do next? The manuscript fell open and Caoimhin eagerly read the inscription on the vellum.

'Say only a little but say it well,' he read aloud.

Disappointed, he tucked the book away, briefly glancing at the cover of another manuscript he knew to be titled the Book of Letters. He'd glanced at it when he'd inherited the books after the death of his teacher. But he'd not had the opportunity to make a close study of any of the manuscripts.

All around the yew there were dozens of the strange purple-black flowers he'd seen earlier and which Sianan had warned him not to pick. But she wasn't here now and his heart was pining for me.

So he did a most dangerous thing. He picked them all. Then he settled down against the roots of the yew to weave me a garland as a gift. I suppose he had it in his head to bring me something back from the Otherworld, either to prove to me he'd been there or simply as a token that I'd not been out of his thoughts for a second. He was a sweet lad.

When he'd finished his garland he carefully packed it into a wide pocket of his book satchel where it would not be crushed. Then he shut his eyes to get a little rest. But as I've told you before, my dear, there are some things you should never do when you're travelling in the Otherworld. And one of them is to shut your eyes to sleep. For there is nothing more troublesome than a dream in the Land of Dreams.

It shouldn't surprise you to learn that Caoimhin fell immediately into a brief but vivid vision-dream. In this sleep he opened the Book of Letters and, following the instructions contained therein, constructed a strange sign made up of many letters melded into one.

As soon as he'd done that he scribed the sign into the bark of the very tree against which he was sleeping. Suddenly a host of warriors appeared from out of nowhere. They knelt down before Caoimhin and offered their allegiance to him. They promised to defend the Killibegs down to the last warrior among them. And they looked much like the Redcaps he'd just encountered.

In the next instant he was seated by a dark pool where he had the sense he'd just engaged in a very frustrating conversation. A stranger was seated beside him. He was soaked to the skin. Caoimhin removed his cloak to cover the man and keep the cold air off him. Then the monk realised he was dressed only in his undershirt.

He looked up as he heard a frantic flap of wings. A great black raven flew down from on high and perched upon the branch above him.

'At last I've found you!' the bird cried jubilantly. 'You must follow me. We go to the Killibegs with all haste. A terrible disaster has befallen us. There is no time to lose. Sianan has been searching for you. She will be overjoyed I have found you.'

Caoimhin got the impression the raven was not addressing him but the stranger wrapped in his cloak.

'I have an army,' Caoimhin offered.

'And you will need every one of them by your side if you are to save the Killibegs and all who dwell there. This night is hardly over. Dawn will be a bloody red.'

The raven spread its wings and cackled one last thing before departing.

'Say only a little but say it well.'

Caoimhin woke as soon as the bird had finished speaking. He was startled by the clarity of the dream. He opened his satchel without a second thought to retrieve the Book of Letters.

Now I'm sure you've realised this Book of Letters was another version of the Book of Signs Mugwort had found among the manuscripts Guy stole from the Killibegs. As I've said, the theory of sign magic is very simple.

Take a desire, distil it, then express it in a sign which coalesces the wish into a symbol. Mugwort's method involved burning the sign, whereas Caoimhin's book recommended keeping the finished sign about one's person or leaving it to hang up. Both methods prescribed forgetting the original purpose the Sigil was created for.

Now our lad Caoimhin was already gifted in the dreaming department. It's through that dreaming state that sigils are best crafted if they are to work properly. That's why many books on the subject advise one to forget the wish and commit nothing but the sign to memory.

It didn't take Caoimhin long to read the opening chapter which explains this to the reader. And because he'd just had a dream about this book and its magic he didn't think he needed to read the chapter of warnings. Why is it no one takes any notice of the warnings?

In a few seconds he had his charcoal writing stick unpacked and was making notes in the margin of the manuscript. First of all he wrote down his wish. He read it aloud once he thought he'd worded it right.

'It is my will that an army shall come to the aid of the Killibegs to save all in their time of need.'

Satisfied this statement was exactly what he desired, Caoimhin started playing around with the letters. First of all he crossed out any that had been repeated. Then he looked for one letter to use as a central form.

If you're thinking this wasn't very monkish behaviour, you'd be right. Caoimhin knew what his teacher would say if he were here. But he didn't care. He was driven on by a sense of love and protectiveness for me.

Yes. The whole reason for him indulging in the dangerous practice of sigils in the first place was out of a desire to keep me safe. So I suppose his teacher, my brother, might have forgiven him. But let's not delude ourselves that he'd have been surprised. Eriginas had owned this book for many years. Am I to believe that he had read it from cover to cover and yet never created a sigil for himself? Not bloody likely. He was as inquisitive as the next man. He would have cast a few sign spells in his time. I'm sure of it. So don't judge his student too harshly.

It wasn't long before Caoimhin had come up with his sigil and once he'd worked it out he was ready to carve it into the tree against which he was leaning. He took out his little scribe's knife, the one he used for sharpening goose-feather quills. Then, with the greatest care and attention to detail, he cut the bark away from the mighty yew into the pattern of his magical sign. When it was done he sat back to admire his handiwork.

For a long while nothing happened. He began to doubt that his dream had been influenced by the Otherworld. He began to worry that his ability to see visions of the future had been impeded by the enchantment of this world.

Crestfallen, he began to pack away the Book of Letters. He placed his charcoal stick and penknife back in the pockets at the side of his satchel. Then he shouldered the bag, making ready to march off in the direction the chieftain had advised him would lead to the Killibegs.

He didn't notice two figures quietly moving around behind the tree to take a better look at him. For they were warriors who knew how to move with stealth. He didn't hear one talking under her breath to the other. Nor did he discern the whispered reply.

Caoimhin leaned on his walking stick that had been a gift from Gobann. He thought heard something moving about in the woods but he shrugged it off as the work of his skittish imagination. At last, with a sigh, he berated himself for believing in a heathen, pagan and quite likely heretical practice such as sigil magic.

'I have strayed from my path as a monk,' he berated himself. 'I can't believe I just cast a spell. I've been deluded by that bloody heathen Druid Gobann.'

He was considering whether to abandon the beautiful walking stick when a hand came down hard upon his shoulder. The monk nearly jumped into the lower branches with the shock of it. But the hand held him firm under its weight. Somehow Caoimhin managed to struggle with his assailant. As soon as he was free of the heavy grip he spun round to face his attacker.

He held the stick up to fend off the enemy and caught sight of the owner of that hand. Then he suddenly relaxed. He'd expected the worst. He'd thought perhaps Redcaps loyal to Aoife must have caught him or some other dark denizen of the woods might be about to devour him whole.

But instead of any of these things it was a woman who stood before him. She was a warrior, to be sure. In many ways she was not unlike the Redcaps, but she didn't look as ferocious as the chieftain or his fighters. Her face was full of joy as she grabbed the monk and hugged him close to her.

'Thank you!' she told him over and over as she kissed him on the cheek. 'You've saved us from the curse of Aoife.'

Srón of the Sen Erainn did not let go of Caoimhin till she had wept tears of joy for her release. When she was finished, her companion, Scodán, had a go at him as well.

'I thought we were doomed to an eternity trapped within those bloody wooden idols,' he bawled, his face wet with tears and his voice choked with emotion. 'You saved us. We owe you our lives.'

'Steady on,' Srón cut in as she separated her companion from the monk. 'No need to go that far. We were still alive within the statues. I know it was a bloody strange, stifling and frightening experience but he didn't save our lives. He merely released us from the curse Aoife placed on us. We owe him a debt. That's enough.'

'You ungrateful bastard!' Scodán responded. 'I'd rather have been dead than stuck as an ugly piece of timber for the rest of my days. The thought of being slowly consumed by wood-worm fairly rattled my splinters. As far as I'm concerned, he saved our lives.'

'Are you sure you didn't already get a touch of woodworm in the head?' Srón shot back.

Caoimhin had by now ascertained that the idols had disappeared. So he came to the conclusion from what he'd heard that he must have been somehow responsible for helping these two warriors escape their enchantment. Perhaps, he reasoned, it had something to do with the sigil he'd carved.

'I don't know what I did exactly,' he told them, unwilling to admit he'd been dabbling in spell-craft. 'But I'm glad you're free.'

Srón turned to him with suspicion in her eye.

'Are you a practitioner of the Draoi?' she asked. 'Are you a Druid?'

Caoimhin smiled. He thought it was fairly obvious he was a Christian monk. He recalled the words of Gobann who had told him he wasn't ready yet to take on the mantel of a Druid.

'I'm not a Druid. Not by half. I've a long way to go before I attain to that office.'

'He is a Druid!' Scodán exclaimed. 'He's humble and practised in the Draoi-craft. He dresses strangely for an Ollamh Eolaí Draoi though.'

Srón touched the hem of Caoimhin's sleeve and rubbed the

black wool. 'The cloth is rough as befits one of his rank. It's surely a sign of humility,' she agreed. 'And he did break the enchantment.'

'I'm not a Druid,' Caoimhin protested. 'I'm a Benedictine.'

The Sen Erainn warriors looked at one another blankly and shrugged.

'What's a Benedictine?' Scodán asked.

'I'm a servant of God,' Caoimhin explained. 'I have given my life to the One True God, Holy Mother Church and to study. I'm a scribe. I copy holy manuscripts in the scriptorium. I wouldn't usually be out travelling alone in the wilds but my teacher died and I was left all alone.'

Caoimhin went on to tell them briefly everything that had happened to him since he'd left Wexford. At the end of his story he added one last sentence.

'So you see, I'm not a Druid.'

Scodán took his friend by the arm and led her out of Caoimhin's hearing.

'Excuse us for a moment, will you?' Srón apologised. 'We're here on secret business. We need to exchange a few words together in private.'

'He's a Druid!' Scodán whispered under his breath. 'He released us from the bonds of Aoife. He might be able to help us in our duty.'

Srón put a hand to her chin as she considered what her companion had said.

'He might be one of Aoife's own people,' she warned. 'I've heard about these Christians. They're cannibals!'

'Cannibals?' Scodán repeated with a quiver in his voice. 'Do they eat their enemies?'

'They feast on the body of their god,' Srón explained. 'Their priests distribute the corpse at their feasts. But I've heard tell their god does not submit to the sacrifice himself. He is represented by a willing victim.'

'Willing or not, it isn't right. How do we know that Christian Druid isn't going to carve one of us up for dinner?'

Scodán was shaking as he went on. 'I'm a warrior so I'm no stranger to blood and battle but this is another thing entirely. Forgive me if I don't feel all that comfortable with having been rescued from Aoife's clutches only to be slaughtered like a lamb for the sake of some heathen practice too abominable to even think about.'

Srón put a hand on his shoulder and leaned in to whisper in his ear.

'Take a look at him,' she suggested. 'He doesn't look like the kind of fellow who could do us much harm. There are two of us and only one of him. I say we take him with us. His Draoi-craft may come in handy.'

'I'm not sure, Srón, my dear. You're not such a fine judge of character.'

'What do you mean by that?' she shot back indignantly.

'Look at who you've chosen for a partner in this enterprise,' he noted with a smile. 'If I'd been you I wouldn't have settled on me to help you out.'

'I chose you because I can trust you,' Srón assured him. 'You may have shortcomings as a warrior but your loyalty and your occasional courage count for more with me than your skill with a war sickle. Of all the host of the nine hundred Sen Erainn I wouldn't have had any other by my side but you.'

'That's very flattering,' Scodán admitted shyly. 'I'll try to live up to your confidence in me.'

'Then listen to my opinion. We should trust the Druid.'

'Find out whether he works for Aoife or not,' Scodán suggested.

Srón turned to Caoimhín and asked him bluntly: 'Are you a servant of Aoife, Queen of the Night?'

'I told you. I'm a servant of God. A man cannot serve two masters.'

'Was that an answer?' Scodán whispered urgently to his companion.

Srón rolled her eyes in frustration. Then she addressed the monk again.

'We've come here ahead of the warriors of our people to find a well which is said to confer a blessing upon those who drink from it. It is our plan to fill as many water-skins as we can carry, then take them to our warriors to drink before we do battle with Aoife's Redcaps. If we are successful we could save our hosts a lot of trouble. They will be immune to weaponry for a while after tasting the waters.'

'We could save many lives,' Scodán added.

'Are you trying to convince me that these waters will confer some form of immortality?' Caoimhin asked incredulously.

'No. But a draught from the well will keep death at a distance for a while,' Srón replied.

'I'm sorry, I find that very hard to believe,' he laughed. 'If God had wanted us to live without death he would have given us that gift from birth.'

'Aoife is immortal,' Scodán noted. 'The Redcaps are immortal. Perhaps your god did not create them?'

'God created all things. God is all things.'

'Then your god also granted the Queen of the Night the curse of immortality.'

'I've never met Aoife,' Caoimhin told him. 'But I've encountered some Redcaps. They didn't seem to be any different to you or me.'

'Redcaps?' Srón hissed. 'You've been among the Redcaps?'

'Yes,' he nodded. 'They were here not long ago. I was their prisoner. But they let me go free. They've gone to Aoife's feasting hall to prepare an ambush.'

'Then we must hurry if we're going to find the well,' Srón stated. 'We've slept in those wooden prisons too long. The trouble is about to begin. Let us make haste, Druid.'

'I can't accompany you, I'm afraid. I'm headed back to the Killibegs,' Caoimhin told them. 'My people need me.'

'Do you know the road to the Well of Many Blessings?' Srón asked. 'If you do, your guidance could save us precious time.'

Of course he'd heard of the Well of Many Blessings. Flidais had called her well by that name. But Caoimhin had no wish to go there now. He wanted only to return to the Killibegs.

'Will you come with us?' Srón begged. 'Your Draoi-craft could be invaluable to our cause.'

'I will go with you part of the way, for my road leads back in the direction of the river. My companion, Sianan, was almost certain the well lay over the bridge at the end of the road which passes that way. I was separated from her. Perhaps she found the well.'

'We'll walk with you until our paths diverge,' Srón agreed. 'And any help you can offer us will be most welcome.'

So they set off back along the road. And though he'd set about constructing the magical sigil and carved it into a tree, our monk still didn't like to think his spell had freed the two Sen Erainn.

That's another of the mighty dangers when you're working with enchantments. If you don't know what to look for you might not even realise you've cast an enchantment at all. It's easy enough to explain Draoi-craft away as good fortune. But believe me, there's no such thing as coincidence. There's no smoke without fire. And there's no enchantment without a result of some description.

Whether the outcome is what the Draoi-master had intended or not is another matter.

SWEET TO LISTEN TO

Sianan and Tóraí crossed the bridge shortly after the two Guys set off with me and Eterscél back to the Killibegs. They missed us, and since they were in a hurry to reach Aoife's hall they didn't notice the bridge-keeper's house was left open to the elements.

That is until the Seer stopped in the middle of the road and raised his nose to the wind.

'I smell something familiar,' he told his travelling companion. 'What do you think it is?'

Sianan sniffed at the air in this direction and that but she couldn't pick up whatever it was Tóraí had caught whiff of.

'I'm sorry,' she apologised.

He sniffed again a few times.

'I'd swear I smell Normans,' he told her. 'That odour of unwashed grime is difficult to forget. Believe me, I've tried.'

He gave a sharp intake of breath and grabbed Sianan's hand.

'It's Guy d'Alville,' he hissed. 'He's been here. Recently.'

'How is that possible?' Sianan laughed. 'I find it hard to believe Guy would be wandering around in the Otherworld. The last we heard of him was after the fight with Robert. He ran off with his tail between his legs.'

'He might have followed us here,' Tóraí shrugged.

'Let's go on,' Sianan suggested. 'We've enough to think

about without concerning ourselves with Guy. But if you catch wind of anything else be sure to tell me.'

With that they doubled their pace. The night seemed as if it had already gone on for three nights. So much had happened. Indeed, that is part of the enchantment of the Otherworld. As I've told you, time runs differently in that place.

'How far to Aoife's chambers?'

'Not far,' Tóraí assured her. 'If you don't mind keeping pace with me we'll be there before you can bark yourself hoarse.'

She laughed at the curious manner in which he measured time.

That was the last chance she had to think about anything but dodging tree roots and avoiding rocky outcrops for a while. After that they were off across country as fast as their feet would ferry them.

Now it would be true to say that before he journeyed to the Otherworld Guy d'Alville was a hard, cruel man. He'd rarely ever considered the wellbeing of his fellow man unless it served some purpose in his designs.

I knew the bastard. I can tell you without fear of contradiction – he didn't have any saving graces. There was not a single feature about his character that folk might class as redeeming. But on the road through the realm of the Otherworld he began to change. I'm not saying this journey marked an immediate turnaround in his character. Not at all. There were some things about Guy that simply could not have been fixed.

Yet he began to develop a sincere desire to turn his life around for the better. And in no small part he had his great-grandfather to thank for pointing him in the right direction.

I listened intently as the two men sparred with one another. Guy the Elder must have been quite a man in his youth. Some of his ideas seemed quaint and old-fashioned so I had to smile when Guy the Younger took issue with them.

'Women are for breeding,' my love protested. 'They have not been granted the mental faculties required to rule a kingdom.'

'Queen Eleanor ruled the kingdom,' I cut in. 'She was wife to King Henry who left her in charge of England while he was off in France. Then his son King Richard left her to reign while he went off to the Holy Land.'

'Queen Eleanor could read and write,' young Guy conceded. 'She was a woman of culture. But there are not many like her in the world.'

'I can read and write,' I smiled sweetly. 'I have Latin, Greek, Norman French, Gaelic and I understand the Anglo-Saxon tongue. Of course I've also studied some Arabic. But I'm not fluent.'

I paused for effect.

'Yet.'

Guy looked at me with a new interest.

'But you are a peasant,' he said dismissively.

'I am the noble daughter of a noble house. For we Culdees are all considered nobles in this country. What is nobility to you Normans? Among your people all a man has to do to claim a title is go off to war, kill an opponent and hold his lands.'

'There's more to it than that,' Guy countered, but I didn't give him a chance to say another word.

I explained it to him as I would have done to a child. The Normans are such children after all. We Irish see nobility in achievement. Thus a musician of great skill, learning and talent may be considered a noble among our folk. Anyone who gives their life to the path of holy contemplation is likewise considered noble. Nobility is not a reflection of what one may own or acquire. It's a measure of one's spirit.

The older Guy cut in between us, whispering furtively to me.

'Don't interrupt!' he hissed. 'I know you mean well but I don't want to frighten the lad off. These things need to be revealed to him gently. I'm not sure he's ever been confronted with the real values of chivalry. Now walk on ahead and leave us be for a while.'

'I'm a warrior,' the younger Guy snapped, losing his patience. 'I'm a knight. I have seen battle. I have known death. Chivalry has nothing to do with those things.'

The old man looked at me as if to indicate these comments proved his point. Then he waved me on ahead.

'The mouth that does not speak is sweet to listen to,' old Guy pointed out.

'Are you telling me to be quiet?' the younger retorted.

The old knight rolled his eyes. 'Someone has to, since you do not know when to be silent.'

'That's it! I've had enough of your insults. You're a stupid old bastard. How could you possibly be my great-grandfather? We're not related.'

'To think my bloodline should fall to this!' the old man sighed. 'This oaf! This arrogant halfwit. This insensitive, selfish sword-sharp. He's not fit to clean my squire's boots.'

'You don't have a squire,' Eterscél reminded the old man.

'You're right!' the elder Guy exclaimed. 'Then my great-grandson shall be my squire. It'll teach him manners.'

'I will not!' Guy scoffed. 'A knight doesn't clean the boots of another man. A noble doesn't stoop to serving those who are less than him.'

'He does if he wants to get by in the world,' old Guy noted. 'Do you want to earn the respect of others? Do you want the unswerving loyalty of your people? Do you want to be worshipped?'

'Of course I do!'

'Then you must learn to serve others. It's the only way to convince them you are worthy of their loyalty.'

'That doesn't make sense,' young Guy shot back.

'Try it. It is the basis of chivalry. Such actions prove you do not suffer from pride. Or sloth.'

Then the old knight whispered something into his great-grandson's ear. The younger d'Alville raised his eyebrows and shook his head vehemently.

'I won't do it!'

'Trust me. It will earn the respect of those you wish to rule,' old Guy assured him. 'The story will spread from mouth to mouth. You'll be remembered for an act of selfless gentlemanly behaviour. You do want to be known as Stronghold, don't you? You do want to become High-King of Ireland?'

The younger knight thought for a few moments. He nodded.

'Then do as I tell you!' old Guy commanded. 'I'm your tutor. You'll do as I say or you'll forfeit the opportunity to rise to the highest office in the land.'

Young Guy started to protest but Eterscél spoke up.

'I must agree with your great-grandfather. I can't throw my support behind a man who doesn't know how to behave properly toward those of lesser rank. And if you can't be chivalrous I certainly won't honour our bargain.'

'We had an agreement!' Guy spat. 'You assured me I'd be in charge of our course through life.'

'And so you will be. But only if you show me how chivalrous you can be,' the spirit told him.

Young Guy swallowed his pride and decided it was worth giving the old man's suggestion a try. He picked up his pace a little till he'd caught up with me.

'Are you tired, Mistress Binney?' he asked as politely as he could manage. It was obvious he wasn't at all comfortable.

I shook my head, wondering what he was on about.

'Are your feet weary from the road?' he enquired tersely.

'Yes of course they are,' I frowned.

'Then I shall carry you for a while,' he stated, casting glances back at his great-grandfather to seek approval.

The old man nodded, gesturing for him to go ahead. Then, without warning, young Guy lifted me up and threw me across his shoulder. He winded me a little but I didn't care. Guy d'Alville, the object of my infatuation, was carrying me. I was ecstatic.

That was the turning point in his life. After that he truly began to mellow.

Srón, Scodán and Caoimhin made their way back along the path with as much stealth as they could muster. Scodán said very little. He was on guard, wary of every sound, listening out for the noise of bees swarming in particular.

Srón asked our lad about his strange attire. She'd never met a Christian monk before. She'd heard of them of course. A few missionaries had come to Inis Mór in the ancient days before the Norse sea-raiders plied the waves, waging war on the unwary. The few who had come to the bleak islands of Aran did not stay long. Not many folk from the world beyond ever stayed among the Sen Erainn for more than a hand-count of seasons. It wasn't because the fisher folk were inhospitable either.

I've been over there myself so I speak from experience. Their welcoming of strangers is the warmest to be had anywhere among the living lands. They are generous with their feasting, boisterous with their drinking and heavy-handed with their hospitality in general. No one leaves that place without the fondest thoughts for the folk who live there.

It's the island itself that dislikes outsiders. The journey across is perilous. Monstrous seas abound with monstrous sea monsters in the straits between Gaillimh and the islands. That in itself might not be such a terrible thing if it were possible to take a sturdy ship across those waters. But there is nowhere for such a vessel to land. So anyone wishing to cross those seas must do so in a small leather curragh. You'd probably prefer not to know that I almost soiled myself with fright the first time I went across. I didn't understand then that I was in no danger. These people are the finest sea folk who've ever dipped an oar. They live by the rhythm of the harsh, unyielding wash of tide and tempest. Salt runs in their blood.

Their lives are short but all their living days are filled with humour, love and gratitude for the gift of life. I have travelled the wide world, you know. I've dwelled among people of the desert and folk of the sea. And the kindest, most considerate, the most content and best hosts are those who must work hard for their living.

I can only guess why this is so. But from my experience those who live easier lives removed from the threat of hunger or the taint of hardship rarely have it in their hearts to be generous with either their time or their worldly goods.

The Sen Erainn are a generous people, as I have said. And if their island would have had me I'd have stayed there on their rocky outcrop with them and spent the run of my days in happiness and contentment. The truth is their islands aren't for the faint-hearted. The wind never ceases to howl across the flat rock of Inis Mór. It drove me mad in the short time I was there, and I was only there little more than a month. One morning just after dawn I ran out from my stone dwelling to scream back at the wind. I could not match its fury but I certainly equalled it in bloody-minded, pointless shrieking. It was then I decided it might be time to leave.

So it's understandable that Srón knew little of the ways of Christians. None had stayed very long with her folk. Of course she knew the story of Christ. Who could have lived anywhere in Ireland at that time and not heard the tale? It a wondrous hero myth filled with all the classic ingredients of the old Gaelic sagas. And wasn't it Cuchulin who was bound to a tree to await death while the Morrigán sat at his shoulder to accept his sacrifice?

Srón had heard of Christ. No doubt about it. She just hadn't met anyone who had given their life to the Church. So she was a bit surprised such a good-looking young fellow could have made a decision to forego the pleasures of the bedchamber.

Of course, Caoimhin was ready to abandon his vows by the time he met Srón. The love philtre I'd administered made his promise of chastity untenable, to say the least. But he was still very shy about such matters. I know what she was thinking. Every woman knows how alluring a shy, humble, inexperienced man can be. For a while.

So as they shared the road she was content to listen to him speak of his days in the monastery and his journey from Glastonbury to the Killibegs. It was quite an adventure, as you know. And Srón had a way of getting folks to talk about themselves.

It wasn't long before Caoimhin had revealed to her he'd come to the Otherworld with Sianan to track down Aoife. He told her about Toothache who had tried to kill him. And how he'd narrowly escaped death at the hands of that Norman foot soldier.

At last he mentioned me. Srón must have known straightaway that he held me in some affection. She must have sensed there was something amiss with him. He'd spoken so

339

passionately about his vows to the Church and to the Benedictine rule and yet he held a deeper desire for a woman of the Killibegs.

She stopped him in the middle of the road and put a firm hand on his shoulder.

'The poison is still within you,' she told him. 'Whether it be some residue of that tincture which nearly took your life or whether it be some other, you are not yet healed.'

Srón held his head still with both hands and stared into his eyes. Then she forced his mouth open to observe the colour of his tongue. His hands fell under her scrutiny next. She checked his nails, his palms and fingers for stains.

'You've never lifted a sickle in anger,' she smiled, almost in disbelief. 'You've never hauled a fishing net nor leaned upon an oar. You have the hands of a little child, so soft and weak.'

Caoimhin was already nervous at her close proximity. He snatched his hands away from her.

'Come on!' Scodán whispered urgently. 'We must keep moving or the Redcaps will find us. There is a time and a place for flirting.'

'I'm not flirting!' Srón shot back with real indignation. 'The lad is ill. He's been poisoned.'

'Poisoned? And what manner of poison is it?'

'A minor enchantment,' Srón explained, reaching out to touch the monk on the cheek again.

'What manner of enchantment?' Caoimhin managed to ask despite his breathing coming hard and fast.

Srón replied but she did not answer his question.

'You must come with us to the well. If you do not there's no telling what will happen to you.'

'I must go back to the Killibegs,' he protested. 'Binney is waiting for me.'

'If you go back home without first having tasted the waters of the Well of Many Blessings, there's no telling whether you

340

will live long. This is the kind of enchantment that causes men to lose their wits, endanger their lives and throw all caution to the wind. Your body may not be tainted but your mind has been sorely affected.'

By all the hairs of Saint Michael's Unkempt Beard she was right. She'd described the effects of a love philtre down to the last detail.

Our Caoimhin must have sensed he wasn't entirely himself. 'Sianan mentioned something of it to me before we were separated,' he admitted. 'I believe you may speak the truth. She, too, told me I must drink from the well.'

'From what you've told me the situation at the Killibegs is dire,' the warrior-woman went on. 'The last thing those folk need in this time of danger is for you to be running about witless and bewitched. You'll be more trouble than you're worth. In a siege it only takes one foolish act to bring about defeat. You owe it to your friends to seek some healing of this ill so that it does not bring about the downfall of the Killibegs.'

Caoimhin thought about her words for a few moments. He knew in his heart she was right. Yet he didn't want to waste any more time getting back to me. His frantic heart, distracted by the effects of the love potion and filled with impatience to set eyes on the object of his desire, railed against what had to be done.

'Hurry up!' Scodán insisted, showing more than a touch of impatience.

'I'll go with you,' Caoimhin nodded. 'Once I've taken the waters of the well I'll return to my Binney and the Killibegs.'

'Then we must make haste,' she warned him. 'There's no telling what permanent damage the poison has done to you. With every breath that passes from your body the enchantment takes a firmer hold.'

With those words she grabbed him by the sleeve and pulled him on down the path. He stumbled for a few steps, dragging his feet as doubts assailed him. Then he pushed all misgivings to the back of his mind. He lifted his pace to keep up with the two Sen Erainn warriors.

And when she knew the young monk could not see her face, Srón smiled broadly.

FOR GOD AND QUEEN AOIFE

Robert FitzWilliam waited hidden in the bushes by the entrance to the cave. Without doubt he knew this was where he'd find Aoife's feasting hall. And here he'd also find Flidais, who was plotting some act of rebellion against the queen.

As is the way in the Otherworld he had not the slightest idea how he'd come here. Whether he'd been led on by some enchantment or had stumbled on the place, he could not tell. In fact, as I'm sure you've guessed, Aoife had placed him there. She wasn't about to take any chances he'd get himself lost in the forest. He had an important part to play in her plans.

It should be a simple matter, the knight told himself, to seek out Flidais and put an end to her life. He would simply cut off her head, stuff it in a bag and present it to the queen. Quest completed.

Now, you may well ask, what had come over gentle Robert who of late had so earnestly questioned whether he was cut of the right cloth to be a warrior? Here he was, ready to cut the head off a woman he'd never even met at the say-so of another woman he'd only encountered once.

This is the same fellow who had been mindful the Ten Commandments disallowed killing of any kind. Not that the Holy Writ had ever stopped him from slaying the enemy in battle. It's just that lately he'd taken the view that all killing was unacceptable.

Strange it is, I'll grant you that.

But Aoife had played a bit of a trick on him. Indeed she had played more than one trick and not just on Robert. You'll see what I mean. When Robert had supped the honey-scented liquor from the cup he believed to be the Grail, he was swallowing more than he bargained for.

Inasmuch as a drop of ale may cloud the senses or the judgement of a man or woman, so too can the liquors of the Otherworld. Of course, as you would expect, the intoxicants of the Realm of Dreams have a considerable kick. Much more than anything you could expect to encounter in the land of mortals.

So while Robert wasn't flat on his back like a Roman emperor who's downed his first barrel of mead, the honey-scented liquor of Aoife had confounded his senses.

And I'm not even going to go into detail about what tricks Órán had played on him. My goodness! The poor fellow. He must've been well confused.

He took a deep breath, drew his sword then rushed into the cave mouth. Thus he entered the depths of the Redcap fortress.

There were torches to light his way along the corridors so he was able to set a cracking pace. However, it soon became evident he would have a devil of a job getting to the feasting hall without help. There were side tunnels and crossover corridors all along the way. The main tunnel narrowed here and there, making him wonder whether it was going to finish in a dead end.

The first Redcap he encountered made him step back out of sight for fear. The warrior didn't see our Robert. The knight hid in the shadows of a doorway, his heart beating in his chest with terror, until the burly warrior had passed by.

He stayed there for a long while, surprised at his reaction, until he came to the conclusion he had nothing to fear from these folk. After all, it was their queen who'd set him this quest.

It wasn't long before another Redcap came barrelling down the tunnel in his direction. So Robert took a deep breath and stepped out to confront the creature. The warrior hadn't expected to be stopped in the middle of his journey. He pulled up to a halt and stood looking at the white knight with an expression of shock on his face.

'Can you lead me to the feasting hall?' Robert asked politely. 'Queen Aoife has sent me here on a quest.'

The Redcap cocked his head this way and that. He clearly didn't understand a word that was being said to him. He raised his sickle high and growled to force the knight out of his way. Robert lifted his sword instinctively to parry a blow.

The Redcap saw this as a sign of threat, so in the next moment he swung his long-handled weapon round to slice at the stranger. The knight slipped beneath the arc of the blade then thrust his point hard at the warrior's throat. Blood gushed out. The Redcap clutched his neck and his eyes bulged.

Suddenly Robert remembered the only way to kill one of these creatures was to cut off its head. He could see the warrior was full of rage. He knew he wouldn't be able to hold him off for long.

'I don't want to fight you,' he soothed. 'I'm sorry for hurting you.'

The Redcap screamed, lifted his sickle then swung it down hard with a blow that would have cut Robert in two if it had found its mark. But the white knight deftly stepped out of the way so the blade struck the ground.

Robert took his sword in both hands, swinging the weapon over his head. With consummate skill he brought the blade down with all his force upon the exposed neck of the warrior. There was a crunch and a surprised gasp. Then the Redcap fell lifeless to the floor.

Robert had hardly exerted himself but his heart still beat hard in his chest. He sheathed his sword as he bent over to drag the Redcap into the shadows. But this fellow was huge. Robert couldn't shift him.

In the end he had to reluctantly leave the corpse lying there in a pool of blood. He knew it wouldn't be long before his comrades found him. Then the dæmons of this underworld would be set loose to hunt him down.

Indeed, he hadn't run on a further hundred paces into the tunnels when horns began to sound on every side. Voices were raised in anger in the distance. Feet were on the run and they were the feet of outraged Redcaps.

Robert FitzWilliam realised he now had only a small chance of survival unless he made it to Aoife's hall. He could not hide forever down among the Redcap tunnels, in their very midst. He struggled to slow his breathing and calm himself.

The time to strike at Flidais would be of his choosing, he decided. He wouldn't wait for chance to thrust him into the fight. He abandoned all thought of escape from this underworld. Once he'd killed Flidais he fully expected to meet his death.

He found a crevice in the wall where the masonry had subsided. The crack was wide enough to conceal him and deep enough that no Redcap would be able to glimpse his presence as they rushed by in the corridor. So he withdrew into this dark haven for a while to gather his thoughts.

How long he waited there in the half-light I can't tell you. But by the time he finally chose his moment, he'd rehearsed in his mind every detail of the plan down to the smallest possibility.

A figure flitted by the cave passage further down the incline. Robert prayed the Redcap was on his way back to the main chambers and slipped out to follow him. He was a master, our Sir Robert. There's no warrior alive in the world now nor was there then who could have matched him. He followed his Redcap along the winding narrow passages he'd traversed earlier without the warrior ever suspecting he was being tailed.

Whenever another Redcap approached either from behind or in front, Robert concealed himself down a side passage or in the shadows of a doorway. In this manner he came close enough to the great chamber that he could hear music being played for a dance.

He sharpened up his pace a bit more then. He stepped out as quietly and as far as he dared to gain ground on his Redcap. Suddenly the fellow was right in front of him and the two of them were coming to a widening of the tunnel into a junction chamber where several paths met.

Robert held back. He didn't want to have to fight. A skirmish would attract too much attention.

The Redcap had crossed into the junction chamber when he suddenly stopped dead in his tracks to sniff the air. He spun round before Robert had a chance to conceal himself. He growled a threat, levelled his sickle, then issued a challenge in the uncouth dialect of the ancient Fir Bolg.

The Redcap screamed at the top of his lungs. Robert saw he had no choice but to silence the creature. He leaped out into the chamber with his sword raised high. Then he gave a most unusual battle cry.

'For God and Queen Aoife!'

The Redcap raised the broad sickle blade, sliced it through the air a few times and grunted another challenge.

Robert stood steady as he shifted his blade into both hands. He'd taken up one of the defensive stances of the Sword Dance in readiness for attack. His eyes did not leave his opponent's for a second as he stepped forward to swing his weapon.

As Órán's blade sliced the air the spirit within sang a wondrous sighing melody which echoed within the confines of the chamber. The Redcap was taken slightly aback at that. But when the empty space filled with a white light emanating from the young FitzWilliam's body, the poor creature was dazzled.

The Redcap dropped his weapon with a clatter to shield his eyes just as Órán struck off his head. He slumped forward to his knees then fell at Robert's feet. The head rolled off into the darkness and so out of my story.

Robert was left breathing hard and heavy with surprise at what had just happened. He hadn't intended to kill a Redcap. All he'd wanted to do was defend himself. And he hadn't expected Órán could have such a devastating effect on the enemy.

'That was a fine thing,' he told the sword. 'And it was a little too easy.'

'Would you like me to make things more difficult for you?' the spirit of his sword asked. 'I can do that easy enough.'

'Why would you do that?'

'Maybe you'd enjoy the challenge?' Órán offered. 'How should I know? I can make this as easy as you like or as difficult. It's up to you. But if you think I'm going to risk your life for your sense of adventure, think again. I've invested too much of myself in you over the generations to let that happen.'

'You've said all this before,' Robert noted. 'At the risk of sounding impudent, you're starting to affect my nerves with all that talk.'

'By the way, you should make up your mind,' the Frightener advised.

'What are you talking about?'

'You can't go round yelling out, "For God and Queen Aoife." You have to choose between them. One or the other. If you continue to invoke the two of them you're going to alienate them both.'

Robert sighed heavily before he replied.

'Whenever you emerge from that scabbard there's some trouble waiting for me! I'm tired of you. If you keep

348

interfering, how am I going to be able to think clearly enough to escape this underworld of dæmons?'

'Now that's where you've made a fundamental mistake,' Órán noted. 'You see, you're not going to escape this underworld of dæmons as you call it. Not until you've fulfilled your quest, married Aoife and secured her promise that you will be next High-King of Ireland.'

'I don't really want to be High-King of Ireland.'

'I wish you'd make up your mind. How do you know you don't want to be High-King? Have you already had a stint with a crown on your head? Or have you read something that's put you off the idea? Don't trust anything written down in a book. Believe me, I should know. Most of what's written in books was inspired by some Frightener or Enticer and is completely unreliable.'

'I have no desire to be king!'

'That's what you say now. But give it a try. You never know, you might warm to being a royal. What better opportunity for you to show the quality of your leadership? What sort of a man do you think will take the throne if you don't? It won't be a man like yourself whose heart is good, that's for certain.'

'I'm not worthy,' the knight protested.

'You really should cease that false modesty. It doesn't suit you at all. You have a chance to make a real difference in the lives of your fellow Irish folk.'

'I'm not Irish. I'm a Norman,' Robert corrected him.

'For good or ill you've ended up in this land. The place has changed already in your lifetime and there's plenty more changes afoot. There's no looking back for any of us. It doesn't matter whether you were born from the womb of a Gael or not. You're destined to be High-King. I have planned for these events since long ago. I have nurtured your clan and bred your ancestors together judiciously. You are the final result of all that effort down the centuries.'

Robert frowned, dropping the point of his sword to the ground and leaning lightly on it.

'You'll be a magnificent king!' Órán told him. 'You'll be just, honourable and true to your word. You'll not make war unless called to the defence of your realm. And then you'll be a terrible opponent. Your people will worship you as the very ideal of kingly virtue. During your reign all will prosper, hunger will flee and joy will enter every heart.'

'Shut up, Órán,' Robert whispered. 'Do not tempt me.'

'What did you say?' the spirit flashed with mockery. 'You have ideas above your station, Master Robert! You are no saviour come to redeem creation. You may not bestow redemption. You are a mere mortal. And I am not the Devil either, who would take delight in tempting you out of your cosy little shell of foolish, childish, monkish beliefs.'

Órán lowered his voice. 'There is nothing you can say that will change your destiny now. Your course has been set and you must lean hard against the tiller if you're going to bring the boat of your soul around in this swell. Fulfil your quest quickly. Then we can get on with the work that has to be done.'

At that instant the knight caught a distant echo in the passage ahead. He realised that perhaps this was not the best place to be having such a discussion. Just as this thought crossed his mind another Redcap ran headlong into the hall. The creature stopped with a sliding shock, widened his eyes, then turned around.

Before Robert knew what had happened the Redcap was gone again off in the direction of the echoes. There was no sense trying to catch that fellow. He knew he wouldn't have a hope of pacing a Redcap who was running for his life. So our knight addressed Órán.

'It seems you are right. My destiny is sealed. But I won't accept that my life is out of my hands. I will stand here and fight the Redcaps until they strike me down or until there are none of them left to deal with. Do you understand?'

'What?' Órán asked, clearly showing in the barely restrained tremble of his voice how frustrated he was that Robert was wasting so much time. He wanted to be getting on to the feasting hall of Aoife. He wanted to get this quest over and done with. 'You will not fall while I am with you. I will be at your side.'

'Then these tunnels will be cleansed of all their Redcaps. And we shall do this deed together.'

Not another word was spoken between them for a long while afterwards. For as Robert spoke the last word of that sentence the first of several Redcaps entered the chamber. And this fearsome fellow held his sickle high above his head to strike at the deadly intruder.

But our Rob was too swift for the Redcap. A parried blow was quickly followed by another, then a broad sweeping hiss of Órán's blade brought another head to rest upon the floor, separated from the trunk which once supported it.

Robert had just dispatched that fellow when another appeared before him, then another. Each Redcap fell before the weapon as easily as if our Templar had been cutting stalks of wheat. And that was what he found unnerving.

For the first time in many years since he had started studying the Sword Dance he felt as if there were something deeper to the whole practice that he had never before grasped entirely. He sensed an all-pervasive awareness opening itself to him. Instead of experiencing the world as separate from himself, it seemed he was melting into the existence of everything to become part of a greater whole.

This granted him the unnerving sense that he could read the responses, fears and even thoughts of his opponents. As a test of this notion he took careful note of the next Redcap who confronted him.

The warrior was frightened even before he entered the

chamber or glimpsed the headless bodies of his comrades scattered about. Robert could feel that for certain. There was no question in his mind this Redcap was horrified.

Then he felt the rush of anger course through the very being of his enemy as the creature's eyes lit with hatred and his blood pumped hard. Robert knew the warrior's intent to raise a sickle and before the Redcap could do so he easily slipped behind the fellow's guard and struck off his head.

Suddenly he knew the pain, fear and fleeting panic which accompanies any soul who is unexpectedly dispatched from the world. Our gentle knight was appalled. His whole body tensed in readiness for the next assailant, yet his thoughts were racing. These Redcaps were not ugly dæmonic creatures. They were men very much like himself.

He hadn't expected the Redcaps to have feelings like his own. He'd not thought for a moment these monsters might share anything in common with him. An awful possibility crossed his mind. What if, apart from their legendary immortality, the Redcaps weren't in any way different from him at all?

He recalled vividly the exaggerated tales he'd heard of the Saracens before he left Ireland for the Holy Land. He'd gone off to Outremer the first time expecting to meet all manner of uncouth barbarians. But to his surprise he'd found the Saracens to be a courteous, cultured people who valued the pious folk among their number and respected the word of God. Everything he'd been told about their ways had been proved wrong in time.

To be sure there are good and bad among all folk, no matter what their faith or ambition. That was the lesson Robert had learned in the Outremer. And now he was beginning to understand these uncouth folk might be viewed in much the same way.

'Who are these warriors who call themselves the Redcaps?' he asked Órán.

'They are a degenerate people who have lapsed into barbarism,' the spirit replied. 'They are of no consequence.'

'It's obvious they're of no consequence to you,' FitzWilliam retorted sharply. 'They are not mortals but were they once men and women?'

'There was a time when the usual span of winters among their people was no more than ninety as a rule,' Órán informed him. 'But then they got their hands on the Quicken Brew which was given to them in payment for aiding Eber Finn of the Gaels in the war against his brother Éremon of the north.'

'What brought them to this?' Robert asked as he prodded one of the corpses with his sword point.

'They soon turned bitter when they came to understand immortality is not such a great boon. It is more of a burden. A few hotheads among them thought it amusing to terrorise the Irish with their appearance and horrific whispered tales about their ways. Rumour begat rumour. Untruth lay down with exaggeration and before long they parented an offspring named legend.'

The spirit took a moment to allow his explanation to sink in.

'They look fearsome, to be sure,' Órán admitted. 'But if the truth be known they are no different from any mortals you might care to meet. There are still a few hotheads among their number and it's them you have to blame for any general misbehaviour by the remainder. For those hotheads are their kings and chieftains.'

'I will not fight these people,' Robert decided.

'What?'

'There's no sense in killing the Redcaps. Wherever I cut the head off one, another dozen will spring up to attack me. I cannot hope to prevent them overwhelming the defences at the Killibegs. But I may be able to win their confidence and parley with them for peace.'

'You're a noble-hearted soul indeed you are!' Órán exclaimed. 'But alas you are mistaken.'

As he spoke another Redcap appeared from the main passage. Through the effect of his new-found awareness Robert immediately knew there was murder in the heart of this stranger. He parried a deadly blow from a huge sickle, then pushed the Redcap back against the wall.

The warrior's wide wet green eyes were wider still as he struggled for breath. Our knight held his forearm against the throat of his adversary, marvelling at how weak the Redcap became. Yet he did not die. Robert released his grip, stepped back then raised his sword to strike.

But as the creature was expecting the death blow from the spirit blade our knight hesitated. The Redcap lunged forward in a flash, wielding his sickle round in a great arc. Before he knew what was happening, Robert was caught in a desperate struggle. He didn't want to kill the Redcap but he didn't want to be cut down himself. He was torn between what he desired most to do and what he had no choice *but* to do.

In exhausted exasperation the knight swung his sword high above him to bring it down deep into the shoulder of his opponent. While the warrior was still reeling from the blow he slipped his blade out of the Redcap's body then struck off his head with another broad sweep.

Robert put the point of sword to the floor and rested, puffing and panting from the exertion of the fight.

'That's enough!' he declared. 'No more! There must be another way to approach this problem.'

'There's always an alternative to any unpleasantness,' Órán agreed. 'Why do you insist on taking the difficult road? Why can't you see that I've prepared the way for you? Trust me. I know you well. I wouldn't lead you into any situation which compromised your high moral standards.'

'Wouldn't you?' the knight cut back sharply. 'Then why did

354

you try to stop me going out onto the battlements of the Tower of Glass to accept my quest?'

'I wasn't trying to stop you. I was merely pointing out to you what sort of trouble you were getting yourself into. And I wanted to urge you to get your quest over with quickly so we could move on to greater things.'

The Frightener's voice mellowed to a more soothing tone.

'The fright in these few Redcaps has been very tasty indeed,' he told Robert. 'I thank you for these morsels of fear. But we have bigger birds to broil my dear.'

'You see these poor folk as nothing but nourishment. In the same breath you speak of high moral standards.' Robert pointed to the lifeless bodies scattered about the floor. 'I seem to remember that senseless murder doesn't fall within the range of behaviour I'd consider morally acceptable. Yet you've led me to this place where I'm slicing up Redcaps like a boy with a stick knocking the heads off sunflowers.'

'This was your doing, not mine. I told you to listen to me. I would have shown you a different way.'

'Show me the way now. I want to avoid further bloodshed.'

'Well you can't avoid it. You've accepted a quest to kill Flidais.'

'Will you help me avoid having to kill other Redcaps?'

'I won't,' Órán declared petulantly. 'I'm enjoying their fear. And I want you to understand the nature of our relationship. You rely on me as much as I do on you.'

'Very well,' Robert hissed. 'Then we shall see if this white knight ever ascends to the High-Kingship of Ireland. I wouldn't count on it if I were you.'

'What are you talking about?'

Robert didn't reply. He simply held out the sword in front of him.

'What are you doing?' Órán shrieked.

Then Sir Robert FitzWilliam dropped the blade that had

been his father's. He let go of the Frightener spirit which
dwelled within and he left himself defenceless against the next
Redcap to enter the chamber.

'Let them come,' he said with determination as the weapon
clattered on the floor. 'I'm ready to die.'

Órán was in a panic and no mistake. It seemed no matter what
he said or did he couldn't get Robert to see that everything
would turn out for the best. He'd never known a mortal like
this fellow. Ungrateful, he seemed. And arrogant.

The Frightener spirit wrestled with the possibilities. What
was he to do? He couldn't let the young knight throw away his
life like this. Robert FitzWilliam had taken three hundred
winters to create. Órán couldn't just abandon him because he
was proving difficult.

And that's a thing about Enticers and Frighteners you
should be aware of. They don't give up on their targets. Ever.
They may seem to take a step back from you or even to agree
to leave you alone forever more. But they never keep such
promises. They don't feel obliged to us. We're just a source of
food for them.

So, knowing his host was a simple man of pious inclination,
Órán decided he'd have to resort to another course of
deception. He didn't want to do it because such open deceit is
generally very exhausting for spirits. They're much better at
subtle lies than the obvious.

The Frightener withdrew himself from the sword to take
the material form of the old man who'd met Robert at the
gates to the forest. As his body took shape he shook himself
vigorously.

'That's better!' he sighed. 'I always feel much calmer once I've got the blood flowing.'

'You won't change my mind,' Robert said.

'I'm not going to try,' Órán shrugged. 'I can see you've made up your mind. I've taken material form to wish you well before I depart. There's no sense in trying to convince you to do anything your conscience won't allow.'

Robert squinted; he was beginning to suspect some sort of ruse.

'I'm going to leave you now,' Órán went on. 'I won't be returning. After I'm gone I want you to think very carefully about what you've abandoned here today in this chamber.'

'What have I abandoned?' the young FitzWilliam asked bitterly.

'You've thrown away your one chance at attaining to all your secret dreams. You've laid aside your wish to one day have a hall and home of your own. You've denied your inner desire to be the patriarch of a noble lineage. You have walked away from any hope you ever had of finding a woman who will be your wife and a mother to your children.'

'I'm a Knight of the Temple,' Robert pointed out. 'I've already made my vows. I've promised my hand and heart to God. I am not free to marry. Nor am I permitted to own a hall. I long ago renounced my secret dreams.'

'It doesn't have to be that way,' Órán whispered, seeing he might yet be able to convince his host. 'Look at what happened to Alan de Harcourt. His memory was affected so he could not recall his vows to the Temple. That freed him to marry. And what a woman that Mirim is! You could have the same thing happen to you. It's easily arranged.'

Robert turned his gaze to Órán and stepped close enough so that their noses were almost touching. There was a weariness in his reddened eyes that told the Frightener this one was close to giving in. He'd seen it a thousand times before.

'I've told you,' Robert whispered. 'I'm not interested. Now go away! Leave me to my fate if that's what you're going to do. If you're going to stay, do me the courtesy of keeping your mouth shut.'

Órán allowed the smile to drop from his face as he started to walk away.

'I'll go. There's no sense in prolonging this foolishness. I'm grieved you did not measure up to my expectations. I suppose my mistake was in turning to the FitzWilliam clan in the first place. None of you has ever really been worth the effort. And if you're the culmination of their breeding then all I can say is the blood line is flawed.'

'Go!' Robert bellowed.

As he yelled he spun to face the Frightener. But Órán had already gone. Robert was utterly alone now. He swallowed hard, pushed the regrets from his mind and prepared to face his enemies and his death.

In the distant corridors there was very little noise. It was as if the Redcaps had been completely distracted from him for the moment. He knelt down before the sword he'd thrown away and offered up a prayer. He crossed himself solemnly before he spoke his words to God.

'I beseech thee, O Lord, bring the enemy here to me to make a swift end of my life. I have failed you. I have entertained temptation. I have had dealings with dæmons. I have regretted my promises to you. I have sought ways to change my life from the path of the spirit to the road of the flesh. I am no longer worthy of this life you have given me.'

His words echoed through the chamber as he opened his eyes. There were no sounds coming from the depths of the caverns. He was alone with the corpses of his victims.

Robert looked down at the sword he'd discarded. He could no longer sense the presence of the Frightener spirit which had dwelled within it for three hundred summers or more. He had been abandoned.

'I deserve no less,' Robert declared. 'I am unworthy even of such a spirit as Órán'

As he spoke the young knight felt a tingling sensitivity spread from the nape of his neck around his skull and over his shoulders. It was an uncanny, unnerving feeling similar to that he'd experienced in his younger days whenever he'd been visited by the Blessed Virgin.

He thought back now on those times and suddenly wondered whether Mary the Virgin had visited him at all. What if all along it had been Órán impersonating the Mother of God?

Had Órán been presenting himself as a holy vision in order to be able to manipulate him into joining the Templar Order and thus learn the arts of warfare? It was certainly true that any aspirant to the High-Kingship of Ireland would have to be a capable warrior at the very least.

Every belief he held, every sense of the sacred in his life was suddenly called into question. What if his vocation to the Knights Templar had been nothing but a trick brought about by the meddling, manipulative Frightener that had attached itself to him?

'You fiend!' Robert shrieked, shaking his fist at the ceiling but intending the gesture for the absent Órán.

As those two words rang out a soft blue light began to fill the chamber. Robert grabbed his sword and stood up.

'Go away Órán!' he bellowed. 'I won't be so easily tricked again.'

But even as he spoke he began to feel an overwhelming sense of divinity such as he'd never known before. His entire being began to vibrate with an indescribable joy. His vision was acutely more sensitive. He could hear the tiniest shuffle of his shoes on the floor. More than that, Robert felt as if his body were being lifted up on a string attached to his heart. His head dropped back. His chest was dragged upward and forward until his feet barely touched the ground. His whole body was arched now in an ecstatic dance of the soul. Robert could hardly breathe for the unfathomable joyousness that filled him.

It was in this state that he became aware of another presence in the chamber. Another soul was there with him, observing passively everything that was happening.

'Who are you?' Robert managed to gasp.

His tongue refused to do his bidding and his lungs would not push the air out to give any strength to the words. But the stranger had heard him.

'I'm no Enticer,' the deep resonant voice replied. 'I'm no Frightener either. Indeed, I am unlike any other spirit you are likely to encounter even in the Otherworld.'

There was such a sacred tone to everything the stranger said that Robert frowned deeply. Could this be a visitation from the Holy Spirit? Could this be the voice of God?

As that thought came to him the knight caught the scent of roses in the air. But it wasn't merely an aroma. It was as if the very elements of everything that is a rose had been distilled into an ethereal essence. The flower buds bloomed in that scent. And the petals fell as the blossom perished.

'Who are you?' Robert repeated, eyes rolling back in surrender to this joy of joys.

The stranger did not reply. The knight struggled to turn his head to get a glimpse of whatever spirit it was that held him in this state. Then he realised he was no longer floating on the tips of his toes. He had been lifted up high off the floor.

'Stop!' he cried.

In an instant he was released from the hold. His feet struck the floor hard and his legs buckled under him with the weight of his body so his knees struck his chin.

He'd become accustomed to a kind of weightlessness. Now he felt heavy and clumsy again.

Robert managed to drag himself to his knees, clutching his chin. He had recovered control of his body and he breathed easier for that. It was a relief to be on familiar ground again. And despite the ecstatic experience he was still deeply suspicious of Órán's part in this encounter.

'Who are you?' Robert repeated for a third time as he turned his head slowly toward the source of the blue light.

The illumination was blindingly bright. But as Robert shielded his eyes, as you might from the sun's ferocity in the desert, he could discern the vague shape of a woman.

'Show yourself.'

The light faded immediately as the form of a noble lady stepped forward. She was dressed in a long gown of deep blue, though her feet were bare. Her veil was purest white and her face shone like the brightest silver star in the heavens.

Anyone else in Christendom would have instantly recognised her as the Blessed Virgin Mary. But Robert saw her for who he thought she really was.

'You will not tempt me,' he whispered under his breath as he crossed his breast.

Although his words were softly spoken, barely audible, the apparition heard him well enough. The blue light intensified again, building to an eye-scorching crescendo so that Robert had to turn away.

'Be gone, thou dæmon!' he shouted.

The light diminished to a tiny point of searing white. Robert peeked out from behind his hands to see the brightness fade into nothing.

For a few breaths the chamber seemed such a dark place. Without the beautiful dæmonic presence everything was dull and devoid of life. The sense of joy had been replaced by grief and loss.

His heart was racked with guilt for feeling so ecstatic about a dæmon. He was still on his knees so he offered up a prayer to atone for his wayward thoughts.

'Mea Culpa,' he began, which is how all Roman Christians begin their most earnest submissions unto their God.

The phrase is an admission of shame, of guilt, of culpability. If you were brought up in the traditions of Rome or had spent time in the convent as I did, you'd know that of course. But in my day the influence of the Roman Christians did not extend beyond the Norman-occupied areas of Ireland.

The Culdee folk who followed the teachings and tales of Christ did not place too much emphasis on the punishment of sins. It's probably difficult for you to believe that but it is true. Our people plied the esoteric tributaries of the river of Christianity.

In our teachings there could be no sin. There was no original sin. There were only mistakes. In my understanding God is forgiving of our silliness, our self-interest and our sly dealings.

You see, there is no better way to learn a lesson than through making mistakes. It's a way of reaching perfection, if you like. And since God has set innumerable tests for us to endure, is it not most likely that His purpose is to teach us well and truly that which He wishes us to learn?

Take my advice, throw off the shackles of guilt. Live your life with a pure, innocent and shameless heart. Fear not the ravages of Hell nor any threat of eternal punishment any priest may try to weight upon your spirit. The God of the Culdees is not a harsh judge, nor is He a deity who concerns Himself with punishments or rules or laws.

To my way of understanding God is my guide and my inspiration. He is a target to be aimed for rather than a stern parent to be frightened of. And along the way, if I falter, I know the God of All Things will be there to give me a helping hand whether I ask for it or not, whether I choose to believe in Him or not. At the end I will return to the hearth of God. Indeed, I have never really been away from His home.

At his heart, in the very depths of his soul, Robert knew the same truth. He'd seen enough of the world by then to have come to some conclusions of his own about the nature and nurture of God. So it was hardly surprising that those two words he spoke which proclaimed his guilt rang empty to his own ears.

'Do not upbraid yourself,' a male voice declared and the tones were deep, soft and soothing. 'You have proved yourself already to me.'

Robert clasped his hands in front of him and shut his eyes tightly to hold back the tears. He suddenly felt entirely lost and alone. Even this strange, calming, disembodied voice did not banish doubt. He began to wonder whether he had lost his mind completely.

'Do not forsake me, my Lord,' he begged and he instantly knew that fear was unfounded.

'I will not seek revenge nor recompense for the actions of your life,' the voice assured him.

Robert knew this to be the authentic speech of the Almighty. I don't know what made him so certain. Perhaps the manner of the manifestation convinced him. I can't tell you. Whatever gave him the impression he was listening to the words of God, he certainly knew it with all his heart.

'What must I do, my Lord? Where would you have me go? What path would you have me follow? I am yours to command.'

Then the voice told him a most remarkable thing. Let us not forget that Robert had passed into the Otherworld. Even though he wasn't entirely conscious of it, he was kneeling on the soil of another country, a place he'd never before visited. And in that land the impossible and the unbelievable seem more real and probable than any dream in this world.

The voice said to him that he should follow that which spoke to his heart. This teaching is at the core of the Culdee ways. I know there are many folk these days who call themselves Culdees but, believe me, they are not. They're merely using the holy reputation of our people to justify their own theology.

Anyone who calls himself a Culdee yet preaches abstinence from the world or decries the sinfulness of the flesh is not a true Culdee at all. Any man who claims every sin must be paid for is not a Culdee neither.

And those who reckon the only road to Heaven is paved with countless laws for this and that aren't Culdees. Those who quote petty prohibitions against every insignificant aspect of joy except those they imagine God approves of, they aren't Culdees either.

My life with the people of the Killibegs taught me that God wants us to be ourselves. That's why we were all born into this world of material wonders. It isn't to sit back in fear of accepting the precious gifts God grants us. After all, everyone agrees that God created everything.

Everything.

The springtime bloom is his invention as much as the battle cry. The glorious sunset was made by him no less than the stench of decay which overcomes the body after death. The holy ascetic who lives apart from others but dwells close to divinity in his heart is no less a child of God than the warrior who spills the blood of his enemies in war.

We are each given a part to sing in the choir of life. It is when we raise our voices with passion that all the many voices join in one harmonious chorus. That is the song God wishes us to know.

Those who are ashamed of their singing voice or too shy to sing out loud will never know the joy of joining in the music of creation. And at the end of their lives they will be sorry they didn't follow their hearts. There is no evil here on this Earth. There is only the Creator.

I won't burden you with my views any further. I know it is dangerous in these times to express such opinions. I'm sadly aware few folk could grasp what I'm on about.

As I was saying, since Robert had been led along the warrior path, the holy voice had inspired him to follow it with enthusiasm. His inner voice was speaking to him now. It told him, 'Do your best. Indulge your ambitions. Experience all you may. For that is the only way to learn.'

'Thou shalt not kill,' Robert replied in a firm tone, seeking confirmation from the voice that all killing was wrong.

'Thou shalt not kill,' the voice repeated in confirmation. 'But a warrior who has learned his craft and is wise in the ways of the world need never take another life. You have slain your enemies in the past. That was your part to play also.'

'What of Flidais?'

'All things must pass. The burden of the flesh is a terrible one to bear. Do not mourn for those who have shed it.'

'I have sinned.'

'But it is your true intention never to take another life ever again. For you have laid down your blade in submission. Is that not so?'

'That is true.'

'There is no death. What seems so is no more significant than a change of attire. Do you believe me?'

'I do.' Robert was sobbing.

'Then hear my command,' the voice boomed.

Robert looked up to the ceiling of the cave, hoping to catch a glimpse of some physical form. But there was only the torch-lit rocky outcrop above and the flickering shadows dancing across the chamber.

'A quest waits for you,' the voice continued. 'Take up your sword and finish it. Then go forth into the world. Seek out all that your heart desires most. Raise yourself to be a lord over other mortals. Find yourself a wife to be a mother to your children and a companion through the voyage of existence. Be just and compassionate in all your dealings with your fellow creatures. Do not stint at living your life to the full in every regard.'

'How can this way lead to a holy life? I seek the road of sanctity,' Robert stated, dumbfounded.

'Life is holy whether it is lived well or not. The way of sanctity is best lived by example. Do not preach nor presume that you know the mind and purpose of God. Pride does not suit you at all, my dear Robert. Strive to be an inspiration to others and to pass into the storytellers' repertoire as a just ruler possessed of a compassionate heart. Then you'll be assured of a place in Heaven. If you earn the love of others through respect rather than fear, you will attain to the greatest joy of all. For there is no greater reward in this life than to love well and to be well loved.'

Robert closed his eyes, knowing the words to be true. But he'd witnessed so many theological charlatans in his life, and he had prayed so fervently for guidance in the past without any apparent reply, that now he seriously doubted whether God would waste His time answering his questions.

'Do not doubt,' the voice assured him. 'I am He whom you seek. The Gaels call me An Té a bhi agus atá, which means He Who Was And Is.'

And when Robert heard those words he no longer questioned the truth of this revelation.

'I am yours to command, O Lord,' he replied. 'May I prove to be a worthy vessel for your purpose.'

With that Robert immediately sensed the presence of the spirit had departed and he was left alone on his knees in the cave. The dearest wish of his heart had been fulfilled. Perhaps you may wonder that he did not doubt the truth of the holy visitation. You might think to yourself perhaps he should have been a little more sceptical. But that's only because you haven't known such a thing yourself. Nor have you yearned for it with the fervour our Robert had known.

So as he knelt there in silence with his hands clenched together tightly in front of him, Robert smiled. The Redcaps were no longer on his mind. They did not concern him. All he wanted now was to press on to his goal and to fulfil his quest. He picked up his sword, turning the blade down so it touched the floor. The cross of the hilt was level with his face.

'I will go on,' he promised. 'I will go on.'

Then he stood up shook the dust off his tunic and set off in search of Aoife's feasting hall.

The Drowning of King Caoimhin

While Robert was making his way down through the tunnels of Aoife's underground city, Caoimhin, Scodán and Srón crossed the bridge over the river. They had made good progress, though they could not have realised the well was within a hundred paces or so.

The monk was surprised he'd been able to keep up with the two warriors. Indeed, he'd been taken aback at his ability to keep pace with Sianan when they first set out from the Killibegs. After all, he'd been bedridden with the poison only a few hours earlier. Now he was marching along without so much as a puff of exhaustion to slow him down. He still didn't realise that he'd been given a draught of the Quicken Brew. Sianan hadn't told him. She'd made a decision to break the news to him at an appropriate time. She'd sensed it would be a great shock for him, he being a Christian of the Roman Benedictine variety. And she wasn't wrong, let me tell you.

He may have been immune from death but he wasn't immune from enchantments and Draoi-craft. The Quicken Brew did not offer such protection. And as I may have mentioned, the love philtre was one which grew stronger in effect the longer one was separated from the object of one's desire.

They were making their way along the road when they came to a narrowing of the track which Caoimhin thought was familiar. A short steep path led on from there down to the place where the waters bubbled out from a cleft in the rock, shaped into the form of a face.

He climbed down carefully, growing more excited by the moment as he recognised this place from his vision. Recent rain had muddied the path. It was hard going in the mud. He was so intensely absorbed in keeping his balance he ran straight into the back of Srón who had come to a standstill halfway down the track.

Below them lay a pool formed around the sacred spring. Caoimhin waited a few breaths for Srón to move on. But she didn't show any sign of continuing her descent.

'What's the matter?' he whispered, fearing that Redcaps were waiting in ambush.

She did not reply.

'Is there danger?' he asked under his breath.

Still the warrior-woman did not reply. So Caoimhin put a hand upon her shoulder to get her attention. Slowly Srón turned round to look at him. Her face was pale, her eyes filled with tears.

Scodán caught up with them then. He came to halt against Caoimhin's back as he let out an almost inaudible cry of anguish. Then the blood drained from his face also.

'What's going on?' Caoimhin insisted.

Srón lifted her arm to point. Her hand swept around in a wide arc on her left side. Then she pointed to the right. It was at that moment Caoimhin saw them and I wouldn't be surprised if the blood drained from his face too as he realised what he was looking at.

All around them on the slopes of the hill leading down to the pool were hundreds of carved wooden idols, their faces contorted by pain, fear and rage. They were crudely shaped as if by some long-forgotten savage folk. This forest of woodland spirits stood silent, guardians of the path to the pool. Some were covered in moss, others leaned this way or that. All about their feet were piled great gatherings of leaf fall and soil washed down by the rain.

Caoimhin had to lean hard against Srón when the shock set in.

'They look just like you did before the enchantment was broken,' the monk noted in a quiet tone for fear of disturbing the sleepers within the statues.

'Behold the hosts of the Sen Erainn,' Srón declared. 'Here stand the nine hundred who came across the water to face down Aoife and the Redcaps of the North. Our people have been enchanted.'

'If this is the Well of Many Blessings, how did they find it before us?' Scodán asked.

'They passed us by while we were under the idol enchantment,' Srón told him. 'I saw a host out of the corner of my eye, though I could not turn my head to get a better look. Your face was pressed into the soil. So you couldn't have seen them at all. All is lost.'

'All is not lost,' Caoimhin told her.

'The Druid will free them!' Scodán declared with relief.

'I'm no Druid.'

'You set us free.'

'I don't know how I did it. If I did.'

'Then all is lost,' Srón repeated.

'Did you not come to this well seeking its healing waters?' Caoimhin asked.

'Yes,' she replied. 'But what good are those waters now? None of my folk may drink of them. In order to taste the healing spring one must have a tongue. To imbibe the virtues of the pool one must have lips and a throat. These poor souls are things of wood, lifeless.'

'We used to have an abbot at Glastonbury who loved to sprinkle holy water all over the brothers at mass as a blessing,'

Caoimhin told her, refusing to give up hope. 'After a long day spent hunched over a book copying the words of scripture, I used to look forward to that soaking. It refreshed me. It revived me. Truly it was a blessing of sorts. Perhaps it is enough that these waters merely touch the one they are to heal. How do you know the water must be tasted?'

Srón half turned on the track and grabbed his arm tightly. Scodán took her hand in his as they searched one another's expressions for doubts.

'He might be right,' the warrior-woman admitted to her companion at last. 'I've never heard it said the *only* way to gain any healing from the waters is to drink them.'

In the next second the three of them were running recklessly down the path headed straight for the pool. They were travelling so fast that when they came to the flat space at the bottom it was all they could do to avoid falling headlong into the waters.

Once they were standing on the pebbled shore Srón and Scodán looked to their monkish friend.

'Is this the place you know as the Well of Many Blessings?' Srón asked him in between gulped breaths.

Caoimhin bent over, leaning hard against his knees in an attempt to calm his breathing. He struggled to look around at the pool, the spring and the surrounding rocks.

'It is,' he replied.

With that confirmation they didn't waste another word. The two Sen Erainn threw off the water-skins they'd been carrying. Caoimhin picked up an armful of the leather vessels and knelt at the water's edge. He wrenched a cork from the first skin then plunged it into the cold dark waters to bubble and fill with precious healing.

When that one was full he corked it, then reached for another. He'd just got that second one under the surface when a sinister voice challenged them.

'What do you think you're doing? Who gave you permission to steal the sacred waters of the Well of Many Blessings?'

The three of them stood back from the pool, looking from one to the other as Srón pointed silently to the stone head at the well-head. The spring that had emerged from its mouth in a steady stream had ceased to flow.

'Who are you?' the head asked, its features stern with the challenge. 'By what right or reason do you dare fill your skins from this pool? You will answer to me unless you empty them out again. Do you hear me? You'll suffer for your thieving if you don't pour out that water.'

The head suddenly spat out a great stream of water with such force that it splashed against the rocks on the other side of the pool. Then he held back the rush of water and went on.

'Speak up! Do as I say! I am Mallacht, Guardian of the Well of Many Blessings. None may drink of this spring without my leave.'

Of course Gobann had just been cheeky drinking from the well without permission. And Tóraí-Oat-Beer had been a dog when he took a sup. Try stopping a dog drinking from a spring when he's been running half the night.

'And how may we be granted your leave?' Srón asked politely.

'You must give me a gift.'

Then the head lifted its chin to spit springwater at each of them until they retreated up the pebble bank where he couldn't reach them. The water was icy and it stung their skin where it touched.

'What do we do now?' Scodán moaned. 'What gift could we give that monster that would satisfy it? How do we release our kindred without the help of the healing waters?'

Caoimhin gritted his teeth with frustration. His fingers brushed against his book satchel. Then he had an idea. He quickly removed the garland of flowers he'd made as a gift for me at the yew tree. He removed the delicate purple roselike flowers from the pocket. After he'd made a few hasty repairs to the weave, he held them up.

'This will do nicely,' he declared with confidence. 'I'll just have to find something else to give Binney as a gift.'

He paused for a moment, having second thoughts about parting with the flowers, then he handed his book satchel to Srón. She took it solemnly with a silent promise to look after it. Caoimhin removed his poor monk's shoes and his stockings. But as he only wore a long knee-length linen shirt beneath his robes he decided it would be best to leave his monkish habit on.

When he was ready he placed the garland over his head. Then he walked down to the waterside, gingerly stepping this way and that to avoid the smooth pebbles which threatened to bruise his feet. At the very brink of the pool he stopped.

The stone head had returned to its mundane duty of spraying water out from the spring through its pursed lips. It was ignoring him. Caoimhin coughed. Mallacht did not look up. So the young monk stepped into the water to cross to a part of the pool where he could climb up. Once he'd got that far he made his way around to the side of the stone head, carefully climbing along the rocks in his bare feet.

At last he was close enough to Mallacht that he could reach out to slip the garland over the stone head. He leaned forward to do so and the flowers fell down across the stone face with a graceful elegance.

Mallacht was so surprised he stopped spitting the spring.

'What's this?' he cried, his voice full of suspicion.

'A gift for you in payment for your waters,' Caoimhin explained.

The stone head strained his eyes to look at the beautiful purple flowers. Indeed they suited the statue well. It was as if he'd suddenly sprouted the most vibrant purple hair.

'I can't see them!' Mallacht complained. 'What use is a gift I can't see?'

Unexpectedly the stone head shifted slightly to spit at Caoimhin. The monk put up his hands to protect his face, slipped his footing and fell headlong into the water with a great splash.

His two companions rushed to the waterside to offer him help but they were driven back by the savage spitting head of the guardian spirit.

'Stay back!' Mallacht warned them. 'Or I'll drown you both too. None return from the depths of my pool unless I let them. So watch yourselves!'

They did as he demanded, though their hearts called out for action. Scodán had to restrain his companion with all his might. Finally he dragged Srón to her knees on the pebbles, her fists clenched in anguish, her face red with tears.

As for Caoimhin, he managed to take in a hasty breath before he was dragged down into the dark depths. His monkish robe of wool was soon waterlogged and his linen undershirt doubled in weight once it was wet.

He fought against his fate by kicking out. He flailed his arms until he was thoroughly entangled in his clothes. Then he felt the weeds at the bottom of the pond tickle his ankles. He opened his eyes as his hands laid flat on the mud.

If he expected everything to be dark down there he was certainly surprised. There was light everywhere. It was little more than a soft luminescence, a greenish glow which bathed everything in a sickly aura. But it was enough to see by.

Before him, entirely entangled in weeds and water grasses, was a young man. He'd been wrapped up with vegetation for his shroud. His face was pale. His black hair floated about his face with every little movement Caoimhin made in the water. It was cut in the same style Gobann wore: shaved about the sides and back; another band of hair had been taken off the top of his head from ear to ear.

His eyes were shut tight and his hands were folded across his chest. Behind him on a rock ledge a beautiful harp lay upon its back. Caoimhin could not have imagined an instrument such as that one. The fore-pillar was fashioned with the heads of two serpent-like creatures. Both carved creatures had eyes of crystal which sparkled in the green underwater glow. There was another clear oval crystal set in the very top of the fore-pillar and other stones inlaid at intervals around the serpents.

But it was the wires of this harp that really caught Caoimhin's eye. They seemed to be of pure gold. And as the water shifted around the instrument he thought he could hear a weird moaning hum as they gently vibrated.

This was Mawn. There was no doubt about it. His archaic purple tunic, shaped around the neck with scalloping and embroidery, marked him as a man of wealth. His fine knee-length boots were unlike any Caoimhin had ever seen. If he had held any other doubts as to the identity of this prisoner they would have been dispelled by the presence of one article of clothing the stranger wore about his shoulders. It was the most magnificent cloak of the blackest raven feathers. It was exactly like the one Gobann wore. This alone marked him as a Druid.

Caoimhin was so awed by the presence of this man in the depths of the pool he hardly realised he was drowning. He'd already expelled all the air from his lungs and his vision was blurring. A wonderful sense of peace began to descend upon him such as he'd never known.

Then the strangest thing happened.

At that same moment his two companions sat on the pebble bank with their shoulders hunched over in sadness, shock and exhaustion. They'd come through all sorts of dangers only to reach this point where they were powerless to help their friend and unable to rescue their people.

375

'He's gone,' Scodán sighed. 'No one could hold their breath that long. Not even deep-water divers can stay down for such a drawn-out interval.'

'We shouldn't have let him go alone,' Srón cried. 'We should have dived in after him.'

Her companion put an arm about her to soothe her.

'We would've been drowned too,' he reminded her. 'What use would that have been?'

'What use are we now?' she retorted. 'It would've been better if we had drowned. He saved us in our time of need. But when he needed our help we let a spitting stone head deter us from our duty. I am no longer worthy of the title warrior. And neither are you.'

Scodán bent his head in shame as Srón let the tears flow. He had to agree with her. They'd been chosen from among all their folk to find the Well of Many Blessings. And here when they were put to the test, when the fate of their people lay within their grasp and the life of a friend was threatened, they had let fear get the better of them.

The two of them huddled close together, burying their faces in one another's tunics as they lamented the loss of Caoimhín and along with him their honour.

'It is well that our kinfolk are turned into slabs of wood,' Scodán noted, his voice cracking with emotion. 'For I could never face my comrades again after this.'

'And all because we feared to get wet!' Srón bellowed.

As she spoke she suddenly became aware that her arm was soaking. There was water rolling off her hand and her sleeve was saturated. She looked up, expecting to see that rain had started to fall. But instead she was treated to a shock.

Caoimhín was standing before her in his drenched linen shirt. He was soaked to the skin. Stranger than that, his hair had grown long and matted. It was no longer golden honey coloured. It was a light brown.

For all the world he looked just like the ghost of a drowned man. The young ones of Aran used to be told horrific stories about what happens to the soul after a drowning so they'd not wander too close to the shore on their own.

A long thin straggly beard had sprouted on the ghostly chin. His fingers were capped by sharp yet rounded nails like the claws of an animal. His eyes were unearthly large and bluer than they had been before his drowning.

Srón was so startled that she shimmied up the pebbles backwards, kicking little stones this way and that. Scodán looked up as she slipped out of his grip. When he saw Caoimhin he, too, was off up the pebbles to get away from the apparition. His eyes never left the ghost for a second.

'Don't harm us!' he cried out. 'We didn't mean to abandon you!'

The warrior slipped on the loose stones and hit his head hard. He must have lain there no more than a few seconds, but when he opened his eyes again Caoimhin was standing before him with a hand held out.

'Let me help you up,' the monk offered. 'Are you hurt?'

That was enough for Scodán.

'He's going to drag me into the pool to drown me!' he screamed. 'He's going to end our lives just as his was finished off. We're doomed to die under the water!'

'Shut up!' Mallacht bellowed. 'Why must you make so much noise. That one wasn't drowned.'

Srón stopped her retreat.

'What do you mean, he wasn't drowned?' she asked, her voice weighted with scepticism. 'He was under the water for a terrible long time.'

'Immortals can't be drowned,' the stone head explained.

Suddenly the two Sen Erainn warriors relaxed. They stood up, still wary of Caoimhin but a lot more comfortable than they had been.

'Why didn't you tell us you're an immortal?' Srón asked suspiciously.

'Because I'm not an immortal,' Caoimhin protested. 'I don't even know whether I believe there are any such folk in the world. I've met one who claims to be a Fanaí, but she's not that much different from you or me.'

'Then how do you explain the fact that you spent so long underwater without drowning?' Scodán ventured.

The warrior approached Caoimhin to test the temperature of his skin.

'I can't explain it,' the monk shrugged.

'He's warm,' he noted. 'He's not a ghost then.'

'Of course I'm not a ghost,' Caoimhin laughed.

'Fishes and the dwellers of the deep may stay beneath the water that long,' Srón told him. 'And immortals may do so also. But none others. You are neither a fish nor a dweller from the deep places.'

Caoimhin looked at her, frowned, then laughed again.

'I don't know what happened. I stayed down there until I had the presence of mind to slip out of my black wool robes that had weighted me down. Perhaps the waters have some quality which allows one to live beneath them for a longer time than usual.'

That explanation seemed to make sense to both the Sen Erainn.

Scodán sighed with relief as he spoke. 'Perhaps that's why your hair has grown so long also. It was the enchantment of the pool that prevented you from drowning.'

'That's it,' he told Srón. 'We came here looking for these waters because they are reputed to stave off the effects of injury in battle. It stands to reason that if young Caoimhin here took a mouthful of water it was enough to preserve him against death.'

Srón wasn't entirely convinced. But she reasoned to herself

that they were now wandering in the Otherworld – the laws of the mortal lands did not always apply in this place.

She approached Caoimhin warily, placed a hand on his arm to check that he was indeed warm and alive, then hugged him close to her.

'I'm sorry,' she sobbed. 'We should have come to your rescue. I promise I will never let you down again. I owe you my life. I've learned my lesson.'

'No harm done,' the monk noted cheerily.

But as Srón touched the back of his neck she noticed the monkish tonsure on the crown of his head had disappeared. Where there had been a bald patch of skin there was now a thick vibrant growth of hair.

'You've changed since you took your bath,' she told him.

Caoimhin touched the back of his head. Then he stroked the thin beard at his chin.

'If the waters could do that to me, is it so unbelievable I could have survived drowning in the pool?'

Srón seemed to accept this but Mallacht was not so easily mollified.

'He's a bloody immortal, I tell you!' the stone head insisted. 'I've seen enough of his kind to know. Only immortals come out of that water with any breath in them. Mark my words.'

'We'll have to disagree on that,' Caoimhin cut in. 'With the greatest respect to you, Mallacht, I am not an immortal and that is that. Until you can produce proof for the existence of the immortal kind I cannot even accept there are such folk walking either in this world or the next.'

'What more proof do you need, you stupid boy?' the stone head snapped. 'You Christians all think you're the cream of the dairy, don't you? Well you're the bloody cream all right. You're the thickest of all your kind.'

Srón took another step back as doubt shaded her eyes again.

'Don't listen to him,' Caoimhin countered. 'Can't you see he's trying to sew discord and mistrust between us?'

'Is that what you're doing?' Scodán asked Mallacht. 'Are you just trying to stir up trouble?'

'Maybe I am,' the head conceded. 'Maybe I'm not.'

In that instant Caoimhin recalled his vivid vision of this place. In the dream Gobann had advised him not to be intimidated by creatures such as the well-head. The Druid had picked up a pebble and tossed it at the guardian.

In a flash of inspiration Caoimhin selected a pebble from the shore and threw it at the stone head. The little rock thwacked Mallacht in the centre of the forehead then splashed into the water.

'Ow!' the stone squealed. 'That hurt!'

'There's more where that came from,' Caoimhin warned him.

The monk picked up another pebble and threw it. This stone also found its mark. Mallacht cried out again in pain and struggled to spray water at the monk. But Caoimhin was standing beyond the malicious stone's reach.

Srón and Scodán soon held little rocks in their hands. Then a veritable rain of pebbles came down upon the well-head. Some struck Mallacht in the mouth, many hit him in the cheeks, a few thumped against the top of his head. And one sailed through the air to thud into his eye.

'That's enough!' the stone cried in outrage. 'I won't take any more! If you don't stop that stone-throwing I'll be forced to do something really nasty.'

'And what would that be?' Caoimhin laughed, choosing another pebble from the array around his feet. 'You don't seem to be able to do much but spit water. How nasty can that get?'

Then, without hesitation, he hurled his pebble. It sailed through the air in a graceful arc. Mallacht could see it coming.

He turned his head this way and that, desperately trying to avoid the vicious missile, but he couldn't escape it.

The pebble struck him hard on the forehead with a resounding thud. 'Aoife told me there'd be days like these,' the stone winced. 'I wish I'd never got on her bad side.'

'Did Aoife turn you into a well-head?' Srón asked.

'Indeed she did,' came the mournful reply.

'She turned us into wooden idols,' Scodán told him.

'You were lucky,' Mallacht hissed. 'I'd give anything to be a dumb lump of carved wood with no pool to protect and no water springing out of my mouth all day long.'

As he finished that sentence the stream forced its way out again.

'I can't hold a decent conversation with anyone,' he complained. 'I hardly get a dozen words out before . . .'

His sentence was cut off by a sudden burst of springwater.

'You see what I mean?'

'What did you do to upset her?' Srón asked.

'I didn't do anything!' Mallacht screeched. 'I was one of her Redcap captains. I was her favourite. One day out of the blue for her own amusement she changed me into a well-head.'

He paused to let the water flow for a few seconds.

'She never explained why. She just did it.'

He thought for a few moments as the water spouted through his mouth again. Then he asked a question.

'What did you do to upset her?'

Scodán replied without realising he should have been a little more sensitive to Mallacht's feelings.

'We were part of a host of the Sen Erainn. We came here to the realm of the Otherworld to take part in the great rebellion against Aoife. She caught us before we could do her any harm.'

'Are you enemies of Aoife?' Mallacht snapped.

'Yes we are.'

Mallacht let out a terrible moaning call that turned into a

bubbling gurgle when he could no longer hold back the spring from spurting out his mouth.

'I was her loyal servant,' he sobbed. 'I never put a foot wrong. Now I don't have feet at all. I stood by her through thick and thin and this is how she repays me.'

The water had its way with him again.

'She treats her enemies better than she treated me,' he noted with venom. 'After all my loyal service I ended up worse off than a rebel.'

Once more the spring interrupted the flow of his speech.

'And how did you break free from your bonds?' he asked.

'Caoimhin set us free,' Srón told him.

'The immortal did it?'

She nodded.

'I'm not immortal,' Caoimhin protested.

'Then how did you free them from Aoife's curse?'

'I don't know,' the monk shrugged. 'Maybe it wasn't me at all. I just happened to be there when the enchantment wore off.'

'I saw him scribbling on a piece of paper,' Scodán told the well-head. 'I wouldn't be surprised if he's a master of the Draoi-craft.'

'I'm not a Druid!' Caoimhin stated irritably.

'What did I tell you?' Scodán said to the well-stone. 'He's humble, talented and a master of enchantment.'

'Stop it!' the monk cried.

Out of sheer frustration Caoimhin tossed the pebble that was resting in his hand. It sailed toward Mallacht. The well-head shrieked as he watched the pebble coming for him.

'No! That's enough!'

But his screams didn't deflect the rock. It hit him hard in the left eye.

'That hurt!' he bellowed. 'Ouch! He can't be a bloody Druid. He's too cruel.'

'Let us fill our water-skins,' Caoimhin demanded. 'If you allow us to do that we will stop pelting you with pebbles.'

'No.'

Three rocks flew across and hit him so fast he hardly had time to shout in dismay.

'All right!' the stone head shrieked. 'Take as much water as you like. But Heaven help you if Aoife catches up with you. She doesn't look too kindly on folk who steal her waters.'

'Is this her well?' Srón asked.

'It is,' Mallacht confirmed. 'She calls it the Well of the Goddess. But lately Flidais has been dwelling here. She's been gathering her rebels round this spot readying for the fight to overthrow Aoife. She's the only real goddess of this well.'

'Are you part of that conspiracy?' the monk probed.

'That depends on who's asking me. Tell me true, are you one of Aoife's folk?'

'She's no friend to me or mine,' Caoimhin stated truthfully. 'She's raised a force of Redcaps to overrun the Killibegs. She's planning a terrible slaughter there. I came to the Otherworld with a friend hoping to put a stop to her.'

'In that case I'm with the rebels. I'm with Flidais.'

'We must work together,' the monk argued. 'If her enemies unite against her, Aoife has no hope of success.'

'You may take what you will from this well,' the stone head declared. 'But you must promise me that if you fall under Aoife's interrogation you will not divulge my part in this rebellion.'

'I will not.'

'Then approach, friend, and take your fill of the waters of the Well of Many Blessings.'

Caoimhin went down to the water to retrieve the one water-skin he'd filled. He weighed it up then drank a mouthful of the sweet waters. He suddenly realised that since he'd emerged from the depths of the pool his head had been so much clearer. His thoughts were not focused on me any longer.

Infatuation is a terrible debilitation. It drains the life out of its victims as surely as any Enticer spirit may do. Caoimhin's mind felt sharp and alert again. His vision was clear. That's why a certain thought struck him.

'Perhaps we don't need to fill all the skins,' he mused aloud.

'What do you mean?' Scodán asked.

The monk simply smiled at him and winked.

'Follow me.'

They went up the path, climbing to where the mud was slippery and difficult to traverse. There Caoimhin left the track and approached a wooden idol that was standing alone. It was the lowest statue on the hillside. All the others were fanned out above it toward the crest of the hill where the main body of idols stood.

Careful not to waste a drop of the precious water, Caoimhin removed the stopper from the water-skin. He held the vessel under one arm as he squeezed down on it with his elbow and pointed the neck at the statue.

Water sprayed out over the timber, immediately leaving a dark stain. The three companions stepped back to see if the enchantment would be easily broken. They didn't have to wait long for the healing waters to have an effect. Before their disbelieving eyes the wooden grain of the statue disappeared to be replaced by textures of a different sort.

Where there had been awful hideous bulging bulbs there were suddenly soft wet grey eyes full of life. In less time than it took Caoimhin to shout, 'All we have to do is wet each idol down,' the first of the Sen Erainn warriors was free of the enchantment.

The fellow sucked in a deep breath as the life returned to him. His skin at first grey soon refreshed to a healthy pink. His face was bright with consciousness, his muscles stretched into motion as every sinew woke from wooden slumber. He doubled up then in momentary pain as a wave of cramp struck him. Srón was at his side in an instant to offer comfort and a deep draught of water from the well.

Before the warrior had fully recovered Caoimhin was already on his way round the timber company of idols spraying water on each and every one. Scodán followed on after him comforting distressed comrades as they regained their bodies of flesh and bone.

In a short while there were a dozen warriors of the Sen Erainn eagerly filling water-skins at the pool. Before long there were fifty warriors working to bring their comrades back to consciousness. The hillside was abuzz with activity, cries of jubilation and groans of pain as atrophied limbs were pressed back into service.

The Sen Erainn worked hard to free their warriors from the binding of Aoife's spell. Caoimhin, Srón and Scodán were just beginning to tire when the last warrior fell out of the timber to gasp the sweet fresh air of freedom.

Nine hundred they were. So you can imagine the terrible din they raised as they gathered on the pebble shore to wash the splinter memories out and to drink of the healing spring. Some of them jumped into the pool in their joy. A few swam silently back and forth across the water in celebration.

The stone head protested of course. He shouted. He bellowed. He threatened. He cajoled.

'Get out of my pool!' Mallacht demanded.

No one took the slightest bit of notice of him.

'I was a bloody chieftain once!' he screamed at the top of his voice. 'I had a thousand like you under my command!'

But it was to no avail. The warriors of the Sen Erainn were not going to be ordered around. Their ire was up. Their blood was warm again. And their chieftains were already talking heatedly among themselves about what to do next.

There would be no stopping them now. Aoife had thrown her net about them once. It would not happen again. Inasmuch as it were possible to sneak a force of nine hundred warriors through the forests of the Otherworld undetected, the chieftains decided that is what they must do.

The only way to beat the Redcaps and their queen was to surprise them. They would march to meet with Flidais and her warriors at the feasting hall.

Caoimhin was seated by a fire on the pebble beach with Srón and an exhausted Scodán when he realised the stone head was calling out to him. It addressed him as 'that bloody immortal'. He stood up and walked wearily toward the water, finally ending up ankle-deep in the pool so he could hear what Mallacht had to say.

Srón sat by the fire watching the monk as he spoke with the head. She couldn't hear a word of their conversation. The noise of nine hundred warriors cooking, cleaning, rejoicing and cursing is fairly overpowering, as I'm sure you can imagine.

She saw Caoimhin throw up his arms in a gesture of helplessness. Then she watched him shake his head again and again, but she could not tell what it was he was refusing to do or agree to. At last the monk bowed to the well-head respectfully then returned to their fire.

He was just about to sit down again when a warrior crunched across the pebbles near Srón and barked an order.

'You three will come to the chieftains. Now!'

Scodán dragged himself wearily to his feet as Srón came close enough to Caoimhin to whisper.

'What were you talking about with that stone bastard?'

'I'll tell you later,' he replied mysteriously and left it at that.

Halfway up the hill track the seven chieftains of the Sen Erainn had arranged themselves in an arc. They sat on roughly cut portable benches which the Sen Erainn always carried with them when the chieftains were off travelling. These were arranged in a semicircle around a fire. The three companions were ushered to stand before them.

As Srón, Scodán and Caoimhin bowed, the seven war-leaders stood up, drew their elegant fighting sickles and upturned them with blades to the ground in salute. Then each warrior laid their weapon down on the ground as they returned to their seats.

Srón gripped Caoimhin's arm so tightly he could feel the blood struggling to pump through to his hand.

'What's the matter?' he whispered. 'What's going on?'

'We summon Scodán of the Slua Sen Erainn,' one of the war-leaders began.

He was a grey-bearded, heavy-boned old man. His head was shaved at the sides and back and across the top of his skull from ear to ear. The remainder of his hair was knotted into long locks tied at the crown. Caoimhin was once again reminded of Gobann's hairstyle.

The old man's face was painted with small blue dots in patterns quite similar to those the Redcaps wore in red. His clothes were dark blue. A practical war tunic with elbow-length sleeves was his undershirt. On top of this he wore a coat of silvery armour plates which overlapped one another like the scales of a fish. His cloak seemed to be made of fishing net, though the weave was much tighter than any net Caoimhin had ever seen.

'Who is he?' he asked Srón under his breath.

'That is the mighty Becc mac Dé,' she answered. 'He is a War-Druid and a leader of our people.'

'Scodán of the Ocean Shoals,' the old man intoned as a summons. 'Scodán of the Fisher Folk. This council names you chieftain. You have proved your worth to us nine hundred fold. We welcome you into the Shoal of the Salmon.'

As he was speaking another chieftain stood up. She was a rosy-cheeked old warrior-woman hardened by her life near the ocean but not bent down under the weight of her seasons. She held up a fine new coat of scale armour that sparkled and shimmered in a way that would certainly have made any fish envious.

She placed the armour over his head, adjusted it then threaded a belt through hooks at the waist to fasten the beautiful armour. When that was done she took Scodán by the hand to lead him to the bench where two chieftains made room for him to sit.

'Srón of the Inner Harbour,' Becc mac Dé declared. 'Srón of the Fisher Folk. This council names you chieftain. You have proved your worth to us nine hundred fold. We welcome you into the Shoal of the Salmon.'

The old woman chieftain produced another coat of armour. This one was of finer make than Scodán's. Each scale was much smaller and they all tinkled together like tiny bells. The polish was much finer too. The war-coat reached down below her knees.

'This armour was worn by your ancestor,' the old War-Druid told her. 'The Fish-Poet Aenghus mac Ómor. He was the last great King of the Sen Erainn. He swore allegiance to Eber Finn, monarch of the Gaels. Since his day when the tribes were sundered the seven chieftains have ruled in place of kings among the fisher folk.'

The old man paused as Srón was led to her seat with the other chieftains, leaving Caoimhin to stand before the assembly alone. He had tears of pride in his eyes for the honour done to his new-found friends. Becc mac Dé now stared directly at the monk as he continued speaking.

'Since his glorious death in battle there have been no kings among the Fisher Folk of the Sen Erainn. Our immortal brethren took kings but we do not recognise them. The red caps of war have not been worn by our people since the two tribes of the Sen Erainn set off on their different paths. Those who took the Quicken Brew now wear that headgear every day. We put it on only in time of war.'

Caoimhin was surprised to hear these people were the same blood as the Redcaps.

'Tonight we will put on our red caps again and go to fight for the first time in many generations. And the wearing of the red caps is not the only ancient custom we intend to revive.'

The seven chieftains took out their red headgear and solemnly placed the caps on their heads. Srón and Scodán were presented with fine pointed hats exactly the same as the other chieftains wore. Caoimhin marvelled that he would not now have been able to distinguish these folk from the Redcaps of Aoife but for the fact that they were much more pleasing to look at than their fierce outlaw relatives.

'There are nine chieftains now,' Becc mac Dé continued. 'As there were in the days of Aenghus. Nine chieftains constitute a royal council. So it is time to elect a king.'

He paused again as the old warrior woman brought forward another coat of armour. This one was the most magnificent of all the three Caoimhin had seen that evening. It sparkled silver as if it had been made entirely out of that metal. The scales were so tiny they could have been plucked from a fish.

Two other chieftains stood up beside her bearing other clothes. One man carried a dark blue tunic of rich soft wool over his arm. It was embroidered with silver fishes swimming about the collar and the cuffs of the sleeves. He also held a fine pair of britches made of black doeskin and a pair of long black soft leather boots.

The other chieftain carried a fine helm of bright silvery metal with a shroud of mail rings hanging around the back of the neck. Set upon a spike at the very top of the helm was a long flowing black horse-tail.

'This helm was a gift to our people from the King of the Gaels,' the War-Druid explained. 'It was given in honour of Aenghus mac Ómor who fell fighting for Eber Finn and his people. No King of the Sen Erainn has ever worn it. Aenghus was the last royal ruler among the mortal Sen Erainn. We brought this helm and the royal armour with us to this fight because we thought this would be the last stand of the Slua Sen Erainn.'

He pointed to the tunic.

'These are the finest garments we can muster, considering we are so far from home.'

Then he looked at Caoimhin directly again.

'We could not help but notice that you sacrificed even the clothes you were standing in for the good of our people,' the old man declared. 'The warriors are saying you cannot be drowned. That is a fine omen and an auspicious attribute.'

He paused to observe Caoimhin's reaction. Then he continued.

'You have brought our war host back from the enchantments laid upon them by Aoife. If you will do us the honour of accepting these tokens in gratitude for all you have done, then it would please this council greatly.'

The monk was amazed at the richness of the gifts. Before he could find the words to politely refuse, the War-Druid went on.

'Will you accept our humble gifts?'

He saw that these people were doing him a great honour and that it might offend them if he did not graciously accept. He was a monk, he reminded himself. Robes of war were not meant for one such as him. Then he recalled his teacher had often said it didn't matter what clothes he wore as long as he was a monk in his heart.

'I will humbly honour your gracious endowments,' he answered.

A great tear had welled in his eye and was rolling down his cheek. No one had ever honoured him so. He could hardly believe anyone could be so grateful to him for anything. In his estimation it had only been a small thing he had done.

The warrior-woman chieftain stepped forward as her

companions dressed Caoimhin in tunic, britches and boots. Then the coat of sparkling armour was slipped over his head and belted tightly at his waist.

A coif of soft padded linen was laid over his long hair and fastened beneath the chin with a knot. At last Becc mac Dé stepped forward to place the silver war helm on his head. When that was done the War-Druid stepped back and smiled with fatherly pride at the monk.

'There once was a fisherman who loved to fish in the deep waters,' he said. Caoimhin expected he was going to be told a story. 'One day a bright ocean-going fish snagged in his net, and though it weighed as much again as that fisherman, he hauled it in to his sturdy leather curragh. His boat creaked and complained with the burden. Nevertheless he took that fish home. And it fed his family for a month. I have a sense this fish will feed his kinfolk for a year at least.'

Caoimhin smiled. He didn't understand the poem but he thought it would be best to show his appreciation for the thought behind it. He bowed low to the chieftains.

Srón stood up and all the other chieftains followed her example.

'My ancestor would have put it this way,' she began. 'I was becalmed and you summoned the breeze. My oar was washed overboard and you lent me yours. Therefore I will share my catch with you this night and every night forever if you will hold a lantern at the stern of my leather boat to light my work. And that way if I come home smelling of fish oil then so will you.'

The gathering hummed approval. There were whispers that Srón had inherited the legendary talent of her ancestors. Caoimhin caught himself blushing as he noticed the sparkle of pride in Srón's eyes.

Becc mac Dé raised his arms in the air as all fell silent.

'Hail to the Fisher-King!' the chieftains suddenly shouted in one voice. 'Hail to King Caoimhin!'

Midnight on All Souls Eve

While the Sen Erainn were acclaiming their new king Sianan and Tóraí were crawling into the entrance of a low cave. The interior was darker than dark. It was blacker than pitch. Sianan stepped in and even with her excellent eyesight could see nothing whatsoever.

'We can't possibly go on!' she mourned. 'How will we find our way without a light?'

'We don't need eyes when we have my nose,' Tóraí told her.

He snatched her hand and led her down a long winding stair deep into the bowels of the Earth. Sianan lost count of the steps. Her whole mind was concentrated on keeping her footfall steady in the overwhelming blackness of the cavern.

By and by she noted that the shadows had lifted a little. She put that down to her eyes adjusting to the dark. But it turned out there was a flaming torch set in the wall at the bottom of the staircase.

When they reached the entrance hall where the torch was hanging Sianan stayed close to the wall. Her instincts told her it was deadly dangerous for them to be wandering around in this Redcap cavern without the leave of the queen.

Tóraí wasn't so timid. He sniffed the air this way and that. Then he took her hand again.

'The passage leads out to the main hall. Beyond that another tunnel leads directly to Aoife's feasting hall. Tonight there is to be a great celebration. Guests are coming in from near and far. It is to be a masking.'

'A masking?' Sianan asked.

She understood well enough what that meant. But I suppose you wouldn't know what a masking is. So I'll tell you. In the ancient days of the long ago, before the Gaels, our ancestors, came to this land, the Fir-Bolg and the Tuatha-De-Danaan dwelled in Ireland. They celebrated the same fire festivals as our folk for we are all kindred to one another if you trace back far enough. Only the details of the ritual ceremonies differed between our clans. To the Fir-Bolg, who were Aoife's people and who are also known to us as the Redcaps, Samhain Eve was a time of mystic significance. Even among the Culdees of my kinfolk this was so. But we didn't go in for the elaborate ritual which took place amongst the Fir-Bolg.

You see, it's like this. It was well understood since the ancient days that the body which each of us inhabits is no more than a suit of clothes. The face we wear is little more than a mask. That's how a certain custom grew up among Aoife's kinfolk.

At Samhain everyone would don a mask to attend a great party. These masks were more than simple emblems or trifles as they are among the Norman folk. It was believed that anyone who wore a mask was literally transformed into the creature it represented. Thus it was considered very bad manners to attend the festivities in a mask without a complete change of attire to go along with it. The masking of one's everyday appearance granted licence to behave according to the whims of the character portrayed by the new face.

Thus emotions that had, by convention, been left unexpressed for the year, such as anger, jealousy, lust or mocking derision, were allowed to surface. And since no one could tell who was who, these potentially dangerous expressions could find a safe release.

It's a very complex tradition. I can't say I understand it fully myself. I have attended a few of these celebrations on Inis Mór since the events of this tale took place. I can say with certainty they are marvellous affairs. There's dancing, frolicking, fighting, flirting and fun to be had as long as you follow the rules. And it is understood that although you are no longer walking in the form of your current incarnation, you are also expressing an aspect of oneself.

Though I might put on a fish-head mask, that doesn't mean I am transformed into a fish. I have simply decided to give full expression to those qualities I have about me which are fish-like. If I know myself well enough I may also recall a previous incarnation in which I was indeed a fish. But that's rarely a conscious decision. It is the mask which draws these things out. The mask chooses you, if you like.

'That's how Flidais plans to ambush Aoife,' Tóraí explained. 'Everyone will be masked, including the entertainers. If we hold any hope of entering that celebration at the feasting hall we will have to find ourselves some masks as well.'

My experience of life has been that quite often when you set your sights on attaining something the means are made available to you almost immediately. What you choose to do with those means is what really influences the outcome.

So it was with Tóraí and Sianan. The very moment she realised they would need some sort of festive disguise they were provided with one. And it happened in a most interesting manner.

They had been carefully traversing the cavern tunnel which led toward the feasting chamber when Tóraí suddenly placed a firm hand on Sianan's chest. It was already too late for him to explain why. At the next corner two strange folk were seated on a stair drinking from a large bottle made of the rarest blue glass.

And if that were not enough to make the hackles stand up at the back of Sianan's neck, they were both dressed in costumes.

One had a mask which depicted the long snout and floppy ears of a red Sotar dog. And the other wore the long beak, black feathers and pointed skull of a raven.

'They're drunk,' Tóraí whispered to her.

Then, without a word about what he intended to do, he strode forward to greet the strangers.

'Good evening, my dears!' he offered. 'I see you're ready for the feast. It'll be a fine one tonight.'

'Indeed!' the pair of drunken revellers replied in chorus. 'The queen will be a goddess on the morrow. And she has commanded us all to attend her party.'

The fellow dressed as a Sotar leaned close to Tóraí. There was a terrible stench of wine on his breath.

'I'm a performer,' he confided. 'So is he. We've been commanded to juggle for the queen. But I don't think I'll be going.'

'Why not?' Tóraí asked.

The stranger never replied. He simply fell forward unconscious, numbed by a surfeit of the blue-bottle inebriant. His companion frowned, burped loudly, looked at the bottle as if it were poison, shook it, handed it to Tóraí then collapsed on top of his friend.

By then Sianan was looking over her companion's shoulder in horror.

'What did you do to them?' she hissed. 'You've murdered them!'

'They're well capable of murdering themselves,' he assured her. 'Come on, let's get these two up the stairs and out of sight.'

They each dragged a drunkard up a dozen steps into the darkness and there they relieved them of their masks and beautiful costumes. A short while later Sianan emerged from the staircase dressed in a raven mask and a glorious cloak of feathers. She clicked her beak and waddled as she'd seen Lom Dubh do so many times.

Then Tóraí appeared in the mask of a dog. Of course it wasn't such a difficult thing for him to play the red Sotar. He'd already had a lifetime of experience in that role.

'Who are those two?' she asked her companion. 'They seem to be mortals. They certainly aren't Redcaps.'

'They're travelling players,' he explained. 'They've been employed to entertain the crowd at the feast.'

As he spoke Sianan looked at her companion with amusement. When he finished she let out a little laugh.

'I don't want you to take this the wrong way,' she confided, 'but for a man you make a fine dog.'

'But if I were a raven,' he replied, 'I'd know in an instant you were a lady.'

Sianan knew this wasn't a comment on how unconvincing her raven-waddle appeared. He was actually paying her a very sweet compliment. So she was glad the mask covered her face. Tóraí couldn't possibly have noticed her blushing and smiling with delight.

She raised the blue mead bottle in her hand to indicate they should press on. Tóraí bowed low and then he was off ahead of her, taking full advantage of this opportunity to allow his Sotar nature to shine through.

They hadn't gone a hundred paces when they came to a large set of double doors, one of which was slightly ajar. Within the chamber beyond there were lights and music and raucous dancing. The laughter of many folk flowed out into the corridor mixed with the heady scent of roasted meats.

Sianan's mouth began to water. It was Samhain Eve. Even among the Culdee folk this was a night for wild celebrations. She'd been looking forward to this evening all year long. It was a pity, she told herself, the festivities at the Killibegs had been called off. But what better place to spend this holy eve than in the feasting hall of the Queen of the Night?

Tóraí waited for his friend beside the door, poking his

inquisitive mask nose through the crack far enough to take in the joyous atmosphere beyond. As Sianan approached he turned to her with anticipation.

'What a night we're going to have!' he exclaimed, barely able to contain his excitement.

'We're not here to have a good time,' she reminded him, and herself, I'm sure, for who wouldn't have been tempted to indulge in a little party in that hall?

As she spoke those words a huge Redcap guard opened the door and stepped out. He was wearing the most ridiculously small badger mask and a tiny animal skin on his back. Neither concealed his identity at all. He leaned heavily on his long-handled war sickle as he spoke.

'That's right!' he told Tóraí sternly. 'You're here to give a good performance and entertain the queen.'

'What?' the dog-man stuttered.

'You're late!' the Redcap snarled as he repeatedly pointed a finger hard into Tóraí's chest with each syllable. 'You're lucky she isn't here yet or she'd have your blood for a breakfast beverage.'

The guard put an enormous firm hand in the small of Tóraí's back and pushed him into the chamber. Sianan squeezed past the guard before he had the opportunity to shove her along in the same manner.

The sight that met her eyes as she entered the hall was one you would never forget if ever you saw it. And she never did. Indeed, in later years she delighted to describe it to me again and again. So even though I wasn't there I have a clear picture of the scene in my mind.

The chamber was huge. Ten men could have stood shoulder upon shoulder to the ceiling. To walk from one end to the other would have been a span of some two hundred steps and the same from side to side. Eight sets of double doors led into the room, two at each wall. There were no windows so the air

THE WELL OF THE GODDESS

did not circulate well. To compensate for this there was a huge censer swinging back and forth across the centre of the chamber billowing huge gusts of rose and frankincense smoke.

At either end of the hall two enormous candelabra were set into the ceiling to light the chamber. Each one of these fantastic gilded ornaments supported two hundred candles. Every candle had a tiny reflector behind it to add a little to the strength of its illumination.

Tables were arranged around the walls loaded with food and drink of every kind. There were further candelabra placed on stands at intervals on these tables. No one had sat down yet to eat.

The guests were mingling in the middle of the floor, chatting, laughing and generally running amok as one is wont to do on Samhain Eve. At the far end of the hall a group of musicians were playing on a raised platform but Sianan had to strain her ears above the noise of the crowd to hear what they were playing.

'Bloody typical,' she muttered to herself. 'I finally get the chance to attend a real Faerie feast and I can't hear the bloody band playing over the noise of the cackling feasters.'

Just then she brushed past a seated figure wearing the astonishingly vibrant likeness of a man for a mask.

'You'd better be careful what you say, Sianan,' the wearer warned her in a familiar cackle. The eyebrows of the mask rose and fell unconvincingly in time with his words. 'You don't want anyone to recognise you. Do you?'

She narrowed her eyes in suspicion. It was a few moments before she managed to put a face to the voice and then a few more before she recovered from her surprise.

'What are you doing here?' she growled with genuine anger. 'You're supposed to be off fetching the Morrigán! I can't rely on you to do anything.'

'There, there, my darling Sianan,' the figure laughed. 'Calm down. You're attracting attention to yourself.'

'You black-hearted bastard!' she snapped. 'Just wait till I get hold of you.'

'Now, now!' he warned her. 'You make a fine raven by the way. I've never looked at you in this light before. You're really quite attractive. Perhaps we should put our differences aside for a while and get to know one another better.'

'Lom Dubh,' she retorted, gritting her teeth as she spoke, 'if you were the last raven on Earth I wouldn't waste my time with your talk. You're a lying, split-beaked, mangy-feathered son of a cuckoo if ever there was one. Why aren't you off looking for the Morrigán as you promised?'

'I got distracted,' he explained. 'First of all Robert FitzWilliam wanted me to pass a message on to you. But I couldn't find hide nor feather of you anywhere. When I returned to meet him at the appointed place he didn't turn up at all. Most frustrating it was.'

'Where is he now?'

'How should I know?'

'You should have come searching for me,' Sianan grunted in reprimand. 'It can't be helped. Now I want you to fly back to the Killibegs with some news.'

'What? And miss the best party of the year?' he sputtered, or as near to a sputter as a raven can manage. 'Actually, there won't be another shin-fling like this for a good long while. Aoife's celebrating her ascension to the title and status of goddess tonight. That doesn't happen every Samhain Oidche.'

'I know all about Aoife, you black-eyed bundle of bones! I'm here to put a stop to her. Remember?'

'Oh yes,' Lom Dubh recalled. 'You're not very happy with the queen, are you?'

'What about the Morrigán?' Sianan demanded. 'Where is she?'

'She's over there,' the raven informed her. 'That's her

dressed as a Druid woman. She's leaning on the arm of that fellow who's dressed as a fish. That's Sorcha and Dalan. Sorcha has been the reigning Morrigán for two thousand, seven hundred winters. She retires next year. Dalan is her consort. I've known them since the old days when he was the Druid advisor to my father King Brocan. Even then I had a feeling he'd go far. Nice chap too. Always has a good word to say for everyone. He's renowned as a Brehon judge and he's got an abiding love of Sen Erainn poetry. Spends a lot of time on Inis Mór listening—'

'Shut up!' Sianan cut in. 'I'm not in the mood for one of your interminable history lessons. Introduce me to the Morrigán.'

As you'd know if you'd heard any tales when you were a child, the Morrigán is an ancient one who watches over the battlefield. She is the Queen of the Ravens and she has responsibility for raising up wars.

The raven lifted his mask a little with one wing.

'Are you sure you want me to do that?'

'Yes!'

'She won't be happy about it. It's her feasting night.'

'Just do it!'

'Very well,' the raven shrugged, or as near to a shrug as a carrion bird can approximate.

Then he let out a piercing whistle that had Sianan covering her ears with pain and Tóraí running to her side.

'What's the matter?' the dog-man asked excitedly. 'Is something happening? Are we going somewhere? Is this a game?'

Lom Dubh leaned forward to confide in Sianan.

'I know he's dressed as a red Sotar but he's taking the role a bit seriously, isn't he? Where do you find these folk who follow you round?'

Sianan grunted under her mask. 'You dusty-coated, carrion-breathed, spindle-clawed descendant of a pigeon! I have a good mind to pluck your scrawny back to patch my cloak.'

'It's a fine cloak by the way,' Lom Dubh complimented. 'It could almost pass as a Druid cloak of the old days.'

Sianan was going to let him know she'd had enough of his empty promises. He was a self-centred, evil-hearted creature without any conscience at all, in her opinion. But she didn't get the chance.

A hand was at her shoulder and she half turned to see a Druid woman with long matted brown locks leaning on an intricately carved staff.

In an instant the abbess was down on one knee paying homage to the Morrigán.

'Get up!' the raven queen insisted. 'This is the one night of the year when I don't have to attend to the duties of my office.'

Sianan arose slowly but averted her eyes to the floor out of respect as she did so. Every reveller in the immediate vicinity noticed her. And tongues began to wag.

'You're attracting attention to yourself,' Lom Dubh warned. 'Don't you know anything about Faerie etiquette?'

'Is this a friend of yours?' Sorcha the Morrigán asked him. 'She's a bit green to be out before midnight on Samhain Oidche, isn't she?'

'Forgive me, my lady,' the raven explained. 'She's been wanting a word with you regarding Aoife's ascension to the rank of goddess.'

'Has she?'

'She was hoping you'd intervene on behalf of the Culdee folk of the Killibegs who will surely be slaughtered this night by Aoife's Redcaps.'

'Was she?'

'I told her you were the Queen of Carrion and that you wouldn't deprive your subjects of their Samhain feast. But she thought she could persuade you to relent.'

401

'Did she?'

Sorcha touched the raven-feather cloak Sianan was wearing.

'Where did you get this?' she asked. 'This is one of the ancient Druid cloaks. Only a poet is entitled to wear such a garment.'

'I found it,' the abbess replied. 'On a drunken entertainer. He relinquished it to me when he fell into a stupor.'

'Who is this woman?' the Morrigán asked Lom Dubh. 'I seem to recognise her voice.'

'This is Sianan,' the raven answered in a low voice, for it was Samhain. It was considered very impolite to reveal a masked reveller's identity. 'She is a Gael. She is one of the Fánaí who are also known as the Wanderers.'

'That's where I've heard her voice!' Sorcha exclaimed.

'We've never met,' Sianan cut in.

'But I've sat on the roof of your chapel in my raven form and listened to you talk to your people,' the raven-queen told her. 'And I was one of those Druids who administered the Quicken Brew to you.'

Then Sorcha shook herself like a bird throwing the dust off its feathers.

'Tonight I am permitted to take my woman-shape again. I don't have to parade around in the form of a bird. I've only got one more cycle of the seasons to serve as carrion-queen. I'm tired. What makes you think I'd want to help you save the lives of a few mortals?'

Sianan didn't know what to say. If the Morrigán wouldn't help, then who would?

'I'm surprised you're still bothering with them,' the raven monarch went on. 'Aren't you bored with their petty struggles yet? Perhaps it's time you started associating with immortals. Try to enjoy yourself tonight. Meet a few folk. Get to know your peers. You're a new face. We haven't beheld a new face in our company for an age.'

'I belong with the mortal kind,' Sianan protested. 'I made a vow to stay among them to preserve the lore and law of my people.'

The Morrigán stepped closer and put a sisterly arm around her shoulder.

'My dear,' she began, 'that is a very fine sentiment. I applaud your sense of duty. If only there were more folk like you among the immortal kind. Have you ever considered training to become the Morrigán? I think you'd make a marvellous carrion-queen.'

'Me?'

'Yes, my dear. You. As it happens, tonight is the night I must announce my successor. I had a few folk in mind for the job. I even considered Aoife for a while. But she's far too self-obsessed to take on such a demanding regency. You, on the other hand, would be perfect for the role. What do you say?'

'What of my duty to the Gaels?' Sianan objected. 'What of my promise to preserve and protect our songs, stories and poems?'

'I don't imagine there'd be any conflict,' Sorcha replied. 'The Morrigán is as much a part of Gaelic culture as she is of Fir-Bolg, Danaan or Raven. You'd be doing your people a great service. Not many Gaels remember the Morrigán in these times. The Norman folk are everywhere. It would be very sad if their concept of the raven as merely an evil harbinger of death were to swallow up all the many aspects of the office or of the old ways.'

Sorcha shrugged her shoulders and made an observation. 'The cloak of raven feathers suits you very well. I would have thought you were born to wear it.'

'I was just telling her what a fine raven she makes,' Lom Dubh cut in. 'She'd be an exemplary Morrigán. Just the kind of new blood we need on the throne.'

'Be careful, Lom Dubh,' Sorcha shot back. 'I'm still the queen.'

'I apologise, Your Majesty,' he bowed. 'I only meant that –'

'I know what you meant. You're still under my jurisdiction while you walk about in raven skin. A man-mask doesn't make you man. Though, I grant you, there are many men who would disagree with me on that point.'

The Morrigán turned her attention back to Sianan.

'What do you say?' she asked. 'Would you like a unique opportunity to serve your people? Would you be up to the task? Would you be the one to lead the Raven-kind?'

'I'll have to consider your kind offer,' Sianan answered politely, still taken aback.

'Of course you will,' Sorcha nodded as she patted Sianan's shoulder. 'We'll speak again before midnight. Think carefully. Try to enjoy yourself here tonight. It's your first Samhain among your own kind.'

'My own kind?'

'You're an immortal,' Sorcha laughed, amused that Sianan did not think of herself as one of these people. 'Most folk here this evening are of the undying kind also. Mortals are not your real kin.'

Her eyes sparkled with compassion.

'I'm sure this is difficult for you to accept,' the Morrigán told her. 'Those who are doomed to die are not the same as we are. They are short-sighted. They are selfish. They are petty. That's why we conceal ourselves from them. That's why we take on disguises and forms which confound their understanding.'

She sighed and stepped back to take the hand of her companion Dalan.

'He and I have drawn breath since the days before the Gaels came to this land,' Sorcha revealed. 'Dalan and I saw the ships of your ancestors arrive on these shores after their voyage from the Iberian lands. We shared table with kings and poets who are but legends to you. And although the seasons have passed without number we still remember what it is to be mortal.'

Dalan smiled at the raven-queen. His fishy eyes were full of admiration and love for this woman.

'The fate of mortals is not our fate. The ways of mortals are not our ways. We have a duty as guardians of the land. The mortal kind would cut the forests until there was no timber left standing.'

'Bough-splitting bastards!' Lom Dubh interjected.

Sorcha ignored him. 'The mortal kind would build towns, hunt out the forest folk, fill the rivers with their filth, choke the air with their hearth smoke, scour the land with their ploughs and scar the country with their fires. If we let them.'

'The people must feed themselves,' Sianan protested. 'They must have timber for building and grain for their bellies.'

'They live only a few seasons,' Sorcha retorted with a dismissive wave of the hand. 'We will still be here long after they have stripped the Earth of all its goodness. We will live on when the melody of their songs is but a distant echo. And it is our folk, the immortals, who will have to look on the results of their devastation when the mortal kind are no more.'

'Bark-stripping brigands!' Lom Dubh muttered.

There was such venom in the raven's voice that Sianan could hardly recognise him. Now I don't know what it is to be immortal. But for what it's worth, here's my opinion.

I can understand what Lom Dubh and Sorcha the Morrigán were on about. Even in the space of my short life there has been a noticeable change come over the land of Ireland. There are fewer forests. That goes without saying. The Normans are renowned axemen and they do not stint with the ringing of their blades.

There are less deer in the woods, because there are not so many woods. Nevertheless a host of hunters roam about the country. The rivers are full of rubbish which is the detritus of town living. The solid floating waste of too many bowels has driven the fish away. The sunrise is too often marred by grey-brown wood smoke.

The bogs which were once the domain of countless birds and wondrous flowers are being shovelled into the fireplace to be burned as turf fuel. Why has bog turf replaced timber as fuel? Because there isn't enough timber left to burn.

Scarred tracts of land are all that is left of what was once virgin bog full of the sweet odour of the peat. The birds are leaving this wasteland never to return. The country is being transformed.

There was a time when there were no towns in Ireland. All our people were like the Culdees who wander from place to place making their homes without disturbing the fragile balance of the countryside.

But who would care to live such a life these days? The Normans stop the travelling folk with fences and boundaries. I challenge you to cross the lands of a lord with all your worldly possessions on a cart. You'll soon see what I mean. You'll have a sword at your throat and an arrow in your back before you can say, 'I'm not trespassing. I'm just passing through.'

The farmer wants to produce more than he can eat so he can pay his taxes and sell his excess to the townsman. The towns-man wants more and more food because he's got too many children and because it is fashionable to be fat. And because he has to pay his dues to his lord. The lord wants the latest fashions in tunic embroidery. He wants the finest food and the best horses. So he increases the taxes. The king wants to be one step ahead of his nobles in the tunic-embroidery race so he demands more taxes from the lords. And the Pope sitting in Rome far removed from the farmer takes a tenth of everything and as a consequence wears very fine tunic embroidery indeed.

All this greed bleeds the countryside of life. And one day, mark my words, the land will turn up its toes and die. It will reach the limit of its tolerance, rebel against our ways and starve us out. Then the lords can try eating their lovely tunics. I hope the fine gold embroidery sticks in their teeth.

The immortal kind have always known there was going to be trouble if our numbers grew too great. They have to live with the terrible short-sighted destructiveness with which we foolish mortals indulge ourselves. Little wonder the Old Ones hold us in such contempt.

And why do they keep apart from us? That's easy enough to answer. Mortals, as I said, are short-sighted. Their eyes are full of greed visions of their own enrichment. If it were common knowledge there were ever-living ones among us, many mortals would soon desire to share the accursed gift of life eternal.

How would the immortal kind keep the secret of the Quicken Brew? It wouldn't be long before there were too many ever-living ones walking the Earth. There'd be hunger among their kind. And there is nothing, my dear, absolutely nothing, so terrifying a thought as the pain of a hunger which cannot and will not be relieved.

Can you imagine what it would be like to go on living in the agony of famine with no hope of release? The immortal kind suffer hunger too, you know. So they're well frightened of famine that finds no end in death. That's why they see our childish ways as nothing short of disastrous.

The Morrigán and the Raven folk perform a valuable service to the immortals and to the Earth. The Queen of the Ravens stirs up wars which keep the population of mortals within manageable restraints and so relieves the burden on the land. Her subjects clean up the battlefield, turning the slain into nourishment for themselves and the soil.

You may think this a brutal way to look at the world. But consider what I say. I knew a tree once that had stood a thousand summers. From acorn to oak that magnificent creature had seen more life than you will ever understand. His wisdom was far-reaching. Mortals such as you or I could not hope to fathom his knowledge. He'd seen fire, flood, tempest, forest and farmland.

He knew he was not merely an oak. He knew he was an expression of the All. His understanding was in the terms of an oak tree. He was but one branch of the great tree of creation. As we all are.

After a thousand years of life and living he was cut down in an hour. In a day he was cut up. In a week his body was no more than a memory, his soul had fled, the soil of his home had been turned up to plant oats. And do you know what they did with his heart? The bloody Normans fashioned an iron-bound gate from his flesh and splinters to keep their enemies out.

We mortals are but passing flickers of the candle. When the wax is all gone and the wick is burned out, the flame of our lives must pass to another candle or it is completely extinguished. But the immortal kind are like the sun. In their ever-burning silence they look down on us. They are among us day by day. Mark my words they are there, often masquerading as mortals. You may even know a few of them without realising their true nature. But for the most part the ever-living ones have long ceased to reveal themselves to us.

Even in my lifetime most folk have stopped believing in them. The Old Ones have chosen to withdraw from us. They are patient. They know that if we go on with our greed we will be gone soon enough. And then this Earth will be their domain alone.

When our towns are deserted the forests will reclaim the streets. The woods will swallow up all the striving and the greed and turn it into nourishment for the saplings of the future. What seems like an age to us is but a moment to the Old Ones. What takes a lifetime for a king to build may be swept away in a breath and returned to the soil.

As I said, many of the immortals withdraw completely from the world to await our passing. Some work toward hastening our destruction either in subtle or nor so subtle ways. A few try to labour in alliance with our folk to heal the damage of our greed. Only one or two reveal themselves in the hope that all the wanton destruction of our people might be averted.

As the Morrigán touched Sianan on the shoulder once again she mystically imparted all these revelations and more to her. The abbess was suddenly aware of many things which had never crossed her mind before.

'You have dwelled too long among the dying and the dead,' Sorcha told her. 'Now it is time to walk among the living who are your true kin. When the petty passions of the mortal kind are turned to dust, who will give you comfort? Only those who are your eternal brothers and sisters.'

Sianan was lost for words.

The Morrigán smiled as she added one last thing. She spoke in a joyous conspiratorial whisper. 'Awake! Dance in celebration this night. You are born of the Ever-Living Ones. Do not mourn for the folk of the Killibegs. Do not mourn ever. You cannot avoid your nature so you must embrace it. Whether you do so this evening or later in your long life makes no difference. One day the mortal kind will be but a memory and you will return to the bosom of your true kinfolk.'

With that her escort and consort, Dalan the Brehon Judge, took the raven-queen's arm and they strode off toward the far end of the hall to dance. All the way the two of them were laughing. Their eyes were jewels of enjoyment. Their souls shone with love for one another.

'You'd do well to take careful note of all Sorcha has to say,' Lom Dubh suggested as he watched them take up the dance.

'Whose side are you on?' Sianan asked, the frustration clearly expressed in her voice.

'I am Lom of the Fir-Bolg,' he reminded her. 'I was a king among my people once, before these accursed feathers sprouted from me. My sister is Aoife. Sorcha has been the Queen of the

409

Raven-kind since I first took this form. I have watched countless generations of the mortal kind come and go. I hold some of them in great affection still. But I no longer allow myself to become attached to them. They are no more than leaves which fall then return to the soil to nourish the tree.'

He clicked his beak under the mask he wore before he spoke again.

'Perhaps she's right. Maybe it's time you let go of your attachment to those who suffer death. It's not healthy for you to tie your fate to them too closely. All your efforts will come to naught. For they will die and you will not.'

'Are you advising me to abandon the people of the Killibegs? Are you telling me I should let the Redcaps overrun the settlement to murder everyone in cold blood? Do you suggest I sit back and watch while Aoife uses the fear caused by the deaths of all those innocent people to further her own cause?'

The raven shrugged. That is to say he moved about under the costume so it looked like he was shrugging.

'The people of the Killibegs are beyond your help,' he soothed. 'Whether they perish tonight or at some other time, they will certainly die, every one of them. As for Aoife, it remains to be seen whether she will indeed persevere with her plan to terrorise the country into acclaiming her a goddess. There are still many obstacles in her path which must be overcome before that happens.'

Tóraí touched Sianan on the arm to get her attention. The abbess turned to look at him and as she did so Lom Dubh took the opportunity to slip off the high chair he'd been seated upon and disappear into the crowd.

He'd had enough of all this seriousness. He wanted to enjoy the celebration. He had spotted two good friends who'd just arrived in the hall. They were sporting the forms of a man and woman rather than their usual awful worm shape.

'If the Nathairaí are allowed an evening without their

punishment I don't see why I shouldn't do the same thing,' he muttered to himself.

Amidst the growing excitement in Aoife's hall no one noticed Lom Dubh withdraw to a corner to transform himself. In a few seconds he'd changed into a young man with long jet-black hair and a thin pointed goatee beard. His clothes were of dark green, closely woven wool over which he sported a cloak of deepest crimson fastened with a large silver brooch and pin.

He adjusted the cloak a little. Then he produced a circlet of silver from his tunic and placed it on his head to hold his hair in place. Satisfied that he was ready to present himself in polite company, he put up a hand to catch the attention of the Nathairí.

'Lochie! Isleen! Over here! It's me!'

Sianan didn't notice the change any more than anyone else in the hall. She was much more interested in what Tóraí had to say to her.

'He's here,' the dog-man whispered, loud enough so she could just hear him. 'Robert FitzWilliam has arrived.'

Indeed it was true. Robert FitzWilliam was wearing Aoife's gift, the helm of shining silver with its strange face plate shaped like the beak of a bird. And he had just been admitted to the hall through the same door Sianan and Tóraí had entered.

He was dressed as a Knight of the Temple, to be sure, as I described to you earlier. But there was nothing else about him that might have distinguished him as Sir Robert. So how did Tóraí know it was him? That's easy to answer.

Tóraí had a nose for these things.

'He has a tinge of long-distance travel about him,' the

411

dog-man explained, taking short sharp sniffs at the air. 'And there's still a hint of boiled milk clinging to his person. A cheese maker may wash diligently every day but he will never scrub the odour of curds from his skin.'

'Don't let him know we've recognised him,' Sianan whispered. 'We'll follow him round a while until I'm ready to make my move. I don't want to attract any unwanted attention from Aoife or her Redcaps.'

As she spoke a hand came down on her shoulder.

'You're up,' announced the Redcap who'd been standing at the door. 'Mugwort's just about to start his show and you're on after him. I hope you've got a good performance planned. The queen has strict instructions that we're to deal severely with any entertainers who fall short of the mark this evening.'

'Severely?' Tóraí repeated with obvious discomfort. 'What do you mean by severely?'

The Redcap brought the great crescent of his sickle in close around the dog-man's shoulders without quite touching the blade to Tóraí's neck.

'Do I really need to explain myself?' he grunted.

'Not at all,' he gulped. 'I'm a Seer. I understand perfectly what's on your mind.'

'I think you must be mistaken,' Sianan protested, intervening to push the sickle out of harm's way.

The Redcap lifted up his badger mask to leer at her.

'I don't think I am,' he assured her. 'The last time I was mistaken, I mistakenly took off the heads of two entertainers.'

He frowned menacingly.

'I make no secret of it. I despise your kind. You're the lowest of the low. And if you're part of Mugwort's company you're worse than the worst.'

'I don't know anyone called Mugwort,' Sianan shot back.

'You don't? Aren't you the jester called Feverfew?'

Sianan realised she could be in trouble if the Redcap discovered she wasn't among the invited guests.

'Of course I am,' she told him, thinking quickly. 'I've just had a bit too much to drink. I'm not myself. I probably shouldn't have stayed up so late last night. I'm all at sixes and sevens; muddle, muddle, that's me.'

Suddenly a hand came down on her other shoulder.

'Stop stealing my lines!' a voice demanded.

When Sianan looked to see who it was she saw a strange man dressed in traditional troubadour garb but wearing no more of a disguise than an exceptionally long, droopy and obviously false nose.

'Who are you?' the Redcap bellowed.

The troubadour lifted the false nose up from his face.

'It's me.'

The Redcap screwed up his face then shook his head to show he didn't recognise him.

'Mugwort!' the jester barked.

'So it is! Master Mugwort! Well I never! I didn't recognise you. That's a brilliant disguise!'

'Thank you,' the entertainer bowed.

The Redcap adjusted his badger mask as he spoke.

'I was just telling Feverfew here I thought you were the worst of the worst. But it appears you're not so bad at disguise, subterfuge and costuming after all. You certainly fooled me!'

'You may leave us now,' the jester informed the guard imperiously. 'We must prepare for our performance and you are keeping us from our profession.'

'Of course, Master Mugwort,' the Redcap bowed and then he was off to stand his post at the door.

Mugwort stepped closer to Sianan and grabbed her by the raven-feather cloak.

'I know you've been using my lines!' he rebuked her. 'You'd

better watch yourself. If I catch you doing that again I'll use the Book of Pictures on you. So be warned.'

Sianan lowered her head to indicate she would do as he demanded and thanked her guardian spirits Mugwort hadn't realised she wasn't Feverfew at all.

'You'd better get ready to take over from me,' he told her. 'The queen will be here soon. When I've finished my performance you'll be on stage straight afterwards. We mustn't keep her waiting. Have you been practising the juggling I set you to?'

Sianan shrugged.

'Juggling the small sickles!' he half shrieked in rage.

She nodded.

'Good thing too! Now go to your places, the both of you. I'm going to prepare myself for the accolades of the queen.'

Then he was off pushing through the crowd toward the raised stage where the musicians were still playing. A fat new satchel of red leather was on his shoulder. And he carried a large bundle of blank parchment under his arm.

By the time he'd gone Robert had also mingled in with the crowd. Sianan stood on her toes to search over the heads of the gathering but she couldn't see him anywhere. She turned to Tóraí. He was gone too. So she started pushing her way through the crowd toward to the stage.

The young FitzWilliam was conducting a search of his own. He realised he had no idea what Flidais looked like. How was he going to find her in amongst all these strange masked folk? Then, once he found her, how was he going to take off her head without being prevented from doing so?

414

Being the kind of valiant fellow he was there was no thought in his mind for his own safety. He was completely committed to his quest. As he used to say, there's no problem that can't be solved. Or as I always say, you can't sup on chicken broth without you must pluck a few feathers.

So he resolved to approach someone in the crowd and ask them to point Flidais out to him. This was actually a riskier undertaking than he perhaps realised.

To reveal he didn't know what Flidais looked like without a mask was one sure way to prove he didn't belong among this company. But to be ignorant of the fact that this was a masked feasting where identities were not supposed to be revealed would be proof positive he was not an invited guest.

As chance would have it Robert's legendary luck was riding at his shoulder that night. He came to a point in his wanderings through the crowd when he was confronted by three ordinary enough looking folk. They could have been mortals for all he knew, they were so out of place among the many other outlandish guests.

So he decided to ask them his question.

'Good evening,' he began.

The two men bowed to him. The red-haired woman in the long green gown raised her eyebrows and offered her hand for him to kiss.

'Good evening,' she purred, her eyes sparkling with excessive mischief and a mystical fire of passion. 'Where did you spring from, my dear? I do hope that armour is hiding what my imagination has filled it with.'

Robert took her hand and carefully raised the visor of his helm just far enough so that he could touch his lips to her fingers but not far enough that she could glimpse his face.

'Calm down, Isleen,' one of the men sighed. 'I know it's been a while since you were allowed to walk about in this form. But you're making a fool of yourself.'

'Shut up, Lochie!' she snarled out of the corner of her mouth. 'I've been trapped in that worm body for more winters than I care to recall. Aoife allowed me to take on my womanly form tonight for the first time since accursed Danu imprisoned us. I'm going to take advantage of these few hours before I have to be a worm again.'

She turned her head sharply to her companion.

'If you're going to waste your time, that's your business. Leave me alone!'

Robert coughed uncomfortably before he broached the difficult subject.

'Could any of you kind people point out the Goddess Flidais to me?'

'Who wants to know?' Isleen snapped, her jealous side finding expression immediately.

'I am merely a humble admirer of hers. I was hoping to kneel down before her in worship.'

Lochie laughed. 'He's not interested in you! He's come looking for a younger maid.'

'Shut up!' Isleen grunted back. 'She's only a few thousand winters younger than me.'

'Just a moment,' the other male cut in as he scrutinised the armour and the white tunic Robert wore. 'I know your voice from somewhere. What's your name?'

'You shouldn't ask questions on a night like this,' Lochie reprimanded him. 'We're all here to have fun. No one wants to be reminded of their day-to-day form.'

Then the Nathair turned to Robert. 'I hope you will find it in your heart to forgive my friends,' he said. 'They've spent a long while trapped in the form of a raven and a worm. They've forgotten what good manners are. Indeed, I too have been a worm these many winters. Don't hold our brashness against us.'

'I know his voice!' the other man insisted.

'Shut up, Lom Dubh!' Lochie hissed.

'Lom Dubh!' Robert exclaimed. 'Is that you?'

Then the knight raised the face plate of his helm.

'It's me,' he whispered. 'Robert FitzWilliam.'

'Robert!' the raven-man exclaimed in terror. 'What are you doing here?'

He took the knight by the arm to lead him toward the door.

'You must leave immediately. It's dangerous for you to be here tonight. If she finds you the queen will have your hide for a hearth rug.'

'Aoife commanded me to come here tonight,' Robert explained. 'I've been set a quest to fill.'

The two Nathairaí looked at each other in dismay. Then they turned to Lom Dubh.

'There's going to be trouble,' Isleen decided. 'Terrible trouble.'

'We'd better leave,' Lochie suggested. 'It could get very uncomfortable here in the hall.'

Lom Dubh turned his attention back to Robert.

'Why are you seeking Flidais?' he pressed.

'I am to take off her head,' he confided.

Lom Dubh felt the blood drain from his fleshy face. Isleen leaned hard against Lochie as they took in this frightening piece of news.

'Look,' Lom Dubh began when he'd recovered slightly from the shock, 'this is the first time in an age since the three of us have been allowed to walk around in our man or woman form. We just want to have a drink or two, sample the cuisine and flirt with any eligible immortals we happen to meet.'

He lifted Robert's visor to catch his eye.

'The last thing we want is a bloodbath. Do you understand? We get enough of that in our monstrous forms.'

'I must fulfil my quest,' the knight replied dumbly. 'I gave my word.'

As he spoke two rather gruff and poorly disguised Redcaps wearing stag masks pushed in behind them. Lochie took the raven-man by the forearm and whispered into his ear.

'Those two behind the young FitzWilliam are Redcaps who follow Flidais!'

'How can you tell?'

'The masks!'

Flidais was the Goddess of the Hunt, you see. So she loved to dress her loyal followers in the trappings of male deer. Every goddess has her signature animal of the forest, it just so happened Flidais was drawn to stags.

'What are we going to do?' Lom Dubh shot back at his friend.

'We're going to help him,' Isleen declared. 'I never liked that huntress anyway. If she's planted her Redcaps here in the feasting hall it can only mean one thing.'

'What's that?' Lom Dubh asked.

'She intends to make an attempt on Aoife's life, you eedyit! Why else would there be so many of her warriors milling about in stag masks?'

It was true enough. As Lom Dubh and Lochie looked about them they counted at least fifty warriors very poorly disguised as stags of the forest.

'I'll show you which one is Flidais,' Isleen told the knight.

'Don't get involved!' Lochie warned her.

'Listen! If we let Flidais murder Aoife, where does that leave us?' Isleen asked. 'Aoife promised to release us from the bonds of our imprisonment. Flidais wouldn't do the same. We must ensure the Queen of the Night is kept safe from all harm. If that means helping this handsome, young, lithe and willing knight to murder Flidais, then so be it. I for one will gladly stand by and watch him do his work with a combination of fascination and relief.'

She placed a forefinger under his chin for a second then took hold of Robert's visor and hauled the face plate down over his face.

'There you go, my lad,' she hummed with delight. 'We don't want anyone recognising you, do we?'

She took the knight by the hand and led him through the crowd in search of the Goddess of the Hunt.

A blast sounded on a horn. The assembly hushed, turning all their attention to the stage where Mugwort was already standing with his red satchel by his side and his hands high in the air.

'Ladies, gentlemen, creatures of woodland and river, lough and bough, mountain, cave, ocean and Otherworld, welcome. My name is Mugwort, troubadour of the highest standing, entertainer, poet, musician, balladeer, confidant of kings, paramour of queens, envy of princes and daydream of the fair maidens.'

'Get on with it!' someone shouted.

The jester lost his train of thought for a moment. He struggled to remember what he'd been going to say next.

Before him there were folk dressed in hare costumes with long white ears and dark sparkling eyes. There were twenty or so badgers, albeit unconvincing, standing round the doors. A greater number of stags were sprinkled round the assembly, their antlers standing up above the rest of the crowd. There were one or two ravens, a dozen salmon, six boar, forty or so cows, three rather self-satisfied looking bulls, a couple of wary mice and three dogs of various breeds. That's not to mention the countless folk who were attired in mortal form as men and women. Then there was the scattering of goats, horses, does, sheep, geese, ducks, puffins, seals and a single walrus. Aside from that there were one or two small trees, a hag, three folk dressed as diminutive Redcaps and two standing stones.

Mugwort raised his eyebrows when he saw the stones, wondering whether they were part of the decoration of the chamber or genuine disguises.

'Get on with it!' the same voice shouted and that was enough to wake him out of his musings.

'I am Mugwort,' he repeated and there was a collective groan. 'I have been commanded by the queen herself, Aoife of the Redcaps, Sovereign Lady of the Night, to perform for you her honoured guests.'

'Get on with it!'

The jester coughed. There were scattered laughs. Then he dragged a fine lute around from where it hung at his back. With a flourish he bowed, elegantly placed the fingers of his left hand upon the frets at the neck and with a flick of his fingers he strummed a chord.

Now as every musician will tell you it is an optimist who commits himself to any melody on an instrument which has not been recently tuned. The lute sounded the most hideous discordant clang of disharmony imaginable.

A few folk laughed.

'I won't be a minute!' Mugwort told them. 'I should have done this before I came up on stage.'

He twisted the tuning pegs this way and that, stretching the strings with whining hums until they all seemed in tune. Then he strummed another chord. But somehow the instrument seemed less in tune than it had been before.

'I don't know what's wrong with me,' he apologised. 'I'm not myself tonight. I'm very nervous. It's all the pressure of performing for the queen.'

More of the audience laughed.

'Can anyone tune this for me?'

Giggles all round but no one offered to take the instrument from him. So he slipped the shoulder strap off and placed the lute at his feet.

'I'll come back to that later,' he assured everyone. 'I probably just need to warm up a little.'

'We'll build a bonfire for you,' some wit replied. 'With a stake for you to stand at.'

The jester laughed nervously. 'I'll recite a poem,' he told them with a cough to clear his throat. 'There once was a shimmering salmon tree, with a smile as broad as bed linen. He asked around for a bucket where a half-grown man could snuffle. They said there was only a cattle trough and it had been stuck in a puddle. So they slaughtered a bright yellow cabbage and the rest of the morning the butterflies made merry.'

Mugwort swallowed hard. He knew even as he spoke the words that the verse hadn't made any sense at all. But what was he to do? His once refined skill at spontaneous poetry had fled him. Only gibberish came to his mind.

But the audience didn't care. There was applause and laughter all round. Encouraged by this he picked up the lute again, strummed a terrible excuse for a chord then put it back down again quickly.

'I'll play some music later,' he promised.

He glanced down at the bundle of parchment he'd brought with him. Mugwort decided it was time to show off his skill with the sigils. He searched about in the leather pouch at his belt for a piece of charcoal. When he'd located one he pulled it out.

'Do you know what this is?'

'A shard of half-charred birch bark,' the answer came back from the same heckler who'd interjected earlier.

'That's right!' the jester replied. 'I will now display my uncanny ability to make wishes come true,' he declared. 'Has anyone got a wish?'

The room was full of murmurs of excitement as everyone called out their own personal desires. These ranged from the downright defamatory to the utterly undignified but Mugwort couldn't distinguish one from the other.

In the midst of all this noise and hullabaloo a horn sounded out loud and clear. The gathering fell silent as Aoife appeared at the rear of the room. Two great Redcaps poorly disguised in badger masks led her through the parting guests with sickles held high.

Everyone who had knees or whose costume allowed it, knelt down in respect as she passed them. Mugwort swooned. He could see by her cold stare that she had some terrible surprise in store for him.

Dressed in her favourite green gown the same shade as the butter of a love potion, Aoife approached the stage. And as she did so the jester also fell down on one knee with his head bowed.

'Greetings, my lady,' he managed to say without stammering. 'May Samhain Eve bring you all you desire.'

'I desire to discover who disentangled Guy d'Alville from my enchantment,' she retorted sharply.

Mugwort found he could not reply. There was a lump of pure terror in his throat and no words could get past it.

'It was you, wasn't it?' the queen pressed. 'You helped Guy escape.'

'It was a mistake!'

'Do you really expect me to believe that?' Aoife asked. 'How did you do it?'

'I didn't mean it!'

'How did you do it?' she repeated in a firmer tone.

'I'm not even sure it was me,' Mugwort insisted.

'How did you do it?' the queen said again in a voice that was full of fire, threat, rage and hatred.

'It was the sigil book,' the jester admitted. 'I made a word picture. I didn't mean to let him go. It happened by accident.'

Every light in the chamber dimmed as he spoke. The effect was so dramatic that Mugwort gave a little yelp of fright. Everyone else had raised their eyes from their deferential bows. Aoife's face glowed with a blue tinge that made her features seem so frightening that Mugwort clutched his chest, sure he was going to faint with terror.

'Don't kill me!' he pleaded. 'Don't turn me into a tree! I'll make amends. I promise.'

'That's for certain,' the queen declared and her voice was that of a dæmonic creature. 'You'll pay a recompense to me. And the payment will be to grant me a wish. If you should fail I will punish you.'

Suddenly the candlelight brightened again, the blue glow around Aoife disappeared and everyone in the chamber breathed a sigh of relief. Except Mugwort of course.

'Listen carefully and I'll tell you my desire,' Aoife told the jester. 'And if your skill with the sigils is that great you will grant it to me instantly.'

'My lady,' he protested, 'I'm no sigil master. I'm merely a dabbler. I can't guarantee I'll be able to grant your wish.'

'Then you will suffer for it,' she shrugged with a smile.

The queen put a finger thoughtfully to her chin. 'Let me see,' she mused aloud. 'What is it I desire most in this world?'

'A castle!' someone suggested.

She shook her head. 'I've got one.'

'A handsome knight to be your plaything,' another cut in.

Aoife thought about that for a little while. 'I have one of those already.'

'Revenge!' Lom Dubh suggested.

'Now that's interesting!' the queen agreed. 'But I've visited my vengeance on everyone who's earned it.'

'Perhaps there's someone who hasn't earned it yet,' the raven replied.

Aoife smiled.

'Thank you, my brother. Now I know what I would wish for.'

Mugwort waited in apprehension, certain he would be the target of her wrath. So when she spoke again he fully expected she would have him cast a sigil against himself. That would've been typical of her sense of humour. It would've have suited her perfectly.

'It is my wish that death should come to any goddess here tonight who would seek to oppose my rule.'

The jester breathed a deep sigh of relief, wiped the sweat from his brow, lifted his charcoal and scribbled down the wish.

'Thank you, my lady. Thank you,' he muttered as he wrote. 'As you wish so it shall be.'

In a minute he'd formed a sigil from the condensed letters of her wish. Then he took a new piece of parchment, drew out the sign and handed it to the queen with a flourish.

'What now?' she asked.

'For the sigil to be effective you must memorise it,' he told her. 'Then the parchment must be consumed in flame.'

Aoife glanced at the drawing, quickly committing it to memory. Then she held the parchment up with one hand. In a flash of blue sparks the sigil burst into bright flames and was reduced to ashes in less time than it took the gathering to gasp in astonishment.

'How long do I have to wait before Flidais is dead?' the queen enquired. 'Now your sigil has been constructed and destroyed, will the enchantment be instantaneous?'

The Goddess of the Hunt pushed her way to the front of the crowd in outrage that she'd been named by Aoife. She tore off the doe mask she'd been wearing and cast it aside in a fury.

'How dare you accuse me!' she shrieked. 'What evidence do you have? Who has smeared these allegations on my noble character?'

Aoife turned to face the Huntress with a sneer.

'You've brought fifty of your thugs into this assembly,' the queen noted. 'You disguised them as Stags but they're Redcaps just the same. Rebel Redcaps, I might add. You had a mind to murder me. Didn't you?'

'That's simply not true!'

Flidais put her hands on her hips and stared Aoife down but it was clear the queen had struck on the truth. Everyone in the gathering moved to take sides. The loyal followers of Flidais backed away from the queen. The more astute folks took to Aoife's side of the room.

'Do you deny you brought a force of Redcaps to my hall hoping to slaughter my supporters and myself at the first opportunity?' the queen asked.

'I deny it!'

Flidais showed no hint of fear on her face but her voice wavered just the tiniest amount. That was enough for more folk to quietly desert her side and slink toward Aoife's supporters.

'Is it not true that you approached my own brothers with this treachery, hoping they would come to your aid?'

'It is untrue,' Flidais replied but there was little conviction in her words now that she knew who had betrayed her. 'I came here for no other reason than to celebrate your ascension to the rank of goddess.'

'No other reason?'

Flidais looked at the faces all about her. Even among those who had guaranteed her their support there was a sense of defeat. One or two previously loyal supporters shrugged as they moved to Aoife's side.

Flidais realised that if the sickles started to fly she would not be able to count on anyone to stand by her. So the Huntress decided to bluff this out as best she could. Disaster could still be averted.

'I came here to drink my fill and eat to my heart's content of the feast of Samhain,' she laughed nervously. 'And I admit there was one other reason I decided to attend your celebration.'

'What was that?' Aoife demanded to know.

'I heard there would be a knight here this evening,' the Huntress declared. 'I was told he was a valiant, handsome, chivalrous and alluring man. I wanted to see this legend for myself. And perhaps lure him to my bedchamber.'

'Who is this knight of whom you speak?' the queen smiled sweetly, throwing her arms wide. 'Is he among us? Surely we'd all like to become acquainted with him.'

'His name is Robert FitzWilliam,' Flidais told her.

'Then you are in luck,' Aoife shot back as the smile dropped away from her face. 'He is standing behind you.'

The Huntress spun round to look on the knight wearing his strange helm. Flidais blushed with anticipation as she bowed her head to the stranger.

'It is my pleasure to meet you at last,' she gushed, half out of relief at turning Aoife's attention away from her and half out of genuine excitement at standing before this famous warrior. 'I hope we will get to know one another much better.'

'Alas you will not,' Aoife promised. 'For Robert has been set a quest.'

As the queen spoke the young FitzWilliam raised the sword he carried. He shifted the weight of the weapon so he grasped it firmly with both hands. Then he brought the blade down with all his might in a sweeping slash across the neck of the Goddess of the Hunt.

There was a terrible gnashing split of flesh as the sword parted the head of the Huntress from her neck. Blood spattered across Mugwort still kneeling on the stage. The next thing the jester knew he was watching the lifeless head of Flidais roll across the floor to come to a thudding stop at the foot of the raised stage.

It was more than three long slow breaths before the folk gathered in the feasting hall reacted. Some fell down to their knees again. Others backed slowly away to the door. The Redcaps dressed in stag masks tore off their disguises and lifted their sickles. Dozens of Redcaps in badger masks poured into the room, sickles flashing, to form a circle around their queen.

'Submit to me!' Aoife commanded. 'All those who would have followed Flidais must submit to me. Those who kneel down now will be forgiven. Those who defy me will be banished from the ranks of the immortal kind.'

A few voices were raised in protest but there was no conviction behind any of the objections. As much as the ever-living ones may carp on about the curse of immortality, there are few who'd willingly give up their lives to embark upon the cycles of birth again.

'It is unlawful to take the life of a fellow immortal!' one proud and powerful woman declared above the murmurs of submission.

All eyes went to the Morrigán.

'Sorcha has spoken well,' her companion Dalan confirmed, stepping forward. 'It is an affront to the ways of our people to cut down a rival and thus deprive them of the benefits of the Quicken Brew. There must be recompense for this killing. And as if that were not enough, there is no worse crime than to violate the laws of hospitality. A fine must be levied and a punishment brought down for this bloody deed.'

'I did not kill her,' Aoife pointed out. 'He did.'

'He is your servant!' Dalan shot back as he tore off his fish mask. 'You put him up to it! You are as guilty as he is.'

All the joy had drained from his eyes. Now there was a harshness about his features that reflected the seriousness of the charge.

'Be careful what you say!' Aoife warned him in a low voice. 'I did not wield the sword. I did not take that pretty head from those treacherous shoulders. She planned to murder me! What was I to do? Let her take *my* head off?'

Dalan stared into her eyes. 'Then you admit you planned this killing?'

'This knight was protecting me out of loyalty,' she told him sharply. 'I cannot be held responsible for the fact that my servants hold me in high esteem and would not have me murdered. He was merely doing what he thought was right.'

'You set him a quest.'

'Yes,' Aoife shrugged.

'It is unlawful for any immortal to take the life of another immortal,' Dalan insisted. 'He must pay.'

'He is a mortal,' the queen declared. 'Thus no laws or precedents have been broken. He will not be fined or punished. That is the law. You said it yourself.'

'I call down a fine against him nevertheless,' the Brehon judge declared. 'He will pay the worth of Flidais in fines to her clan.'

'She has no clan,' Aoife laughed. 'She's older than you or me. All her people are long gone.'

'Danu is her mother,' Dalan smiled. 'As she is mother to us all. The fine will be paid to her. And if he does not pay the fine he will be handed over to the servants of Flidais and they will take the payment out of his mortal hide. This is my judgement. Let none disregard it.'

Aoife's expression changed instantly. It was as if a sheet of ice had formed across her smile and a cold wind had howled in her spirit.

'You are a Brehon judge,' she conceded. 'You are learned in the law. And we must all respect our judges. Your judgement will stand. But I will pay the fine for him. Since he is my servant and he was acting out of loyalty to his queen, it falls to me to support him in this hour of need. No sovereign who loves her people would do less.'

It was Lom Dubh who spoke up next.

'All hail Queen Aoife, Goddess of the Night!'

The words were repeated with trepidation around the feasting hall as Dalan bowed, stepped back and then took his place at Sorcha's side again. The two of them were the only ones to remain silent and aloof in the chamber.

The raven repeated his cry with an emphasis which suggested it would be wise to show some enthusiasm. This time the hail was shouted. And the third time the assembly cried out their praise there even seemed to be some genuine love in their voices.

The queen held up her hand to cease the adulation and turned to Robert.

'You have fulfilled your quest and proved yourself worthy. Great will be your reward.'

Then she faced Mugwort.

'You have granted me my wish. I congratulate you. Now I commission you to write down all you have learnt about the sigils. The finished book will go to Sir Robert as token of my appreciation. I forgive you your earlier transgressions against me.'

Mugwort stood up with tears of relief in his eyes. Robert had fallen to his knees along with everyone else. Now he was up again as all the gathering got to their feet and started chattering about the events of the evening.

Sianan decided this would be the best time to leave. She tapped Tóraí on the shoulder to get his attention but as she did so Sorcha appeared before her.

'Have you made up your mind?' the Morrigán asked.

'Do you really need an answer from me tonight?' Sianan replied.

'I'll give you till dawn to make up your mind,' Sorcha conceded. 'I know it's not going to be an easy decision. But I've a feeling you'd make a wonderful raven-queen.'

Truth to tell Sianan was a little overawed at meeting the legendary Morrigán. And she was quite flattered at the attention she been given too. Even a wise old soul like her is easily beguiled in the feasting halls of the Otherworld. I wouldn't be surprised if she'd completely forgotten about Mawn for a moment.

'Till dawn then.'

'I'll seek you out,' the Morrigán assured her. 'I've heard there's to be a great battle at the Killibegs. There are thousands of Redcaps marching there even as we speak. It should be a marvellous slaughter! The Raven-kind are gathering also.'

The delight in her voice was disquieting. Sianan shuddered at the raven-queen's cold, hard blood lust.

'I shall be at the Killibegs,' the abbess declared. 'I shall make my last stand amongst my own people. And where they fall you will find me.'

Sorcha reached out to draw Sianan close to her in a warm sisterly embrace. The gesture was so unexpected the abbess could not resist.

'We are your people now,' the Morrigán told her.

Then Sorcha melted back into the crowd to leave Sianan looking blankly into the crowd. It was Tóraí who shook her out of her daze.

'What do we do now?' he asked her.

'We must go back to the Killibegs and warn the people that they are in grave danger.'

'What of the spell to bring Aoife down?' the dog-man asked.

Sianan searched his eyes.

'Tell me,' she said, 'you have the gift of Seeing. Can you discern whether Aoife can be brought down by such an enchantment?'

He looked away.

'I fear that she cannot. Though I can't tell you for certain.'

'Then we must go back to the Killibegs, help with the defences and call upon the Goddess Danu, mother of us all, to intervene. She is our only hope now.'

With that the two of them slipped out of the feasting hall, unnoticed by anyone except Lom Dubh who took note but said nothing. Then by a combination of stealth, good fortune and trickery they made their way up through the Redcap tunnels to the surface. And from there they sought the road back to the forest gateway which would lead them to the Killibegs.

While all that was taking place in the feasting hall Caoimhin was being carried down to the pebble shore by the spring at the Well of Many Blessings on the shoulders of the Sen Erainn warriors. Their cheers filled the air so that his protests could not be heard above their adulation.

At last they placed him on his feet at the very edge of the water then retreated up the shore to stand tightly packed in a crescent of arms and armour. The nine chieftains, including Srón and Scodán, took their places in the front of their war party.

As they did so Becc mac Dé walked out to where Caoimhin stood, hugged him close, then turned to face the host of warriors. He raised both hands high to indicate they should come to silence. Then he dropped his hands to his side slowly to tell the warriors to sit.

They did so in absolute quiet. Satisfied, the War-Druid stepped back behind Caoimhin and spoke under his breath.

'You must address your people, my king,' he told the new monarch.

Caoimhin's mouth was dry with nervousness. He couldn't imagine what they might want to hear from him. It isn't every day a lad is proclaimed king. I'm sure he must have been quite taken aback. I mean, they'd not really explained to him what the fine armour signified until he was well and truly dressed up as their king.

'Speak from your heart,' Becc mac Dé advised him gently. 'They will understand such words.'

Caoimhin looked around at the expectant faces. Some leaned heavily on swords or sickles, others sat small round shields in front of their crossed legs. But every eye was on him. He glanced at Srón, noticing she was smiling broadly with admiration. She nodded to him to offer encouragement.

'Warriors of the Sen Erainn,' he began. 'You do me great honour to account me as one of your own. I am but a humble traveller and am undeserving of your praise or your crown.'

Nine hundred voices raised as one.

'No!'

Caoimhin was taken aback.

'Speak from your heart, my king,' Becc mac Dé said again. 'That's what they want to hear.'

The new monarch thought about that for a second then went on.

'I was once trapped in a prison much the same as you were,' Caoimhin told them. 'My prison was my black Benedictine robes. My movement was restricted. My life bound by strict laws.'

Everyone hummed approval at his speech.

'But I have been set free,' he went on. 'My heart has been unlocked. Now I am at my liberty to wander where I will. For love is the key and the lock was of my own making.'

There was another hum but not so enthusiastic. Not everyone understood exactly what he was getting at. I tell you, the love potion had changed his life. Once you've experienced love there's no going back.

'Now there is one thing on my mind,' the new king declared. 'There is a settlement called the Killibegs. This night Aoife intends to bring the full force of her Redcaps down upon these people who nursed and nurtured me. My heart dwells in that place for I have a loyalty to those folk. And I will go to stand among them when their enemies descend in force.'

'Then we will come too!' Scodán shouted and the entire host raised their voices in affirmation.

Caoimhin lifted his hand to still them again.

'You have named me your king and I am proud to bear that title. But it seems to me that you have no need of a sovereign. It is the Queen of the Night we must deal with. She is our common foe. If you will come with me to the Killibegs and defend the folk of that place at my side, then I vow I will serve you faithfully until the day Aoife ceases to be a threat to our peoples.'

A great cheer rose up from the crowd as Caoimhin lifted his hand again. It took a little longer for the host to settle this time. Then he turned to Becc mac Dé.

'What do I do now?'

'You must name your council of three and appoint the commander of the warrior host.'

'I name Srón, Scodán and Becc mac Dé to be my council of three,' he declared without needing a moment to consider the options. 'But as to the commander of the warrior host, I wish to bring one among you who is your brother. His kin were sundered from yours many generations ago. But he knows the Redcaps well and has no love for Aoife.'

'Who is this warrior?' the War-Druid hissed. 'If he be a Redcap he may not serve as our commander. There is a long-standing enmity between our clans. They chose their path an age ago. We will not follow after one of their kind.'

Caoimhin was surprised. He hadn't expected such hostility toward this idea after all his other edicts had been so warmly accepted.

'Perhaps you should interview him yourself,' he told Becc mac Dé. 'His name is Mallacht and he is the guardian of this well. It was he who allowed us to draw the water from the spring which brought the hosts of the Sen Erainn out from the stupor of Aoife's enchantment. If it had not been for him you would all still be stood up on that slope looking down on the pool as helpless as nine hundred fence posts.'

The old War-Druid grunted.

'I was a war-leader,' Mallacht piped up. 'I fought alongside Aenghus mac Ómor. I saw him cut down by the warriors of Éremon. I was among those many who took the Quicken Brew and thus gained everlasting life. But I swear to you I was not among those accursed folk who raised their swords against their brethren of the Sen Erainn.'

He paused to spout water through his mouth. When he was finished he went on.

'I was a Redcap but my hat was not stained with the blood of our kin.'

'We are no longer kin,' Becc mac Dé shot back. 'Our paths went off in different directions long ago.'

'Yet unless we unite we cannot hope to defeat Aoife's ambitions,' Mallacht told him. 'I have fought countless battles. I have never been defeated. Who among you has ever even raised a blade in anger?'

The assembly was quiet as the stream of water poured forth from Mallacht's mouth. It was true. None of them had ever been to war. It was not the Sen Erainn way to resort to such a dire and deadly consequence unless forced through necessity. They were a people who lived by diplomacy and compromise, reason and respect.

'How do you hope to stand against the Redcaps and win?' the stone head pressed. 'You are but mortals. You will fall like wheat before their sickles. They will harvest your warriors for blood with which to dye their caps.'

The War-Druid cast his glance down at the deep waters of the pool. For a moment he thought he saw something stirring within the depths but it was just a fleeting glimpse so he paid it no heed.

'I will stand with you. I will direct your war fury. I will guide your people into battle. And if you doubt me or my loyalty for a second you may relieve me of my command at any time. But you must trust me.'

Now you or I might have been left scratching our heads that this lump of stone could talk. But if it had asked you to trust it, what would you have said? When you're travelling in the Otherworld many things that would be considered incredible seem perfectly reasonable. That's the real danger of that place.

'How do I know we can?' Becc mac Dé asked as the stone head spat a steady stream of water.

'Because I have been placed under the same curse as you were. Only my travail is worse than yours. I am a wellspring. Do you think it's pleasant having to spit water all day long and all night too?'

The stream gushed out of his mouth as if to emphasise his point.

'It's not easy to keep up a decent conversation,' he added before letting the water continue its flow.

'You seem to be trapped,' the War-Druid conceded. 'How do we release you from your bonds?'

'Aoife is cunning,' Mallacht replied. 'There is only one way to break the enchantment.'

'What's that?'

'Forgiveness. I must be granted full forgiveness.'

'That's how she ensured you'd be here for a long time,' Becc mac Dé realised aloud.

'She thought only *her* forgiveness would release me,' Mallacht added excitedly. 'But you also hold me in contempt. If you and your people were to forgive me then my misery would surely be at an end.'

He stopped speaking to allow the built-up pressure of the stream to pour out. Then he continued.

'Release me and you will have a loyal servant. Let me go from this enchantment and I will work to bring about the downfall of she who imprisoned me.'

Caoimhin placed a hand on the War-Druid's shoulder.

'Mallacht has been here guarding this spring for an age already,' he reminded the old man. 'If we forgive him he will be free. Don't forget that it was he who helped to release your people from the bonds of enchantment. If you won't accept him as your war-leader then at least grant him some peace.'

Becc mac Dé looked hard into Caoimhin's eyes, searching for the slightest hint of treachery.

'You have spoken at length with this creature,' he noted. 'Do you trust his word?'

'I do,' Caoimhin nodded.

The War-Druid turned his attention back to the stone head.

'I forgive you, Mallacht of the Wellspring. And all my people also offer their forgiveness. Any transgressions you have ever made against our ancestors or our kinfolk have been annulled by your actions this night. May you find peace.'

The host of warriors seated on the pebble beach and the hillside gave their word as one in affirmation of the War-Druid's pledge. The stone head smiled to hear their collective murmur of forgiveness. Then he laughed.

'Thank you!' he cried out. 'Thank you!'

But they were the only words he had a chance to say. His eyes widened and he toppled forward, landing in the water with a great splash of white foam. Then he sank immediately and swiftly to the bottom.

Where he'd been set in the rock wall a great gush of water erupted which soon enough subsided into a trickle again. Then all was quiet. And if you hadn't seen old Mallacht stuck in the wall, you wouldn't have known he'd ever been there.

Down, down Mallacht tumbled until his face found the mud at the very bottom of the pool. It was dark there among the crushed reeds and gritty pebbles. And the first thought that struck him was that the enchantment had not been lifted at all.

He let out a muffled underwater scream at that realisation. Then he felt a hand on his shoulder. A dark shape vaguely resembling the outline of a man turned him over in the mud. But the silt was so stirred up that Mallacht could not make out the man's features.

It was in that instant he realised he had a body again. Hands, feet, legs, belly, arms and every muscle flexed into life with a jerk. He wasn't just a face any more. He was a man.

A hand gripped him tightly, drawing him up off the floor of the pool. Then he felt himself dragged along the bottom of the mud until he could go no further. His limbs, unaccustomed to movement, were unable to respond. They were weak and rebellious.

The stranger took him over his shoulder then and walked on beneath the water toward the shore.

Caoimhin, Becc mac Dé and the warriors and chieftains of the Sen Erainn stood by helplessly waiting for Mallacht to emerge. None dared go down there among the reeds and darkness to help the stone head.

Soon enough, though, Caoimhin began to feel very concerned for the well head. He strode into the water to his knees until a strong hand held him back.

'Go no further,' the War-Druid told him. 'Mallacht is an immortal. He cannot be drowned.'

Caoimhin had a flash of his own moments underneath the waters of that pool. He saw again the strange figure trussed up

437

directly beneath the spring. Then he recalled the wonderfully decorated harp that had rested nearby.

Almost as soon as that picture was clear in his mind there was a great bubbling and the waters of the pool began to roll in turmoil. Caoimhin looked down into the depths and caught a glimpse of a dark-haired figure dressed in purple tunic and raven-feather cloak. His hair was in the same style as Becc mac Dé. And he bore a harp in one hand.

Over the other shoulder this dweller of the deeps was carrying a man. The monk-king knew who they both were immediately. Without a thought for his own safety he removed the helm and handed it to the War-Druid.

Becc mac Dé could see what was on his mind.

'You must not go down there,' he advised his king. 'They must rise up together without your aid.'

By the time he'd spoken those words the two figures had emerged from the waters of the pool. Caoimhin and Becc mac Dé helped them to the pebble shore. Mawn placed the harp down carefully on the stones as Mallacht lay down. His arms and legs were still weak from centuries trapped within the stone. Mawn soon joined him, rubbing his calf muscles and stretching his neck. He'd been a prisoner a good long while himself and standing around at the bottom of a pool for any amount of time is going to stiffen your limbs somewhat.

Then the monk-king knelt down at the side of the dark-haired fellow with the Druid tonsure. His eyes were large and strange, just like Sianan's.

'My name is Caoimhin,' he stated. 'Welcome to you, Mawn. Your enchantment is ended.'

He turned to the other man who was dressed in the same style as the Redcaps he'd encountered earlier. His brown beard was long and matted but his smile was wide.

'Welcome to you, Mallacht of the Well,' he bowed.

The man took his hand in a strong grip of greeting. Then he spoke a few stern words of warning.

'If ever you should throw stones at my head again, King Caoimhin of the Sen Erainn, rest assured I will throw them back at you. For now I have my hands again I will toil unceasingly toward the downfall of Aoife and anyone who raises their hand against me.'

With those words spoken the two pool men were given cloaks to keep them warm and then they were placed by a fire. A broth was served to them and neither of them spoke another word until the bowls were drained.

Mawn kept his harp close by. He was not eager to trust these folk. But Caoimhin was determined to gain his confidence.

'Will you play for us?' he asked. 'I've never seen a harp like that one. And it's been my lifelong desire to play upon such an instrument.'

Mawn looked up into Caoimhin's eyes. His expression was distrustful but this was soon swept away as he noticed something deep within the monk-king.

'Do I know you?' he asked.

Caoimhin shook his head.

'I've seen you before.'

'I fell into the pool,' the monk told him. 'I was nearly drowned. I saw you imprisoned there.'

'And how did you know my name?'

'Sianan told me.'

The stranger's eyes lit up with joy as he gripped Caoimhin's tunic.

'You've seen Sianan?'

'I have.'

'Where is she?'

'I don't know,' Caoimhin admitted. 'We were separated. But we are going to the Killibegs and I'm sure she will be there by the time we return.'

'Then lead me on to the Killibegs,' Mawn sighed. 'I have been a prisoner far too long. It's time I was reunited with my soul-friend and my duty.'

'I dreamed about you,' Caoimhin confided. 'I saw you down there in the pool in my dream-vision. I spoke with Flidais who would have trapped me also. She is fearsome. I've never known such fright in all my life. Will she be angry we've released you? Will she hold these folk accountable?'

'Flidais is dead,' Mawn stated coldly. 'For if she were still drawing breath I would not be free of the bonds of her enchantment. I know she would never consent to release me. Therefore she must be dead. And if that is so then there is a danger come upon the world of mortals such as has never been unleashed before.'

Mallacht cut in then.

'He speaks the truth,' the Redcap confirmed. 'If Flidais is dead, which indeed she must be, then there is no one left in the Otherworld who will stand against Aoife. The rebellion has been crushed. We can only hope that Aoife either spares us in her mercy, which is unlikely, or overlooks us in her frenzy.'

'We march to the Killibegs,' Caoimhin told them.

'We must not waste a moment,' Mawn confirmed. 'Not another moment.'

The Well of the Goddess

The three strongest forces in this world are the force of water, the force of fire and the force of hatred. Yet one who wields the first two guided by the force of love may be a one to be reckoned with.

Listen well, my dear. I speak as one who has travelled to the Otherworld and returned. Few come back who tread the uncanny paths of that strange country. Of those only a small proportion manage to keep their heads. None return from the Otherworld unchanged. I am one of the few who came back. I am one of the fewer who has not gone completely mad as a result. But to be sure, I was profoundly changed by my experiences in that place.

And so was Guy d'Alville. He came back with a great-grandfather, a sword, a sweetheart and a new name. Stronghold.

While Aoife was rounding up rebels in her feasting hall, Eterscél was leading us back through the paths of the forest to where the two oak trees intertwined. It was just before midnight on the eve of All Souls when we emerged into the Lands of the Living again.

Old Guy fell upon the grass to kiss the Earth. So great was his joy at being freed from his enchantment that we had to haul him forcibly to his feet. His great-grandson was just as glad to have returned. Though of course he said nothing.

I was ecstatic. With Guy, his great-grandsire and a Frightener on our side, my kinfolk of the Killibegs now held some hope of fighting off the Redcaps and the Hospitallers. My heart was fit to burst with pride at my true love.

Meanwhile Sianan and Tóraí were also on their way back to the Killibegs. Caoimhin and his warriors of the Slua Sen Erainn were marching to the forest gate. The rath of my people was fortified for war. All would soon be ready to fend off Aoife's assault. And yet there were so many more surprises in store for us.

All this I've told you tonight took place between the hours of sunset and midnight. As you'd know by now time runs different in the Otherworld. And I am thankful that such is the case. Otherwise we would never have made it back to the Killibegs before the Redcaps.

But I've said enough for this evening. I'm tired. I'll go to bed soon. Tomorrow night I'll tell you the next and final part of the story. I'll just say one last thing before I retire.

As the old tales tell, there are many wells in the Otherworld. Some confer healing. Others grant wishes. Most will leave you reeling with some form of intoxication. But there are wells in the Land of the Living also.

Some of those wells are enchanted. Some spring up for only a brief period then dry up entirely. Many are made by enchantment. I'll never forget how happy I was as we crossed back beneath those two oaks from the Otherworld. I'll always recall the joyous infatuation for Guy which filled my heart.

We of the mortal kind who will never know the benefits of the Quicken Brew live short, mean little lives. There is only one sweetness in all the misery of this birth. And that is love. Drink of its healing. Taste of its joy. Warm your heart by its flames. Listen in the quiet hours of the night to the call of its trickling spring.

Even though I know my heart was skewed by a love potion,

I can't deny the power of the experience which was the result. And though you might think me an old fool for saying so, I thank all which I hold sacred that the love philtre I drank was nothing less than a draught from the waters of the Well of the Goddess.

**POCKET
BOOKS**

Also by Caiseal Mor

The Well of Yearning

Book One of the Wellspring Trilogy

Guy d'Alville had been a Knight of the Hospital
before he was expelled from the prestigious military
order for failing in his duties. He blames the loss of
his fortune on one man: a Templar knight named
Robert Fitzwilliam.

But in his quest for vengeance, Guy discovers ancient
forces afoot. The mysterious Otherworld is astir with
rumours of war. The beautiful and terrible Aoife,
Queen of the Night is gathering her armies to assault
the realm of mortals. Recognising a shadowed soul
when She sees one, She promises Guy the High-
Kingshop of Ireland in exchange for his help.
And, in time, the crown of England.

But Guy has unwittingly unleashed the frightening
fury of the Nathairai, whom some call the Watchers.
Imprisoned for centuries within the Well of Dun Gur,
once these malevolent creatures are free, their
rampage will know no bounds.

ISBN 0 7434 6856 2
PRICE £6.99

POCKET
BOOKS

Also by Caiseal Mor

The Well of Many Blessings

Book Three of the Wellspring Trilogy

Robert Fitzwilliam and his fellow adventurers have
found, in their own way, what they were seeking in
the mystical Otherworld. But their intrusion into that
sacred country has stirred the wrath of Aoife, Queen
of the Night. With her legions of Redcap warriors,
she is planning to march on the realm of mortals
with one aim: the wholesale destruction of Ireland
and the enslavement of all mortal-kind. The people
of Killibegs band together to face their fearsome foes
in a last desperate stand. They have one chance to
defeat the Redcaps: a flimsy, untried strategy that
will pit the faith, courage and strength of the heretics
against the cold vengeance of the dark ones.
Friendships are forged in this struggle; warriors are
put to the test and alliances strained to the point of
collapse. But in the end, no matter what happens, it
will be those who drink from the Well of Many
Blessings who will triumph.

ISBN 0 7434 6857 0
PRICE £6.99

**POCKET
BOOKS**

This book and other **Pocket Books** titles are available from your local bookshop or can be ordered direct from the publisher.

Please send cheque or postal order for the value of the book,
free postage and packing within the UK, to
SIMON & SCHUSTER CASH SALES
PO Box 29, Douglas, Isle of Man, IM99 1BQ
Tel: 01624 677237, Fax: 01624 670923
E-mail: bookshop@enterprise.net
www.bookpost.co.uk

Please allow 14 days for delivery.
Prices and availability subject to change without notice.

The black-hearted Guy d'Alville has tasted
humiliating defeat. But all is not lost. For he now
possesses the sacred books of the holy community of
Killibegs – much sought after by the officers of the
Holy Inquisition. D'Alville resolves to take the
manuscripts to Rome in the hope of restoring his
reputation, titles and lands.

But in fleeing the Killibegs, Guy makes a serious blunder.
Passing through a doorway to the Otherworld, he finds
himself trudging through a strange landscape of myth,
spirits and mischief.

A small band of adventurers led by Robert FitzWilliam
sets off in hot pursuit. In the course of this dangerous
quest, the Wanderers are reunited, three magical wells
are encountered and Robert learns a lesson that will
change his life forever.

As for Guy d'Alville, his life will take an unexpected
turn the moment he takes a sip of the mystical waters of
the Well of the Goddess . . .

'The voice of a born storyteller' AMAZON.CO.UK

Cover illustration © Caiseal Mór
Cover images © Getty Images

Pocket Books
FICTION
£6.99

www.simonsays.co.uk

ISBN 0-7434-685-89

9 780743 468589 >